Joanne Rock credits her decision to write romance after a book she picked up during a flight delay engrossed her so thoroughly that she didn't mind at all when her flight was delayed two more times. Giving her readers the chance to escape into another world has motivated her to write over eighty books for a variety of Mills & Boon series.

Karen Booth is a Midwestern girl transplanted in the South, raised on '80s music and repeated readings of *Forever* by Judy Blume. When she takes a break from the art of romance, she's listening to music with her nearly grown kids or sweet-talking her husband into making her a cocktail. Learn more about Karen at karenbooth.net

Discover more at millsandboon.co.uk

THE REBEL

JOANNE ROCK

A CHRISTMAS
RENDEZVOUS

KAREN BOOTH

MILLS & BOON

First Published in Great Britain 2019
by Mills & Boon, an imprint of HarperCollinsPublishers,
1 London Bridge Street, London, SE1 9GF

The Rebel © 2019 Joanne Rock
A Christmas Rendezvous © 2019 Karen Booth

ISBN: 978-0-263-27198-0

1119

MIX
Paper from
responsible sources
FSC™ C007454

This book is produced from independently certified FSC™ paper to ensure responsible forest management.

For more information visit: www.harpercollins.co.uk/green

Printed and bound in Spain
by CPI, Barcelona

THE REBEL

JOANNE ROCK

For Stephanie Hyacinth, Ann Thayer Cohen and Anne Martel. I'm so grateful for your support and kindness. I'm never parting with my gold star!

One

Marcus Salazar would have enjoyed the afternoon trail ride a whole lot more if he'd left his cell phone back at the ranch.

He'd set the device to vibrate after ignoring two calls from the office, but he still found himself checking it. He couldn't help it. He'd come to Mesa Falls Ranch, a Western-style luxury corporate retreat here in Montana, for the most important business meeting of his life: to hammer out a deal with his half brother, Devon, that would finally give Marcus full control of Salazar Media. Their negotiations couldn't start soon enough to suit him.

When his phone began buzzing again, he plucked it from the breast pocket of his canvas jacket and saw that it was Devon calling. Maybe his brother had finally arrived. Marcus reminded himself to be civil and start things on a positive note. He and Devon might have opposing views on the future of Salazar Media—and just about everything else—but there was no need to revisit old ground this week. He'd simply discover how to buy out Devon's investment and they could sever ties at last. He swiped the screen to answer the call.

"I can meet you in the great room in twenty minutes," Marcus said without preamble, grateful for the cooperative Appaloosa who didn't seem to mind his busy hands. He tried to keep a level grip on the reins with one hand while he held the phone in the other, remembering basic horsemanship from his prep school days. "I took one of the horses out while I waited for you, but we're almost back to the main lodge now."

Squinting into the late-afternoon November sunlight, Marcus could see the pine-covered ridge that sheltered the stables on the six-thousand-acre ranch. The acreage was situated close to the Bitterroot River, a place his father, Alonzo Salazar, had visited often, and he'd talked of bringing Marcus and Devon there for a trip on several occasions.

When they'd been kids, there'd been bad blood between their mothers that had made the trip too difficult to orchestrate. And later there'd been plenty of enmity between the men themselves. Now it was too late. Marcus and Devon had said their final goodbyes to Alonzo Salazar last summer after a battle with pancreatic cancer that was over far too quickly. Their father was gone, and he'd been the only reason the brothers had been civil to each other outside the family business.

They probably could have dissolved the rest of their ties without coming here, but they were fulfilling a deathbed promise to their father to meet at the ranch before they went their separate ways. For reasons Marcus still didn't understand, their dad had been determined to get Marcus and Devon to this corner of western Montana.

"I'm not in town yet, unfortunately." Devon's voice competed with a lot of background noise. An announcement over a loudspeaker. The hum of other voices. "I'm still in the airport in Mumbai."

"Mumbai?" Marcus leaned back in the saddle, stopping the horse on the trail so he could give the call his full attention. "As in the other side of the globe?"

Frustration simmered in his veins. His brother wouldn't arrive for at least another day.

"I would have called sooner, but my phone and passport were both stolen and I was...*detained* by customs." His brother sounded pissed. And exhausted.

"Did you recover the phone?" Confused, Marcus checked the caller ID and saw his brother's face, only to realize Devon had contacted him through a social media messaging service, not a regular call.

"No. I bought a new one at an airport kiosk." Devon's voice rasped like a man who'd been talking for hours. "I've got a message in to the embassy to get some help returning to the States, but in the meantime, I—" there was interference on the call, as if Devon was walking through a wind tunnel "—should be in Montana soon."

"I missed that." Marcus nudged the Appaloosa's flanks, wondering if the cell signal was weak in this heavily wooded section of the trail. The mare started forward again. "I just finalized the deal to bring on Mesa Falls Ranch as a client." He'd been working on that angle with the ranch owners ever since he'd realized the trip here was inevitable, and he'd received a verbal agreement from one of them earlier in the day. "I can take an extra day to work on their account personally, but if you're not here in forty-eight hours, I'm flying back to Los Angeles."

Marcus handled the West Coast office. Devon was his copresident in New York. Only their father had outranked them, and he'd been a mostly silent figurehead CEO.

"There's no need. I—" Devon's words faded as the connection cut out again "—as an emissary. She can speak for me—"

A loud crackling noise hissed through the device.

"Who?" Marcus strained to hear what his brother was saying, the tinny voice over a loudspeaker drowning out some of Devon's words and the poor call quality muting even more. "Is someone coming to the ranch for you?"

"—will message you. Sorry about this."

The connection cut out completely.

Marcus glared down at his phone to see Devon's social media photo staring back at him. How could Devon have waited until the last minute to get on a flight to Montana? Even on the company jet—and he didn't have it in Mumbai—the trip would have been eighteen hours, give or take.

Although, having been detained in customs overseas himself, Marcus knew it wasn't a picnic. Besides, maybe Devon's guilt over not making their meeting would play into Marcus's hands in helping him win control of Salazar Media for good. The company had been his brainchild, after all. His father and brother had only signed on for financial support, with their father assuming the CEO position simply because he'd been effective in brokering an accord between his warring copresident sons. With their father's death, there was a power vacuum that Marcus planned to fill. As the creative founder, Marcus deserved the CEO role, and he planned to have it or he'd leave the company that he'd started.

Jamming the phone in his breast pocket, he urged his mount faster, racing hard toward the main lodge on Mesa Falls Ranch. The retreat had undeniable appeal. The fact that the mountains and the wide-open spaces could distract him from his frustration for even a moment was a testament to the place's beauty. A consortium of owners—six in all—had maintained the lands and shared the cattle for the last eight years, with each of them having a home on the acreage. But the group had decided to open the land to guests a year ago, in an effort to fund their move to sustainable ranching. Sensing a business opportunity for Salazar Media, Marcus had opened a dialogue with the group, hoping to secure their account. The owners had made a verbal commitment to six months' worth of social media advertising with Salazar, with an option for extending the contract if they were pleased. Marcus planned to set up a few appointments with key members of the ranching staff—to make his presence felt here—and then head back to LA once the finalized contracts were signed.

His conscience would be clear that he'd at least tried to meet Devon at the retreat. If Devon couldn't bother showing up, that was on him.

As Marcus reined in behind the stables, he could see a shiny black Escalade pull up to the huge main lodge. A liveried driver hopped out and jogged around to the back, where tinted windows prevented Marcus from seeing inside. His brother's words floated back to his brain—something about an emissary.

Could Devon have sent someone to the ranch in his place? It galled him to think his brother had managed to arrange for a replacement, because he would have had to make the arrangements hours ago. Clearly, phoning his own brother to let him know he was delayed hadn't been his first priority.

He slid down to the ground and handed over the Appaloosa's reins to a waiting stable hand. He thanked the guy and kept his eye on the Escalade as the back door opened and a decidedly feminine leg appeared.

A black high heeled boot. A slender calf. A sliver of gray pin-striped skirt.

She can speak for me...

The words blasted back into his mind as the only woman who was ever allowed to speak for Devon Salazar stepped fully into view.

Lily Carrington stood tall on the tarmac in a black overcoat left unbelted over her pale gray suit and lavender-colored blouse. A tiny patent-leather handbag dangled off her arm. She was the most perfectly proper woman Marcus had ever met. Never a silky dark hair out of place. Efficient. Articulate. Clients praised her up one side and down the other. She'd been Devon's right hand in the business during the crazy years that it had doubled, then tripled in size, working her way up to the COO position, effectively the number two person in the New York office.

She was the antithesis of everything Marcus normally liked in a woman, cool and composed when he usually went for passionate, artsy types. Yet for some irritating reason, he'd always fought a fierce attraction to Lily.

Lucky for him, she was engaged to another man and safely off-limits.

Not so lucky for him, she still roused a surge of lust

just standing in the driveway looking like a movie star in sunglasses that covered half her face.

"Marcus." She gave a polite smile as she caught sight of him, edging past her driver to head toward him. "What an impressive property for a retreat." Tipping up her sunglasses, she gestured toward the massive lodge-style building newly constructed as guest quarters. Her gaze swept over the pristine stables, the welcome center and attached paddock, and the rolling hills that turned into mountain vistas behind it. "It's breathtaking."

He found the view of her far preferable to the autumn landscape but kept that opinion on lockdown. He was already calculating how fast he could leave town without compromising his bargaining position with Devon. He'd done things he wasn't proud of in his life, but indulging an attraction to a woman wearing another man's ring was a line he wouldn't cross.

"It should photograph well," he acknowledged, turning his attention to the views instead of Lily's pliable mouth or pale blue eyes. "Since Devon couldn't bother to show, maybe we can spend our time here setting up the ranch account and gathering some on-the-ground intel the team can use to fine-tune the marketing approach. I'll text you an agenda so we can both get back home as soon as possible."

She was quiet for a long moment. For so long, in fact, he needed to turn and look at her again for a hint of what she was thinking.

"We could do that," she admitted slowly, staring at him with newly wary eyes. "Or we could start a dialogue about how to fill the CEO position, since that was the original intent of this meeting. Maybe you and I can come up with some workable options for the future of Salazar Media—"

"That meeting was planned for Devon and me. Not you." He wondered where she saw herself in this negotiation for power at Salazar Media. Was she hoping to carve out a better position for herself? Oust Marcus completely and take over the West Coast office?

If not for the fact that the Salazar brothers were on opposite coasts, the business might have tanked years ago. But they'd made it this far by operating as independently as possible from each other in New York and Los Angeles.

"I have a stake in the outcome, too," she reminded him coolly. "And now that your father isn't around to negotiate your differences, I hoped maybe I could facilitate a conversation about the future."

"Did my brother ask you to talk me into rolling over on this?" He realized his thwarted sexual tension was making him speak more sharply than he might have otherwise. "Did he think you had a better shot at enticing me into doing what you want?"

Marcus had compromised his vision for the company too many times over the years, playing it safe while good opportunities passed them by because Devon had a different approach.

"Of course not," she replied adamantly, shaking her head. "However, I am familiar with some of the frustration on both sides—"

"No, Lily," he said, cutting her off, unwilling to walk down that conversational path with her. "You can't possibly know the level of my frustration."

Their gazes met and held for a long moment while he let those words sink in so she could chew on them for awhile. He guessed the moment when she suspected his underlying meaning. There was a soft intake of breath. An almost silent rush of her surprise before she gave a slow blink.

Had she truly been unaware of the attraction?

Not that it mattered either way. He had enough grievances involving his brother. He wasn't going to try to wade through the haze of lust that Lily conjured for him. So instead, he tipped the driver who had delivered her to the ranch, sending the car on its way. When he turned back to Salazar Media's COO, she seemed to have plastered a new mask of indifference on her lovely face.

"In that case, I'll wait to hear from you when you're ready to meet." She held her small purse in front of her now, which was a laughable defense. There could be a whole conference table full of people between them and he'd still feel the tug of desire.

Nodding, he turned on his heel to retrieve his horse, grateful as hell that he'd chosen to stay in a guesthouse separate from the ranch's main lodge.

The more distance between him and Lily Carrington, the better. The woman was a serious threat to his concentration when the future of his company was at stake.

What had happened back there with Marcus?

Lily asked herself the question again as she sank deeper into the claw-foot tub in the bathroom of her guest suite, indulging in a post-travel soak that she hoped would clear her head. The suite was beautiful, with hardwood floors and reclaimed barn beams in a nod to the Western setting, but incorporating plenty of contemporary touches like the glass-encased tile shower next to the vintage tub. She'd clicked on the fire in the sleek hearth as soon as she'd arrived, even though it wasn't all that cold outside. She wanted the whole mountain experience.

Lily brushed a hand through the bubbly, rose-scented water, upset that she couldn't fully savor the beauty of Montana and the unexpected trip because suddenly there was something odd between her and Marcus Salazar.

Something hot and unexpected.

Closing her eyes as she breathed in the steam-drenched air, Lily thought back to those moments after she'd arrived in front of the huge lodge. She'd been glad to see Marcus, if a little wary. She knew about the long-standing estrangement between the half brothers, although she'd never fully understood it. If they disliked each other so much, why had they launched a joint business with the help of their father? Then again, their talents went well together. Marcus was the creative genius with expertise in the digital media world, while Devon had the business savvy that kept the company in the black.

Devon had been her friend as well as her direct supervisor for five years, but he'd never shared much about his personal life. And Marcus remained a mystery even though he ran the West Coast branch of the company.

Since she'd interacted very little with Marcus directly, she'd been cautiously optimistic when Devon had asked her to take his place at this meeting. She'd wondered— naively, perhaps—if she'd be able to generate a dialogue between the Salazar men now that their father was gone and the future of the company remained up in the air. The business was still privately held, jointly owned by the Salazar brothers, so there was no board of directors to please or strict timeline to fill the CEO slot. Yet as months had dragged on in stalemate, some of their clients were getting frustrated at the lack of a single decision maker in the company. The struggle for power between Devon and Marcus could hurt the whole company. The business needed strong, united leadership.

But whatever had happened in the driveway at her arrival was going to hamper her efforts to make that happen. Marcus had inspired something she had no business feeling as an engaged woman. His dark hair and even darker eyes were so unlike his brother's. His tall, athletic build…

Swallowing, she halted her thoughts about his body, not letting herself linger on that path.

Wrenching her eyes open, she lifted her left hand from the bathwater to stare at the heavy Asscher-cut diamond on her ring finger, a family heirloom Eliot Winthrop had given her two years ago when he proposed. The five-carat piece was flawless, the facets catching the light from the bathroom sconces.

Until recently, she hadn't really questioned the long engagement, since they were both busy building their careers—he with his family's wealth management firm and she with Salazar Media. They'd been childhood friends; their families had both built their fortunes in the financial world and had always been close because of it. Eliot had also made her feel like less of an outsider after the scandal of her birth. Lily's single mother had refused to tell her parents who the father was and ultimately had given up responsibility for her child altogether, leaving Lily with her grandparents when she was four years old. As a result, Lily had never really felt like she belonged in the opulent Newport world she grew up in.

Later, she and Eliot were high school sweethearts. When he'd gone to college, she'd assumed they'd both move on. But she'd been disappointed by the drunken frat boy atmosphere even at her high-tier school, so when Eliot had proposed, she'd jumped at the chance, knowing they would make a good team. Not necessarily a romance to set the world on fire, but a solid partnership grown in mutual understanding.

They'd talked about uniting their families' respective businesses with a merger once they wed. She'd always taken strength from their friendship, certain it would grow into the kind of love her grandparents shared. But right now, with the memories of Marcus's eyes on her stirring an unexpected heat, Lily wondered why she'd never felt that kind of pull with Eliot.

Drying her hands, she reached alongside the tub to retrieve her cell phone. Once she called her fiancé, she would put the incident with Marcus out of her mind. Hearing Eliot's voice would remind her why they were right together—even if they still hadn't set a date for the wedding.

Lily punched the heart icon on her phone—the image she'd tagged him with in her contacts—but the call went straight to voice mail. Somehow, hearing his prerecorded message didn't provide the same reassurance as speaking to him personally. If anything, it only served to remind her of how often she checked in without getting ahold of him. Was that normal for a couple in love?

After leaving him a message, she ended the call and tried to put the worries out of her mind, settling the phone on the pile of towels near the tub. Whatever had happened with Marcus was surely a fluke. A fleeting feminine interest she wouldn't dream of acting on.

Her mother had been the kind of woman who could be tempted into relationships based on physical attraction, a trait that had made Maggie Carrington choose a lover over her own daughter. Lily knew better than to count on something as temporary as lust. Chemistry was a smoke screen that only confused people, complicating the real factors that needed to be considered for a long-lasting relationship. Like shared values and goals. Mutual respect and affection.

Satisfied she could salvage this trip and put that moment with Marcus behind her, Lily stepped out of the tub and dried herself with one of the fluffy bath sheets, her body steaming with the scent of roses. When Marcus texted her with an agenda, she would be ready to work. Clearly, he wanted to keep things professional and focused on business as much as she did.

No doubt he would keep those long, sizzling looks to himself for the remainder of their time together in Montana. And if a tiny piece of her still craved the way that moment had made her belly flip, she would simply channel it where it belonged—into her relationship with her fiancé.

Professional armor in place the next day, Lily strode through the foyer of the main lodge on her way to meet with Marcus. The building where she was staying was strangely quiet since the property wasn't open for a retreat this week. She was the only guest that she was aware of, yet there must be maids at work, since she'd had turndown service the night before when she went out for an evening walk in the moonlight. She'd also discovered on her walk that the stables were staffed and she was welcome to ride anytime.

She was curious to see some of the ranching operation itself. The lodge and welcome center looked like a luxe mountain resort, but she'd read up on Mesa Falls Ranch and knew they'd been successful raising cattle and sheep.

She stepped into the great room, where the tile floors were softened with colorful Aztec rugs, the reds and burnt oranges repeated in the throw pillows and framed prints on the natural log walls. A small bar held top-shelf liquors under the watchful eye of a stuffed American bison standing near the pool table. Bar stools padded in black-and-white cowhide were all empty save for the one where Marcus was seated.

She allowed her eyes to roam over him for a moment before he saw her. His dark hair was a shade deeper brown than his older brother's, and he wore it longer, too. Dressed in a blue button-down, he typed fast on his tablet keyboard, a pair of earbuds tuning out the world while he worked. When he turned his brown eyes toward her, she steeled herself for whatever it was that had happened between them yesterday. But the thing that had sparked last time was shuttered now.

Tapping off his screen, Marcus withdrew the earbuds and shoved them in the pocket of his suit jacket resting on the back of the bar stool.

"I didn't expect you so soon." He stood and gestured to the bar.

"I'm here to work," she reminded him, stopping next to a wooden game table and keeping her distance.

"Here to work, or here to gather information for Devon?"

"Any information I gather would benefit you both, since I work for Salazar Media and not exclusively for your brother." She didn't enjoy playing word games with him, but she planned to defend herself and her position.

Her job was too important to her to get on the wrong side of a man who still owned half of the company.

"Right." He acknowledged her point with a nod. "But you got your start in the business by being Devon's right hand. I don't think that instinct to look out for him is just going to disappear."

Impatience and indignation squared her shoulders.

"Do you want to work or question my motives?" She set her laptop bag on the game table, unwilling to be cowed. "Just so I'm clear."

Marcus took a step closer. "I prefer to work, but I don't think I can relax enough to do that until I understand why Devon would send you to a meeting slated to determine future control of the company."

His nearness brought trouble with it. She could see the bristled shadow along his jaw. Read the mistrust in his dark eyes. Feel a charge in the air that made her skin tighten. Lily drew a deep breath to set him straight, but she caught the scent of his aftershave, spicy and male.

"Devon wants to be here himself. You know that." She scavenged for the right words that would make things go back to the way they used to be between them. "But after he found out his passport had been stolen, he asked me to be on-site in case you need help closing the deal with Mesa Falls."

Her position allowed her to oversee the day-to-day operations in New York but gave her the flexibility to work directly with clients, as well. She'd learned two weeks ago that Marcus had approached Mesa Falls Ranch as a potential client, because he'd requested proposal material from her office. She'd researched the place immediately, liking to stay up-to-date on all their current and potential accounts. So she'd jumped at the chance to visit the ranch herself and escape her grandparents' growing pressure to set a wedding date.

His eyebrows shot up. "In case *I*—" he tapped his chest "—need help sealing the deal? I got confirmation we won the account before you even arrived on the property."

She suppressed a sigh of frustration. Men and their egos. She hesitated, unsure how much to share and wary of stepping on his toes again. "Devon didn't know the deal was sealed at the time he called me. And quite honestly, he was afraid you would be on the first plane back to Los Angeles unless he showed you some kind of good-faith effort."

"You're the good-faith effort?" His voice hummed along her senses, suggesting things at odds with his surly words.

She restrained the urge to lick suddenly dry lips, confused by whatever seemed to be happening between them. "Like it or not, yes."

He stood there, entirely too close to her. Assessing. Then his gaze shuttered, his expression revealing nothing.

"Unfortunately for both of us, Lily, I work more effectively on my own," he informed her quietly. Then he turned and retrieved his tablet. "I suggest we divide and conquer the tasks for setting up Mesa Falls Ranch as a new account and leave it at that."

Blindsided by the abrupt turn in the conversation, she didn't even know what to say to that as he tapped open his screen.

"Do you care at all about this company?" She'd always had the impression that he didn't trust her fully. But he'd never come out and admitted he didn't want to work with her. "Because you're doing it a grave disservice to cut me out of the loop."

She could see the muscle in his jaw flex, his mouth flattening into a thin, determined line before he spoke again.

"That's never been my intention. I can send daily briefs on everything that happens here. But I'd prefer we get the work done so we can fly back to our respective coasts, where we can turn our attention to our own projects."

Anger simmered, but she locked it down to maintain professionalism.

"And I respectfully decline." She gathered her things, knowing it would be wisest to retreat until cooler heads prevailed. But first, she leveled her gaze at him. "I plan do to my job right here, where my presence is clearly needed."

Two

Braking to a stop in one of the ranch's utility vehicles the next morning, Marcus switched off the ignition and hoisted himself up to lean on the roll bar for a better view. The ranch foreman had offered him the choice of horse or vehicle to tour the property today, and Marcus had opted for the two-seater with no cab and a little wagon in back. He hadn't informed Lily of the tour, leaving before dawn. He knew that was a mistake. That he was hurting the company because he couldn't keep his emotions under control. Right now, he needed space to clear his head and figure out his next move.

As the sun rose higher in the sky, he reached for his camera on the passenger seat and withdrew the wide-angle lens from his bag. He had a couple of possibilities for a shot from this vantage point, and he lined up the first one, focusing on some dried wildflowers in the foreground.

Taking photos of the ranch was the best distraction, a pleasure in an otherwise tense trip. Adjusting the settings for shutter speed and aperture, he calculated what images he still needed for the social media campaign before he could head home.

Devon had messaged him during the night, saying the US Embassy was working with him to get his credentials reissued but that no progress would be made over the weekend. Marcus had resisted the urge to fire back a scathing response, unwilling to alienate Devon when he needed to convince him to let Marcus buy him out of the company. Later today, he'd tell Devon they needed to reschedule the Mesa Falls Ranch trip for another time.

Without Lily Carrington.

Just thinking about her spoiled his first shot of the wildflowers. Because he suspected her of spying for Devon? Or because Marcus wanted her for himself? Both options messed with his head.

While he'd always been drawn to Lily—in spite of his concern that she owed her loyalties to his brother—he'd been able to rein it in since they worked on opposite coasts. Being with her in person, when he was already grappling with his frustration with Devon, brought an unwelcome fiery element into his emotions for her. That's why he'd let her take the meeting with the ranch manager alone this morning while Marcus toured the place on his own. He got a better feel for clients by seeing what they had to offer—in the case of Mesa Falls, by exploring the ranch—than by listening to them. In his experience, customers were often too close to their product or service to be able to see the subtle facets of what made it unique. Long before Salazar Media became a national brand—and before Devon got his business school "best

practices" involved with every aspect of the company—
Marcus had excelled at finding his clients' individuality.

He wanted to bring the company back to that original
goal—giving each account a distinctive voice and image
that stood out from the rest of the media noise. And now,
peering through the wide-angle lens to see a herd of elk
step into the golden field, Marcus knew he could do that
here. Swapping to a zoom, he zeroed in on the elk with
video and stills, already seeing a way to set Mesa Falls
Ranch apart in the marketplace.

He was almost finished when the hum of another
nearby motor distracted him. He turned and saw a second utility vehicle approaching, a cowboy at the wheel,
a tall, slender brunette dressed in dark jeans and a long-
sleeved T-shirt in the passenger seat.

It was Lily. She gripped the roll bar, her big sunglasses
shielding her face from the sun now at its zenith. Her
lips were pursed, her hair uncharacteristically flyaway,
the dark strands dancing around her face as the vehicle
picked up speed. When they braked to a stop near him,
she stepped out with tense shoulders, her tall boots with
high heels better suited to a fashion runway than a Montana meadow.

"Hello, Marcus," she greeted him, impatiently swiping her hair away from her face. She kept her voice low,
for his ears only. "You missed the morning meeting."

"I left it in your capable hands," he told her before
turning his attention to the burly rancher dressed in worn
jeans and a dark Stetson who strode at a more leisurely
pace behind Lily. "You must be Coop?"

"Cooper Adler, at your service." He tipped his hat and
shook Marcus's hand.

They'd spoken on the phone a few times while Marcus had been planning the trip. The ranch manager was responsible for the environmentally friendly practices taking root here, and they'd discussed how a social media campaign to document Mesa Falls' move to green ranching would hold a lot of appeal for potential guests.

"I was just taking some photos to inspire the creative team when I return home. We're going to start work on a company narrative next, and I'll send a team out here to take more footage once we firm up our approach."

Lily hovered at his elbow as he spoke. Every now and then the breeze stirred a long strand of her hair to brush against his shoulder. A silky, barely there touch.

"Just let me know whatever you need." Coop nodded but didn't seem all that interested in the whys and wherefores of the social media profile for the ranch. "I drove out here to see you in person since Ms. Lily told me you might be leaving soon?"

"My brother couldn't make it, so I'm afraid—"

"The ranch owners really wanted to have a welcome reception to meet you and your brother. Weston Rivera has asked to firm up a date with you both." Coop frowned, his forehead wrinkling as his eyebrows knitted. "And, more importantly, Weston wanted me to let you know that he has papers to deliver to you and your brother. But he says he needs to give them to the two of you together."

"Papers? From who?" Marcus was surprised the man had never mentioned it in their preliminary phone conversations. Beside him, he felt Lily tense.

Had she known about this? And, more importantly, did she know what was in those papers?

Coop scratched a hand along his jaw. "From your father. He left them with Gage Striker—one of the other owners—the last time he was up here."

Lily cleared her throat, softly drawing Coop's attention before Marcus could demand answers.

"Cooper, did Alonzo Salazar spend time here very often?" she asked, her expression perplexed.

Marcus found himself wanting to know the answer, too. And why the hell had his father entrusted documents that belonged to him to one of the owners of Mesa Falls Ranch before his death? At least it appeared that Lily didn't know about the documents, though his rising anger eclipsed any relief he might have felt.

The rancher tipped his face toward the sun. "As often as he could once he found out about the cancer. Before that, maybe twice a year."

Marcus missed whatever Lily said in reply, his brain too stuck on that revelation. His father had always been a man of mystery, disappearing in his study for days on end when Marcus had been a kid, or traveling to destinations unknown for work he'd never shared anything about. To the outside world, Alonzo had been a teacher at a private school, until he retired and took the role of CEO at Salazar Media. But privately, even before Salazar Media took off, he'd always seemed to have another source of income. In the last few years, Marcus had asked his dad to visit him in Los Angeles plenty of times, but his father hadn't wanted to travel much after the cancer diagnosis. Or so he'd said. Apparently he'd had enough energy to fly to Montana.

Had Devon known about those trips? Could he have accompanied their father? But Lily seemed caught off guard by the news, too, and he suspected she would have been privy to Devon's schedule.

"I was unaware Dad left anything for me here." He would have thought any paperwork would have gone through the lawyer, but then again, Alonzo Salazar had never been a rule follower. Devon's mother had left him when Alonzo had argued a marriage certificate was no more than a "piece of paper," and Marcus's mom had discovered sharing a child with Alonzo didn't mean sharing a life with him. "I'll stop by your office when I get back to the ranch and pick up whatever my father wanted me to have."

Overhead, a low-flying plane stirred the treetops, creating a rustle all around.

"Your dad was very specific about the paperwork, I'm afraid." Coop gave a wave to the plane, as if he knew the pilot. "Gage left it in a safe, but he won't share the code until you're both here together."

Marcus stifled a curse, realizing his business in Montana wouldn't be as brief as he'd hoped. And he wondered how long Lily would remain at Mesa Falls, regretting the way his thoughts wandered right back to her.

"In that case, I'll see what I can do to expedite my brother's trip." He chucked his camera into the open bag on his passenger seat, wishing he could get in the vehicle and drive until he was off the ranch and far away from the mystery of what his father wanted. And even farther away from the tempting woman on his left.

But before Marcus could indulge that plan, even in his mind, Cooper Adler jumped in his own vehicle and bade them both a good day, leaving Lily standing on the hillside with Marcus.

He glanced over to see her glaring at him, sunglasses perched on her head, her arms crossed.

"What?" he asked, curious why she'd be upset with him already.

"You left me to handle the meeting with the ranch manager on my own this morning, even though yesterday you said you'd be there." She tugged the glasses from her head and stuffed them inside her leather handbag. "They're trying to plan a welcome reception to introduce Salazar Media to the owners, and I didn't know anything about it. I would have appreciated being better briefed on the client."

"Bear in mind we're both having to deal with unexpected circumstances this week." He had no desire to cross swords with her now, not when he was still angry with his brother for being a no-show, and with himself for not knowing how important the ranch had been to their father. "The next time Devon sends you on a spying mission, Lily, just tell him no."

"I'm not a spy," she retorted, her blue eyes taking on a darker hue now that she was upset. "We've been over this. When I filled in for Devon, I foolishly hoped I could help the two of you reconcile and maybe save the company in the process."

"If you represent his interests and not mine, how are you a good choice to negotiate a reconciliation? And either way, that's not happening." Marcus was taking the company, end of story. He moved around to the driver's side of the utility vehicle and slid into the seat. "Why don't you get in touch with Devon and ask him to send you back to New York?"

She hesitated then, after a moment, moved toward the passenger seat and sat down. It was a good thing the vehicle had no doors, excusing Marcus from ushering her in and out in a gentlemanly fashion, because her near-ness got under his skin.

Whenever she moved, that damn diamond ring on her finger refracted light beams into his eyes like a weapon of deflection.

"I asked him that already." She reached down to one side of the seat and retrieved the safety belt, tugging it around her narrow waist. "He refused." When the latch clicked, she glanced up at him, her blue gaze sliding right past his defenses. "So it looks like you're stuck with me."

Lily was grateful Marcus didn't try to talk to her on the ride home.

Sulking about her job felt like the right thing to do on this day when nothing had gone right. Her fiancé had awoken her with a text message at three in the morning to let her know that his obligations to the family busi-ness in the UK were going to continue into spring, so unless she wanted to come to London for the holidays, they wouldn't be seeing each other anytime soon. An-other time, she might not have been so upset, since she had a lot of new work obligations herself, but in light of how hard this trip was testing her, the blasé tone of Eliot's message had filled her with doubts. Wouldn't he miss her? Did he have any plans to ever discuss the wedding date her grandparents kept pushing her for?

Of course, when she fell back asleep, she had wildly inappropriate dreams about Marcus, which filled her with guilt and left her exhausted. Then there had been the morning meeting Marcus had skipped to take a private tour of the ranch, and her message exchange with Devon, who had told her in no uncertain terms he needed her in Montana this week.

Not to spy, obviously. But like his father, Marcus could be a bit of a wild card. He was a charismatic leader, and she guessed that Devon worried he might try to start his own company and take "his" clients with him. Lily guessed that, aside from helping Marcus set up the new account, she was also on-site to keep a dialogue open between the Salazar men. To remind Marcus that the branches of the company had worked together effectively in the past, and could do so again.

After indulging her frustrated thoughts for ten minutes, Lily forced herself back to the present, only to realize that Marcus wasn't heading back to the main lodge. The scenery around them had changed, going from sweeping vistas to dense fir trees. The earthy scent of damp leaves and pine needles filled the air as small brush snapped under the vehicle tires.

"Where are we?" She sat straighter in her seat, trying to see through the network of branches.

She'd seen hints of the ranch pastures earlier on her ride with Coop, but this looked very different.

"We should see the Bitterroot River soon." Even as he said it, the vehicle broke into a clearing, and a wide expanse of water came into view. "You looked like you needed a breather as much as I did."

"I—" She didn't know how to respond to that. They were the first words she could remember him speaking to her on this trip that weren't confrontational. "Thank you."

He braked to a stop close to the river's edge, along a narrow strip of rocky beach. The water glittered in the sunlight like a jeweled ribbon winding through the land.

"I could use a few shots of this." He reached alongside her leg, his brief touch startling her for a second before she realized he was retrieving the camera bag at her feet. "Do you mind spending a few minutes here?"

His attention was fixed on his camera, where he turned dials and adjusted settings. She watched him for a moment, intrigued. She tried not to think about the fact that her knee still tingled from the barest contact with his knuckles. She'd never thought of Marcus in *that* way until yesterday, and now she wasn't sure how to ignore the attraction that lurked too close to the surface. Something strange had happened between them yesterday. Something more than just Marcus accusing her of spying for his brother.

"Sure." She told herself to go for a walk along the water's edge. Anything to put physical distance between them. But she couldn't seem to stop watching him as he lined up a shot of the river partly framed by a wavy tree branch. She could see the whole image on the screen that took up most of the camera's back. "That's a great shot. You have a really good eye for composition."

His hands stilled on the camera for a moment. Then he turned his gaze her way.

"My brother once informed me that I have a talent for art because I only have to please myself, whereas he has the better disposition for business because he cares what other people think." He went back to work on his camera, shifting a few dials to take the same picture with different settings.

She knew Devon could be cold. Calculating, even. But she'd always appreciated his levelheaded practicality. She was wired the same way.

"Do you think there's any merit to that idea?" Lily knew she'd never have any hope of helping these two warring siblings reconcile their interests unless she understood Marcus better. She told herself that's why she wanted to know.

Overhead, a bird wheeled in circles before diving into the water with a splash. The air was cold today, but the sky was a perfect, unspoiled blue in every direction.

"I agree Devon is a people pleaser, and I'm not. That doesn't necessarily mean he possesses a better head for business." He clicked the shutter a few times, capturing new images of the water before refocusing on another bird searching for a meal.

It was interesting to watch him work. Salazar Media had its roots in the digital world, with the brothers on the forefront of engaging online audiences in constantly changing ways.

"Devon excels at pitching our services to big business. You drive the creative side." She couldn't understand why he didn't see that the two of them needed each other. "That gives the company balance."

"But I'm not interested in balance." He shot images in fast succession as the bird dived to the water. "I don't care about generating the biggest possible bottom line. I care about challenging myself and finding new outlets that interest me. That's what keeps art vibrant. That's what puts our business on the cutting edge."

Setting the camera on the seat between them, he turned toward her, giving her his undivided attention.

"But the business shouldn't be all about you," she said softly. The company had grown rapidly in five years, and they now had satellite offices around the country. They were talking about going global.

She'd climbed the ladder fast at her job, and she owed much of that to how quickly Salazar Media had expanded.

"Why not? It was my brainchild. My work that started

it. The company wasn't meant to be a business opportunity for the whole family, just an outlet for my art. Now I can afford to buy my brother out." He leaned closer, warming to the topic. "I'm done compromising my vision for his."

In the river, a fish jumped and splashed in the slow-moving water.

"Salazar Media isn't just you and Devon anymore. There are whole offices full of employees whose livelihoods would be hurt if you scaled back." She wondered if he'd thought this through.

"You think I should let Devon buy *me* out of Salazar Media and start over on my own?"

That's what he'd taken away from her comment? She'd never met anyone who thought like him before.

"Of course not. You've earned a strong reputation and the respect of industry professionals. You wouldn't want to walk away from that."

"Which isn't a problem for someone who doesn't care what other people think, remember?" He leaned back against the door, studying her from farther away. "Maybe you've got too much in common with my brother to understand that. You're a people pleaser, too."

She stiffened.

"It's not a matter of pleasing others." She wasn't sure why they were talking about *her*. She wasn't the one threatening to break up the family business. "But I do care how my choices affect others."

"An artist can't afford to care about that. I have to be impervious to criticism in order to keep creating art." His knee bumped hers as he shifted, reminding her of that keen awareness she had for him. "I have to passionately believe in my choices in spite of what anyone else says."

"That makes sense." She crossed her ankles, giving him more room. Only to be polite, of course, and not because she was worried about the way his touches affected her. "But you don't need to become so completely self-absorbed that you discount the preferences of others."

"But creating work that I'm proud of requires me to be relentlessly honest with myself." His dark eyes seemed to laser in on hers. Challenging her. "If the court of public opinion fell away, and there was no one else in the world to approve or disapprove of what I'm doing, would I still make that same choice?"

His gaze seemed to probe the depths of her soul as he spoke. As though his words, somehow, applied to her.

The people pleaser.

"If you're suggesting that Devon and I both make our decisions based on larger factors than personal desire, I couldn't agree more. Your brother tries to do what's best for Salazar Media." She felt defensive. Of herself. Of Devon.

"What about you, Lily?"

"I don't own a stake in the company," she reminded him.

"I realize that," he said, more gently. "Consider it a hypothetical question to help put yourself in my shoes." He stared out at the Bitterroot River again, perhaps sensing that the conversation was getting under her skin. "If you weren't worried about other people's opinions, would you still make the same choices?"

No.

The answer was immediate. Definitive. Surprising her with its force.

She had made so many decisions based on people's expectations of her that it would be difficult to point to those few that she'd made purely for herself. Though her job was one of them.

Still, she would never be able to discount what her grandparents wanted. They'd raised her, taking her in when her mother had quit caring about her. And she would always owe them for that.

But she couldn't deny that she may have given them too strong of a voice in her future—in everything from her job and her education to, yes, her pick of fiancé. That didn't make it a mistake, did it? They wanted what was best for her.

In the quiet aftermath of Marcus's question, she didn't like the new lens he'd given her to view her own decisions. Because what she saw through his eyes was not the woman she wanted to be.

The autumn breeze off the water suddenly brought a deeper chill, and Lily was grateful when Marcus turned the vehicle back toward the ranch.

Three

Just because Marcus had made a valid point didn't mean she needed to reassess her whole life, did it?

Lily wrestled with his words while she repacked her bags late that night, determined to fly back to New York despite Devon's insistence that she remain in Montana. Devon might be the person she reported to in the New York office, but his directives held equal weight with his brother's since they were copresidents. And Marcus wanted her gone. Hadn't he made that clear from the start? She'd just have to tell Devon that she'd received an order contradicting his. Another reason why the brothers needed to settle their battle themselves.

But that wasn't her problem. She couldn't stay here when Marcus had deliberately caused her mental anguish. Accusing her of spying. Stirring an unwelcome attraction. And then, to top it all off, intimating she'd chosen her fiancé for convenience. For ease. Because Eliot checked all the right boxes.

Not that Marcus had said it in so many words.

She rolled her socks together, lining them up in neat pairs along the bottom of her suitcase, taking no comfort from a ritual that usually helped her feel more in control before she traveled.

"Damn you." Stressed and out of sorts, she chucked the final pair of socks at the steer horns mounted above the queen-size bed in her suite.

Was she cursing herself? Marcus? Her fiancé, who hadn't answered the last three messages she'd left for him? She didn't even know. But it bothered her that Marcus's words resonated so deeply inside her, even hours after their talk at the river's edge.

She needed to get away from him and all the feelings he stirred. That had been half the reason she'd started packing. But would that even do any good?

Truth be told, Marcus Salazar didn't know much about her or her life outside work. He certainly didn't know anything about her romantic relationship. So she needed to take some ownership of the fact that she'd interpreted his words today as some kind of judgment about her engagement. *She'd* pulled the meaning out of that conversation.

Which meant…

She was the one with doubts.

Her knees folded, and she dropped down to sit on the edge of the bed.

Staring down at Eliot's ring on her finger, Lily wondered how long she'd been questioning her decision to marry a man who'd always been more of a friend to her than a romantic partner. Maybe that's why neither of them had been able to commit to a date. Why it had always been easy to extend their time apart from each other, the way Eliot had done the day before. Perhaps her initial acceptance of four more months apart was another important clue that he was not the right man for her. And that was something he needed to know sooner rather than later. No delays.

She needed to call Eliot again. And keep calling until she got through. Because the engagement had gone on long enough. It was time for them both to move forward with their lives and give up the pretense that a marriage was ever going to happen. She hoped he would see that, too, because she truly didn't want to hurt him. They'd been friends for a long time before the engagement, and she hated the idea of causing a friend pain. But she knew this was the right thing to do. She slid the heirloom diamond off her finger and placed it on the nightstand, at peace with her decision.

Picking up her phone, she hit the button to contact him through the video call app.

He answered on the first ring, his dark blond hair and gray eyes flickering to life on the screen. "Just the woman I wanted to speak to. Hello, Lily."

He wore a tuxedo shirt and black bowtie, though he looked thoroughly rumpled as he sat in an unfamiliar setting. A hotel lobby, perhaps? She saw a few other people in the background, but no one else was dressed like him. His eyes were sleepy and a little unfocused, reminding her it was roughly five in the morning on his end of the world. Was he just returning to his hotel? The dark shadow of bristle on his jawline suggested as much.

Nerves surged as she paced a circle around her suite.

"Hi," she managed after an awkward pause, surprised

to have him suddenly on the line. "I really need to talk to you."

"Are you upset that I had to extend my stay here?" he asked wearily. "You know I can't ignore my dad's wishes when it comes to this stuff." He plucked at his bowtie, loosening the knot that had already been crooked.

"I'm not upset, Eliot," she assured him, pausing her pacing to ensure her video image was still and focused on his end. "But I've been thinking about our engagement. About our mutual willingness to delay it inevitably. And I really think it's a sign that we need to call it off."

He seemed to shake off the weariness, his gray eyes widening as he leaned forward in the seat and shoved a hand through his hair.

"End the engagement?" he asked, a new urgency in his voice, still wrestling with the knot in his tie.

"Yes." She knew it was the right thing to do, but her stomach tensed anyway. "I'm so sorry to do this long-distance but—"

"What about the merger?" he blurted, forgetting all about the bowtie as he gestured with his hand. Then, as if hearing the way that sounded, he shook his head. "I mean, as much as it hurts to think about ending the engagement, we have more at stake here than just our personal happiness."

Frustration mingled with wariness and a touch of wounded pride. But, in all that tangle of emotions, she felt relief that "heartbreak" didn't seem to be an issue for either of them.

"I realize that." Releasing a pent-up breath, she sank into the window seat, careful not to crush the drawn damask curtains. "But marriage is too big of a commitment for us to make it just for business reasons."

"We make a great team, though, Lily." His gaze shifted to something beyond his phone. Or someone. Because he held up a finger as if to say *one more minute* to a person she couldn't see. His gaze flicked back to her. "We should at least consider other options before we walk away from the engagement."

A hurt deeper than wounded pride surprised her. Perhaps it was because Eliot didn't seem remotely concerned about the loss of love or companionship in his life—just the merger. Maybe he'd never felt anything deeper for her than friendship and fondness.

It didn't help matters that her intuition told her he was gesturing to a female companion. Not that it mattered now.

"Either we want a real marriage or we don't." Lily articulated the argument she'd been having with herself—quietly—for months. "After this conversation I feel certain that you're not any more ready for that step than I am."

In the background, she heard a woman's tinkling laughter. Eliot glanced up in the direction of the sound—aggravated—before refocusing on Lily.

"Lily, please—"

"Rest assured, I'll return the ring next week. And I'd like to wait until then to break the news to our families." She wouldn't keep a priceless family heirloom. Especially from a man whose interest in her seemed more mercenary by the moment.

"They're not going to be happy with this decision," Eliot warned her. "Not your family or mine."

"Which is why I'm going to wait to discuss it with my grandparents until I'm back home next week." Swallowing hard, she didn't want to think about that talk yet. "Thank you for understanding."

"I'm not sure I do." His eyes went back to whomever he was with. "I've got to go, though, Lily. We can talk about this later."

"That won't be necessary," she assured him, grateful to have the conversation over. "Goodbye, Eliot."

She felt no guilt about punching the disconnect button. If he was actually with a woman, Lily was a little surprised he'd taken the call at all. But she was relieved, more than anything, to have ended things with him.

As Lily felt the weight of the engagement fall away, a new burden settled on her shoulders. Eliot was right that her grandparents were going to be upset with her. Disappointing them was something she'd avoided her whole life, and she knew without question that they would disapprove of the broken engagement. Furthermore, a little voice in the back of her head reminded her, they definitely wouldn't be happy about how this might endanger the merger of the family businesses.

As she shut off her phone for the night, she began unpacking her suitcase. Maybe staying in Montana a little longer wasn't such a bad idea. Just until she figured out how to handle things on the home front.

It wasn't that she was hiding from them. Just…weighing her options for the future. Besides, she had a job to do at Mesa Falls Ranch. If things really fell apart with her family and the worst happened—if they disowned and disinherited her the way they did her mother—then Lily would need her job more than ever to pay her bills and secure her future. So right now, keeping Salazar Media intact seemed like the best use of her time.

Even if it meant facing Marcus again.

* * *

Enjoying the access to the stables at Mesa Falls Ranch, Marcus found himself on horseback for the third time in as many days. He'd attended a private boarding school where his father had taught, and horses had been an integral part of the program. Incoming freshmen bonded over a three-day trail ride, and the students' relationship with the school's animals grew from there. Every day at the Dowdon School, there'd been riding.

So he was comfortable enough on the Appaloosa as he filmed video footage of a team stringing a portable electric fence on a new patch of pasture for the ranch's cattle. Besides, this excursion took him away from the main lodge, where he'd be sure to run into Lily. To hedge his bets, he'd left at dawn again, shadowing the ranch manager all day.

Coop had explained that moving the animals more frequently, to smaller patches of grass, was a key element in the green ranching model. In the years that Mesa Falls had been adhering to the practices, they'd seen a strong increase in the health of the grasslands and the wetlands. This model involved changing the grazing areas and, of course, stringing fence a whole lot more often. Marcus was filming whatever parts of the process interested him.

When his cell phone vibrated, he shut off the camera and grabbed for it fast, seeing it was a call from his brother. He'd left messages for Devon an hour ago, following up on a long email he'd sent the day before about the paperwork their father had left for them.

"Any idea what the hell kind of papers Dad would have left with a Montana ranch owner instead of giving to his lawyer?" Marcus asked, not even bothering to say hello first.

"I wish you'd come straight to the point for a change," his brother deadpanned. "But no. I don't have a clue. And it seems strange—even for Dad—to keep the whole thing a secret."

"He was so careful laying out all his wishes for divvying up the property and his assets."

Devon gave a sarcastic laugh. "He had to be, since he knows you and I don't spend more than five minutes in a room together unless a client is involved."

In the background of the call, there were shouts and horns honking, completely out of sync with the yellowed field surrounding Marcus, where the only sounds he heard were dry grasses rustling in the cold air and the creak of saddle leather.

"Maybe the papers pertain to his mystery business," Marcus mused. "And we'll finally learn something about his unidentified sources of revenue."

Although Alonzo Salazar had taught English literature at the high school level, he'd always had a lifestyle that suggested he had a sideline, even long before he collected a paycheck with his sons' company.

"If the will didn't reveal anything, there's no way some musty papers in Montana are going to contain any surprises. It's something more sentimental. A letter to his grandkids or something."

The idea punched him in the gut, since Marcus had zero intentions of marrying, let alone fathering children. He'd seen firsthand how fast a family could disintegrate.

"No matter." Despite his father's failings, Marcus hated to think he'd died disappointed. But Devon was the last person he'd share his regrets with. "At least this explains why he made us promise to come to the ranch together. Clearly it's something he wants us both to learn at the same time."

"I'm working on getting there, believe me," Devon muttered. "In the meantime, can you lay off Lily? She does a hell of a job for the company, and she's got enough on her plate without you making her feel unwelcome."

Marcus wondered how tough the life of a pampered Newport heiress could be, but he didn't voice that thought.

"I'm giving her a wide berth. I can't promise I'll do more than that." He was doing her a favor by staying away, remembering how he'd gotten under her skin the day before. He genuinely hadn't set out to make judgments about her or her life when they'd gotten into the discussion at the river's edge. But he'd seen in her eyes when he'd struck a nerve.

All the more reason for him to let her be.

"While you're at it, you could stop accusing her of spying for me. If I wanted some kind of secret updates on you, I think I'd send someone who doesn't…stand out as much as Lily."

A surge of something—defensiveness? Jealousy?—roared through him. The horse must have felt it, too, since she gave a long shudder with a sharp head shake.

"What the hell is that supposed to mean?" Did Devon know that Marcus was attracted to Lily? What if he'd chosen to send her to Montana just because she had a way of messing with his head on another level rather than just spying?

Regardless, Marcus knew he needed to get his attraction for her under control. But it was a lot easier to manage when they were on opposite coasts.

"We both know Lily doesn't exactly blend into the

background." There was a scuffling sound on Devon's end of the call before he returned. "Look, I've got a situation here. I'll let you know what news I hear from the embassy tomorrow." Then he abruptly disconnected the call, leaving Marcus more aggravated than before.

It would be easy to pass off the discontent as part of his old standoff with Devon. And no doubt, that accounted for some of it. But Marcus couldn't help the underlying concern that his greater frustration stemmed from having Lily too much in his thoughts. He'd upset her enough that she'd mentioned it to Devon, apparently.

Yet, if she understood what was at stake—that Marcus was using all his restraint to stay away from her— maybe she'd see the situation differently. He didn't want to impede her ability to do her job. And he still believed they could work together effectively as long as they maintained what had worked in the past—conference calls, emails or group chats. Maybe he'd been too subtle about what he felt for her.

This time, when he got back to the ranch, he needed to draw the line in a way she couldn't possibly misunderstand.

Lily toured the ranch's private spa on her own, having obtained the key from the head of housekeeping. With no retreat guests this week aside from Lily and Marcus, the spa wasn't currently staffed. But she had wanted to explore as many aspects of the retreat as possible, and this decadent facet of the business was a feast for the senses, from the scented soaps and candles for sale in a display case to the soothing sound of water burbling in the stone fountain.

After peeking into the various treatment rooms, Lily

stood at the front counter and perused the list of spa services, wishing she could indulge herself. The last eighteen hours since she'd called off things with Eliot had been a relief, but stressful, too. He'd messaged her twice, asking her to reconsider, never once mentioning that he loved her or couldn't imagine life without her. That shouldn't have hurt her, considering she'd been the one to break things off. And yet it underscored that she'd been blind to what had been missing in their relationship for years.

And of course, she was worried about what would happen with the merger they'd planned for their families' companies. Would they be inviting the same kind of corporate unrest that the Salazar brothers experienced?

She couldn't answer that. And part of the reason was because she hadn't told her grandparents about the split yet. Yes, it had business implications that would resonate throughout Carrington Financial and Winthrop Wealth Management. But that fact didn't have to dictate how she handled her love life. She closed her eyes for a moment, breathing in the scent of lavender and chamomile that permeated the room. The ceiling fan stirred the plants around the stone fountain, the sound calming her frayed nerves.

Then she heard the thump of boots reverberate on the tile floor behind her.

Straightening, she whipped around to find Marcus in the spa with her, the main door falling silently to a close behind him. He cast a long shadow with the light falling behind him. A shadow that hovered over her.

"I've been looking all over for you." He ran a hand through his dark hair. She noticed his cheeks were a deeper tan than the day before. He was dressed for riding in jeans and boots as scuffed and well-worn as any of the ranch hands'.

"I thought I'd check out some areas of the property that you might overlook." She felt oddly naked around him without her ring on her finger. Or maybe it was just being near him in this private place. She tucked her hands in her pockets. "But if you'd rather photograph the spa, I can find somewhere else to go."

He'd made it clear from the first day that he was trying to avoid her. That he'd rather she were back in New York. So she planned to stay well out of his way. Even if she owed him a debt of gratitude for helping her to view her engagement in a new light.

She wasn't ready to thank him for that just yet, especially when he still believed she was spying for Devon. The idea was an affront to all the hard work she'd done for the company.

"No. That won't be necessary." He sounded emphatic. "I wanted to speak to you."

He took a step closer, and she remembered she was still clutching the menu of spa services. She turned back to the counter to set it aside, wishing her heart didn't gallop quite so much around him. It was one thing to break off her engagement because of a conversation she had with Marcus. It would be quite another to…have anything more to do with him. They were coworkers. Nothing more.

She remembered all too well what her grandparents thought of her mother when she'd run off with a lover, turning her back on the family.

Choosing romance over responsibility had devastating consequences.

"I'm listening," she said simply, wishing they could

have the conversation in a more businesslike setting, preferably with a conference table between them rather than in a space flanked by massage tables and hot tubs.

"Devon asked me to lay off where you're concerned." His eyes glittered with something dark and unreadable. Something compelling. "His words."

She'd never met someone so willing to wade right into the fray. To prod at difficult topics and demand answers. There was a reason Devon usually handled the clients, not Marcus.

"I made him aware that I couldn't do my job well since you don't trust me." She wasn't sure how else to respond. "That makes my presence here counterproductive." She fisted her hands deeper in her pockets, braced for wherever this was heading.

"The lack of trust I could work around," he clarified, closing more of the distance between them. "It's a matter of me being attracted to you that is presenting the problem." He stopped less than an arm's length away from her.

With any other man, she could shut down this line of discussion in no time flat. She understood professional boundaries and knew how to enforce them. But the problem that dogged her with Marcus was that she was attracted, too.

Her mouth went dry as she struggled for words. "I—"

He didn't seem to hear. Or maybe she hadn't actually made a sound. Either way, he continued.

"I fell short of making that clear to you the first day, hoping to find an alternative way to address a problem that is one hundred percent of my own making." He stood so close she could have counted the bristles along his jaw. If she'd been so inclined. "But at this point, I feel like I owe you an explanation—an apology, actually—

for my behavior when it's having a negative impact on your job. I'm sorry."

"You're attracted to me." She thought back to her conversations with Marcus before today, sliding in the new piece of information to see how it fit. Realizing it explained a whole lot. "I'm not sure how to respond to that."

"I'm still dealing with the ramifications myself." His brows swooped down low, his gaze narrowing. "The ethics of the situation are clear. Salazar Media put a mandatory disclosure policy on work relationships for a reason."

She nodded awkwardly, still taking in what he was saying. "We don't have a relationship," she reminded him. "So there's nothing to disclose. And even if we did, you aren't my direct supervisor."

She knew company policy backward and forward after sitting in on the committee to revise the standards the year before. Not that she was contemplating a relationship of any sort since she'd just ended one. Her thoughts were just jumbled.

"That's splitting hairs, as I'm sure you know." His jaw flexed. "It's a professional line I can't cross. And on a personal level, even if we didn't work for the same company, I'm not the sort of man who would ever make a pass at a woman who is…otherwise engaged."

His dark eyes glittered with a spark of heat that he didn't bother to hide.

"I'm sure you're not—" she began, hoping to divert this line of conversation. Unwilling to acknowledge her newly discovered awareness of Marcus until she knew how to handle it.

"I'm not that kind of man," he repeated, his voice lowering. "But with you, Lily, I'm tempted."

Her breath caught. Held. She blinked back at him,

feeling awkward about sharing the news of her broken engagement when they stood this close. Then again, keeping it to herself when he'd just made a wrong assumption felt uncomfortably close to deception.

And wasn't she trying to overcome his lack of trust in her?

"I'm actually—" Her voice cracked, and she cleared her throat, telling herself it wasn't a big deal to share the truth with him. Telling Marcus was nothing like facing her grandparents. She pulled her left hand from her pocket and showed him her bare ring finger. "We decided to call things off."

For a moment, Marcus's eyes remained on hers, not tracking to her raised palm. But then, as he refocused on her hand, she saw his expression shift, transforming from wary tension to something more resolute.

Determined.

"You ended your engagement." His dark gaze tracked back to hers, and she could feel the attraction he'd talked about. His. And yes, hers.

Which was highly inconvenient. Uncomfortable, even, given what he'd just shared with her. She felt an invisible barrier between them fall away and wondered how she'd ever recover her defenses.

Or if she even wanted to.

"I did." She didn't recognize her own voice, too breathy and uncertain. "I just wanted you to know because it seemed dishonest to pretend otherwise when—"

"Lily." Something in his voice gentled, undoing her completely.

Her name on his lips, so softly spoken, drew her to him like steel fragments to a magnet. She felt all the fractured, uncertain pieces of her leaning toward him, responding to the heated promise in his dark eyes. And it didn't matter that they walked a tightrope of professional responsibility. She took a step closer.

"I'm glad I did it." She didn't know if she was reassuring him or her, but standing here with Marcus right now underscored how necessary it had been to end her engagement. "I didn't understand why I was so compelled to pick up the phone and inform him of it yesterday, but it's starting to make sense."

Marcus shook his head in silent denial, but he lifted his hand to her cheek, grazing a path down to her jaw. Even when her heartbeat kicked faster, she knew she could still stop this unwise moment before it happened. It wasn't too late to crush all the needy feelings stirring inside her. She could never allow herself to be one of those women who threw everything away for the sake of sizzling chemistry and heated embraces.

But since she'd also never felt anything like the draw of Marcus Salazar, she thought it couldn't hurt to see what it might be like *just once*.

It was simple curiosity. Normal human want. Just this one time, she could step into the fire of combustible attraction and experience the burn.

The flames licked up her already, torching away reason. And by the time his lips met hers, the heady sensation was the most exquisite feeling she could have imagined.

So good, Lily could almost forget she was playing with fire.

Four

There had been times in Lily's life when she'd listened to her girlfriends gush about a new guy, had seen them glowing with a kind of radiance, yet she'd never fully comprehended what all the hype was about.

Until now.

Marcus's kiss delivered all the fanfare and more. She saw stars. Her knees went weak. Her every nerve ending was on overload. With his lips moving over hers, she understood every breathless confidence about romance in a way she hadn't before. Because while she respected and admired her former fiancé, he'd never made her feel like she might spontaneously combust from the pleasure of his hands on her waist. Or from the searing heat of his body suddenly pressed to hers.

She reached for Marcus's shoulders to steady herself. To draw him closer. To make sure this was real and not a dream…

Only to have him pull away abruptly with a ripe curse, softly spoken.

She couldn't process it, though, not when her senses still reeled and her body tingled with hot desire. Her brain too scrambled to speak yet, she steadied herself with a hand on the cool granite countertop of the spa's reception desk. Anchoring herself in a world tipped sideways.

"I didn't mean for that to happen." Marcus shook his head, his hands falling away from her. "Or at least, not to that degree."

Flustered at his withdrawal, she wasn't quite sure how to interpret that.

"It felt like you meant it." She folded her arms across her breasts, needing a barrier between her body and his when she felt so raw from just a kiss.

How could he revert to conversation so easily after what had just happened? She hadn't suspected that level of heat lurked beneath the surface between them, but now that she knew, she didn't have a clue how to pretend she hadn't felt it for those few tantalizing moments.

"I've been wanting to do that for a long time," he acknowledged, pacing away from her toward a shelf full of dried flowers and white scented candles. "But that doesn't mean I should have acted on the impulse. I'm sorry, Lily."

Feeling off balance, she flexed her fingers against the granite while his back was turned toward her. "We'll figure out a work-around."

She hoped. Now that she understood some of the reason for his behavior toward her, she could surely figure out a way to get back on level ground, professionally speaking.

"And I should have asked you how you're feeling

before I—presumed to kiss you." He turned to meet her gaze again. "I'm sure it must have been a difficult decision to end a significant relationship, and I wouldn't want to take advantage of you at a vulnerable time."

She was surprised by his thoughtfulness, considering how antagonistic things had been between them. She tried to understand this new facet to Marcus's personality.

"I'm fine." Or at least, she would be once she adjusted to letting go of her family's expectations. And once she'd assured herself she could put Marcus's kiss into perspective. "In retrospect, I should thank you. It was our conversation by the river that helped me see I was holding on to the engagement because it was easy. Expected, even."

"Expected?" Frowning, he sniffed at one of the candles on the shelf. "By who?"

"My grandparents. Eliot's family. Our marriage would have solidified a longtime business relationship between the Carringtons and the Winthrops. Once we had wed, we were going to unite our families' respective financial services businesses." She grazed her fingertips over her lips, then stopped herself once she realized what she was doing.

She didn't need Marcus to know how much the kiss had rattled her. He certainly didn't appear as if his world had been rocked the way hers had been. Was it because he was better at hiding his emotions? Or because the kiss hadn't been as big of a deal to him? She bristled at the thought.

"How imperative was the merger? Is your family's business struggling?" He slid the candle back onto the shelf and walked toward her again.

Her nerve endings danced in anticipation. So much so that she took a step away, bumping into the spa's front counter.

"We'll be all right." She hoped. Her head ached with the new worry. "And even if we aren't, I can't justify remaining in an engagement for the sake of the family business."

He stared at her for a long moment. Assessing her.

"Are you sure about that?" His dark eyes wandered over her, rousing a whole host of complicated feelings.

Desire. Awareness. Guilt.

"Positive." She nodded, unsure of her footing with this man. She'd come to Montana hoping to help Marcus and Devon resolve their business differences and keep the company together. But Marcus's attention was proving too distracting. Too tempting.

And she needed this job more than ever.

"So what else did Devon have to say?" She needed to refocus on her professional obligations. Fast.

Marcus leaned on the counter beside her, his long legs close to hers. "He expects to hear from the embassy tomorrow, but I'm not holding my breath."

"Did you tell him about the papers your father left here?" she asked carefully, unsure how much he would be willing to share about it.

"I did. He was as surprised as I am that Dad didn't leave them with his attorney." He studied her for a long moment. "And I don't want to press you about the broken engagement if you'd rather not discuss it. But since you gave me credit for opening your eyes to the fact that you don't love him—"

"It's not that," she clarified, feeling a sudden defensiveness. She straightened from the spa counter, pacing over to the fountain, where water babbled down a rock wall, wishing she could find peace in the serene sound. "I've been friends with Eliot forever, and I hope that doesn't change."

Then again, what if he really had been seeing someone else? She didn't like what that said about Eliot's character.

Still, it seemed disloyal to talk to Marcus about the details of her failed relationship.

"You still love him," Marcus observed.

She ran a fingertip along the surface of the spilling water, letting the cold wash away the mix of guilt and awareness. Or else just hoping it could.

"Not the way I should. Neither of us was in any hurry to set a date, and we've been actively avoiding any discussion of wedding plans." She knew that indefinite delay had meant something. "Our friendship is really just that. A friendship."

Marcus came up behind her. She felt the warmth of his body just inches from her back and suppressed the urge to turn and face him. To repeat the sensual contact that had her off balance even now, minutes after their kiss.

What if she couldn't stick to the *just once* bargain she'd made with herself?

"I realize my kiss was ill timed and impulsive, given what you must have been through in the last twenty-four hours." His voice tickled along the back of her neck. "And that doesn't begin to address the professional transgression, which I'm still at a loss about how to handle."

Her breath caught.

"I can't afford to lose this job," she reminded herself as much as him. "So if you'd like me to disclose a relationship to HR because of one momentary indiscretion, I will. But we're both adults, Marcus. We aren't the first people to overstep that line in a professional setting. And bottom line, we still have to work together this week."

"You won't consider returning to New York now that I've been honest about what makes this relationship problematic?" His voice sounded even nearer now.

She held herself very still, her fingertips resting on the waist-high rock wall where the water pooled. "I need to be here."

He huffed out a frustrated breath, his body close enough to hers that she didn't dare turn around and look at him when her emotions were all knotted. "Then we'll have to find a way to make it work."

She closed her eyes, letting the feel of his nearness sweep over her, tantalizing her for one heart-stopping moment.

Would she be foolish enough to let him touch her again? Even knowing the power of his kiss?

She was grateful she didn't have to make that call when he turned on his heel and walked away, leaving her in the spa with her heated thoughts.

Exhaling a pent-up breath, Lily took stock of her situation. She couldn't fail at her career so close on the heels of failing in her personal life. Her work was the one place where she was independent, earning only what her skills warranted and not what her last name afforded her. She prized that. So the attraction to Marcus was going to make her workweek more than a little difficult, especially since Devon had specifically sent her to the ranch to help keep Salazar Media intact.

She'd simply have to redouble her efforts to forget about the kiss—and somehow convince Marcus that remaining in business with his brother was in his best interest.

* * *

Her tennis shoes sinking in a pile of dead leaves, Regina Flores tucked deeper into the woods behind the spa building at Mesa Falls Ranch, needing to stay hidden. She'd worn dark clothing for today's reconnaissance mission, but she was hardly invisible. There was always a chance someone on the property would see her. She'd had a good view of the couple in the spa from her spot outside one of the treatment room windows, especially with the help of her camera's zoom lens. But she'd had to leave the vantage point once Marcus Salazar stalked out of the building.

She couldn't allow him to see her. Not before she'd worked out a cover story.

A light snow began to fall as she slipped her camera inside her jacket, holding her breath while he mounted his spotted horse. Regina wished she could have heard his conversation with the pretty brunette. Had they spoken about anything significant? Anything that would help Regina's cause? She couldn't tell.

Their kiss had looked—new. Both of them had seemed surprised about it. Thanks to her zoom lens, Regina had observed the stunned desire in Marcus's eyes when he pulled away from the woman. And although Regina hadn't been able to see the brunette's expression afterward, she could read the body language well enough. There'd been an awkward aftermath to that kiss. The woman had been uneasy, restless in her own skin.

Yet before that, there'd been a telltale lean toward Marcus. As if she wanted more from him.

Maybe none of that mattered in the big scheme of things to Regina's mission here. But since she wasn't entirely sure what she was looking for at Mesa Falls

Ranch—only that the long-sought answer to a puzzle was here on this property—Regina wouldn't discount any clue, however small. She needed to know what Marcus and Devon Salazar were planning once both brothers arrived on-site.

They were fulfilling a request from their dying father to be here.

That alone made it imperative for Regina to figure out why. Did it have anything to do with the ill-gotten gains that Alonzo Salazar had made at the expense of Regina's family? She refused to see any Salazar profit from her misfortunes—even Alonzo's heirs.

He had been her greatest enemy, and now he was gone. His death had robbed her of the direct revenge she craved. But if there was a chance that the dead man had funneled the tainted revenue stream to his heirs, Regina would find a way to stop it.

First, however, she needed information.

Watching Marcus Salazar ride away from the spa building, Regina drew a breath once again, filling her lungs with the fresh, pine-scented air. Another time, she might have enjoyed the rugged beauty of the Montana landscape. The Bitterroot River rushed fast in some places and meandered slowly around big, rocky curves in others, the mountains rising with a jagged majesty in the distance.

This was no vacation, however. No joyride through the western states. She was only at Mesa Falls Ranch to learn everything she could about the Salazar heirs and their plans for their father's estate.

Alonzo had destroyed her family with his thinly disguised "fictional" novel based on her family. He'd never claimed the story, written under a pseudonym, as his own, but she knew he was the author. The private investigator she'd hired had finally found irrefutable evidence after years of digging. That book had torn apart her parents' marriage, revealing her mother's infidelity and Regina's real father in a way that had severed her relationship with the man who'd raised her—the only father Regina had ever known. So even though Alonzo was dead, she would find a way to make sure his heirs didn't profit any more from that story.

Her story.

But she wanted to get to know them first to determine if they could be reasoned with. After what their father had done, though, she was doubtful they would be trustworthy, having been brought up by such an awful person. Alonzo hadn't restricted his hurtful deeds to just her father or her mother. He'd harmed her, too, and she'd only been a teen at the time.

Her father had turned her out of her home.

Marcus Salazar was fair game if he could lead her to answers, especially since she suspected his business had been built on income from her family scandal. As for the pretty brunette who lingered inside the spa, she could be an important piece of the puzzle. A way to get close to the Salazars. Regina watched as the woman brushed a tentative hand along her lips, as if remembering Marcus's kiss even now.

Regina needed to figure out who she was and her connection to the Salazar family. If she was important to Marcus, that made her important to Regina. For entirely different reasons.

A twinge of conscience stung at the thought that the woman might be innocent. But Regina tamped it down by reminding herself that if the woman really was innocent, Regina would be doing her a favor to keep her out of the Salazar web. And clearly, the man meant something to her, which made her biased about the Salazars. Someone not to be trusted.

With Marcus well out of sight, Regina sidled around to the front of the building and searched for a way to let herself inside. The sooner she learned more about what the Salazars were doing in Montana, the sooner Regina could enact her plan for revenge.

In the middle of a stern mental talk with herself, Lily heard a rustling sound near the front door of the spa.

"Marcus?" She straightened from her spot at the counter, instantly alert. "Is that you?"

It was frustrating to see how quickly her heart rate ratcheted right back up.

"Hello?" The feminine voice coming from the foyer quickly deflated those thoughts. Then the voice's owner, a petite brunette in dark work clothes and tennis shoes, strode into the room. "I'm looking for the manager?"

"I'm a guest of the ranch. Lily Carrington." She extended her hand.

The woman smiled, dimples flashing in a way that transformed her face from pretty to stunning, all without an ounce of makeup as far as Lily could tell. The rich olive tone of her skin seemed to make her silver-gray eyes stand out all the more.

"Regina Flores." The newcomer squeezed Lily's palm quickly before letting go. "I live nearby and thought I'd see about a job here."

"The ranch manager is Cooper Adler. He could probably help you. His office is in the main guest lodge." Lily pointed in the general direction.

Regina nodded, hair sliding over one shoulder. "I'll

definitely check in with him." She hesitated, her quicksilver eyes taking in the spa features. "So no one is working in here today? I'd love to book an appointment sometime, but I'll bet all the services cost a small fortune."

"I'm not sure." She didn't know how to answer that since she didn't think the spa was going to be open to the general public, just to guests. "The ranch manager unlocked the building for me to look around because my company is doing some advertising for the ranch."

"Lucky you." The woman's gaze darted to Lily as she gave a conspiratorial grin. "Maybe having a job here will help me get access to the spa, too."

"Would you like me to take you over to the guest lodge?" she offered. "I can introduce you to Coop."

"No need, but thank you just the same." Regina waved off the proposal, and as she did so a paper fell from her pocket. "I'll go in a minute."

"You dropped something." Lily bent to retrieve the brightly colored drawing from the white tile floor. It looked like a map.

"Oh. Right." Regina took the paper quickly, blushing as she tucked into her pocket. "I've been trying to memorize the trails around here before I put myself in front of the ranch manager. I really do need a job, so I want to be able to fit into whatever role they need. Trail guide. Animal care. Cattle driver."

Regina's willingness to accept any of those jobs said a lot about how much she wanted—and needed—the work. Lily felt a swell of empathy for her, knowing that without her grandparents' support, she would have been in a similar situation. They'd cut off Lily's mother completely, which had occasionally put Lily in the impossible position of mediating between them.

Would they be as quick to withdraw their support of her now that Lily had made a huge decision that would affect Carrington Financial without consulting them? A deeper sense of doom resounded through her as she considered the broken engagement in that light.

"Are there many trails for riding?" Lily asked in an overbright voice, determined to redirect her thoughts back to her job. "I've been meaning to explore the whole property."

She needed to make her position at Salazar Media unassailable, no matter which Salazar brother walked away with control of the company. She had to be indispensable.

"There are tons, especially on the side where the ranch borders the Bitterroot National Forest." Regina pulled a packet from her other pocket while tucking her personal papers even farther out of sight. "I have an extra map of the area, if you'd like one. It has a few public trails marked around the perimeter of the ranch."

"Thank you." Lily opened the packet, which looked like it might be from a welcome center or local chamber of commerce. "I appreciate that."

After a few more polite exchanges, the woman departed to seek out Coop, leaving Lily to her own devices again. She would study the property in more detail tonight and plan for a ride the next day. It would keep her focused on her job, which was critical right now. And as an added bonus, it would keep her away from the ranch, ensuring she didn't fall into Marcus's arms again.

What the hell had he done?

Restless and edgy from the kiss he'd shared with Lily, Marcus urged his horse to go faster as they headed toward a high point on the Mesa Falls Ranch property. He'd intended to make his interest in her crystal clear so she'd stay away from him. Instead, she'd stunned him to his toes by flashing that bare ring finger of hers.

She'd ended things with her fiancé. In part because of something he'd said in his ramble down by the river. But was that all there was to it? Or had the attraction between them played a role?

Marcus bent low over his mount's neck, feeling the Appaloosa's deep, even breaths as she surged higher up the hill. Together, they broke through a last stand of trees, emerging into a rocky clearing at the top. The horse slowed her pace naturally, and Marcus eased back in the saddle, gathering his bearings.

Jumping down to the ground, Marcus let the horse catch her breath while he walked to the edge of a cliff overhang to check out the view. A cold Montana wind stirred snow flurries from the trees. He tipped his head into the icy flakes, needing the crisp air to blow away the cobwebs in his brain. Or at least let him recover enough brain cells to figure out what had made him kiss Lily like his life depended on it.

Damn.

The move had been unwise at best—mixing his personal and professional worlds wasn't a good idea—and downright risky to his goal of maneuvering his brother out of Salazar Media. Lily was Devon's friend. Devon's confidante. And no matter what she said to the contrary, she was almost certainly Devon's spy this week.

Why else would his brother send the chief operating officer in his stead when he got stranded in India? If Devon had truly been concerned about his brother closing a deal, he could have sent their best account rep.

Turning from the view of the river valley, Marcus

stalked toward the opposite side of the hilltop to peer back down in the direction he'd come from. Through the trees, he could see a few ranch hands creating a new pasture area with electric fencing, a never-ending task with the sustainable ranching model Mesa Falls had adopted.

Beyond that, farther down the long slope, Marcus glimpsed a corner of the spa building where he'd left the newly single Lily Carrington. He could make out a gabled roof over the side door and a hint of the gray slate pathway bracketed by snow-dusted bushes on either side.

In fact, was that her now, hurrying down the steps?

A dark-haired figure in black rushed down the path and darted out of view so quickly he almost thought he'd imagined her. Was it Lily? She'd been wearing a silky pink blouse when he'd been with her earlier. He remembered the feel of the fabric against his fingers when he'd pulled her to him and tasted the lips he'd dreamed about too many times. She could have a black jacket, though.

As he lingered there, reliving the kiss he probably shouldn't have claimed but couldn't ever regret, Marcus spotted a flash of pink. Lily—even from this distance he knew it was her—strode out of the spa at a more leisurely pace than the woman he'd just seen. She turned back toward the door briefly, as if checking the lock or making sure she hadn't left something behind. While he watched, she zipped up the placket on a plum-colored coat.

Had there been someone else in the spa when he'd spoken to Lily? Had someone witnessed the kiss? Not that it was a huge secret or something forbidden. But it rankled him to think someone might have been there without them knowing. His brother's words from an earlier phone call rattled around his brain.

*If I wanted some kind of secret updates on you, I think
I'd send someone who doesn't stand out as much as Lily.*

Could Devon have done something like that? It seemed
far-fetched, even for Devon. The woman was more likely
someone who worked at the ranch. He put her out of his
mind for the moment as his gaze tracked Lily until she
disappeared from view on the gray stone pathway.

Even from this distance, she drew him.

And now that she was unattached…

Cursing himself for letting his brain wander in that direction, he turned away from the cliff's edge and stalked
back toward his horse. He had enough trouble of his own
without borrowing the kind Lily Carrington would bring
into his life. He should be focused on finding a way to
buy out Devon's share of Salazar Media. Or figuring out
how to obtain the papers that his father had left for Devon
and him to open together.

But memories of Lily in his arms taunted him. The
flash of heat in her pale blue eyes before he'd kissed her.
The astonishment he'd glimpsed there afterward. Had it
been surprise because he'd kissed her in the first place?
Or might she have been rattled at how much it had affected her?

She'd felt so damned good against him, her subtle
curves tempting his hands to explore every inch. And
in turn, her fingertips had been hungry and restless as
they'd skimmed over his arms.

A crow cackled in a nearby tree. Glancing up, he found
the bird perched in a ponderosa pine cawing down at him
like a troubled conscience, as if it was chiding him over
how foolish it was to think about Lily when he needed to
leave her alone. Marcus called to the Appaloosa, know-

ing it was time to get back to civilization when he was starting to find meaning in random bird noises.

Mounting the mare, he patted the horse's neck and steered her toward the path back to the ranch. He had work to do, for starters, and he would just avoid Lily for the next few days. She was bound to be upset by the broken engagement, so he had no business confusing her with the attraction he felt for her. It was just lust, pure and simple.

Strong as hell, yes. But lust nonetheless.

It had to be. Because Marcus knew better than to feel anything more complicated than that for a woman with strong ties to his brother, her very presence threatening what he held most dear—his business.

Five

Lily sat at a game table in the great room of the lodge the next afternoon, poring over maps of the ranch. In theory, she was plotting a ride around the property to get a better feel for the area and the client's needs. Her encounter with Regina Flores, the helpful local who'd lent her a map, had given Lily the inspiration she needed to quit brooding about the unexpected kiss from Marcus and the inevitable fallout with her grandparents when they learned she was giving Eliot back his ring.

As long as she was in Montana, she might as well make the most of it. Shuffling the paper maps, she reminded herself she had work to do. Marcus may have made light of her role here, but she planned to do her part to help Salazar Media secure Mesa Falls Ranch as an account long-term. In particular, she wanted to find a way to share the experience of this beautiful property with the world. Her company had often kicked off a client's social media campaign with an event. The photos made for great posts and invited additional engagement. Lily had a few basic ideas, possibly with a charitable tie-in, but she wanted to see more of the land herself to find a unique angle or backdrop. Talking to people who worked the ranch could help, too.

Moreover, riding the ranch herself would give her time to enjoy the beauty of western Montana and provide some distance from Marcus. The man seemed to lurk in every corner of her thoughts since that heated encounter in the spa.

Her cell phone vibrated on the game table, sending a rush of anticipation through her before she could quell it. No doubt Marcus would want to meet again soon.

But the caller ID screen showed Devon's name instead. An odd mixture of relief and disappointment swirled through her.

"Devon?" She shifted her focus to business. "Has there been any word from the embassy?"

"I've been cleared to travel," he told her, his words spoken over a rush of other voices in the background. "I'm at the airport now."

"That's great news." She wondered briefly what that meant for her. Should she pack her things? "I think the meeting with Marcus is better left in your hands."

Maybe she'd recover from the crazy attraction once she was back in her office on the other side of the country.

"Actually, Lily, I'd prefer you don't mention my travel status to my brother." The background noise grew louder for a moment and quieted down.

"Why?" She felt a sinking sensation in her chest, hating to be put in a position of keeping secrets, given Marcus's distrust of her. "It's important for you to both be here since your father left paperwork—"

"I'm aware of that." Devon sighed with a hint of impatience. "I've got to board soon, so I won't be in the States until tomorrow anyhow. But I have some urgent business errands to run before I head to the ranch. I'm worried about—"

The call cut out.

Lily checked her screen and saw the phone showed the connection was still live. "Devon? Are you there?"

"Sorry." His voice came back with a crackle. "I need some more information about that paperwork before I sit in the same room as Marcus to hear whatever bombshell Dad might have dropped."

Nervous tension had Lily on her feet, pacing around the table, her riding boots quiet on the Aztec rug.

"I don't understand." She glanced toward the entrance of the room, ensuring she was still alone. "You think he knows what those papers contain?"

"I heard rumors about my dad's secret work for years," Devon said cryptically. "But I thought a lot of that was because my mother—well, there were a lot of hard feelings between her and my father. I just know I need to investigate a couple of possibilities before I get blindsided right in front of Marcus."

Lily recalled Marcus's expression when Cooper had informed him of the paperwork. He couldn't have faked that surprise. "I really don't think he knows anything."

"But he wants to buy me out." Devon's words were clipped. Brusque. "Marcus will use anything to get control of the company. I can't risk giving him the upper hand." For a moment, a loudspeaker announcement in the airport muted anything Devon said. "I'm boarding now, Lily. Just keep quiet that you heard from me, okay? And—most importantly—be careful of Marcus."

The call disconnected.

Be careful? Just what did that mean?

Worried about her new role keeping secrets from Marcus, Lily felt a kink in her neck that spiraled down into both shoulders. When she was back in the office, she would give Devon a piece of her mind. She might still report to him, but she was no longer his assistant, and she didn't appreciate being dragged into corporate politics. She'd earned her promotion because she was supremely well qualified for the job. Devon had no right to take advantage of their friendship.

She tapped her phone against her chin, thinking.

For now, she supposed it couldn't hurt to do as he asked. She just wished he hadn't called her at all and put her in this position.

She heard footsteps on the hardwood floor outside the great room, and Marcus appeared in the archway. Her belly did a flip as she tucked away her phone.

Dressed in dark jeans and boots, he looked as if he'd been out riding again. She'd seen him on horseback multiple times since arriving, which surprised her. She'd always thought of him as more of a tech guy with his knowledge of the digital side of their business. He set aside his snow-dusted jacket on a bar stool, his long-sleeved T-shirt stretched tight across his shoulders.

"Lily." He stopped near the empty bar, watching her. "I didn't know you were in here."

Could he make it any more obvious that he was giving her space? Or did he simply regret that kiss?

Rattled for more reasons than she cared to pick through right now, Lily moved toward the table and began gathering her papers. She should be pleased that Marcus was wary of her, since it would make it easy for her to be careful around him, as Devon had put it.

But what if she didn't feel like being careful every moment of her life? a rebellious part of her asked. An overinflated sense of doing the right thing had sent her into a two-year engagement with a man who had barely winced at losing her.

"I was just leaving," she said, lifting her chin to look Marcus in the eye. It might not be totally his fault that she was feeling exasperated. But he certainly played a role. "You can have the room all to yourself."

"What's wrong?" His dark brows swooped together, his expression puzzled as he moved deeper into the room. "You seem upset."

She took her time folding one of the larger maps into sections. "Do I? Not surprising, considering how difficult you're making it to do my job. You gladly ignore me, except for the moments when you claim tremendous interest in me, followed by more cold suspicion and distance." She managed a tight smile. "I'm actually delighted to work on my own. Without you."

She hadn't realized how much she'd craved the chance to tell him exactly what she thought of his hot-and-cold routine the day before. But she recognized now how much his behavior had weighed on her, and it was a relief to have her resentment out in the open.

"I didn't know you had a sarcastic streak." An amused smile played across his lips.

"There's a great deal you don't know about me." Flustered, she jammed the remaining paperwork into her bag, unwilling to take the time to smooth out the folds. "But then, your assumptions are always so accurate, why bother to really get to know anyone?"

She plowed past him, her eye on the exit.

"You're right. I've been hell to work with and unfair to you, Lily. I'm sorry."

The stark honesty of the words slowed her step. She found it impossible to keep the full head of steam when his apology had just stuck a pin in her anger. She pivoted to face him.

"Thank you for acknowledging that," she said stiffly, feeling adrift in this relationship unlike any other she'd been in.

Marcus wasn't just a professional colleague anymore—not after that kiss they'd shared. But they didn't have a friendship. Or a romantic relationship. And they couldn't really be enemies with that apology hanging between them, softening the edges of what she'd been feeling. Whatever she was navigating with him sure felt like uncharted terrain.

"What would you say to a fresh start?" He took a step closer. "We clear the slate, forget about the assumptions and misunderstandings, and begin again?"

Wariness mingled with the attraction she couldn't seem to escape.

"You make it sound easy." She couldn't imagine clearing her mind of all the preconceived notions she had about him. And she was pretty sure that damned sensual awareness of him wasn't going anywhere.

"Maybe it won't be." The deep resonance of his voice was like a caress. "But since we took on the ranch as a high-profile client, I think there's too much riding on our working relationship for us to fail."

She took a deep breath to steel herself and ended up

catching a hint of his aftershave. She resisted the urge to close her eyes and savor it.

"Agreed." She didn't want to mess up the career she'd built. Besides, she needed it now more than ever to prove to her grandparents that she could stand on her own two feet. She had too much pride to go running to them for help.

"Good." A glimmer of satisfaction lit his dark eyes as a smile kicked up one corner of his mouth. "Why don't we start by you telling me where it is you're trying to go with all those maps? Chances are, I can help you get there."

For a breathless moment, her brain conjured tantalizing images of what that might entail. She suspected Marcus possessed a great deal of knowledge about getting her where she'd like to go.

But then he pointed to the papers sticking out of her bag at odd angles, redirecting her thoughts. Cursing her wayward imagination, she reached into the tote and hastily rearranged the maps.

"I want to tour the whole ranch," she admitted, grateful to focus on something other than Marcus's hands or his compelling voice. "I thought I'd try to gather some inspiration for a kickoff event, possibly something set on the ranch."

"Let me take you," he offered. "Do you ride?"

She met his gaze, wondering what it would be like to spend the whole day with him. Alone.

"I do." She pushed the words past the dryness in her throat.

"Good." He backed up a step, offering her a clear path to the exit. "I'll meet you at the stables in half an hour."

Nodding her agreement, she darted past him and headed to her room to change. She'd need every moment of that half hour to figure out how to make a fresh start with him, all while keeping his brother's secret and somehow guarding herself against any more sizzling kisses.

Two hours later, Marcus steered a spirited quarter horse named Evangeline along a high ridge on the westernmost border of the ranch. The weather was clear and warm, a perfect autumn day in Big Sky country, the canopy of blue so crisp it looked like you could reach up and touch it. He'd been ignoring the urge to take photos in deference to his riding companion, making an earnest effort to learn more about Lily.

She rode a half step behind him on a quieter mount the foreman had suggested for her. Penny was an older paint with an easy disposition, and Lily had accepted her with thanks, although it was quickly obvious to Marcus that she was an excellent horsewoman. She sat in the saddle with the proper form that came from training and the ease that resulted from many hours of riding.

He hadn't asked her about that yet, however, carefully keeping the conversation on work as they took in the ranch sights. Her accusation about him making assumptions had hit close to the mark. His father had once pointed out something similar about his character. At the time, Marcus had ignored it. But today, when Lily had flung the words at him in anger, he'd recalled his dad's gentle suggestion that he look deeper than the surface.

You do that so well with a camera, son. You get to the heart of things with a lens. Without it, you sometimes miss the big picture.

The memory had slammed him unexpectedly. His father's death had been too swift for Marcus to appreciate all the ways he was going to miss Alonzo Salazar's quiet presence in his life. Now, months afterward, memories like that one could blindside him. Taking Lily on the tour of the ranch felt like a concession made to his father. An effort to be a better man.

Or, hell, maybe he was simply rationalizing the need to spend more time with Lily. Sure, he still found it difficult to trust her. But he couldn't deny he was attracted. And they damned well needed to get work done this week.

"Oh, how pretty." Lily breathed the words reverently. "Marcus, look at the fox."

Reining in, he turned to look where she was pointing. In the valley below them, a large red fox picked her way slowly through the golden fields while three energetic kits frolicked around their mom. The little ones playfully jumped at each other, their heads appearing and disappearing over the tops of the dying meadow grasses. The mother slowed at the edge of a brook to take a drink.

"That's a lively crew mama fox has to look after." He watched the animals for a moment, but the curve of Lily's appreciative smile was more of a draw for him. She seemed to be enjoying herself after their tense exchange at the lodge.

She'd worn a long anorak with fitted khakis and tall riding boots for the trip, an outfit that gave him renewed appreciation for her curves. She had an athletic leanness about her, but she was still distinctly feminine.

"Sometimes I tell myself that having a sibling is overrated, but that little group sure makes it look fun." Her blue gaze flicked to his while her horse's ears twitched.

"I wouldn't know. Devon and I were destined to be enemies, having mothers who were locked in their own conflict." He hadn't meant it as a swipe at Devon. It was a simple fact that had set them at odds early on. But in deference to Lily's friendship with his half brother, he changed the subject. "Have you noticed all the little feeder streams we've passed in the last hour and a half? Coop said the revival of the wetlands is one of the best indications of the local environment's renewed health."

"They're doing something right here." She hesitated, and for a moment he thought she was going to redirect the conversation back to the topic of siblings. But instead she said, "Aren't foxes a pest for ranchers?"

"Coop said they're trying to grow the whole ecosystem, pests and all. Within reason, of course. The theory is each level of predator has one higher up on the food chain, so a balanced system stays in balance." He'd been reading a lot about the ranching model since taking on the client. It beat brooding about Devon's long delay in arriving.

Or his mistrust of Lily's motives.

"Would you mind if we stopped for a few minutes so I can make notes?" She pointed toward a cliff with a few jutting scrub trees behind them. "There's a low rock wall over there."

"Of course." He dismounted and ground-tied Evangeline. He would have helped Lily down, but she was already on her feet, digging through a saddlebag to retrieve a notebook and camera. "You ride very well," he observed, trying not to linger on the sight of her long legs encased in soft twill.

"It was part of the curriculum at my boarding school." She arched a dark eyebrow at him. "Another gift from my grandparents that I'll never be able to repay."

"The Carringtons are one of Newport's oldest families. I doubt they need to be compensated for educating their granddaughter."

"In theory, no." She moved toward the cliff and dropped down to sit on the flat rocks under a juniper tree. "But in the same way that your mother and Devon's mother have always been at odds, my grandparents have never forgiven my mother for making foolish romantic decisions. And since I'm her daughter, I've always felt like their words were a warning directed at me, a reminder that I need to be a better person than their disappointing daughter."

He wouldn't have guessed that someone like her— born into one of the nation's wealthiest families—would battle those kinds of feelings. But how damn naive of him to think that. Every family had its own issues, its own fierce divisions and rivalries.

"It's sad that any kid is blamed for the actions of their parents," he said carefully, still feeling his way in this new attempt to broker a peace with her.

He swept aside some fallen leaves to sit beside her on the stacked rock wall. He crossed his ankles and stared out at the view, the light flurries giving the mountain vistas a gray filter.

"Sad, but common." She tapped a few things into her phone and then set it aside to pick up her paper and pen. "I've always tried to tread lightly with them, really weighing what to accept in terms of help. I couldn't argue about the boarding school since I was too young. But I opted for a college that was paid in full by scholarship instead of an Ivy League. And I took the job with Salazar because it was something outside the family realm of influence."

"I wondered why you didn't go to work at Carrington Financial." He had a new respect for her choices; working as the COO of a company like Salazar Media would never rival the kind of salary and influence she surely would have wielded at her grandparents' company.

"I sit on the board to represent the family, but I don't take a paycheck." She shrugged. "Of course, my grandparents like to remind me that they never took one, either."

He couldn't stifle a laugh. "As if they needed to."

"Right?" She glanced over at him, mischief in her eyes.

It was a shared moment of connection that would have been nice if it hadn't been followed—almost instantly—by a lightning bolt of heat. He felt it blast through him, and he guessed the same thing hit her, too, because her smile faded. Her gaze dropped to his mouth.

And the heat redoubled.

He wanted to pull her close and taste her, but he'd barely walked away from the last kiss with his sanity. Their chemistry was far too potent. Unpredictable. And no matter how much he wanted to justify an affair in his mind, he couldn't get around the fact that she worked for his company.

"I'll get my camera." He seized the idea like a lifeline as he sprang to his feet. "I can snap the photos you wanted."

He took his time going back to his horse and retrieving the camera, wishing he could find some restraint before rejoining Lily. He dragged in long breaths, hoping the pine-scented air swirling with flurries would cool his jets. When he'd stalled as long as he could, he turned around to face her.

She chewed her lip, her pen and paper forgotten beside her. She'd drawn her knees up and looped one arm around them. Her dark hair was caught in a ponytail, the end trailing over one shoulder.

"Can I ask you something?" She studied him with thoughtful blue eyes.

He nodded, still wanting to kiss her until they forgot everything else. To the point where he didn't trust himself to speak.

"Just a minute ago, when you were right here." She pointed to the spot he'd vacated. "I thought for a moment—" She hesitated. "Maybe I imagined it—"

"You didn't." His voice was hoarse, his fingers tightening around his camera. "I felt it, too."

Her eyebrows rose, and she gave him a look of genuine surprise.

At least, that's what he thought he saw. He was trying his damnedest to appreciate the bigger picture. To not make assumptions.

Could she be that innocent, where she didn't recognize the most elemental hunger? Or maybe she'd simply been sheltered in her relationship with the ex-fiancé she now labeled a friend. The possibility that this level of chemistry was new to her pleased him more than it should have. Tantalized the hell out of him.

"So we're right back where we started—things between us are either hot or cold," she mused, although there was a hint of breathlessness in her voice. "No middle ground."

"On the contrary, I'd argue that's where we are right now. I'm not walking away, but I'm not sure I trust myself to come closer. So…yeah." He couldn't take his eyes off her. "We're right in the middle."

She straightened as she seemed to think that over. Weighing the words. Trying the idea on for size. He could almost see the wheels turn in her head as she processed it. Around them, the birds sang and hopped from tree to tree, oblivious to their dilemma.

Then, suddenly, Lily was on her feet, her riding boots cutting through the dry grass as she charged toward him.

"I don't like how that feels one bit," she announced, only stopping when they stood toe-to-toe. She was so close he could see a tiny spray of freckles along her nose, so close he could catch a hint of her rose scent.

His pulse sped faster, urging him toward her. But he told himself to be sure. To listen to what she was saying, and to be certain about what she wanted before he acted.

"Considering that we've misunderstood one another in the past, I want to be sure I'm clear…"

He quit talking when she tugged his camera out of his hand and set it on the ground, safely tucked between two tree roots. When she returned to face him, he could see the heated intention in her eyes, right before her hands slid up his shoulders.

"How's this for clear?" she whispered, arching up on her toes to kiss him.

Six

Lily knew this wasn't wise.

And still she couldn't scavenge a scrap of restraint where Marcus was concerned. Because just once hadn't been enough. That first kiss had been too fleeting. She hadn't really been able to savor the onetime thrill.

Was it so wrong to want a do-over now that she knew what a kiss was capable of? She'd never experienced the kind of melting heat he made her feel with just a look. Never dreamed that a sensual connection could manifest this kind of power over her. It was daunting. Irresistible. What better time to explore it than here, two thousand miles from home, when she needed to reevaluate her whole life anyhow?

At least, that's what she told herself when she closed her eyes and fell deeper into Marcus's arms.

His hands roved over her with a possessiveness that

thrilled her. She may have initiated the kiss, but he took it over, nipping her lower lip gently between his teeth, licking soothing strokes with his tongue afterward. She clung to him, her arms wrapping tighter around him, dragging him closer.

The meadow and the horses fell away until Marcus was her whole world. His touch. His breath in her ear as he kissed his way along her jaw and down her neck. Pleasure spun out from every place he touched, the heat flaring hotter and wilder. She speared her fingers into his hair, testing the texture of the thick, dark strands. It was silkier than she'd imagined.

A low growl in his throat felt like wordless approval as his fingers clamped on her waist before venturing lower to cup her hips. She felt dizzy from how much she wanted this. Her arms banded around him, anchoring her body to his.

"Lily." Her name was a whisper against her damp lips.

"Mmm?" She pried her eyes open to answer him, her heart beating madly.

"I don't want to take advantage." He sounded so serious. And sincere.

"You wouldn't be," she assured him, still dazed from the pleasure flooding her veins. Still trapped in the combustible heat and wanting to stay there. "I kissed you first."

"A technicality." He tipped his forehead to hers, his hand cupping her cheek. "The bottom line is things are going to get out of hand in a hurry unless we…rein it in."

A cloud of disappointment descended on her, snuffing out some of the heated thrill, but not all of it.

"Back to the middle ground," she mused, wondering why that sounded so difficult with Marcus when she'd never had a problem maintaining professionalism around him in the past.

It was like their time together since her arrival at the ranch had opened the door to a secret side of herself she hadn't known existed. Now, she wondered how she could have missed out on this kind of pleasure for so long.

He chuckled softly as he edged back from her. "Only for as long as you want to keep things there." His dark eyes roamed over her in one final caress. "It has to be your call whether or not we move forward from here."

A shiver rippled over her skin. As reason started to return, she recalled the secret she was keeping from him—that Devon was on his way to the States, but apparently not coming to the ranch right away. Keeping Devon's confidences while sharing kisses with his brother was not going to end well. Steeling herself against the sensual undertow threatening to pull her under, she huffed out a pent-up breath.

"You're letting me decide?"

"I already know I want more," he clarified. "So my decision is made. We declare a relationship to protect ourselves at work. Sign the form that says it's voluntary, for all the good that does. If you're okay with it, I really don't care about any of the rest since we'll fly back to our respective coasts in the end." He shook his head slowly, giving her a thoughtful look. "But I also recognize you aren't used to indulging in the kinds of relationships that I have."

She was on board with everything he'd said right up until the end.

"What kind are those, exactly?"

"The simple variety. Where the rules are clear and no hearts get broken." He took his time explaining it. To ward her off? Or so she knew what she was getting into? "It's easier that way."

Simple. Clear. Who did he think he was kidding? The stakes were already too high for them to deceive themselves about this unwise attraction anymore.

"I'll keep that in mind. And thank you for the…er…decision-making power." Her pulse slugged harder. Faster.

She would think about it, certainly. She wondered if she would think of anything else.

Slowly, she became aware of their surroundings again. Birds calling as they searched the cold ground for food. Tall grasses rustling in the cold wind. She breathed in the scents of pine and dead leaves, hoping to clear her head of the sensual fog enough for her to finish making notes about the ranch. She should be focusing on finding the perfect spot for a launch event to showcase Mesa Falls Ranch.

"Good." Marcus scooped up his camera from the ground and returned it to his saddlebag. "Then we understand each other. Unless you decide you're ready to move forward, we find a way to work together and navigate the middle ground."

He drew Lily's horse closer so she could mount for the rest of their ride. He even held out a hand to help her, but she waved him off, preferring to handle the animal on her own.

Besides, with the way she was feeling right now, the slightest touch could send her free-falling into a decision she would only regret.

Long minutes passed in silence as they turned north and followed a grassy lane worn smooth by truck tires. The paint she rode needed little guidance from her, content to follow wherever Marcus's quarter horse led.

"We should be close to one of the owners' houses," Lily remarked once she'd regained her composure. "The map Regina gave me showed one of the homes backing up to Bitterroot National Forest."

"Regina?" He glanced back at her over his shoulder. "Is that someone in the New York office?"

"No. Sorry, I forgot to tell you. When you left the spa yesterday, I met a local woman, Regina Flores, who came in looking for the ranch manager to ask about a job." She rushed through the words since they brought to mind the off-the-charts kiss she'd shared with Marcus just before Regina arrived. "She seems to know the area well, and she had Weston Rivera's house marked on the map. I think this must be his part of the property."

Lily had wondered about that later when she reviewed the papers that Regina had given her. On an inside flap, there was an X marked on two spots along the ranch perimeter. One was labeled *Rivera*, a name Lily recalled from a document she'd read about the collective that owned the ranch. She assumed the other X related to another owner's home, but information about the ranch owners had been decidedly difficult to unearth. Had Regina been trying to locate one of them to ask for work?

"It is." Marcus slowed down so they could ride side by side and speak more easily now that the trail had widened. "And Weston Rivera is one of the few owners who spends much time on-site, so he would be the one most locals would connect with Mesa Falls."

"I wonder how your father came to be so fond of the ranch. Montana is far from where he lived, and the landowners don't seem inclined to invite many people here. It's only been open for corporate functions for the past year." She knew that Marcus's father had been a teacher before taking over as CEO of Salazar Media, but not much else about him. It seemed unlikely that Alonzo Salazar would have been a guest on one of the business retreats here.

"Devon never told you?" Marcus frowned as he glanced her way. "Our dad taught at a boarding school on the West Coast. All the owners of Mesa Falls Ranch attended Dowdon. They were a few years ahead of me, though, so I don't know them personally."

"You went to Dowdon?" Lily had heard of it. It was an all-male institution, although perhaps that had changed in recent years. She knew it wasn't easy to get in and that it was an Ivy League feeder school. She'd attended a girls' academy with a similar legacy on the East Coast. "I went to Abigail Leonard, and I was stressed to the point of illness for four years straight. Although I liked the horseback riding."

Marcus laughed. "No wonder you can hold your own on a horse. The riding was the high point of school for me, too."

Her perspective of him shifted yet again. They were more similar than she'd realized. She imagined Marcus acing everything he touched at school. He was supremely talented and had the perfect blend of art and business sense. All the entry-level creatives in the New York office followed him online and looked up to him as a kind of digital media guru.

But behind that tremendous success and personal achievement, he would have had a normal childhood not tainted by the wealth that her grandparents controlled. The Salazar men had made their own fortunes with their company. Marcus would have attended the prestigious boarding school not because his parents paid the huge tuition, but because his father taught there.

"I can't believe Devon never told me he went to Dowdon." She'd met him on the board of a charity fund-raiser shortly after she'd finished college, and they'd bonded over their shared frustration with roping friends into buying tickets. When he'd heard her concerns about moving into the family financial business, he'd promptly offered her a job with him instead.

Their friendship had always been easy, and their work style was both compatible and effective. There had never been the slightest hint of the tumultuous attraction that she felt for his brother.

The man who preferred his relationships "simple." She couldn't deny the notion held some appeal. Obviously, Marcus had made it work with other women in the past. He must have come by his strategy through experience.

"Devon didn't go to Dowdon." Marcus pointed to a strange-looking brown-and-white bird in a dry field to the east. "That's a sage grouse, by the way. Do you mind if we stop?"

He was already getting out his camera, and Lily distractedly recalled reading about conservationists' efforts to attract the species to western sagebrush lands. Its return, she knew, was another indication of a recovering ecosystem.

"Of course." Lily didn't even need to rein in her horse. Penny stopped as soon as Evangeline pulled up. "But I'm surprised Devon wouldn't have attended the school if your father taught there."

Marcus remained on horseback as he raised the viewfinder to his eye and focused the camera. She followed the lens to where the odd-looking bird puffed its chest with a distinctive whooping whistle, its tail feathers fanned out and its neck ruff fluffed. The shot would be pretty with the sun lowering in the sky and casting a golden glow across the field.

"Don't forget that by the time Devon was heading to high school, his mother and mine were in a feud of their own. Devon's mom didn't want Devon anywhere near me or our father."

"How sad for you both." She wondered if Devon's mother had thought about how hard it might be on her son to alienate him from a half sibling. But then again, maybe she just thought she was protecting him.

Lily hadn't known Alonzo Salazar well, since he'd hardly been around when he was CEO. But she knew he had a reputation. He was someone her grandfather would have diplomatically called "a charming rake."

"Devon's mother is from a wealthy family." Marcus clicked away before he reset the focus. "They didn't like my father to begin with. So when she left him, they rallied around her. Devon never lacked for opportunities."

Lily weighed that with what she'd come to know of him. She would agree that he seemed accustomed to a level of luxury and comfort, even though he worked tirelessly for the company. She wanted to ask more about Alonzo Salazar and his connection to the owners of Mesa Falls Ranch, but just then Marcus set aside his camera, seemingly finished with his work.

"Speaking of my brother, have you heard from him today?" Marcus swung his dark gaze toward her. "I've messaged him twice with no response."

The reminder of the secret she was supposed to keep tied her tongue. It wasn't in her nature to lie. She felt her heart rate increase in direct proportion to her nervousness.

So she dodged the question altogether.

"I can't imagine where he is," she said honestly, since he could be flying over the Pacific, Alaska or a Hawaiian island and she wouldn't know.

"No?" Marcus's eyes narrowed briefly before he picked up Evangeline's reins and urged her forward. "I'm thinking I'll call the embassy myself and see if I can speed things along from this end. I'm not leaving Mesa Falls until I know what my father left for us, and that means I need Devon here."

Lily felt a blush creep up her cheeks, hating deception in any form.

"Good idea," she returned, knowing she couldn't prevent him from finding out the truth if he really followed through on calling the US Embassy.

She just hoped he didn't quiz her any more about his brother's whereabouts, since the information wasn't hers to share. And she sure hoped Devon wouldn't make any more cryptic calls before he put in an appearance on the ranch.

That evening, Marcus paced around the second-floor patio of his guest cabin. Restless and edgy, he'd damn near worn a path in the wide cedar planks near the wrought iron rail where he could look out over a picturesque bend in a creek that met up with the Bitterroot River. He'd been making calls to no avail for the last two hours since he'd returned from his ride with Lily.

While Lily had a suite in the main guest lodge, Marcus's quarters, a four-bedroom guest residence with its own heated pool and small stable, were more spacious and remote. Of all the amenities, it was the stable that Marcus most enjoyed. This way he could keep a horse close to make the best of his time in Montana.

Although, perhaps he should be more grateful for the physical distance from Lily Carrington. If they'd been sleeping under the same roof, things would have been even more complicated between them. As it was, he'd left her at the guest lodge after their afternoon ride and suggested they meet for dinner to finish discussing event ideas.

To his surprise, she'd agreed. Because she wanted to keep close tabs on Marcus? Or did her commitment to business simply outweigh the attraction they grappled with?

Or maybe there was a third reason—that she still underestimated the powerful draw between them despite all evidence to the contrary. He knew they'd been a single touch away from combustion both times they'd kissed. But there was a chance she didn't realize how closely they walked that line. He'd meant it when he said what happened next was up to her. But she'd been every bit as invested—every bit as lost—in that last kiss they'd shared.

So he kept one eye out for Lily's imminent arrival while the catering staff set up dinner downstairs in the glassed-in sunroom overlooking the heated pool. There was a lighted stone path around the backyard, connecting the outdoor spaces to the pool and sunroom where he could see the caterers putting the finishing touches on the space. A natural tree slab polished to a high shine served as a table under an elk-horn chandelier suspended from post beam rafters. The narrow bar held a champagne bucket with a vintage he'd chosen earlier. Everything was ready for his guest.

If only he could have gotten in touch with Devon, he might have enjoyed the evening more. He checked his phone for at least the fifth time, acknowledging that it was too late to contact the embassy in Mumbai. He'd already left another message for Devon and phoned a California congresswoman's office to see if she could facilitate bringing his brother home.

For now, as the sun sank lower in the sky, there was nothing more he could do but wait for Lily. She'd resisted his offer to pick her up at the main lodge, reminding him the evening wasn't a date.

He wondered if she would rethink that once she saw the candles flickering under glass globes. Or the fresh flowers that wreathed an archway leading into the sunroom. He'd stopped himself from hiring a live musician, however, preferring to have her all to himself for as much of the evening as possible. The waitstaff had to be there, but once the meal was over, he intended to send them on their way. Then Marcus and Lily would be alone.

Tonight, if she chose to pick up where they'd left off with the afternoon kiss, there would be nothing standing in their way.

Checking his watch, he went inside the master suite to drop his phone on the nightstand and retrieve a gray tie from the valet stand. He didn't want to be too formal, because then Lily would be aware of the lengths he'd gone to for the evening. He wrapped and folded the silk into place as he headed down the stairs in a black suit and white shirt. He glanced in the mirror at the base of the stairs long enough to straighten the knot, then headed outdoors by the pool for a breath of fresh air. Even out here, classical music played over the sound system. No soothing Mozart or Brahms tonight. He'd opted for a playlist heavy on Bach, the layered melodies as complex as the woman he waited for.

"Marcus." Her voice called to him, seemingly out of nowhere.

Swiveling around to find her, he scanned the pool area, confused as to how she could have arrived without him hearing her, or seeing her, for that matter. He'd been watching the gravel lane from his upstairs patio.

"Over here," she called again, and this time he realized she was at the opposite end of the pool area, on the far side of the cabin's property, away from the road.

She stood at the edge of the field in boots and a long rust-colored coat over a yellow dress belted at her narrow waist. Her dark hair was piled on her head and pinned at haphazard angles, a soft coil with loose strands that teased her chin and her collarbone.

Something about her exposed neck sent a stab of hunger through him that was almost painful. He dragged in a breath of the cool air and headed toward her.

"I'm sorry I didn't hear you arrive. Did you park out front?"

"I walked." Standing in the high grass, she lifted her hem slightly to kick out one foot, revealing her turquoise-colored cowboy boots. "It wasn't that far."

"You walked." He stopped just short of her, resisting the urge to touch her, taste her. He wanted to skip dinner and feast on her instead. "That must be at least two miles."

"Nearly three." She shrugged. "I was glad for the time to air out my head." She glanced up at him and away again quickly. "Plus, I wanted to think through event ideas for the ranch."

"I would have been happy to pick you up. Come have

a drink." He couldn't resist touching her, guiding her forward with his palm on the small of her back, but only for a moment. "The appetizer course is almost ready."

She had only barely stepped onto the smooth stone path that wound around the pool when she stopped again.

"Oh, Marcus. This is beautiful." Her gaze took in the sunroom, glowing with warm light as dusk began to turn the sky purple. "Are those canna lilies around the sunroom?"

"I might be able to identify a sage grouse across a field, but I draw the line at discerning one flower from another." He took her arm and tucked it in his. "Let's go take a closer look."

He heard her quick intake of breath, which made him think of more intimate encounters. He wanted to hear that soft gasp again tonight, under far different circumstances. But he tamped down that thought—and a whole lot of others—and tried to simply enjoy the feel of her forearm on his, the delicate fragrance of her soap and shampoo.

"You didn't have to go to all this trouble for dinner." She admired the table setting through the clear glass walls before leaning closer to the flowers that made a hedge between the pool and sunroom. "Although, it all looks so beautiful, I can't help but enjoy the effort."

"Good. That's reason enough to spend a little extra time on a meal." He opened the sunroom door for her and took her coat, inhaling her rose scent as he revealed her bare arms beneath tiny cap sleeves of yellow lace. Hanging the coat on a wrought iron rack, he led her to the table and withdrew a chair, the wooden legs gliding smoothly along the floor.

"This doesn't feel like a business meal." A line of worry snaked between her brows.

"So we should eat rubber chicken in the local hotel's conference center instead?" Marcus strode to the bar and pulled the champagne bottle out of the ice bucket. "I won't apologize for enjoying my work."

He used a linen napkin to cup the cork before twisting it off with a satisfying *pop*. At the sound, one of the waiters hurried over to take charge of the task. Marcus gave the younger man the bottle and took his seat opposite Lily.

She smiled politely while the drinks were poured. But as soon as the waiter disappeared, Lily's gaze tangled with his.

"I just don't want to muddle our working relationship any further," she confided. "I know we got sidetracked earlier today with whatever was happening between us, but I think it's important we figure out an event for Mesa Falls Ranch. I'm here tonight to work."

"As am I. And I've been very clear that you're in charge of what happens next between us, if anything. In the meantime, however, I plan to make sure you enjoy yourself whenever you're with me." He hadn't realized how much he meant that until he spoke the words aloud. No matter how often he reminded himself that Lily's first loyalty was to his brother, or that a relationship between them would cross a professional line, Marcus wanted her anyway.

Her lips were pursed; she looked deep in thought.

Before she could plan a rebuttal, he lifted the faceted crystal champagne flute. "In fact, let's toast to a perfect fall evening. The atmosphere is sure to hatch the exact right event idea."

At the mention of their work, a slow smile curved her

glossy pink lips, and she clinked her glass lightly to his. "Cheers."

The swell of victory in his chest was undeniable. He sipped the champagne and savored the sight of her across the table from him. He wanted to touch her again. To skim her bare shoulders with his hands and hear her breathy sighs in his ear. To pull every pin from her hair until it cascaded over him like a silk curtain.

The hum in his veins was about more than just this one small victory. It was the growing anticipation of everything the night might bring.

Seven

Two hours later, swirling dark port in a dessert wine-glass, Lily tried not to fall any further under Marcus's spell.

It wasn't easy, given his charming side she'd glimpsed during dinner. He'd obviously put a lot of thought into the evening, from having the dinner in the sunroom with its breathtaking mountain views at twilight, to the discreetly placed patio heaters that ensured they would be warm enough to linger over the meal. A fire also blazed in the huge stone hearth.

The food had been exquisite, thoughtfully prepared by an innovative chef the ranch owners were working with to open a seasonal restaurant nearby. Marcus had not only hired him for the evening meal, he had also convinced the chef to retain Salazar Media's services for his other restaurants in Miami and Los Angeles.

"Are you always working?" she asked after a careful sip of the port.

She'd indulged very little during the meal, wary of letting her guard down around a man who intrigued her on every level. She needed to protect her professional standing, and an affair with one of the owners of the company seemed unwise in the extreme. Although, she had to admit, she'd weighed the idea often enough over the last two hours. Memories of his kiss were never far from her thoughts.

Was she deceiving herself that she could spend time with this man and not cross the line she walked so warily? She had been so certain she could come here tonight and focus on the job, on firming up plans for an event at Mesa Falls Ranch.

"When you enjoy what you do for a living, is it really work?" he asked, pulling his dark gaze from the crackling fire to meet her eyes across the table.

The shiver of awareness she experienced wasn't a surprise anymore. She'd come to expect it.

"You really find that much fulfillment with the company?" She noticed the server heading their way.

"Most of the time. The only aspect I don't like is reining in good ideas to fatten the bottom line or make our performance stats look more impressive." Marcus offered her his hand. "Would you like to take a walk around the grounds?"

She took in his dark suit, surely custom-tailored because it fit him perfectly.

"That sounds nice." She left her port behind on the table and followed him to the coatrack, where he retrieved her lightweight cashmere jacket.

His hands lingered a moment as he settled it on her shoulders. Or had she imagined it?

Before she could decide, he took her hand and wrapped her fingers around his forearm so he could steady her as they walked.

A chivalrous touch.

Maybe that's why she couldn't will herself to let go as they followed the line of the four-rail fence around the huge guesthouse. She was hyperaware of where her fingers rested on his forearm.

"I've got a suggestion for the event." Marcus stopped close to the stables, where two horses stood in roofed stalls open on both ends to let air flow through. "Although it's probably over budget."

With the help of a low-hanging full moon, she recognized Evangeline and an Appaloosa he favored.

"I'm listening." She tipped her face into the breeze blowing in off the mountains.

"What if we hold the party on the ranch, but host two simultaneous galas in New York and LA, with staggered starts to accommodate the time difference." Marcus laid his other hand on top of hers and, in a gesture that seemed almost instinctive, stroked a thumb along the backs of her knuckles, stirring her senses.

He'd told her that what happened next was up to her. Yet she didn't want to pull away.

Instead, she tracked the path of his touch with her eyes. "I'm not sure how we could generate enough interest for such a big undertaking. Unless it's a benefit." She had already considered a charitable tie-in.

"What if we entice two major corporations on each coast to hold the satellite events by offering them a cut rate on their first retreat?" His touch stilled on her fingers.

She glanced up at him, his dark eyes enticing her closer when she should be thinking about work. She battled an urge to splay her hands along his broad chest. But she began to see where he was going with the party idea. It would definitely increase their reach—digitally and physically.

"That could work," she admitted.

"Then we offer the guests the opportunity to sponsor a wildlife family. Adopt a sage grouse or a wolf or even a bear—hell, I don't know." He rested his free arm on the fence rail, warming to the topic. "Or, for a small donation to the sustainable ranching efforts, a guest could become a caretaker of a section of the river."

"Like Adopt A Highway?" She'd seen signs like that on major roads before.

"Exactly. Then, when your group visits for the retreat, you can see how your waterway is doing or get reports on the sage grouse population." He guided her toward the sunroom, one palm at the small of her back.

Lily was working out the logistics, focusing on the nuances of his idea as she tried to ignore the way his voice stirred her senses and made her want to lean into him. "But the ranch isn't a charity."

"No. The donation would go to greater conservation and education efforts from whatever nature conservancy group we work with. But offering some kind of tangible return on their investment—like bragging rights that your sage grouse is thriving—would make the efforts more real. Plus it gives people an emotional attachment to the place."

Lily couldn't hold back a smile. "I know there are

green ranching initiatives that we could work with who could put the dollars to direct use." With a few more notes, the idea would be ready to pass off to the staff in the New York office to make it happen. "I think you're really on to something."

She liked the scope of the idea. And the budget they had to promote the ranch was impressive, so they needed an event with real impact for their dollars.

"We could show plenty of video footage at the New York and Los Angeles parties. I think if people saw the land and the creatures who call it home, they'd feel more invested in protecting it. Or seeing it firsthand by scheduling a retreat."

The idea of visiting a part of the country known for its beauty, spending time among people who were working hard to retain that natural splendor, was going to really draw forward-thinking businesses to Mesa Falls Ranch.

"I agree." She felt more invested, too, recharged to do her job tomorrow. "Your creative team is going to have a field day with an event like this."

As they neared the sunroom again, they stopped short of the doors. She knew their time together had probably reached its natural conclusion. She should thank him for a lovely evening and head back to her suite at the main lodge.

But his touch gave her butterflies. And she still needed answers. She wanted to use this week to figure out what she wanted from life before returning to the rigid expectations of her grandparents back home.

When she spun to tell him good night, he was close behind her. Strong and warm, his physical presence was an undeniable draw.

"I should…" She bit her lip, weighing her options

while the breeze blew tendrils of hair to tickle her neck and graze her shoulder. The scent of wildflowers teased her nose. "That is, I'd better—"

Marcus quieted whatever she was about to say by lifting a strand of her hair between two fingers. He didn't touch any other part of her, but the gentle tug at her scalp made a thousand pleasurable tingles race along her spine.

"Would you like me to drive you back to the lodge?" he offered, the look in his eyes melting her insides.

She'd never felt anything as potent as this. It shamed her to think it when she'd been engaged for two years. But better to know now that she'd been playing at romance before. This? It might not be romance, but it was the most seductive feeling she'd ever experienced.

"I'm having a difficult time knowing quite what I want tonight," she confessed, more drunk on moonlight and Marcus than anything she'd sipped over dinner.

Marcus leaned fractionally closer, his voice a low rumble near her ear.

"When it's right, you'll know for certain." He slid his arm around her shoulders and pointed them in the direction of the driveway. "I've got one of the ranch trucks out front. I'll give you a lift, because I don't want you walking back to the lodge in the dark."

He made an excellent, sensible point. And even as she followed him to the truck, Lily knew she didn't care for this sensible path. Yes, it reinforced everything she'd been telling herself all week long.

Don't be too hasty.

Don't kiss Marcus again.

Don't risk the career you need now more than ever.

"Wait." She turned on her heel just shy of the running board of the shiny black 4x4. Here, under the floodlights of the detached garage, she could see him clearly. "I feel like this is the safe, reasonable sort of decision I've been making for my entire life."

She wasn't telling him so much as thinking out loud, feeling the need to talk through the knot of confused impulses, hoping she could untangle them. She paced a few steps away from him, her boots tapping a quick rhythm on the stone driveway.

"No one would ever blame you for doing the reasonable thing," Marcus agreed calmly, as if his dinner companions routinely sorted through pros and cons of their wild attraction to him out loud.

"You do." She pivoted to face him where he lounged with a shoulder against the truck door. "You told me I'm a people pleaser."

"I didn't mean it as an insult," he said carefully. "I was simply pointing out how different we are."

"Because *you* don't always do the reasonable thing." She didn't want to be like Marcus, the creative, fiery genius who was forever tugging the company into new terrain. Did she? "I remember a memo you sent out to everyone last year that said best practices are for people who don't know how to forge a new path."

She remembered rolling her eyes at the memo when it had shown up in her inbox. Because she lived by best practices. They were in place for a reason.

"I believe I was more diplomatic than that." He folded his arms across his chest as he watched her pace.

"I forged a new path when I broke my engagement." She halted as the idea fully sank in. No doubt about it, her grandparents weren't going to view the loss of a Winthrop marriage prospect as following a "best practice."

"Did you?" Marcus straightened where he stood but

didn't move closer. "I think it's all a matter of perspective. And that's strictly between you and the man foolish enough to lose you."

She only partially heard him, as her brain raced in new directions.

"This week is not about doing the sensible thing." She'd already done something that would shake her grandparents' trust in her. And she'd already rattled her own view of herself by going after that combustible kiss with Marcus—a kiss that had ended far too soon.

How much more harm could it do to take this night for herself, to see what she might be missing in a life bounded by others' expectations of her? One night wouldn't magically transform her from a woman who lived by best practices into a woman like her mother, who turned her back on family for the sake of romance.

"What is it about then, Lily?"

She walked toward him with a new sense of purpose. A new certainty.

"Right or wrong, it's about what I want." Clearheaded, single-minded, she laid her palm on Marcus's chest, her fingertips grazing taut muscle hidden only by a fine layer of cotton twill. "And I want to be with you tonight."

Marcus couldn't imagine anything sexier than hearing this grounded, strong woman talk through her thought process like a trial attorney, steering her argument to a logical—and sensual—conclusion. Desire flared hot at the thought of having her in his bed.

"It would be my pleasure and my privilege to honor that request." He stilled her wandering hands, taking them both in his before lifting first one, and then the other to his lips. He kissed the back of each, breathing in the scent of her skin. "But first, let me bring you inside where it's warm."

She gave a quick nod of agreement, and he turned to lead her in the front door of the guesthouse. The catering staff had gone home for the night; Marcus had noticed earlier that their van was gone from the front driveway.

They were very much alone.

Marcus bolted the door behind them and took her coat before Lily slipped out of her boots. Seeing her step deeper into the living area, a pair of thin socks peeping out from the hem of the yellow dress, filled him with a sense of protectiveness and made the line they'd just crossed feel all the more real. He hit a button to lower the blinds around the whole room, and another to start the fire in the hearth. The only light came from a hallway chandelier and the two sconces on either side of a bookshelf, but the low blaze in the gray stone fireplace lent a warm glow to the room.

He'd wanted Lily since the first moment they'd met—at a client meeting four years ago, before she'd gotten engaged. Even then, she'd been off-limits because she was his brother's assistant and friend, so he'd tried his damnedest to stay away. It had helped that they worked on opposite coasts. After he'd heard she was engaged, he'd shoved all thoughts of her even further to the back burner.

Now, suddenly, she was here with him.

His gaze followed her as she slowed her step near the sofa. He didn't want to rush her. Just because she'd committed to the idea of being together didn't mean he was done romancing her. Not by a long shot.

"You're making me nervous," she confessed in a breathless rush, her fingers digging into the cushioned back of the gray sectional. "Are you thinking this is the craziest idea ever?"

"Hell, no." He loosened his tie a fraction of an inch before he stepped into her path, standing inches away from her. The last thing he wanted was for her to feel anxious. "I was just thinking how damn long I've wanted you. I'm also wondering if I've developed some kind of superpower, since I feel like I willed this night into being."

She laughed lightly. "I'm not sure luring women into your arms counts as a superpower."

She still wore her jacket. He peeled the fabric away from her shoulders and let the garment fall over the back of the sofa.

"Most men would beg to differ." He stroked her arms, liking the subtle shiver he felt move through her. "Though I'm not interested in convincing anyone but you."

"No?" Her blue eyes tracked him, a new alertness in her gaze.

"I've wanted you since the first time we met."

"You hid it well. I had no idea."

"Do you remember that day?" He bent to graze a kiss beneath her ear, a tendril of her fallen hair tickling his nose.

Her head tilted, and he felt the rapid thrum of her pulse where his lips lingered. Her fragrance, something lightly floral, intensified as his breath warmed her skin.

"I remember. We had a meeting with a resort chain, and I felt you watching me while I was taking notes."

Straightening, he stared down at her, waiting for her eyes to open.

"I thought you were unaware." He stroked a finger along her cheek while her lids fluttered.

Then she met his gaze fully. "I didn't know what you were thinking. I knew you and Devon didn't get along well, so I guess I thought you might be suspicious of me, too. Looking back, I can see where that feeling was a spark of awareness, but at the time, I had a boyfriend, and I knew from Devon that you were in a relationship, as well." Her fingers walked up his chest, circling around one of his shirt buttons. "Besides, after those first few meetings, you hardly noticed me."

Did she really believe that? He couldn't wait to show her how thoroughly she captured his attention.

"Whatever relationship I was in at the time was forgettable. And I never stopped noticing you. I just grew more discreet."

She pursed her lips, and for a moment he wondered if he'd said the wrong thing or struck a nerve. But then, she returned her attention to his shirt buttons, unfastening one and sliding her fingers up the placket to the next in line. "While I'm not sure that I like the idea of being just another forgettable woman in your life, I'm at the point where I can appreciate something simple. Clear rules. No one gets hurt."

She'd been listening carefully when he'd outlined those points earlier in the day. It was just as well, since Marcus stood by them. He'd seen how fast a family fell apart when a couple decided it wasn't worth trying anymore.

He shut down those thoughts fast, grateful as hell just to have Lily in his arms, where he'd wanted her for a long, long time.

"You could never be forgettable," he assured her, breathing in her scent, craving the taste of her on his tongue.

"I just want to choose something for myself. Something selfish. Something that's just for me."

"Then you're making the very best choice tonight, Lily." He drew her fully against him, hip to hip. Breast to chest. The contact sent a flash fire though him. "And I'm going to prove it to you."

Eight

His lips claimed hers with a heat and possessiveness that turned her knees to water. Clinging to him, Lily let herself be swept away, realizing their previous kisses had been mere tentative precursors to this explosion of need.

She swayed on her feet, anchored by the hard strength of his arms banded around her. Her body melted against his, her curves fitting to his hard planes, her hips cradling the erection straining closer. She lost focus, hungry for more, now, faster.

He seemed to anticipate that need, or else he felt it just as fiercely, because no sooner did she think it than he plucked her off her feet and carried her through the kitchen, never breaking the kiss. Vaguely she registered the quiet hum of a refrigerator as they passed it, the nightlight glowing over a range, and then a darkened hallway before he stepped into a spacious bedroom at the back of the lodge.

When he set her down again, her feet sank into plush carpet and a chill crept along her skin from a whirling overhead fan. He pulled away, and she opened her eyes long enough to see him click a remote for the gas fireplace before he reached to still the ceiling fan. The master suite glowed in the sudden blaze from the white brick hearth. Gray walls and a wooden cathedral ceiling made an already large room feel massive, but the sleigh bed beside her was angled toward the leaping flames in a way that seemed to invite lounging. White pillows of all sizes spanned the headboard while a puffy down duvet draped over the footboard.

She could absolutely see herself lingering in bed here all day. Especially with her potently sexy rival tangling in the sheets with her.

Her heartbeat raced as he made quick work of his shirt buttons, shedding his tie and then his cuff links before shrugging out of the fine white cotton, revealing a powerful chest and toned abs that were even finer.

She heard a feminine sigh of appreciation and belatedly realized it was hers. She couldn't even blink, she was so busy admiring this man.

"May I?" he asked, reaching toward her then sliding his fingers into her hair to remove a pin.

Her throat was too dry to reply, so she settled for a wordless nod, her scalp tingling while he slowly undid her hair. Pin. By. Pin.

Taking her hair down had never felt so seductive. Each tendril that slipped to rest on her shoulders felt like a sensual stroke along her neck and shoulders. When the last silky loop unwound, Marcus dropped the pins on the nightstand and then speared his hands into the waves. Sensation tripped down her spine, pleasurable shivers chasing one after another.

He breathed soft praises against her ear, the low rumble of his voice vibrating through her while she splayed her hands along his bare chest, hungry to feel all that delicious male strength.

"I can't wait to be inside you." His whispered words sent a sharp ache of longing through her, and she let go of him long enough to reach for the button that held the neck of her dress together.

"I need to feel more of you." Her fingers fumbled with the cloth-covered fastenings until he took over the task, freeing her from the yellow silk.

Two more buttons and the whole dress was in a pile at her feet. She would have started shimmying out of her bra and panties if not for Marcus's sudden, fixed attention, his whole body going still for a moment.

"Wait." He halted her hands before she could reach the hooks on the back of the yellow lace, his fingers gently circling her wrists. "You take my breath away, Lily."

Her heartbeat stuttered and restarted at the look in his eyes. A new level of sensual awareness made her somehow feel bold and shy at the same time. Bold because she wanted to explore all of this new heat with him. Shy because his obvious fascination with her made her self-conscious.

"Touch me," she invited, wanting his hands all over her, all the time. "Please."

"My pleasure," he murmured, his fingers tracing the outline of the lace on her hips while his lips lowered to the peak of her nipple where it was visible through the fabric.

He licked and nipped, teasing her there in a way that made a new tension coil tight inside her. By the time he slipped his hand between her legs, she rocked against him shamelessly, needing him there.

The guttural sound he made in his throat was half desire and half pain. Or maybe that's just how she was feeling. The need for completion raked through her while he stroked her sex through the damp lace.

She rolled her hips against him and realized he was still wearing pants. Seized by a new need to have him naked immediately, she worked the belt and fastenings free until he stepped out of the trousers, walking her backward to the bed.

Her gaze darted to his, and she saw the raw desire reflected there. She wasn't the only one teetering on the brink right now.

He flicked free the clasp on her bra and dragged the lace panties off her hips, leaving her naked. She craved his touch everywhere at once, but he pushed her gently back to the mattress, settling her in the middle of his bed.

Only then did he shed his boxer shorts. The heat between them combusted, flaring into a total conflagration. He paused to retrieve a condom from a drawer and toss it beside her on the bed, but she could only think about getting his hands on her again. His whole body on hers.

Aligned. Joined.

But he was taking it more slowly. He angled one broad shoulder between her thighs and kissed her there. Deeply. Sweetly.

The intimate feel of him threatened to make her lose all control. She edged back a fraction, needing to catch her breath, but he pressed closer. The tension built to an unbearable high. She couldn't think. Couldn't breathe. Couldn't do anything but feel.

And then sensation crashed over her in waves, drowning her in a pleasure she wasn't sure would ever end. When it finally did, he kissed his way up her body, lingering on each of her breasts before he finally reached for the condom. Sheathed himself.

She was tongue-tied, overwhelmed, so thoroughly sated she couldn't imagine needing more. Except she wanted to feel him inside her, to give him the same kind of pleasure he'd just given her. She wanted to tell him that, but he was already rolling her on top of him. Guiding her hips down over him.

And just like that, the tension ratcheted right back up. The hunger returned with a vengeance, bringing with it a new ache that only he could satisfy. He entered her, inch by delectable inch. She'd never felt anything so amazing.

So good.

For long moments, she moved with him, letting him guide her where he wanted her. Building the pleasure for them both, he was a generous and skilled lover, sensing what she needed. Giving her more. And she could have gladly followed his lead for hours, exploring what made him feel good. But soon, she felt his hands still. His whole body was taut as a bow and unmoving.

She tilted her hips, arched her spine and found a whole new sensual gear. Her release blindsided her in one lush spasm after another, catapulting her over the edge. Marcus followed her, his shout of completion a hoarse echo of hers before she collapsed against him. Spent. Exhilarated.

Glowing with sensual satisfaction.

For long moments, it was all she could do to breathe. She focused on doing just that while her eyes closed and her heart settled into a more normal rhythm. Marcus shifted her to his side, sweeping away the surplus pillows until they each were left with one, then retrieving the extra comforter from the footboard. He hauled it over them, draping her in soft white down.

She smiled at the feel of it against her bare skin, not wanting to open her eyes yet. Not ready to face the reality of being in her boss's bed for the night.

She felt too wonderful to regret anything.

As he lay beside her and stroked her hair, she couldn't resist glancing his way. He studied her in the firelight, his expression inscrutable. Perhaps he wasn't ready to think about what had just happened between them, either.

She searched for something, anything to say to fill the silence that was growing heavier by the second.

"I am excited about your idea for the gala on the ranch," she finally said, her thoughts turning to the safe topic of work. "I'm going to contact some nature conservancy groups and see who's interested in partnering for the event."

Marcus grinned at her across the pillow. "And you accused me of always thinking about the job."

A trace of guilt smoked through her, even though his smile never faltered. Had that been insensitive? Rude, even?

"I'm sorry." She felt awkward. "I'm not very good at this."

"There's nothing to be sorry for." He pressed a finger gently to her lips. "I was only teasing. And I'm looking forward to seeing what the team comes up with for the ranch gala."

The brush of his skin against her mouth reminded her of all they'd just shared, sending a fresh quiver down her spine. Gazing into his dark eyes, she wondered how long they could dance around what had just happened. Sooner or later she would have to face the fact that she had made an impulsive, romantic decision, not all that different from the ones her grandparents had spent a lifetime warning her against.

For the rest of her time in Montana, though, she planned to indulge. To enjoy more of the pleasures she'd denied herself for too long. So right now, she simply relished the feel of Marcus's caress while she considered how to best do her job.

"Do you think we'll have much involvement from the owners?" She hadn't met any of them yet. "Not just for the event, but with the awareness campaign? I'm just wondering who'll sign off on our plans."

"I spoke to Weston Rivera initially, the one who's here most often. He can approve things, but apparently he does a lot of search-and-rescue work that can make him hard to reach. In that case, we send things to Gage Striker, who's more involved on the business end—" Marcus cut off abruptly, his hand going still where he'd been stroking her hair. "Why?"

"Just curious." She shrugged, wondering why he'd think her interest unusual. "I find the dynamics of the group sort of surprising, don't you? Not many friends go into business together on something like this. Especially when they don't seem to spend a lot of time here."

"Maybe that's why they're insisting on having a welcome reception once Devon gets here. To give us all a chance to get to know each other."

His phone vibrated on the nightstand before she could reply.

"That could be Devon," Marcus said, levering up on his elbow to retrieve the device. "I'd better check."

She doubted it was Devon, who was most likely still in the air. She felt another pang of guilt over how she hadn't shared what she knew about his return trip.

Marcus scowled when he looked at the screen. "Would you excuse me?" He sprang to his feet and dragged on his boxers, then headed toward the door before giving her one last glance. "I'll be right back."

As he padded down the corridor away from her, she couldn't deny a sinking feeling in her gut. He'd pulled away from her abruptly when she'd started asking more questions about Mesa Falls Ranch. Could it be he still didn't trust her? Reaching down to the floor to retrieve his discarded shirt, she jammed her fists through the sleeves and covered up. She wanted to feel indignant at the thought that Marcus might not trust her, especially given what they'd just shared.

Except Devon had forced a secret on her, so she wasn't being totally honest with Marcus. Moreover, Devon had told her to be careful around Marcus. Advice she had ignored. What could he have meant?

While she weighed her next move, Marcus reappeared in the doorway. His expression was thunderous.

"Devon has hired a private investigator to look into our father's past."

Anger churned at the thought of his brother trying to outmaneuver him, leveraging any advantage to take control of Salazar Media now that their father was gone. Marcus couldn't shake the sour feeling in his stomach that he'd somehow been played in coming here. Had the trip been a distraction that gave Devon extra time to probe their father's mysterious past? What if he'd learned things that would give him an edge when they finally received whatever papers Alonzo Salazar had left them?

"I don't understand." Lily's voice pulled him from his spinning thoughts. "How do you know Devon hired someone to do that?"

She was sitting up, propped against the headboard, and had pulled on the shirt he wore to dinner. The French cuffs flapped loose around her forearms as she scraped her hands through her dark hair, sticking a couple of pins through it to hold it in place.

Even as agitated as he felt, he still experienced the sharp tug of attraction. Far from easing the need for her, their time together had only shown him how incredible they were together. She had floored him. At least until the moment that she'd steered their conversation immediately back to work, making him question how much information she might be tucking away to pass to Devon.

"Because I just spoke to Weston Rivera, one of the ranch owners, and he assumed that I knew about the PI." Marcus sat down on the foot of the bed. "The investigator left messages with Weston and two other Dowdon alumni, asking questions about Dad."

He wondered what in the hell Devon was trying to accomplish with the underhanded methods. It was one thing to hire an investigator without telling him. But to let the guy question a new client of Salazar Media? Marcus wouldn't be able to just roll over and let that one pass.

"And how do you know Devon is behind that?" Lily pressed, sounding defensive on his brother's behalf.

"Weston called the guy back and asked him straight out who was paying his bills. The PI admitted it was Alonzo's son, so Weston called me to give me an earful. I know damn well it wasn't me, so clearly Devon is scouring our father's past, looking for clues about whatever paperwork he left us." He spotted the remote for the fireplace on the floor and leaned to grab it so he could dial down the flames.

"But if the investigator freely implicated Devon, your brother obviously wasn't trying to keep it a secret. I'm sure he'll talk to you about it when he arrives." Lily studied him in the dim glow from the fire, the diamond studs in her ears catching the light as she spoke.

She was so damned lovely. He'd never be able to see her again without remembering this night with her. The way she looked in his shirt, the exposed column of her throat tempting him to trail kisses down her neck into the shadowed vee between her breasts. He ground his teeth against the surge of desire.

"*If* he decides to show up at all. While I'm here doing work for the company, he's on the other side of the world orchestrating his plan to oust me from the business." He just wondered if Lily was helping Devon or not. "And he's doing so at the expense of our relationship with a new client."

As soon as the words fell from his mouth, he realized perhaps he shouldn't have voiced his concerns out loud. To her. A woman who was professionally in his brother's camp.

Even so, Marcus was surprised at how much he wanted to trust her. To believe she was neutral in this standoff. But no matter how sizzling their connection, it couldn't trump her long friendship with his brother or her deep roots with the New York office. Could it?

"I'm sure Devon has his reasons. Do you two have to be so suspicious of each other?" she asked, methodically folding back one of the French cuffs on the shirt, pressing it into place as though her hand was an iron. "And what could there possibly be to investigate in your father's past?"

He ignored her first question. He could give a dozen examples of ways his brother had tried to undermine him personally and professionally. But what would be the point?

Instead, he focused on the second question. "My father spent a great deal of time alone, working on undisclosed research."

Lily stopped fidgeting with the shirtsleeve and glanced up at him. "He was an educator. Is that really surprising?"

"I'd understand if there had been published journal articles to show for it. Or correspondence from colleagues or extra books left around the house. But he was incredibly secretive about his work." Marcus thought back to his father's late nights in his locked study. Research trips. Arguments between his parents when they'd still been together. "He almost certainly had a second income of some kind. He had access to cash when he needed it. My mother swears he kept hidden savings accounts open in other names, although I'm not sure there's any proof of that."

Lily pursed her lips, a thoughtful expression stealing over her face. "Did his estate reflect any unexpected assets when he passed?"

Marcus's shoulders tensed. He was wary of responding, even though she would have been able to find out the answer easily enough. From Devon, even. But he couldn't shake the sense that she might be gathering information. Or insights on their father's mystery past that he might not have been inclined to share with Devon.

"No." He raked a hand through his hair, wishing they could dive back under the covers and forget the phone call he'd received. He'd far prefer to have Lily warm and naked beside him right now. "Nothing out of the ordinary. And I think it was on everyone's minds the day the will was read. One of Dad's old friends cracked a joke about Alonzo not being a secret agent after all."

In the silence that followed this comment, his cell phone vibrated again.

Even before he grabbed it, Lily was on her feet. "I should go."

"You don't need to—" he began, until he saw on caller ID that Weston Rivera was on the line.

Again.

"We'll talk in the morning," she assured him, picking up discarded clothing as she breezed out of the room.

"Lily, wait." He stood up as the phone buzzed again. He cursed himself for handling things poorly. With Lily. With his father. And even with Weston Rivera.

But as Lily closed the bathroom door behind her, Marcus realized he could only repair one of those things right now. So he swiped up to answer the call.

"I haven't reached Devon yet—" he began, needing to explain why he hadn't gotten in touch with his brother to find out Devon's endgame for hiring an investigator.

"I did." Weston's voice cut him off. "I informed him in no uncertain terms that I'm opening that safe with your father's papers tomorrow at noon and he can either be here or I give everything to you."

Shocked into silence, Marcus stepped out onto the back deck of the private lodge, needing a breath of fresh air to pull his thoughts together. It was late now, and the temperature had dropped at least ten degrees since his dinner with Lily.

"Excellent," he said after a moment, scratching a hand over his bare chest and wondering how his brother had taken the news that Rivera wasn't going to wait any longer for Devon to show up. "Where should I meet you tomorrow?"

"We'll convene in the ranch's business office." Weston sounded like he was someplace windy. His voice rose as a rush of air distorted the sound on his end. "Coop can escort you if you haven't been there before."

"I'll be at the business office tomorrow at noon," Marcus confirmed. "Thank you, Weston."

"I owe your dad," he said simply. "It's a debt I'll consider paid after tomorrow. The owners wanted to have a welcome reception this week to meet with you both, but if Devon isn't interested in showing up, we'll have to wonder how serious you are about working with us."

The call disconnected. Inside the lodge, Marcus could see Lily emerge from the bathroom, her hair neatly coiled and pinned back in place. He could still feel the texture of the silky locks on his fingers.

It was yet another thing he resented Devon for—interrupting this time with her. Time he could have been learning the nuances of what she liked. Touching her until she came apart in his arms.

Now, he'd have to bring her back to her suite. Find a way to salvage a professional relationship until he figured out her angle in all this. But one thing was certain. He wasn't sharing this latest piece of information with Lily no matter how much he wanted to trust her.

Just in case.

Nine

Pumped full of caffeine and adrenaline the next morning, Regina sat in the ranch manager's office, silently willing Cooper Adler to give her a job as a trail guide.

She'd been awake all night. At first, she'd been researching what job to apply for since Mesa Falls Ranch had several new openings and she wanted to tailor her résumé and interview to be an ideal fit. Once she'd settled on the trail guide position, she had devoted the rest of the night to researching the terrain around the Bitterroot River. She'd brushed up on her local history and quizzed herself on the flora and fauna of the region, ensuring she had enough patter to intrigue even a seasoned ranch visitor.

"You don't say much about your riding experience," her interviewer noted between sips of his coffee from a dinged-up silver travel cup. He eyed her résumé critically, as if he could see right through her fake degree in hospitality. "You really need superior horsemanship in case anything goes wrong with the guests."

"I was on a competitive women's polo team in college." It was true, but she'd been going by her real name then, so she hoped he didn't ask more about that. "Riding is second nature to me."

The ranch manager lifted a bushy gray eyebrow, regarding her silently for a long moment.

"You'll find the horses here don't respond like polo ponies," he warned.

With an effort, she remembered not to bristle at the superior way he spoke to her. After how her father had treated her and her mother, Regina had some major issues with male authority figures. Therapy had helped her recognize that, but there weren't enough hours in a day to have those issues counseled out of her.

"Since the best polo ponies are trained to have some competitive aggression on the field, that's probably just as well." She did her best to give the older man a charming smile. "But if it would help my chances for the job, I'd be happy to put in a few trial days in the stables. You're welcome to see how I handle myself with the animals."

Back in her old, privileged life—before her world had blown apart thanks to the book that exposed her family's scandalous secrets—Regina had had a horse of her own. And even though her family kept multiple animals in the stable, she'd been given her own Arabian on the condition that she would be the one to care for her.

That gorgeous mare, Darla, had been the center of her world for years, and the chores that came with her had kept Regina grounded. She'd always thought it was smart parenting of her father. At least until he'd taken Darla away from her, along with everything else, when he'd discovered that she wasn't really his biological daughter. Back then, she hadn't known the truth, either, and the revelation of her parentage had been a shock. These days, she wore her fake name as easily as any other, since the only identity she had anymore was whatever she created for herself.

"You'd really take on stable work to get this job?" The ranch manager eased his bulky frame back in the leather rolling chair.

His weathered face didn't give much away, but she was sure she heard a hint of begrudging admiration in his voice. He'd set aside her résumé, giving her his full attention.

"Gladly." She would have beaten rugs or washed laundry to get closer to the Salazar heirs. Anything to do with horses was a bonus.

"I'm going to take you up on that offer, Ms. Flores." He leaned his forearms on the desk again. "Although you've already made me a believer, I happen to know that your presence in the stable would give you whole lot of credibility with the ranch hands. And quite frankly, I need my trail guide on excellent terms with them."

She didn't know if she was more relieved that she got the job or that he hadn't asked for references, but she was mighty grateful to Cooper Adler.

"Thank you for giving me a chance." She knew from her two days of observation that Marcus Salazar was in and out of the stables daily. "I can head over there now."

She got to her feet, not sure how she'd get through the day of physical labor on no sleep, but she'd find a way.

"I'll walk with you." The ranch manager rose from his chair, drained his coffee and left the mug on the desk. "I've got a meeting with a guest at noon in the business office, and the stables are on my way. I'll introduce you around."

Instantly alert, Regina gave an automatic response as they headed out of the main lodge. She was fairly certain there were only two guests on the property this week—Lily Carrington and Marcus Salazar. Unless, of course, Devon Salazar had finally put in an appearance.

No matter whom Coop had an appointment with today, Regina wanted to be there.

Because she'd bet it involved the Salazar family. So as soon as Coop left Regina at the stables, she was already plotting her way out of the building to follow him.

When her phone rang shortly before noon, Lily wished she didn't have to answer.

She'd worked from the desk in her suite all morning, pulling together notes for the event she and Marcus had discussed, trying not to think about how awkwardly things had ended between them the night before.

Trying to tell herself that she hadn't torched her career with a single impulsive decision.

But as her phone rang for a third time, she acknowledged she couldn't ignore what had happened last night forever. But flipping it over, she saw it wasn't Marcus calling. It was his Salazar Media copresident, the only other man outranking her in the company.

"Hello, Devon," she answered as smoothly as possible, wondering if the brothers had spoken since Marcus discovered Devon had hired a private investigator.

Marcus had said nothing more on the subject when he'd driven her back to the lodge the night before, remaining silent about Weston Rivera's second phone call. Because he didn't trust her?

The idea troubled her more than it should, considering her attraction to him couldn't go anywhere and shouldn't have ever gone this far in the first place.

"Lily, I'm on my way to Mesa Falls now, but I won't arrive by noon. Is there any way you can stall Marcus?" Devon sounded tense. Terse. Harried.

She'd spent enough time as his second in command to recognize his panic. As his friend and colleague, her first instinct was to help. To say yes and figure out how to accomplish the task later.

But after getting to know Marcus better, she was reluctant to jump into a role that would put them at odds.

"Stall him from what?" she asked instead, setting aside her pen and rising from her seat at the small desk. She walked over to the window looking out onto the pool and courtyard area behind the lodge.

"From the meeting with Rivera. From letting him see Dad's papers before I get there. Didn't he tell you?"

She felt a pang of warning at the back of her neck as she watched a young woman—it looked like Regina Flores from the spa—hurrying along the tree line behind the courtyard.

"He didn't mention a meeting." She couldn't help the trace of impatience in her words. With Devon? With Marcus?

Or with the whole cursed position of being stuck as a go-between?

"Lily, it's almost noon now. Can you please attend the meeting on my behalf? They'll be in the ranch's business office. Rivera said it's in the building near the arena."

Outside the window, Lily could see Regina dart from the trees toward a structure in that precise location. The three-story building had oversize barn doors on two sides, but there were windows at regular intervals on the second floor. Like all the rest of the ranch buildings, the heavy log-frame construction provided a rustic appearance, while the sleek steel accents were contemporary.

"That meeting isn't about Salazar Media, Devon. I can't just waltz in there and take your place to hear information that your father intended solely for you and Marcus." Still, she couldn't deny she was curious about what Marcus would find out. And she couldn't tamp down the frustration with Devon. "Did you really hire a private investigator to look into your father's past while Marcus and I are here?"

"He told you that but he didn't tell you about the meeting?" Devon made a dismissive sound. "For that matter, don't you think it's hypocritical to ask about the investigator even though you say the meeting doesn't concern you?"

Frustration churned inside her. "You're right, it's none of my business. Occasionally our friendship blurs the line of our working relationship, or else you wouldn't ask me to attend a family meeting or to run interference with your brother."

"I just wanted you to stall him," Devon reminded her, a new coolness in his tone. "And what is this new defensiveness about my brother? Does Marcus have anything to do with you breaking up with Eliot?"

Lily gasped in surprise, wrenching her gaze from the window. "How did you know about that?"

"Eliot phoned me. He's obviously upset." Devon and her former fiancé were friends through mutual acquaintances besides her. They'd played tennis many times over the years. "And, of course, he's worried about the merger with Carrington Financial."

Betrayal fisted in her gut.

"I thought Eliot understood I wanted to wait to break the news to our families," she explained, measuring her words while her thoughts raced. A tension headache gripped her temples. "But maybe he's simply telling people who aren't family and expecting the news not to spread?"

She'd been foolish, hiding her head in the sand this week when she needed to figure out an approach with her grandparents. If they found out about her affair with Marcus, it would hurt them all the more.

"I won't say anything, Lily. Hell, you know that." Devon's words reassured her for the space of a moment, before he continued. "It was just so damned sudden, I worried about the timing of me sending you up there with Marcus."

Her reply dried right up. She'd barely wrapped her brain around how to share the broken engagement with the world, let alone what to say about her impulsive—in-credible—night with her boss. She hadn't imagined it was the kind of thing anyone else would ever find out about.

On the other end of the call, Devon cursed softly. "Lily, don't tell me—"

"Devon." She cut him off, unwilling to tread down a path of personal confidences. "I haven't told you any-thing," she reminded him, keeping her voice impassive. Neutral. It wasn't easy, since her heart was racing at thoughts of her professional world imploding. "And since you'll be in Mesa Falls soon, I'm going to let you handle whatever is going on with your brother and the papers your father left for you. I've got a solid plan in place for the kickoff event at the ranch, so if you'd like me to head back to New York—"

"Absolutely not." Devon recovered his professional tone, following her example. If he still suspected something between Lily and Marcus, he'd chosen to drop it for now. "I did hire a private investigator to look into Dad's past, and I'd like you there when I speak to Marcus about that, because we may need a cooler head to mediate."

Lily closed her eyes, her stomach dropping like she'd stepped onto a free-falling ride at the amusement park. And it wasn't one bit amusing.

Her one night with Marcus was going to destroy her career. How would either of the Salazar brothers ever trust her to be the cooler head when she'd leaped into Marcus's bed at the first opportunity? But she couldn't go into that now—not when she didn't have much time to implement some damage control.

"Call me when you're on the ground." She closed her laptop and wondered if there was any chance she could speak to Marcus privately before Devon arrived. "We'll find a time to meet."

She disconnected the call and checked her watch. It was almost noon. If Devon was correct about Marcus's meeting with Weston Rivera today—a meeting Marcus had purposely kept secret from her—Marcus would soon have the answers about his father's mystery paperwork.

Whatever happened, she hoped the meeting ended quickly. She needed to tell Marcus she'd made a horrible mistake the night before. One that she would never, ever repeat.

After that, she'd ask him if there was a way they could put the incident behind them so they could move forward with a professional relationship. She only prayed he said yes, because she had no other options for work right now when she'd just ripped apart her family's expectations of her and probably foiled Carrington Financial's merger.

Then again, if he said yes and she got her wish of burying that scandalous night in the past, she still had zero hope of ever forgetting it.

Checking his watch one final time, Marcus conceded that his brother wasn't going to show for the noon meeting. Would Salazar Media lose the Mesa Falls Ranch account, too, if Devon didn't show up at all this week? He'd been standing in a pine grove with a view of the driveway to the lodge, hoping all morning that Devon would find a way to be here, but it wasn't meant to be.

Maybe it shouldn't surprise him, since Devon had never been like family to him and had never sought Marcus's approval or support for a damned thing outside of business. But he'd believed Devon's affection for their old man was real, and he would have guessed that support for Alonzo—or curiosity about Alonzo's life—would have drawn Devon to Mesa Falls this week. Marcus was done making phone calls about it, refusing to get drawn any deeper into drama with his half sibling when he had a more pressing matter to discuss with Devon—buying him out of Salazar Media. Devon's latest stunt was one more reason Marcus needed to be free of him professionally.

He couldn't help but wonder how Lily would fit into that discussion. With a last glance toward the building where he'd dropped her off the night before, Marcus stalked toward the business office for his meeting. He hadn't mentioned the appointment to her, but he guessed she'd probably learned about it from Devon anyhow. Marcus had never confided his business to a lover in the past, so he wasn't sure why he'd been so tempted to with Lily. Maybe because he recognized her for the professional asset she was. Perhaps he even envied his brother's relationship with her, a bond based on something deeper than what she'd shared with him.

But he couldn't derail himself before this meeting by thinking about that. He tried his best to put her from his mind as he stepped inside the building that housed the ranch's business office. There were stables on the main floor, but they appeared too pristine to be in regular use, with cobblestone floors and wood stall doors painted with images of horses on the front. The place looked more suited to hold champion thoroughbreds than working animals. Huge doors led from the stable area to a paddock and small track surrounded by wooden seating.

Brass lanterns hung at regular intervals on the heavy beams that lined a walkway leading from the foyer. Marcus found a staircase and climbed the steps to the second floor, where double steel doors bearing the ranch name stood half-open. Inside the reception area, Marcus could see the ranch manager in conversation with a leanly muscled younger man he recognized from his research on the property—Weston Rivera.

"I hope I haven't kept you waiting." Marcus strode into the room, his attention focused on Rivera as he extended a hand. "I'm Marcus Salazar."

"Weston," the other man said, shaking hands briefly. At well over six feet tall, he was built more like an athlete than a cowboy, with wide shoulders, narrow hips and long legs. He wore jeans and hiking boots, a pair of aviator shades propped in his dark blond hair. There was something more assessing than welcoming in the guy's hazel eyes. "And thanks for being here. I know your father had hoped both you and your brother would coordinate to be here at the same time, but after six months of waiting for that to happen, I'm at the point where I need to turn over the papers and be done with it. My part-time commitment to search-and-rescue efforts on the mountain makes it tough for me to alter my schedule at the last minute."

Marcus bristled. "In all fairness, we didn't know about the papers until this week."

Weston waved the other men toward another set of doors behind the reception desk, and Cooper Adler stepped forward to unlock them.

"Papers aside, your father took the trouble to secure a promise from you before he died." Weston shot him a level gaze. "I made the mistake of thinking that would have gotten you up here long ago."

Marcus restrained a retort, but only by reminding himself that the group of ranch owners had a relationship with Alonzo that Marcus didn't really know anything about. Clearly, Weston held his father in high regard.

Still, who was he to judge?

"I'm here now," he said between clenched teeth as he followed the other men into a large conference room with a desk and seating area at one end. "Don't let me waste any more of your time."

Coop flipped on the overhead lights but didn't take a seat in any of the gray leather swivel chairs around the oak table. The ranch manager hovered by the steel doors, checking something on his phone and holding the screen at arm's length, as if he had a tough time seeing it.

Weston was already across the room, digging something out from shelves behind the desk while Marcus glanced out the windows overlooking the paddock and show ring below.

"Here it is." Weston straightened, a shallow metal lockbox in his hands. He put the box on the desk while Cooper strode over and set his phone down beside it. "And Cooper got the code from Gage."

Weston punched in something on the fireproof safe's digital access panel, then passed the ranch manager's phone back to him. Without another word, Cooper left the room and closed the doors behind him.

Marcus tensed, wondering about all the secrecy and what the box would contain. How much better had the ranch owners known his father than he had himself?

Weston cleared his throat. "Please, have a seat. I'll leave you alone to review things in a moment, but first let me just say I'm sorry Alonzo is gone. He had a huge impact on my life, and no matter what I said last night about having that debt paid, I'll always owe him something."

Surprised at the outpouring of heartfelt words, Marcus wasn't sure how to respond. "He never said much about his life away from my family, so sometimes I'm surprised at how well other people knew him."

Weston grinned as he slid the lockbox across the oak desk. "Your old man could keep a secret, that's for damned sure. Take all the time you need. Coop will be out front to lock up the room when you're done. And if Devon really does finally put in an appearance, I'll corral at least a couple of my partners into a welcome reception at my house Friday night."

Marcus felt relief steal through him that they might still salvage the business.

"Thank you." Seized with new curiosity, Marcus wanted to dig into whatever his father left. Even though the papers in that box might be something unwelcome.

Or some secret that his sons would now have to keep. Marcus had no desire to hide old skeletons in the closet.

"One more thing," Weston said over his shoulder once he reached the door. "I hope you'll clue your brother in when he arrives. According to the text I got, he'll be here in an hour or less."

"Thank you for the heads-up." Marcus guessed his brother would be driving hell-for-leather to get here now. "I'll speak to Devon as soon as he arrives."

He might not want to share his business with Devon, but he didn't begrudge him whatever their father had wanted them to know.

As soon as the door closed behind Weston, Marcus reached into the box and pulled out a stack of papers.

Twenty minutes later, he still couldn't believe his eyes. His father's secrets were unlike anything he would have ever imagined. His dad hadn't been a secret agent. He'd been an author of pulpy fiction, set in Hollywood with tabloid-esque story lines.

Alonzo had been damned good at it, in fact, hitting bestseller lists under a fictional name that Marcus hadn't recognized. What he couldn't figure out was where all the money from those book sales had gone. There wasn't anything about the literary estate in the files. But there was the name of a lawyer, and Marcus needed to get in touch with the woman pronto.

Because if Marcus was remembering the story line of the popular book correctly, he seemed to recall it had closely paralleled an incident based on real people—a Hollywood mogul and his former actress wife. There was even a clipping from a newspaper about the actress attempting to sue the author of the book, but the sources quoted in the story suggested the family had been discouraged from pursuing legal action since it was tough to win those kinds of cases.

Would the Hollywood clan decide to mount a lawsuit against his estate if they knew Alonzo's real identity? Would they come after Salazar Media?

Emptying the metal safe of all the papers, Marcus shoved them in a manila envelope and charged out of the conference room. He passed Coop in the reception area, then turned to head down the stairs.

Where he ran right into Lily Carrington, her feminine curves more delectable than ever.

Ten

"Oh!" Lily slammed into the very man she'd been searching for.

Marcus's arms went around her, crushing her to him. Because he wanted to? Or to keep her from tumbling right back down the wide oak steps? Her fingers clutched his shoulders as she righted herself, catching her breath and a hint of his spicy aftershave with it. The feel of his strong body plastered against hers was a vivid reminder of everything that had transpired between them the evening before.

The bone-melting kisses. The toe-curling orgasms. In just that brief instant he held her, her temperature spiked from normal to red-hot, her breasts tingling in anticipation of his touch in spite of all her determination to keep her professional distance.

"Are you all right?" He released her slowly, his voice a warm graze of air against her earlobe.

Vaguely, she became aware of the crinkling paper pressed to her spine. A folder? No, an envelope, she realized as he pulled his hand away.

Her gaze darted from the thick manila envelope to his face, his brown eyes unreadable except for the flicker of heat in their depths.

Belatedly, she realized she still clung to him, and she scrambled away so quickly she had to grip the polished wooden banister to keep from teetering backward again. How was she ever going to return to a strictly professional relationship with someone who affected her this way?

"I'm fine," she answered, more to convince herself than him. Then she heard movement on the floor above them, and her shoulders tensed. "Is someone still upstairs?"

The last thing they needed was an audience.

"It's just Coop," he assured her before sliding his free arm around her waist, gently turning her in the opposite direction. "Let's find somewhere else to talk."

She couldn't argue with that. She'd sought him out with the express purpose of having a private, sensible conversation about ending this affair, but she may have underestimated how difficult that would be—the sensible part, anyhow—after how dramatically things had changed between them last night. It would be simpler if she felt a true sense of regret about being with him. But right now, having his strong arm guiding her into an empty tack room that looked more for show than equipping horses, she couldn't scavenge an ounce of remorse that he'd awakened her to a kind of romantic fulfillment that she'd been missing out on all her life.

He let go of her to partially close the tack room door,

leaving it open enough that they could see if anyone entered or exited the building. When her gaze collided with his again, the burst of sparks over her skin sent her scrambling for a neutral topic.

"What is this place?" she asked, running her hands over what looked like a restored western saddle, the leather work showing a level of craftsmanship she'd rarely seen. "I mean, obviously it's a tack room. But why does the whole building look like nothing's ever been used?"

She cursed herself for getting sidetracked. She *wanted* to ask him about the meeting with Weston Rivera, but since he'd kept it secret from her, that didn't seem wise. And she *needed* to speak to him about ending their affair and never telling an earthly soul about it, but that was tough, too, when all she wanted to do was kiss him again.

"I think it's going to be the welcome center and a training area to greet new retreat guests. They'll use the arena to teach basic horsemanship or conduct roping and rodeo demonstrations to entertain guests." Lily followed Marcus's every move with her hungry gaze as he set down the packet of papers on a wooden shelf full of clean grooming brushes. "I remember seeing the description of it in some literature on their website. I think they only just completed construction. But is that really why you're here? To talk about the welcome center?"

She stared down at the cobblestone floor and told herself to get a grip.

"Of course not." She tipped her chin up and met his gaze. "Devon's on his way, and he asked me to be here when the two of you meet."

"It's kind of you to warn me," Marcus remarked dryly. "I appreciate the reminder of where your real loyalties lie."

His broad shoulders took up too much of the room,

making her wish she could seek shelter against them instead of fencing with him all the time.

"Can we not do this, please?" She didn't have much time to sort things out with him. To start cleaning up the mess she'd made.

"Devon must have told you about the meeting with Rivera." He shook his head, his jaw flexing. "No wonder you knew right where to find me."

"Your brother wanted to be here for it," she reminded him, tamping down her curiosity about the papers. "I know he'll be pulling into the driveway of the guest lodge any minute." She needed to get on top of this situation with Marcus before then.

"And what mission did he give you until he arrives, Lily? Does he want you to sidetrack me? Make sure you have me right where he can find me as soon as he arrives?"

He wasn't all that far from the truth, of course. The Salazar men might be business rivals, but they understood one another well enough.

"This isn't about what Devon wants—it's about what *I* want."

Her words produced an immediate effect on Marcus. His restless body went still as his attention narrowed to her.

"And what is it you want?" His voice stirred her senses, the tone somehow plucking taut strings of awareness until she practically vibrated with sensual need.

The air was suddenly sweltering. Oppressive, even. It brought with it the realization that asking for all the things she intended—to end their affair, to never speak of it again, to hide what they'd felt for each other—would only make her a hypocrite and a liar.

Her fingers clenched with the effort not to touch him.

Tension knotted up her back and clamped around her shoulders. Would it feel like this every time she saw him?

"The same thing you do," she replied carefully, certain that Marcus didn't want this affair to derail their working relationship, either. "That is—"

His arms were around her waist then, lifting her against him. The heat that had been building burst into a storm of passion, their hands exploring each other's bodies as if they'd been separated for years instead of hours. His lips claimed hers in a hungry kiss, and she looped her arms around his neck, clutching him tight.

Desire licked over her in greedy, white-hot flames. She pressed herself closer to the source of all that blistering warmth, arching her back, her hips restless, her breasts aching, her pulse throbbing in the most sensitive places...

"Marcus?" The masculine voice from the building entrance poured ice over her.

Edging away from Marcus with a start, Lily glimpsed Devon Salazar framed in the half-open door—and saw her career going up in flames before her very eyes.

Marcus had plotted his brother's demise before, but never with the degree of bloodthirsty enthusiasm he did at this moment.

For once, the instinct was totally selfless, since the tactless bastard had embarrassed Lily. Marcus took his time pulling away from her, doing his best to hide her burning cheeks until she had herself back under control. He saved plenty of anger for himself since he should have never put her in that position in the first place. But he'd never met a woman who could torch his self-control that way.

"What the hell is going on?" Devon glared at him like

he would have gladly gutted him on sight. "Is this what the company travel budget pays for?"

Behind him, Marcus felt the tension radiating off Lily. Guilt stung that he'd exposed her to any possible censure from his brother. A fierce desire to protect her stirred from somewhere deep within him.

"I suggest you think carefully before you start casting stones at the people doing your job for you this week," Marcus warned his brother, holding his gaze until he saw Devon's shoulders ease a fraction. "Nice of you to show up. Too bad you still missed the meeting."

He took in his Devon's black T-shirt and jeans, an unusually dressed-down choice for the man who usually projected an executive vibe.

"You're not getting off the hook that easily. We'll talk about it later when we're not in a place anyone can overhear." Devon glanced behind him to peer at the empty stalls, far more aware of his surroundings than Marcus and Lily had been. "Is Rivera around?"

"He left." Marcus kept his gaze on Devon, a man with green eyes and light brown hair who bore him little resemblance. "I got the impression that he's had his fill of rearranging his search-and-rescue efforts to accommodate your schedule."

Devon swore, but then his attention returned to Marcus, his eyes narrowing. "Do you presume to judge me? I'm not the one breaking up engagements."

"Enough." Lily stepped past Marcus to confront Devon. "If you care to address my broken engagement, I'll thank you to speak to me about it directly."

Marcus watched the two of them face off in silence after that, seeing for the first time that the wordless way they communicated was about more than just a long-

standing work relationship. More than simple friendship. He spied a level of mutual respect that he hadn't
identified in the past. It was evident in the surprising
way Devon backed down before Marcus could leap to
Lily's defense.

Devon gave her a brief nod. It wasn't an apology. More
like an acknowledgment of her point. Whatever it was
seemed to satisfy them both, since Devon moved on.
"Then let's find a place where I can get up to speed on
what's happening at the ranch and what I need to know
from the meeting with Rivera."

Marcus still grappled with a stab of envy for the easy
relationship Lily shared with his brother. Or vice versa.
Seeing that bond with new eyes only reminded him that
if push came to shove at Salazar Media, Lily's support
would be for Devon.

"I realize you trust Lily, but Dad's secrets aren't a
company matter," Marcus cautioned, keeping his voice
low as the sound of footsteps on the nearby stairs echoed
through the floor. "I suggest you read the papers before
we talk about them."

"Fair enough. Who's this?" Devon asked, his gaze on
a pair of boots as they became visible on the staircase.

"That's the ranch manager, Cooper Adler. He's the
owners' eyes on the ground," Lily intoned softly.

Once again, Devon seemed to comprehend the intended message immediately. "I'll speak with him. Apologize for not being here sooner." He spun back around to
face Lily and Marcus. "But afterward, let's talk."

Marcus passed Devon the envelope containing the
bombshell revelations about their father. "Take this for
a little light reading. Bring yourself up to speed before
we get ahead of ourselves with more meetings."

For a moment, Devon stared at the packet like it was a poisonous reptile. Or was it that he hadn't expected Marcus to share the information? Either way, he jammed it under his arm and strode in Coop's direction, hailing the older man with the charm that Devon could slap on as easily as a new hat.

"Let's get out of here," Marcus said under his breath, tugging Lily toward the door on the other end of the tack room, leading her out into the Montana sunshine.

Here the building bordered the fenced paddock area, and it was easy to lift the gate latch and bypass the main entrance where Coop and Devon were talking.

"Where are we going?" Lily asked, sounding wary as she held his hand tightly.

"Far away from Devon." He knew his time with Lily was coming to an end, and he wasn't ready for that to happen. "How about my guest lodge?" His rooms were far more private than hers.

He led her toward the small utility vehicle he'd driven here earlier in the day. With only a roll bar over the seats, the leather bench was sun-warmed.

"You're suggesting we go back to your place?" She slowed her step behind him, letting go of his hand to hold back her hair where it blew in the breeze. She wore a knee-length black skirt with the same cowboy boots she'd had on the night before. And with a blue silk T-shirt and suede jacket finishing the look, she was definitely dressed more casually than usual, perhaps in deference to their ranching client.

He slid behind the wheel but didn't turn the key, waiting for her to decide. "After what nearly happened between us in the tack room just now, don't you think we should consider finding someplace more private?"

Her brows knitted, an incensed expression on her face. But no sooner had she opened her mouth—presumably to give him an earful—than she snapped her jaw shut again.

Instead, she slipped into the passenger seat and simply said, "Hurry."

Her affair with Marcus was ending.

She knew it. He clearly knew it, too.

Yet somehow they'd found this window of time before they needed to walk away, and she didn't want to look back with any regrets that she hadn't taken this one last chance to be with him. After he parked the utility vehicle on the front lawn, they moved in unison toward the door. No words were needed.

He keyed in an alarm code and held the door open for her. She stepped inside the living area, following the same path she had the night before. This time, she didn't wait for him to point the way to the master suite. She slipped off her boots and headed that way on her own.

Marcus was two steps behind her. Until he caught up and swept her off her feet so he could cradle her in his arms.

It was a kind of sweet madness happening between them, and she gave herself over to it one final time. Her body came alive at the feel of his arms around her, his warmth seeping through her clothes and into her skin. By the time he toed open the bedroom door, she was desperate to be naked, to strip away every last barrier between them.

She didn't trust herself to speak, unsure whether she had words for the whirl of feelings that spun through her faster and faster. She could only focus on getting Marcus's shirt off, a task made easier when he set her on her feet again beside his bed.

Pulling open one button after another, she bent to place a kiss on the flesh she'd bared. She couldn't touch enough of him, her fingers skimming along the ridged muscles of his abs and then stroking down the indent at the center. She delighted in the shudder that went through him when she let her lips follow the trail her fingers blazed, a path blocked by his belt.

She worked the buckle with only a little aid from him, and in the end she held one of his hands captive so she could finish the task herself. She took pleasure from peeling away his clothes and freeing him, and even more pleasure from the ragged sound he made when she licked her way around the hard length of him.

With a growl, he hauled her to her feet. He skimmed her hair from her ear to whisper sweet praises there, words that prickled along her skin like a touch.

"I can't wait to have you all around me," he chanted while he drew her shirt off her. "I thought about doing this to you all morning long." He reached beneath her bra to cup a breast in his hand, squeezing lightly. "About touching you. Tasting you."

He kissed his way down her neck to her breasts, ministering to first one and then the other, licking through lace until he unfastened the clasp of her bra and let it fall away from her.

She was ready to come out of her skin by the time he lowered himself to the edge of the bed and drew her down to straddle him. Her skirt rode high on her hips, and he inched it the rest of the way up to make room for himself. She fumbled for the condoms still on the nightstand from the night before, tearing open the wrapper while he teased a touch through her panties.

"Please. Go slow." She wanted him to wait. Needed to feel him inside her when the inevitable happened. "I'm so close."

"Orgasms are free, Lily," he breathed along her neck. "You can have all you want."

His tongue flicked along the place where her pulse fluttered wildly.

She rolled the condom into place while he tugged aside the lace and satin of her underwear. Their eyes met for a red-hot instant as he lifted her hips and positioned her where he wanted her. Her heart thudded hard.

When he lowered her again, joining them, she knew she'd never feel like this again. Ever.

Emotions swelled and broke over her in waves, washing through her with truths she wasn't ready to face. She hid her face in his shoulder, trying to just enjoy the moment, needing to make this time last. She poured herself into the passion, letting it touch her everywhere.

Marcus steadied her, helping her find the rhythm she sought, anchoring her. He rained kisses over her face, stroking fingers through her hair, down her back and, at last—between her thighs.

Her heart wasn't ready for the end they catapulted toward, but her body took control, seeking everything his skilled hands offered. He molded her lips to his, guiding her hips with one hand while he feathered a touch against the tight bud of her sex.

The touch was her undoing.

She flew apart in his arms, her release a shattering completion that left her wrung out and clinging to him, one sensual shudder after another racking her. She could feel his finish, too, knew that he'd found that same incredible, sensual high that she had.

Physically, at least.

His hoarse shout and tense body told her as much. Then with his spent body wrapping hers tighter, she dragged in the warm scent of him, breathing his breath, feeling closer to him than she ever had another soul in the world.

It made no sense.

But the connection was so real she couldn't possibly deny it.

Lily, you fool.

She'd fallen as hard and fast as her mother ever had, ignoring every warning sign that she was wandering down that same path. Even when the evidence of her folly stared her in the face, his gorgeous body still warm around hers, Lily couldn't regret what she'd done.

Only that it was over.

"Lily?" Marcus's voice sounded off as he tensed beneath her.

Was he coming to all the same realizations?

"Mmm?" She lifted her head to look him in the eye, only to discover his attention wasn't on her at all.

His gaze was fixed out the window. They hadn't drawn the shades since it was daytime and there was no other building for miles.

"What is it?" She turned her head but couldn't see anything from her awkward angle.

"Do you know anyone who might show up here in a limo?" He lifted her up with him as he stood.

"A limo?" It took her a minute to redirect her thoughts to the real world.

But as she found her feet and peered down to the driveway beneath them, she saw a liveried driver reach into the back seat. When he emerged slowly, an elegant older woman came with him, setting one delicate designer sandal on the tarmac.

Lily's stomach sank all the way to hell as she recognized the woman's face, even from a distance.

"My grandparents are here."

Eleven

"It's your call." Marcus's voice at her side somehow penetrated the panic buzzing in her brain. "Do you want me to stay with you for this, or would you prefer I leave?"

Her grandparents were outside the house. They'd come all the way from Newport to Montana, and there could only be one reason why—they'd found out about her split with Eliot, and they weren't pleased. As if things weren't already complicated enough with her falling for Marcus while working for his brother.

She started to move around the room on autopilot. Finding her clothes. Dressing. She couldn't possibly think through this until she had clothes on. Her body still ached with the sweet pleasure of what had just happened with Marcus, but her brain was screaming at her to get a move on.

"Lily?" Marcus prodded, reminding her that he'd been asking her something. "Are you okay?"

She blinked her way through the knot of worry and nodded. He was buttoning his shirt.

"I'm fine. I need to face them. I just didn't think it would happen so soon." The doorbell chimed, and her sense of foreboding deepened. She smoothed her hands through her hair, tucking strands behind her ears. "And actually, if you don't mind, it might be easier if I spoke to them alone."

She hated to ask him to leave, but he had offered. The mess was of her own making, so she wasn't going to hide behind Marcus the way she had when Devon discovered them kissing earlier.

"Of course." He followed her down the stairs. "You might as well use the living room here. I'll make my excuses and head over to the main lodge to find Devon."

She appreciated his thoughtfulness and regretted that their last intimate moments together had been stolen out from under her. But she'd always known it couldn't last. Marcus himself had pointed out how different they were that first day they'd spoken down by the Bitterroot River. As a creative person, he couldn't worry about what other people thought. But no matter how much she wanted to carve out a new future for herself, establish boundaries with her grandparents, she would never be the kind of woman who discounted the opinions of the people she loved.

"Thank you." She wanted to say more. To tell him how much these days with him had meant to her.

But the doorbell rang again. For an extended time.

Sighing, she waited while Marcus opened the heavy wood door.

Her grandparents stood as a unified front, her grandfather dressed for travel the way he must have in another lifetime: sleek suit, understated tie, a tweed hat. Her grandmother was the more modern of the two, her ivory-colored pantsuit something a designer had probably sent her last week. Lily hugged them both briefly before Helen Carrington turned her attention to Marcus. Thankfully, he took care of introducing himself and welcomed them to Montana since Lily was still rattled from the surprise of having them show up on his doorstep.

Marcus could be as charming as his brother when he chose to be. He steered her grandparents into the living room, and Lily appreciated Marcus's efforts at small talk while she used the time to remind herself that she could do this. She was a successful woman in her own right, after all. She'd scaled the corporate ranks quickly, and nothing her grandparents said about her choices in life could change what she'd achieved. Part of that success was because she'd been fortunate enough to join Salazar Media when the New York office had been a twelve-person shop. But she'd worked tirelessly to help them become a thriving business with multiple satellite offices and a bottom line that grew at a trendsetting pace in their industry.

By the time Marcus made his excuses to leave, Lily was ready. But no sooner had he walked out the door than her grandmother shot her a withering glare.

Helen Carrington wore her gray-blond hair pinned at her nape with a jeweled comb, and her shoes were from a designer that only a handful of women in the world could afford. None of those beautiful trappings softened the sting of her words, though.

"Is *he* why you chose to throw a Winthrop diamond back in Eliot's face? After all their family has done for you?"

Because the comment was so unlike her grandmother, Lily chose to let it slide. She knew it came from a place of old hurts and fears tied to Lily's mother. Still, it stung.

Her grandfather briefly put an arm around his wife. He was old-school dapper, his gray suit custom-tailored to his shrinking frame, his gray hair thickly pomaded to remain in place.

"We just don't understand this change of heart," he explained more gently, his expression genuinely perplexed. He steered his wife toward the sectional sofa, as if taking a seat would help de-escalate things. "Eliot is already like a part of the family. We thought you loved him."

Lily followed them, lowering herself onto the edge of an oversize wooden rocker near the window.

"I thought I did, too, but we realized there's a reason we keep delaying the wedding. We're better as friends than we are as a couple." That had become even more clear to her after being with Marcus. "And I'm still trying to sort out what to do next, which is why I thought Eliot and I were going to keep the news between us for a little while longer." It hurt to think that he'd gone to Devon and her grandparents almost immediately after she'd told him she wanted to wait to break the news. They'd been friends for a long time before they were a couple.

He'd owed her that much.

"And this is how you sort it out?" Her grandmother took in Lily's wrinkled skirt and bare feet. "By making yourself at home with the man you work for?"

The sting from those words was sharper than before, and it tried Lily's patience. Even though she was sleep-

ing with Marcus, her grandmother was over the line.
Lily was an adult.

"Grandma, that feels like you're passing judgment on
a situation that is mine and mine alone. I love you, but I
don't feel like my romantic life is a place for group decision making."

Her grandfather tilted his head, as if considering the
point. But her grandmother drew in a sharp breath, her
gaze narrowing.

"This isn't just about your 'romantic life.' If you didn't
care for group decision making, perhaps you shouldn't
have gotten involved with the heir to our biggest com-
petitor in the first place." She spoke so forcefully that
she was shaking a bit and had to steady herself by gripping Granddad's arm harder. "The decisions you want to
make by yourself affect many, many people."

The accusation reverberated in her mind, sounding
similar to something Lily herself had said to Marcus
earlier in the week.

*You don't need to become so completely self-absorbed
that you discount the preferences of others.*

Lily followed the memory of that conversation like
Ariadne's thread, finding her way out of this argument.
Marcus had asked her a question that had spurred the
end of her engagement.

*If you weren't worried about other people's opinions,
would you still make the same choices?*

The answer to that had been so sure, so certain, she'd
been rattled to the core.

"I'm truly sorry that I've disappointed you. Both of
you." It really did hurt to know they felt let down. "But
I can't marry a man I don't love for the sake of a business merger."

The words that made so much sense in her head didn't appear to make a dent in her grandmother's displeasure. If anything, Helen Carrington appeared even angrier, her lips pursing with disapproval.

But her granddad jumped into the fray again, patting his wife's shoulders and explaining, "You don't have to marry him forever, darling. A year would do the trick. Hell, eight months would give us time to get the companies merged..."

He kept talking, but Lily couldn't believe her ears. She'd thought her grandparents would be upset with her lack of constancy in breaking up with Eliot. Not for a moment had she considered they might be more incensed that she didn't march to the altar for purely business reasons.

Disillusion slammed her hard.

"You flew all the way to Montana to tell me I should have a marriage of convenience for the sake of Carrington Financial?" She didn't know why she asked. Her grandfather couldn't have been clearer on that point.

"We'd like to think we taught you to put your family first," he said diplomatically.

"We raised you to be the COO of a company," her grandmother added, putting a finer point on it. "We damn well thought you appreciated sound business practices."

Lily shot to her feet, agitated. She paced the floor in front of the wide windows.

"I would never do something so underhanded to Eliot." She needed to end this conversation and shut down that whole line of thinking.

Besides, if she wanted any chance of keeping her position with her company, she needed to tie up her business here so she could rejoin Marcus and Devon. She wanted to help them keep the company together, and now that she understood both of the Salazar men better, she thought she might know a way to help them keep the peace.

"Underhanded?" Her grandmother's eyebrows rose in surprise. "Eliot's the one who spoke to us about the arrangement. I'm sure he was as surprised as any of us that you weren't going through with it."

Shock rippled through her. Had her whole engagement been a sham? Was she the only one who hadn't known it was strictly based on a merger?

"I was unaware," she murmured lamely, restraining the urge to blurt out that Eliot was surely seeing someone else while he was in London.

If her grandparents were this nonplussed about a marriage of convenience, they surely wouldn't be scandalized by her suspicion that Eliot was dating other women.

"So you'll reconsider?" Her grandfather pressed.

"If Eliot wants the merger, why can't it happen without us marrying?" Lily asked.

"His father will never allow it without a marriage," her grandmother supplied impatiently. "Winthrop is in a better position than Carrington Financial, but Eliot doesn't have his father's business sense. I believe Eliot would be glad to turn over some of the burden of running the company to you."

She began to see her grandparents' corporate acumen more clearly as she let go of any illusion that they wanted what was best for her. In some ways, that made it easier to disappoint them.

Especially now that she'd had an opportunity to see for herself what she would be missing out on if she'd wed Eliot.

"I'd like some time to think about it," she said finally,

needing to buy herself time to process it all. "Why don't we have lunch tomorrow and we'll talk about it more then?"

Her legs felt shaky. Or maybe it was the ground beneath her feet that was shifting now that her ethical foundations had been kicked out from under her.

Her grandfather nodded, already agreeing to the plan, but her grandmother leaned forward in her seat, fixing Lily with her gaze.

"Until then, try to remember that marrying one of the wealthiest heirs in the Western world isn't exactly a chore," Helen Carrington said dryly. "It's not like we're asking you to sacrifice your firstborn."

With an effort, Lily gave her grandmother a tight smile before she walked them to the front door. As soon as they left, she found herself wanting to run to Marcus and knew that wasn't the solution. If she couldn't trust Eliot, who she'd believed to have been her friend since childhood, how could she ever trust a man who told her he only wanted relationships that were simple?

With clear rules. Where no one got hurt.

Except she'd developed feelings for Marcus in the space of a few short days. Unwise of her. Not at all sensible. But they were strong feelings nevertheless, grounded in a relationship so different from anything she'd ever experienced.

For all of Marcus's faults, there'd been a real honesty in how he'd approached their relationship. He hadn't lied to her the way Eliot and her grandparents had, allowing her to believe in a romance that had never existed. Marcus had been up-front about the attraction, and about what it would mean for them if they gave into the temptation of it.

She respected that. Appreciated it, even when the fall-out was going to hurt her.

Because with Marcus, there was more to their relationship than just the physical intimacy. It was about the way he'd let her see the real him, giving her a glimpse of how he thought. What he believed. They might be very different people, but she'd seen behind the creative media guru facade.

And she liked what she'd seen.

She suspected she was going to get hurt for being foolish enough to ignore the warning signs that he'd plastered all over himself. Because even with his words and clear rules ringing in her ears, Lily was falling for him anyway.

Marcus hadn't wanted his time with Lily to end like that.

Without a goodbye. Without a conversation about what the future held for them. He'd thought he could find a way to keep seeing her. Find a way to continue a discreet affair somehow. But the arrival of her grandparents had thwarted all that. He hadn't wanted to leave Lily to the wolves. But they were her family, weren't they?

He couldn't get her off his mind as he drove over to the main lodge to find Devon.

Lily was a strong woman, and she wasn't going to let her grandparents bully her into a marriage she didn't want. But he hated that she still faced that kind of pressure. He'd like to think that if he'd been in her grandparents' position, if his business faltered and the only thing that could save it was a merger by marriage, he would have too much personal integrity to coerce his own granddaughter into a loveless relationship. But—despite what it said about him—he could understand the desire to save the business that bore your name. And he suspected Lily was being pressured to change her mind about her ex-fiancé.

As he parked the borrowed ranch vehicle in front of the lodge and got out, Marcus faced the fact that he hadn't wanted to be anywhere near a conversation involving her ex. No matter how much he told her that he wanted to keep things simple with her, she'd slid past his defenses long ago and somehow remained there. For years, it hadn't mattered because she was taken.

Now? He knew that what they'd shared this week had been deeper than the superficial dating he'd done in the past handful of years. If he'd remained in that house with her grandparents, being a part of a conversation about the man who didn't appreciate her when he'd had her, Marcus wouldn't have been able to keep his opinions to himself. The truth was, no one was good enough for her.

Especially not some Ivy League heir to the family throne who didn't appreciate how hard Lily had worked to find her own niche outside the Carrington realm.

By the time Marcus entered the main lodge and found his brother seated in the great room, he was on edge. Spoiling for a fight, even.

His brother sat against a wall near the bar, his Italian leather loafers out of place in the Western-themed room that contained more elk horns than seats. Devon was reading the paperwork that had spilled from the envelope all over the game table next to him. He'd drunk two-thirds of his dark amber drink, the ice cubes clinking against the glass as they melted and shifted.

Marcus dropped down on a bench across from him, not waiting for an invitation to sit. "Why did you hire a private investigator before you came here?"

His brother put down the paper he was reading. "Because I thought maybe Dad was going to reveal he had a secret fortune he was leaving to you and you were going to try to buy me out of the company."

Surprised, Marcus leaned back in his chair, weighing that answer. "That makes no sense. Besides, I have enough money of my own to buy you out. If it was simple to do, I would have tried pushing you out of the company a long time ago."

"I'm well aware you wanted me out," Devon replied evenly. "And beyond finances, I thought Dad might have some secret in here that you already knew. Something that would give you leverage against me."

"Why would you think that?" Marcus heard a scuffling sound outside in the reception area, so he lowered his voice, even though the main lodge was like a ghost town with no other guests except for Lily this week. "Don't get me wrong—I'm not surprised you'd suspect I would use any leverage that fell into my lap, but why would you think Dad had shared anything with me? No one knew what he was up to."

"You went to school where Dad taught—time I never had with him." Devon spoke quickly, but not quite fast enough to hide a flash of pain. "All the owners of Mesa Falls Ranch went to Dowdon, too. Plus, Dad spent a lot of time here before his death. I thought maybe there was some connection to this place for both of you."

Unbidden, Lily's words floated through his brain. *Do you two have to be so suspicious of each other?*

Clearly, the suspicions went both ways.

"This is my first time in Montana. And I knew nothing about the book, let alone why he spent so much time up here."

"Did you read this?" Devon pointed to a letter hand-written on notebook paper.

"I must have missed it." The fold marks on it were deep, so maybe it had been at the bottom of the envelope. "I passed the whole thing over to you before I read everything carefully."

He'd thought he had reviewed all the important things, though. The note was a letter in their father's hand, addressing both of them.

"Take it." Devon pushed it across the table. "That one is more personal and doesn't address the rest of this stuff." He waved a hand over the contact information for the literary attorney, the newspaper clippings and old story notes for the book their father had written. "But first, we should figure out what all this means for the business."

Marcus shoved their father's letter in the breast pocket of his jacket. As he pulled his hand away, a long dark hair came with it, reminding him of the time he'd spent with Lily before her grandparents arrived. The need for her—not just to be with her, but to help her, protect her, talk to her—kept growing the more time he spent with her. A need that wasn't going to disappear just because he got on a plane and flew to the opposite coast.

"Having the company associated with this would be a nightmare." Marcus pointed to one of the news clippings about actress Tina Barnes contemplating a lawsuit. "It's been a secret for this long, I don't see any reason why it can't remain a secret."

"If Dad had a contract to protect his identity, or some kind of confidentiality agreement with the publisher, it probably expired when he died. We need to find out before this explodes on us and we're caught without a plan."

Marcus eyed his brother as Devon took a long swig of whatever he'd been drinking.

"But isn't all of this a giant distraction from why Dad wanted us here in the first place?" He'd come to Montana to make arrangements about the control of Salazar Media and go his separate ways from the brother he didn't trust. "We promised him that we'd come to the ranch and figure out the future of the company, not plan his literary estate that he never bothered to mention to either of us."

Devon frowned. "Lily didn't change your mind about that?"

Marcus stared at him, wariness knotting at the back of his neck.

"Change my mind about what, exactly?"

"About trying to maneuver me out of the company." Devon jammed the remaining papers on the table back into the envelope. "The two of you appear to have gotten on damn friendly terms, so I hoped maybe you'd decided to end your personal war with the New York office."

Marcus swore, anger rising fast that his brother would think he'd mix business with...whatever had happened between him and Lily. He questioned it now, looking back at the affair to see if he'd missed something. "Did you send her here to seduce me?"

The idea would have been laughable considering how much he'd always wanted her anyway. Except it wasn't one bit funny.

"Of course not." Devon set down the envelope, staring at him with what looked like genuine shock. "She's my friend, Marcus. And the last I knew, she was also *engaged*, so I'd never in a million years..." He cut himself off, shaking his head. "You don't know her at all."

"Maybe I don't," he agreed, remembering all the times

his instincts had warned him not to trust her, that Lily's first loyalty was to Devon. "But humor me, will you, and clarify for me why you sent her here in your place?"

"To help you close the deal for the Mesa Falls Ranch account," he said with absolute seriousness.

"We both know I could have closed that deal with my eyes closed, so let's cut the bullshit."

The sense of betrayal cut deep. Not because of Devon, whom he expected it from. But because of Lily. How had he let himself read something deeper into what he'd shared with her?

"I had hoped that you'd stay here until I could get back to the US," Devon admitted, spinning the heavy bar glass around and around on a thick wooden coaster. "I guessed—correctly, I might add—that she would be the one person in the company you might actually stay put for."

"I don't appreciate being manipulated. And I damn well don't like how you used Lily." He wondered how clearly she had understood her role. Maybe she hadn't.

But then again, she knew Devon well. And once she'd broken things off with her fiancé, she'd freely confessed that she needed to protect her position at Salazar Media more than ever.

It cast a dark pall over the affair and all the things he thought he'd been feeling for Lily.

Betrayal burning like bile, he couldn't trust himself to say anything more and keep a civil tongue in his head. Marcus shoved back from the table and made fast tracks out of the room, away from his brother.

Regina scrambled away from the door as fast as she could when she heard footsteps heading her way.

She'd taken off her boots to make as little noise as possible on the tile floors. With no one else in the main lodge besides a maid who'd left the building just as Regina arrived, she didn't need to worry about how odd it looked to sprint across the reception area cradling her boots in her arm.

Silently, she tucked into an alcove that led to a sitting area overlooking a courtyard, her heart racing as she forced herself to be very, very still. What would she say if one of the Salazars caught her spying?

Her breath sounded like giant billows in the small space, the *whoosh* of it convincing her she would be found out any second.

But then she heard the front doors open and close hard—as if someone had used a battering ram on them instead of a human hand. The sound of footsteps faded, giving her the courage to peer out into the lodge's reception area. The massive foyer glowed with afternoon sunlight from the windows in the atrium-style entrance. The front desk was unmanned and discreet enough that it could pass for a sideboard when not in use to check in guests.

Regina put her boots back on, releasing a pent-up breath. She didn't care for spying, and she wasn't particularly good at it. In the last two hours she'd risked her tentative new position at the ranch twice—once by sneaking into the building with the business office and nearly running into Cooper Adler. And a second time just now, listening to Devon and Marcus discuss how much they wanted to bury their father's secrets for good.

Which only proved that they recognized Alonzo's misdeeds for what they were—an intrusion into her family's privacy and rights. But she still didn't know if they stood to profit from the book, or if they had in the past without realizing it.

She couldn't know their intentions until she got closer to them. Or, more accurately, until she got closer to Devon. Marcus was clearly involved with Lily Carrington, and he already knew his way around Mesa Falls Ranch.

But Devon was all alone, and he'd just arrived.

He would need a good trail guide to show him the sights.

Twelve

By the night of the welcome reception for the Salazar brothers, Lily recognized that Marcus had been avoiding her.

She stared out the window of the chauffeur-driven Escalade that had picked her up at the lodge to deliver her to Weston Rivera's home on the Bitterroot River. In the three days since her grandparents had arrived in Montana, she hadn't spoken to Marcus once. At first, when Devon revealed that his brother had left Mesa Falls Ranch for an unscheduled trip to Denver to meet with a client, Lily told herself that Marcus was simply trying to make their inevitable parting easier by removing himself from her presence.

Or perhaps he'd been giving her space to smooth things over with Devon to help her keep her job, although Devon had remained strangely silent about the topic of catching her in the stable that day with Marcus.

Still, despite the hurt of his departure, she'd thought she would try to process everything that had happened over the past week on her own. She'd phoned Eliot to discuss their misunderstanding in detail and had been relieved to learn that her grandparents had missed some of the nuances of their conversation with Eliot about the broken engagement. Yes, Eliot would still be open to a marriage of convenience, but at the time he'd proposed, he genuinely thought their friendship would help them fall in love and make a formidable team. He'd only contacted her grandparents in the hope maybe Lily's mind wasn't made up yet, and he seemed sorry for the problems he'd created for her. He didn't think his father would concede to a merger without the marriage, but he'd been willing to look into it.

She hadn't asked if he was seeing someone else because it didn't matter. She was relieved to have salvaged a tentative friendship and an open dialogue on a merger, which had been enough to mollify her grandparents for now. Lily would use all her business savvy to draw up a merger proposal for Eliot's father when she got back home, and her grandparents would have to be content with that.

Either way, the engagement was behind her. The conversations with Eliot and even her family had left Lily even more certain she wanted more time with Marcus, who'd been honest with her about his intentions and about wanting to be with her. Except now, he didn't seem inclined to give her any more of his time since he'd ceased communicating with her.

The Escalade rolled to a stop outside Weston Rivera's massive modern home built into the mountainside overlooking Bitterroot River Valley. Her grandparents had flown home to Newport the day before, declining an invitation to the welcome reception. Devon told her the gathering would be for fewer than fifty people, but it looked bigger than that from the way guests spilled onto a huge front deck where a tuxedoed bartender was making drinks. White patio lights were strung in a canopy over the deck, giving the gowns and jewels of the beautifully dressed crowd a fairylike glow. The sound of laughter and contemporary rock music filtered softly through the tinted windows a moment before the driver opened Lily's door.

Was Marcus here? She took the driver's hand, allowing him to help her from the vehicle. She'd dressed with care, choosing a pale purple satin-and-lace gown with a big bow tied at the hips. The strapless bodice gave her room for a sapphire-and-amethyst necklace that belonged to her mother, a piece Maggie had left behind when she'd abandoned the Newport lifestyle. Normally, Lily avoided the splash of added jewels, but tonight she'd wanted to embrace her Carrington heritage. The name didn't just belong to her grandparents. It was hers, too. Maybe writing a successful merger proposal would help them respect what she brought to the table for the family business. And if not, that didn't mean she didn't deserve it. Therapy had helped her to understand that.

Besides, the jewels were beautiful. And yes, she wanted to make Marcus eat his heart out.

Lily walked up the carpet runner spanning the stone steps in deference to guests' evening shoes. She spotted her host immediately. Devon had introduced them two days prior when they'd had a meeting to discuss preliminary event ideas for the ranch's social media outreach. She'd had to present Marcus's ideas without him.

"Wow." Weston gave her an appreciative smile, his hazel eyes warm with welcome. "You look stunning, Lily."

He was a handsome man with his lanky frame and thick waves of dark blond hair, but he wasn't the man who filled her thoughts. With his black silk shirt under his tuxedo jacket and his dark dress boots, Weston had a handful of female admirers nearby on the front deck anyhow.

"Thank you." She appreciated the compliment on a night when she was feeling vulnerable. "Have the guests of honor arrived yet?"

"Devon is inside enduring a rare visit from my brother," he said dryly. "Marcus hasn't arrived yet."

Her heart fell at the news. If she'd known Marcus wouldn't be here this evening, she would have found an excuse to fly home.

"I'm anxious to meet your brother," she assured Weston, thanking him for the evening and then entering the house.

Inside, the rock music from the outdoor speaker was less intrusive. But the event remained decidedly unstuffy, with the dessert station featuring cookies painted to look like woodland creatures, a decorative ice sculpture modeled after nearby Trapper Peak and a lively dartboard on a side deck where guests could take aim around a natural waterfall sluicing down the mountain.

She was watching a young woman line up her shot when she felt a familiar presence at her side.

"Hello, Lily."

Despite her preparation for the evening—her care in dressing, her mental pep talks about how to handle this situation—she couldn't help a rush of relief at the sound of Marcus's voice. Or the liquid heat that flooded her veins just from being near him.

Turning, she met his dark brown eyes in the glow of the white lights strung from the pergola-style arches overhead. Right away, she felt the coolness in their depths. She sensed that he'd retreated from her in every way since they'd last spoken.

Because he was that good at keeping things simple and had known it was time to shut down the affair? She wondered if she'd been a complete fool not to listen to him when he'd warned her about that. She could never accuse him of not being honest.

"Welcome back," she greeted him, tempering her need to fling her arms around him and kiss him.

Instead, she knotted her fingers together, clutching her silver purse tighter. He was so handsome in his tuxedo, the classic lines well suited to his broad chest and narrow hips. His thick dark hair framed his face, his expression serious.

"I'm only staying for the party. I have a flight back to Los Angeles in two hours."

"Good of you to make time in your schedule." She noticed his brother was watching them, a concerned frown on his face. How had she ever been so optimistic as to think she could help these two smooth over their differences? Marcus seemed more remote than ever.

"Do you have a moment?" he asked, leaning fractionally closer. "I'd like to speak to you privately."

Her heart sped faster. Foreboding mingled with nerves.

"Of course." She followed him as he led her past a throng of guests, into a foyer and through a room on the opposite side of the house.

They came to tall double doors that were closed. When Marcus opened them, she saw steps that led down into a more casual family room. Beyond that, there was an office illuminated by a small desk lamp.

"Are you sure—" she began.

"I asked Weston where we could speak. This was his suggestion," Marcus informed her as he pulled the double doors closed behind him, dulling the noise and laughter of the party.

Now they were alone in the sunken family room. The gray stone floor was softened by a woven mat in a natural fiber. The floor-to-ceiling windows were covered with bamboo shades. Plants and small trees were the only decorations except for a contemporary sculpture of a young woman seated by the fireplace. Carved in a shiny black stone, the artwork was compelling. Lily would have enjoyed a closer look if she hadn't been worried about whatever Marcus wanted to say.

Privately.

"I realize we went into an affair knowing that it wouldn't last, but that doesn't mean it wasn't significant for me." He launched into his thoughts without preamble, as if he had a prepared statement.

Lily tensed. Whatever he wanted to talk about couldn't be good. He hadn't touched her. He hadn't even suggested they sit, so she stood awkwardly in the middle of the room, feeling off balance.

"It had meaning for me, too, Marcus," she assured him. "It still does."

She wanted to tell him about the realizations she'd come to while her grandparents were in town. How she'd wanted to see him afterward, craved his presence. But his jaw flexed, his mouth drawing into a flat line.

"Nevertheless, I saw our time together in a new light after Devon arrived." His dark gaze flickered with the first hint of passionate feelings—but not necessarily the romantic kind.

Still, she was glad to see he lurked somewhere within the expressionless man who'd asked to speak to her alone.

"How so?" she asked, preferring to get whatever was bothering him out into the light where she could confront it head-on.

She realized her fingertips had fallen to the amethysts around her neck and she dropped her hand, unwilling to betray any need for comfort when he seemed so resolute.

"My brother sent you here to keep me on the premises, knowing full well that I had a long-standing—" he seemed to search for the right word "—interest in you."

She didn't want to believe that of her friend. But then again, Devon had always put his business goals first. Outside the double doors, a burst of laughter felt a world away from their conversation.

"That seems coldly unfair. Even for Devon." She wanted to reach out, to touch Marcus and somehow melt the icy veneer she sensed between them. Just for a moment. "But I would have never come here if I'd had any idea—"

"I know that," Marcus said simply, his stiff shoulders relaxing just a fraction. He paced a few steps away from her and ran his finger over the natural wood mantel built into the stone surround. "I wouldn't have returned to Mesa Falls at all if I'd thought there was any chance you were aware of his motives."

The tightness in her chest eased at the admission.

"Then how did talking with Devon make you view what happened between us in a new light?" She sensed him pulling away.

On the afternoon that she'd asked her grandparents to leave her alone, she'd scoured the ranch searching for

Marcus, ready to tell him she was falling for him. Had she saved herself heartache by not finding him? Or was it simply delayed?

"You may not have been spying for him, but you were almost certainly putting forward his agenda." Marcus paused beside the stone sculpture of the girl, his demeanor every bit as remote. His gaze as flat and lifeless as he stared at Lily. "Which leaves me with just one question for you. Were you keeping his secrets for him all the while you were with me?"

An answering anger lashed through her at the unfairness of the question, at being put on trial for transgressions he hadn't bothered to specify. The music outside the door grew quieter. A muffled sound of a deejay's voice vibrated through a speaker. The party happening around them felt so surreal when she was alone with Marcus and hurting this way.

"Yes," she told him honestly. "Though it didn't matter, since you went on to discover far more about Devon's movements than he confided in me."

"That's all I wanted to know." His nod was brief. Accepting. Only the tight clench of his fingers revealed that he might have been upset by her answer. He moved toward the double doors as if to exit. "It was that simple. That clear. We can fly to our opposite coasts now, and I will stay out of your way. I think they're calling Devon and me to the podium."

His hand was on the doorknob, and he was about to walk out. Anger rushed through her.

"That's it?" Lily's heart ached, but she swallowed down the hurt in order to articulate exactly what she thought. "I knew you wanted simple, Marcus, but I never would have guessed you wanted things *that* simple. One question. Is that really the only chance I get to provide any insight on what I feel or what this week meant to me? Are you really unable to acknowledge that everything isn't black-and-white, to acknowledge the complications I might have encountered because we work together, or because I had just broken off a long relationship?"

He faltered, his hand falling away from the door. Outside the room, she could hear the muffled voice of the deejay again, but she wasn't inclined to put on her public face right now when someone she'd cared about had just shredded her heart.

He stared at her, his dark eyebrows knitted together, as if unsure what to make of the sudden outpouring. Clearly he hadn't anticipated this response when he'd been typing up his speaking notes for the one-question interrogation. Still, he didn't speak.

But he hadn't left, so she took that as a sign to continue. "Three days ago, I was foolish enough to think maybe I could make you rethink keeping things *simple* with me." She doubted she'd ever be able to hear the word again without it hurting. "I thought you were honest and forthright, but now I see that was only because you refuse to look any deeper than the surface. I deserve better than a man who thinks he can analyze my motives or my heart with a single question." She charged past him, opening the door for herself. "Good night, Marcus. And goodbye."

Lily felt the attention of the partygoers from the formal living room on the far side of the foyer. But she kept focused on making it out the door. With her chest aching in a way she'd never experienced during the breakup of her engagement, Lily stepped into the rapidly cooling night.

It was easy to see why it hurt now in a way it hadn't then. She loved Marcus.

* * *

For the first time in his life, Marcus could see the benefit to having a heart of ice like his brother. Because while Marcus was reeling from Lily's words, Devon was able to charm the crowd when the Salazar brothers were called to the small podium.

Marcus had stalked out there like a man held with marionette strings, his brain somewhere else entirely. He'd missed something big with Lily. He'd lashed out at her because he'd been hurting. He'd failed to listen.

He hadn't seen the big picture.

The realization slammed home while he stood among the well-heeled crowd the owners of Mesa Falls Ranch had gathered to welcome Salazar Media to town. The sustainable ranching idea was gaining momentum, and the six men who shared ownership of the retreat wanted to use the place as a way to showcase their successes. Each of those six men had other interests outside the ranch, and supporters from those businesses were here tonight. Weston's brother, Miles, had another ranch in the Sierra foothills of California. Gage Striker was an investment banker and angel investor for any number of companies. If Marcus hadn't been emotionally drained by what had just happened with Lily, he would have been making mental notes about ways to approach some of them for future business opportunities.

As it was, he stood by Devon and let his brother do the talking until the crowd applauded, the music started up again and Marcus could get out of there. He began walking toward the door.

"Wait up," Devon called from behind him.

Marcus slowed his step.

Devon scowled at him, steering him toward a small

media room behind the main staircase. It had four leather chairs facing a big screen and was paneled with sound-proof tiles and cherry wainscoting, a blend of old world and new.

"What did you say to Lily?" Devon demanded as he closed the door behind them. He folded his arms across his chest, barring the door like a damn bouncer.

Marcus wanted to tell him that he hadn't treated her any worse than Devon had.

But was that even true?

He hated to think he'd wounded her even more deeply than the man who'd sent her—while engaged—into Marcus's path. His head throbbed with regret while some of the fight leaked out of him.

"I said all the wrong things. All the stupidest, wrong-headed things." He jammed his hands in his pants pockets, balling his fists. "The worst part of it was I had days to think about what I was going to say. And in my head, I sounded calm and reasonable."

Pivoting on his heel when he reached the end of the room, he paced back toward his brother. Devon had leaned back against the door, still blocking it but not appearing quite as aggressive.

"She looked upset," Devon observed as he stared down at his shiny wing tips.

"And that's helping, thanks."

"It's my fault, too." His brother stroked the two-day growth of beard he'd been favoring for the last year or two, so his jaw was perpetually in shadow. "I shouldn't have asked her to come out here in the first place, but since Dad died…"

Marcus quit pacing, surprised to hear the shift in his

brother's tone, and even more surprised to hear an admission of guilt, however small.

Devon cleared his throat and hefted out a sigh. "There's no one to run interference for us anymore. And she's tougher than she looks, so I told myself it would be okay."

For a moment, Marcus let that sink in. The party outside was barely audible in here. And it wasn't as though Marcus wanted to socialize. Had Lily actually said that she'd been contemplating asking him for more? For something deeper than "simple"?

He'd been unprepared for that. He'd spent a lifetime telling himself that he didn't play games with women. But it turned out that by oversimplifying romance, he'd been playing a kind of game after all. He didn't know how to handle something real.

"She might resign, you know." Which would be a disaster for the company, but was the far lesser of Marcus's concerns.

"I'll fix it," Devon assured him, sounding more confident than he looked at the moment. "At the very least, I'll take over on site to manage the event moving forward. That gives her freedom to do—" his gaze shifted warily to him "—whatever she needs to do."

Marcus had no idea what that might entail. But he knew he needed to talk to her.

"You'd stay on here?" he asked, relieved on that score at least. If Devon set his mind on patching up the Salazar relationship with Mesa Falls Ranch, Marcus knew it would happen.

"Consider it done. I've already got a trail ride scheduled in the morning to bring myself up to speed on the property." He checked a card in his jacket pocket, then held it up for proof. "Regina Flores at ten o'clock."

Marcus nodded. "Thanks for that."

Not that it helped with Lily.

"Did you read Dad's letter?" Devon asked, straightening from the doorway.

"What letter?" As soon as he asked, however, he remembered. "Hell."

He patted his breast pocket even as he recalled it wouldn't be there since he'd folded the note and put it in a different jacket pocket three days go. The letter hung in his closet right now.

Devon withdrew his phone from his jacket and scrolled through images before he passed it silently to Marcus.

"You photographed it?" Marcus enlarged the image.

"I have trust issues," Devon said with a straight face. "I photographed every one of the papers the moment I opened the envelope."

Sinking into one of the leather chairs, Marcus focused on his father's handwritten words, addressed to his sons. Heartfelt and succinct, Alonzo Salazar outlined his regrets about disrespecting Devon's mother by having an affair with Marcus's mother, and his regrets about harming Marcus's mother through an affair with another woman.

I haven't been a good father or a good partner. In the end, I was lonely. Surrounded by friends but no family since my selfish choices made the people around me wary and bitter. I drove wedges between people instead of bringing them together. I wanted the two of you to join forces to form the company so you would have a connection. I know it hasn't been easy working together, but somehow, I still hope maybe you'll try to make it work. It's too late

*for me to have a family, but I'd like to think it's not
too late for me to leave you with one.*

Marcus stared at the letter for a long time, the words
blurring on the screen. It was hard to empathize with his
father, because he had hurt them all. It was why Marcus
had never been close to him or his brother. But there was
a wisdom in what he said. Keeping secrets in the Salazar
family had become such a way of life that it was second
nature for him and Devon not to trust each other. The
fact that Lily had been caught between those two forces
was no fault of her own, and he'd closed the door on their
relationship because of it.

When he stood, he passed the phone back to Devon.

"I'm not him," Marcus said simply. "And I'm not going
to make his mistakes."

He reached for the door, and Devon followed, not stopping him.

"Does that mean you'll consider keeping the company
together?" Devon asked.

Outside the media room, the party was in full swing.
The bar was now filled with top-shelf champagne bot-
tles, which the servers were passing around liberally. On
the exterior deck, someone was taking video of a new
arrival, a hum of excitement in the crowd as a small en-
tourage appeared on the stone steps.

"I'm not sure." Marcus hadn't given any more thought
to Salazar Media. "But I'm not letting Lily get away
without a fight."

Thirteen

Still wearing her evening gown, Lily packed her leather suitcase methodically, determined to take comfort from the ritual of rolling her socks together.

Back in the comfort of her rooms in the main lodge after the disastrous reception, she planned to spend her money very unwisely by driving to the airport and paying for the first available flight out. It was better than asking any favors of her grandparents, even though she'd have a private flight that way, a comfort that tempted her when she felt wrecked inside.

But she wouldn't do that. She'd pack her things and fly business class like a sensible executive. She'd turned off her phone for the first time in months—not because she was avoiding anyone per se. But because for tonight she was done being a go-between. An ambassador. A fixer. She was tired of serving in that capacity for her grandparents and Eliot and the merger they wanted. And she was done playing that role for Devon, who'd imposed on their long friendship without her knowing.

As for Marcus…maybe she was avoiding him just a little.

Because she didn't want to risk another confrontation? Or because she didn't want to risk her heart? She wasn't sure of that, either. The easy answer would be to forget about Marcus, because he didn't want something serious. But she knew what she felt for Marcus was deeply serious. So if she walked away now, was she being as shallow as she'd accused him of being, refusing to take the bigger emotional chance in case he rejected her again?

Staring into the designer suitcase that had been a Christmas gift from her grandparents, she took no satisfaction from the neat rolls of socks. A wave of despair threatened to level her just as a soft knock sounded on the exterior door to her suite.

"Hello?" she called, checking the sleek marble clock over the fireplace as she strode through the living area.

It was too late for housekeeping.

"Lily, it's Marcus." His voice stopped her in her tracks.

Not because she didn't want to see him. But because she did. Desperately.

Biting her lip, she approached the door without opening it.

"Marcus?" Her palm flattened against the dark gray steel barrier. She tipped her head against the wall beside the doorjamb, somehow feeling closer to him.

If she let him in, what was to stop her from flinging herself in his arms? She'd used up all her confrontational words earlier. She didn't have enough left to argue if he'd come here with new questions or hurtful accusations.

"I came to apologize." The words slipped through the crack, winding themselves around her.

Or maybe it was just the sound of his deep, male voice, which she had missed.

She felt her resolve soften.

"I'm listening." Leaning more heavily against the butter-yellow seagrass wallpaper, Lily tried to quiet her hopeful heart beating loud enough to distract her.

"I think you deserve an apology in person." He paused, as if waiting for a reply. Then he added, "So you can see how sincere I am."

Taking a deep breath, she steeled herself for seeing him, knowing already that she wanted to be with him. But she couldn't settle for half measures. She deserved better.

Straightening, she touched the amethysts around her neck. She wasn't her mother, and she wouldn't turn her back on everyone else in her life for the sake of a man. But it was okay to want to be loved.

She unlocked the dead bolt and turned the handle, admitting him.

The remote man she'd spoken to at Weston Rivera's house had vanished. Marcus's tie hung loose around his neck; the top button on his shirt had popped free. His hair curled as if he'd run his hands through it multiple times. His dark gaze collided with hers.

"Thank you." He stepped into the room and closed the door behind them.

"Would you like a seat?" She moved into the sitting area, feeling jittery and anxious, wanting to hear him out but afraid whatever he had to say wouldn't meet the hopeful expectations springing to life inside her.

She needed to just listen.

He took a seat on the tan leather love seat, and his

gaze traveled to her open suitcase in the bedroom. She perched on the armless chair near the window, aware of the marble clock softly ticking over the fireplace.

"Lily, I came to apologize, not just for the way I acted at the party, but for suspecting you of spying for Devon all week long." He sat forward on the cushion, his elbows on his knees. "The issues I have with my brother have nothing to do with you, and it's a problem that I let infect my relationship with you and my relationship with the whole company."

"Oh." She hadn't expected the nature of the apology to be so professional. Was he only here to fix their work relationship? Her heart sank to her toes, and she tried her best not to show it. She nodded, tearing her gaze away from him so he wouldn't see her disappointment. "Your apology is accepted. And thank you."

He was quiet for a long moment while she waited for him to leave. She bit her lip before saying, "It really is getting late—"

"I'm in love with you."

Her gaze flew to his. "Ex-excuse me?"

"I know you might not be ready to hear that yet, but this part actually *is* really simple and clear." He reached across the space between them to touch her hand. To envelop it in his. "I'm in love with you, Lily, and I don't care how complicated that makes things, because being with you is the only thing that matters to me."

She stared down at the place where their hands touched, his darker skin against her pale fingers. Speechless, she wanted to tell him that wasn't sensible or reasonable. But the truth was, she understood him perfectly, because she felt exactly the same way.

So she did the thing she'd wanted to do every moment of the last three days. She flung herself onto him. He caught her neatly despite her lack of grace, one hand going around her waist. His head was temple to temple against hers while she threaded her arms around his neck.

Her heart overflowed with feelings. Joy. Wholeness. Connectedness. The certainty that this was how real love felt.

"Does that mean you forgive me?" he asked against her ear while she breathed in the scent of him that she'd missed so much.

"Not a chance." She closed her eyes, leaning her cheek into his, savoring the feel of him next to her. "It only means I'm in love with you, too."

She felt him smile, his cheek lifting, the bristle of his jaw scratching her gently.

"You love me, but you don't forgive me."

"You left for three days when I needed you," she reminded him. "What if you knocked on my door just now and I didn't answer for three days?"

She felt his smile fade, and he edged back to look in her eyes. There was no mistaking the depth of sincerity in his as he stroked her hair.

"Sometimes I miss the big picture, but I promise you I won't ever do that again." He sealed the promise with a kiss brushed over her lips.

A kiss that soothed all the hurts, big and small, inside her. A kiss that healed and tempted her at the same time.

"Now I feel like I can forgive you." She wanted to learn more about him. Understand him better. Discover everything that made him tick. She couldn't wait for all of those things with him. "What made you change your mind?"

She remembered his expression when she'd left the

party. Her words had jarred him, she knew. But she hadn't expected him to come to her this way. And she'd never, ever expected to hear him confide the feelings for her that she returned in full.

He lifted her the rest of the way onto the love seat, repositioning them so they reclined side by side. "I knew right away—when you called me out for how I spoke to you—that I was wrong. My only excuse is that I've never experienced anything like this with anyone before. I was out of my depth with you because I've had feelings for you for a long time."

Her hair slid into her face, and he swept it aside. Pleasurable tingles tripped over her skin, reminding her of all the happiness that lay ahead for them.

"I knew what I felt for you was real when my grandparents left and all I wanted was to share my feelings with you. To see you, be with you, ask you what you thought." She walked her fingers down his chest, the warmth of him stirring her senses.

"I wish I'd been there for you." He skimmed a finger under the jewels she wore, a caress that left her breathless.

"We both were navigating our way through the surprise of what we felt. We weren't expecting anything like this, but it's a gift." She knew that now—not everyone got to experience this toe-curling joy in love that could be sweet and passionate and aching, too.

Marcus had given her that, and she would always be grateful for it.

"I'll never take you for granted," he vowed with a seriousness that touched her deeply.

"I'll never take this for granted, either," she promised, her voice wobbling but her conviction rock solid. They were both hardworking, focused people. They would channel all of that formidable drive into a relationship so they could build the kind of future they both deserved.

One that would last for a lifetime.

Her fingers twined in the ends of his bow tie, drawing him closer so she could kiss him as much as she wanted, with all the love she had in her heart.

* * * * *

A CHRISTMAS RENDEZVOUS

KAREN BOOTH

For Val Skorup. You are the best cheerleader
a person could ever want, a great friend
and a total rock star.

One

Isabel Blackwell's head had hardly hit the pillow when the hotel alarm went off. The fire alarm.

Frustrated and annoyed, she sat up in bed and shoved back her sleep mask while the siren droned on out in the hall. This was getting old. The luxury Bacharach New York hotel had been her home for nearly two weeks and this was the fourth time the fire alarm had sounded. She'd intentionally gone to bed early to try to sleep away her difficult day. Her brother, Sam, had convinced her to take on a legal case she did not want—saving Eden's Department Store from a man with a vendetta and a decades-old promissory note. So much for the escape of a good night's rest.

"Attention, guests," the prerecorded message sounded over the hallway PA system. "Please proceed to the nearest fire exit in an orderly manner. Do not use the elevators. I repeat, do not use the elevators. Thank you."

"Do *not* use the elevators," Isabel mumbled to herself in a robotic voice. She tossed back the comforter, grabbed her robe, shoved her feet into a pair of ballet flats and dutifully shuffled down the hallway with the other guests. It was not quite 10:00 p.m., so she was the only one in her pajamas, but she refused to be embarrassed by it. Hers were pale pink silk charmeuse and she'd spent a fortune on them. Plus, if anyone should be feeling self-conscious, it was the hotel management. They needed to get their property under control.

She followed along down the stairs, through the lobby past the befuddled and apologetic bell captain, and out onto the street. Early December was not an ideal time to be parading around a Manhattan sidewalk in silk pj's, but she hoped that by now, the hotel staff had finely honed their skills of determining whether there was an actual fire.

The manager shot out of the revolving door, frantic. "Folks, I am so sorry. We're working as fast as we can to get you back inside and to your rooms." He fished a stack of cards from his suit pocket and began doling them out. "Please. Everyone. Enjoy a complimentary cocktail at the bar as our way of apologizing."

Isabel took his offering. She wasn't about to pass up a free drink.

"What if you already have one waiting for you?" a low rumble of a voice behind her muttered.

Isabel turned and her jaw went slack. Standing before her was a vision so handsome she found herself wondering if she had actually fallen asleep upstairs and was now in the middle of a splendidly hot dream. Tall and trim, the voice had a strong square jaw covered in neatly trimmed scruff, steely gray eyes and extremely enticing bedhead hair. It had even gone a very sexy salt-

and-pepper at the temples, pure kryptonite for Isabel. She had a real weakness for a distinguished man. "You had to leave a drink behind?" she had the presence of mind to ask. "That's a very sad story."

The voice crossed his arms and looked off through the hotel's glass doors, longingly. "The bartender had just poured the best Manhattan I've ever had. And it's wasting away in there." He then returned his sights to her, his vision drifting down to her feet, then lazily winding its way back up. As he took in every inch of her, it warmed her from head to toe. "Aren't you freezing?"

"No." She shook her head. "I run hot."

A corner of his mouth curled in amusement, and that was when she noticed exactly how scrumptious his lips were. He offered his hand. "Jeremy."

"Isabel." She wrapped her fingers around his, and found herself frozen in place. He wasn't moving, either. No, they were both holding on, heat and a steady current coursing between them. It had been too long since she'd shared even an instant of flirtation with a man, let alone a chemistry-laden minute or two. Her job was always getting in the way, a big reason she disliked it so much.

"You weren't kidding," he said. "How are you so warm?"

How are you so hot? "Lucky, I guess."

"Ladies and gentlemen," the hotel manager announced, poking his head out of the door. "Turns out it was a false alarm. You may go back inside."

"Looks like you can go rescue your Manhattan," Isabel said to Jeremy.

"Join me? I hate to drink alone." He cocked his head to one side and both eyebrows popped up in invitation.

Isabel had been fully prepared to go back upstairs

and simply take a few thoughts of dreamy Jeremy for a spin as she drifted off to sleep. "I'm in my pajamas."

"Don't forget the sleep mask." He reached up and plucked it from her hair. "Do these things really work?"

She smoothed back her hair, deciding this was only a good sign—he'd invited her to have a drink with him when she looked far less than her best. "They do work. Once you get used to it."

"I've never tried one. Maybe I should. I don't sleep that well."

Isabel fought back what she really wanted to say— that she wouldn't mind having the chance to make him slumber like a baby. Instead, she took the mask from his hand and tucked it into the pocket of her robe. "If you can stand to be seen with me, I'd love a drink."

"You could be wearing a potato sack and I'd still invite you for a drink." He stepped aside and with a flourish of his hand, invited her to lead the way.

Oh, Jeremy was smooth. For a moment she wondered if he was too much so. In her experience, men like that were only interested in fun. She'd moved to New York for a fresh start, so she could pursue a less unsavory line of legal work—adoption law, to be specific—and finally get serious about love. At thirty-eight, she was eager to get on with her life. Still, it was silly to judge yummy Jeremy by a few words in their first conversation. "Good to know your standards." Isabel marched inside and crossed the lobby, stopping at the bar entrance. Despite the generous disbursement of drink coupons from the manager, the room was sparsely occupied, with only a few people seated at the long mahogany bar. It was an elegant space, albeit a bit stuck in time, with black-and-white-checkerboard floors and crystal chandeliers dripping from the barrel ceiling.

"You'll have to let me know where you left your drink behind."

"Over here." Jeremy strolled ahead and Isabel took her chance to watch him from behind. The view was stunning—a sharp shoulder line atop a towering lean frame. His midnight-blue suit jacket obscured his backside, but she could imagine how spectacular it must be. He arrived at a corner table, and sure enough, there was his drink, along with a stack of papers, which he quickly shuffled into a briefcase.

"You really did leave in a hurry," she said. "Is this your first night staying here? I don't take the fire alarm all that seriously anymore. Most of the time it's nothing."

"I'm not a guest. I just had a meeting. I actually live in Brooklyn, but I thought I'd grab a drink before I headed home." He slid her a sly look. "Now I'm glad I did."

Isabel knew she should ask what he did for a living, but that would only lead to discussion of her own occupation. The last thing she wanted to do was talk about being a lawyer, a career she'd once dreamed of but that had since turned into a bit of a nightmare, another reason for moving away from Washington, DC. She'd somehow gone from earnest attorney to a political "fixer," cleaning up the personal messes of the powerful. She was good at it. Very good, actually. But she'd grown weary of that particular rat race. And in Washington, everyone was a rodent of one form or another.

"What would you like to drink?" Jeremy asked, pulling out a chair for her.

Isabel eased into the seat, which was sumptuously upholstered in white velvet with black trim. "I'll have a gin and tonic, two limes." She reached into her robe and pulled out the drink coupon, holding it out for Jeremy.

"Save that for a rainy day. It was my invitation. I intend to buy you a drink."

Isabel had to smile. It'd been a long time since a man had treated her nicely and actually made an effort. She'd been starting to wonder if gentlemanly behavior was a lost art. "Thank you."

Jeremy flagged down the bartender and was back with her drink in a few minutes. He sat next to her, his warm scent settling over her. It was both woodsy and citrusy, conjuring visions of a romantic fire crackling away. "So, tell me about yourself. What do you do?"

She had to make a choice right then and there as to how this night was going to go. Either they would do the same old getting-to-know-you routine that every man and woman who have just met must seemingly pursue, or they would head in a different direction. Coming to New York was supposed to be a fresh start for Isabel and she intended to follow through on that. She would not cling to old habits. She would try something new.

She reached out and set her hand on Jeremy's, which was resting on the tabletop. "I vote that we don't talk about work. At all. I don't think we should talk about where we went to school or who we used to date or how many important people we know."

Jeremy's eyes darkened, but there was a spark behind them—a mischievous glint. He was, at the very least, intrigued. "Okay, then. What do you want to talk about?"

She stirred her drink, not letting go of his hand. She loved that they already had this unspoken familiarity. Like they understood each other, and so soon after meeting each other. "I don't know. A little brutal honesty between strangers?"

He laughed and turned his hand until their palms were flat against each other. He clasped his fingers around hers. How that one touch could convey so much, she wasn't sure, but excitement bubbled up inside her so fast she thought she might pop like a cork from a champagne bottle. It was as if she'd been in a deep sleep and her entire body had rattled back to life. She wasn't the sort of woman who pinned a lot of hope on a man, but she found herself wondering where this might go.

"Like truth or dare, but just the truth part?" he asked.

Isabel swallowed hard, but did her best to convey cool. "Oh, no. I never said I wasn't up for a dare."

Jeremy was so tempted to dare Isabel to kiss him, he had to issue himself a mental warning: *Slow down, buddy.* He was essentially fearless, but he wasn't the guy to make leaps with a woman. Not anymore. He greatly enjoyed their company, but he'd been burned badly by a toxic marriage and the hellish divorce that followed. Since then, he'd learned to employ caution, but he did occasionally need to remind himself.

Still, he didn't want to waste his evening ruminating on his past mistakes. Not now. Not when he was sitting with Isabel, a woman who made him want to employ zero restraint. She was not only a captivating beauty, with sleek black hair framing a flawless complexion and warm brown eyes; she had a demeanor unlike any he'd ever encountered, from anyone—man or woman. What person goes to a bar in pale pink silk pajamas and matching robe and seems wholly comfortable? And the bit about not trying to impress each other? That was like a breath of fresh air. If he had to start talking about his job, he'd just get stressed. Especially after the meeting he'd had in this very bar an hour ago.

"I'm afraid I haven't played truth or dare since I was a teenager," he admitted.

"Me, neither. And almost all of the dares seemed to involve kissing."

It was as if she'd read his mind.

"But we aren't teenagers anymore, are we?" she added.

"Not me. I turned forty this year." Jeremy cleared his throat, struggling to keep up with her. He was usually laser-focused on a retort. As a lawyer, he got plenty of practice. "Okay, then. Tell me something almost nobody knows about you."

She smiled cleverly, stirring her drink. "That could take all night. I have lots of secrets." She bent her neck to one side and absentmindedly traced her delicate fingers along her collarbone.

The first secret Jeremy wanted to know was what was under those pajamas. He wanted to know *who* was under there—what Isabel would kiss like. What her touch would be like, what it would be like to have her naked form pressed against his. "How about three things I need to know about you? As a person. Three things you believe in."

She twisted up her beautiful lips, seeming deep in thought. "Okay. I believe that there is no good reason to lie, but that doesn't mean you have to confess everything. I believe that a good nap will cure most problems. And I believe that love is ultimately the only thing that ever saves anyone."

"Really?" Jeremy found that last part a bit too sunny and optimistic, but then again, he had his reasons for rolling his eyes at love.

"Like I said, a little brutal honesty between strangers. I have no reason to be anything less than ridiculously open and bare my soul."

"You're a therapist, aren't you? One of those people you pay hundreds of dollars an hour to, just so you can reveal the most humiliating things you've ever done."

She shook her head. "Hey. That's against the rules. We said we weren't going to talk about work."

"So I'm right. You *are* a therapist."

"No, you aren't right." She flashed her wide, warm eyes at him. "You aren't wrong, either."

Jeremy had to laugh while he marveled at the puzzle of Isabel. He wanted to peel back her layers, one by one... He suspected there were a lot of surprises to be found. "I suppose you want me to tell you my three truths now, huh?"

"It's only fair."

He had to think for a moment, knowing he had to match the clever balance she'd struck between revealing all and piquing his interest. He would not allow himself to be completely outdone by Isabel. "I believe that taking yourself too seriously is a trap. I believe that apologizing for making a lot of money is stupid. And I believe that there's nothing wrong with having fun."

She nodded, seemingly digesting his words. "Those are all very interesting."

"You're definitely a therapist."

"And you are definitely not good at following rules."

He shrugged. "Most rules are arbitrary."

"Like what?"

"Like the one that says you shouldn't invite a woman wearing her pajamas on a New York City sidewalk out for a drink."

She pointed her finger at him. "Yes. You're so right. That is a stupid rule."

He downed the last of his drink, sensing this was the moment when he had to decide whether he wanted to angle for an invitation upstairs. Fear was a big factor. He didn't want to endure a rejection from Isabel. Something told him she could deliver one in a particularly devastating way. "And yet I went there, didn't I? I took the chance."

"Yes, you did, didn't you? Which makes me wonder what you're after, Jeremy. A drink? Conversation? Or something more?" Isabel sat forward and drew her finger around the rim of her glass, looking at him, unafraid to confront him with her gaze.

He had to break the spell she had him under, but when he let his sights wander, it only got worse. The front of her robe had gaped open, revealing the gentle curve of the top of one breast. Jeremy felt the heat rising in his body, starting in his belly and radiating outward, up to his chest and down to his thighs. It would be so easy to blame it on the drink, but that heat was all created by Isabel. She pulled it out of thin air with her pouty lips, with her dark and sultry eyes, and with her sharp conversational skills. He was not the type to ask for more. Asking for anything only made things messy. It put you at a disadvantage, and he hated not feeling as though he had every weapon imaginable at his disposal. What was it about Isabel that made him want to lie down and give her everything?

"I want whatever you might be willing to give me," he admitted.

She smiled and the faintest blush crossed her cheeks. Good God, she was so beautiful he had to wonder if all of this was really happening. "So I'm in the driver's seat. That's what you're telling me."

"Of course. As it should be, right?"

She nodded, arching her eyebrows in a way that suggested she hadn't quite been prepared for the way their conversation had turned. He loved feeling like he could surprise her, even if the boost to his ego might be completely unwarranted. "So, Jeremy. Since I'm in charge, let me just share one more thing about myself. I don't know how you feel about good views, but I have a spectacular one of the city. Upstairs in my room."

Jeremy felt as though Isabel had just rolled Christmas, his birthday and Super Bowl Sunday into one day. "Funny you should ask, because I am a huge fan of views." He leaned closer and lowered his head, his heart thundering away in his chest like a summer storm.

Isabel drifted closer to him until their noses were almost touching. The rest of the room had faded away. Other people and their surroundings were a distant thought. It was just the two of them, their breaths in sync and their intentions apparently aligned, as well. "Truth or dare," she whispered.

"Dare," he answered without hesitation.

"Good answer." Her lips met his in the slightest of kisses. Her mouth only teased him, softer and more supple than he'd dared to imagine. She angled her head and took the kiss deeper, grasping his shoulder and digging her nails into his jacket. Her lips parted and her tongue skated along his lower lip, making every testosterone-driven part of him switch into high gear. The blood was pumping so fast it was hard to know which way was up.

He reached for her hip, the silk of her robe impossibly cool and soft against his skin. He pulled her closer, clawing at the tie at her waist, needing her. Wanting her.

Like he needed to breathe or eat or drink water. This whole business of not knowing much about each other was so hot. It left him wondering what the night had in store, when he hadn't been willing to gamble on the unknown in a long time.

"You never gave me my dare," he said, coming up for air.

"I dare you to come upstairs and take off your suit, Jeremy. I dare you to rock my world."

Two

It took every ounce of self-control Jeremy had to discreetly walk across that hotel lobby with Isabel. His gut was telling him to take her hand and run as fast as he could, jab the elevator button and get things going between them the instant they were inside. As long as they were alone.

Unfortunately, the elevator was not cooperating. "This thing is so slow," Isabel said, jamming the button a second time. She subtly leaned against him and rubbed the side of his thigh with her hand.

Everything in his body went so tight it felt as though he was strapped to a piece of wood. Blood drained from his hands and feet and rushed straight to the center of his body. He swallowed back a groan and strategically held his briefcase to obscure anyone's view of his crotch. His erection felt like it had its own pulse. He needed Isabel, now.

Finally the elevator dinged and they rushed on board as soon as the other passengers were off. He'd hoped they'd be able to ride alone, but at the last minute, someone shoved their hand between the doors.

It was an older gray-haired woman. "I'm sorry. Thought I'd catch it while I could. Otherwise you end up waiting forever."

"So true," Isabel said. She leaned against the back wall, standing right next to Jeremy. She looked over at him as her hand again caressed his thigh. She bit her lower lip and he thought he might faint. She was too hot for words.

Mercifully, the woman got off the elevator at the fifth floor, but being alone with Isabel only opened the floodgates. He dropped his briefcase as they smashed into each other, kissing hard, tongues and wet lips, insistent hands everywhere. He yanked at the tie on her robe, then fumbled with the buttons on her pajama top. Hers were inside his suit jacket, tugging his shirt out from the waist of his pants. By the time the elevator dinged on the eighteenth floor, they were both in a disheveled state of near-undress.

Isabel picked up his briefcase, handed it to him and dashed down the hall, with Jeremy in close pursuit. She pulled her key card from her robe pocket and Jeremy stole a look down the front of her pajama top, which was already half-unbuttoned. Her breasts were full, her skin creamy and he couldn't wait to have his hands all over them.

Isabel flung open the door and Jeremy again dropped his briefcase, relieved he didn't need to keep track of it anymore. Isabel took off her robe and undid the last two buttons on her pajama top, tossing it to the floor. He cupped her breasts in both hands, her skin even softer and more velvety smooth than he'd imagined. Her nipples tightened beneath his touch. He loved seeing and feeling how responsive she was to him. Her pajama pants hung loosely below her belly button, clinging to her curvy hips. He wanted to see every inch of her and with a single tug of the drawstring at her waist, they slumped to the floor. She had no panties on underneath and that view of everything to come made everything beneath his waist grow even tighter, even hotter.

"You have on way too many clothes," she said as she flew through the buttons on his shirt and he got rid of his jacket. She then seemed to notice exactly how fierce his erection was. "Very nice." She flattened her hand against the front of his pants and pressed hard, rubbing up and down firmly.

He wavered between full sight and blindness. It felt so impossibly good. He only wanted more. This time, Jeremy didn't have to disguise his reaction, and he let out a groan at full roar. Isabel responded by unzipping his pants while he toed off his shoes. A few seconds later, she had the rest of his clothes in a puddle on the floor. She wrapped her hand around his length and took careful strokes while he kissed her. It had been so long since he'd wanted a woman like he wanted her. Something about her left him letting down his guard.

"Do you have a condom?" he asked, realizing that he did not. This was not good planning on his part, but he did not make a regular habit of meeting women after work and going up to their hotel rooms.

"I do. In the bathroom. One minute." Isabel traipsed off and he watched her full bottom and long legs in graceful motion. He couldn't wait to be inside her.

She returned seconds later with a box, which she set on the bedside table after taking out a packet. She tore open the foil and closed in on him, a bit like a tiger stalks its prey. Jeremy liked feeling so wanted. It felt good to know that he still had the power to do this to a woman.

Isabel took the condom and gently placed it on the tip of his erection, then rolled it down his length, all while their gazes connected. She owned every touch, every action of her beautiful body, and Jeremy wanted to drown in her self-confidence. He wanted to live in the world she did—where there seemed to be zero reason to question oneself.

Across the room sat that big beautiful bed, with a crisp white comforter and countless pillows. But Jeremy wanted to make love to Isabel in every corner of this room, and the chair that was right next to him seemed like the perfect place to start. He took her hand and he sat down, easing his hips to the edge of the seat. Isabel didn't miss a beat, straddling his legs and placing her knees on the chair next to his hips. Jeremy reached between them and positioned himself, then Isabel lowered her body onto his. He kept both his hands on her hips while his sights were set solely on her stunning face. Her mouth went slack and she closed her eyes as she let him slide inside. She was a perfect fit. And Jeremy was nothing if not thankful to whatever forces in the universe had brought him to this moment.

Isabel dictated the pace, which was perfect for him. He wanted to know what she liked. Despite the fact that he had so much pent-up need inside him, this was all about her. He would not leave until she was fully satisfied. He eased one hand to her lower back and urged her to lean into him so he could kiss her. Fully and deeply. Meanwhile, Isabel rode his length up and down and

Jeremy struggled to keep up, to keep from reaching his destination too soon. He did not want to disappoint her.

Their kisses were soft and wet, tongues sensuously twisting together. Jeremy caressed her breast with one hand while the other cupped her backside, his fingers curled into the soft and tender flesh. Isabel raked her hands through his hair over and over again, telling him with soft moans and subtle gasps that she was happy. He felt her tightening around him, and that matched her breaths, which had become ragged and torn.

"I'm close," she muttered into his ear, then kissed his neck.

He'd passed close several minutes ago and had since been skirting the edge, trying to ward off his climax. "Come for me."

Isabel planted her forehead against his and went for it, riding his length faster, sinking as far down as she could with every pass. Jeremy was fairly sure he had no blood flow to the rest of his body as he steeled himself. As soon as she let go and called out, he did the same, following behind her. Her muscles gathered around him tightly, over and over again, and the relief that washed over him was immense.

All he could think as the orgasm faded and Isabel collapsed against his chest was that he had to have her one more time. And quite possibly one more time after that.

"I need you again, Isabel." Jeremy smoothed his hand over her naked back and kissed her shoulder, bringing everything in her post-bliss body back to a quick simmer.

"Already?" she asked, slowly easing herself off his lap. She stepped over to the bed, where a mere hour or so ago she'd been attempting to sleep, and pulled back the comforter. She certainly hadn't thought at that time that she'd end up with a man in her room later.

"I'm going to need a minute or two, but I swear that's all." Jeremy padded off to the bathroom.

Isabel climbed into bed and immediately rested her head back on the pillow, staring up at the ceiling. *Wow.* She was glad Jeremy wanted more. That first time had been so hurried. She wanted the opportunity to savor him.

Moments later, he joined her, climbing in next to her and pressing his long body against hers. "You're incredible. Once was not enough."

She could already feel his erection against her leg. She was nothing if not impressed. Jeremy with the salt-and-pepper hair had a very quick recovery time. Of course she was on board. Considering that they hardly knew each other, he had an uncanny ability to hit all of her most sensitive spots. She really appreciated a man who picked up on her cues and followed suit.

"We need another condom," she said, kissing him deeply.

He rolled over and sat on the edge of the bed, took one from the box on the nightstand. Isabel turned to her side and swished her hand across the silky sheets, feeling his body heat still there. She admired his muscled back in the soft light from the window. He was in unbelievable shape and she was happy to reap the rewards.

When he turned back to her, he smiled. "You are so beautiful. I'm still trying to figure out how I managed to talk you into taking me upstairs."

She swatted his arm, then pulled him closer as he reclined next to her. "You're no slouch. Believe me."

He kissed her sweetly, then his approach turned more

seductive, as he opened his mouth and their tongues found each other, swirling and swooping. He was an amazing kisser, there was no doubt about that. Isabel could have kissed him forever; they were in perfect sync. He rolled her to her back and hovered above her, holding his body weight with his firm arms. Isabel ran her hands from his wrists to his shoulders, her eyes closing and opening as he lowered his mouth to her neck, then her breast, taking her nipple between his lips. He was unhurried now, a stark contrast to the frenzied first time.

He positioned himself at her entrance and drove inside slowly, pushing her patience, letting her feel every inch as he filled her perfectly. Isabel rolled her head from side to side, feeling the cool pillow on her cheeks as Jeremy made the rest of her body red hot. She raised her knees to let him in deeper, and he was taking mind-bending strokes just like he had the first time. This was the advantage of a man later in life. He knew what he was doing.

He slipped his hand between their bodies and pressed his thumb against her apex, rolling in firm circles as he kept his even pace. She was surprised how quickly the tension wrapped itself around her, the way he drove her toward the edge of the cliff so perfectly. Right there. The climax was toying with her now, ebbing closer, then pulling away. Each pass brought it nearer and she could feel ahead of time just how intense it was going to be. She heard her own hums and moans, but her consciousness was so deep inside her own body that it came out muffled and fuzzy. Meanwhile, she became fitful and greedy, needing him closer. Needing more. She dug her heels into his backside, pulling him into her, and that was when the orgasm slammed into her, even harder and more intense than last time. This was an order of magnitude she hadn't been prepared for—sheer gratification awash in beautiful colors and hazy, unworried thoughts.

As she became more aware of the here and now, Isabel could tell that Jeremy was also near his peak. His breaths were labored, but light, just like they had been the first time. Puffs of air that seemed to go in one direction. Just in. And further in. In one sudden movement, he jerked, then his torso froze in place, his hips flush against her bottom. She wrapped her legs around him tightly and raked her fingers up and down his strong back, feeling every defined muscle. As her own pleasure continued to swirl around her, she blazed a trail of hot kisses against his neck, wanting to show her appreciation. Jeremy was magnificent. Absolutely perfect.

"Oh, no," he groaned. "The condom. It broke."

Just like that, the spell was broken. "Did you?" she asked. Had she really just been thinking that this was perfect? She should have known better. That did not exist. Not for her, at least.

"Did I come? Yes." He rolled off of her and jumped up from the bed, rushing off to the bathroom.

Isabel closed her eyes and pinched her nose. *Great.* So much for her fun with handsome Jeremy. So much for the idea of a third time. Or a fourth. This was about to come to a quick end, she guessed, at least judging by how quickly he had retreated to the bathroom.

He returned a few seconds later with a towel wrapped around his waist. He paced, running his hands through his hair. "I don't know what to say, other than I'm sorry."

Her instinct was to make him feel better, even when she was feeling worse by the second. "Not your fault. It happens."

Awkward silence followed, and she knew that Jeremy was planning his escape. He had his lips pressed tightly together like he couldn't figure out what to do next. Part of her was tempted to point to the door and save them both the embarrassment. Part of her wanted to put on her sleep mask and convince herself this part wasn't happening. They'd had such an amazing night together. It didn't seem fair that it should end like this. But that was life. Nothing to do about it but move on.

He sat on the edge of the bed, but it was about as far away from her as possible. The divide between them now felt like it was a mile wide. In some ways, she felt like she knew him even less now than she had when they'd first met downstairs. "I don't even know your last name. What if I just got you pregnant?"

Isabel knew that uncertain edge in his voice. She'd heard it before. One time in particular had been so painful she thought she might never recover. That had been over an actual pregnancy, not merely a fear of obligation. Her initial impression of Jeremy had been correct. He came off as smooth for a reason—he was all about the pursuit, not about sticking around. And that was fine. No harm, no foul. They hardly knew each other. It was understandable that he might feel trapped. It was now her job to let him off the hook, if only to allow herself to get on her with her life.

"If it makes you feel any better, my name is Isabel Blackwell."

He glanced over at her. "Oh. Okay. My last name is Sharp."

Isabel grabbed the sheet and pulled it up over herself. Exchanging last names had done nothing to make this situation more comfortable. If anything, it made it so much more obvious that she wasn't built for one-night stands.

Isabel scooted up in bed until her back was against the headboard. "Look. Don't worry about it. It's okay. I keep track of my cycle pretty closely. I don't think there's any chance we're in trouble." She'd undersold that part by quite a bit. She'd been methodically tracking her periods for the last several years. If she managed to meet Mr. Right, she wanted to be able to try for a baby as soon as possible. Isabel prepared for everything in life. It was the best way to avoid surprises and the perfect distraction when you felt like the things you wanted weren't happening fast enough.

"Okay. Well, I wasn't sure if you wanted me to stay…" His voice trailed off, leaving Isabel to make the final declaration.

"No, Jeremy. It's okay. I think it's probably best at this point if you head home. I have a big meeting tomorrow and I'm sure you have things you need to do tomorrow. We probably both need a good night's sleep."

He nodded. "Sure. Yes. Of course." He got up from the bed and began collecting his clothes from their various locales across the room. He let go of the towel so he could step into his boxers, giving Isabel one last parting glance at perfect Jeremy. *Damn.* If only this hadn't started so absurdly. If only it hadn't ended so uncomfortably. He might have been a guy she would have wanted around for a while.

Wrapped up in the sheet, she climbed out of bed and padded past him to the bathroom. She quietly closed the door behind her and sucked in several deep breaths. *You're okay.* Moving to New York was supposed to be her new beginning, especially with men and the notion of having a personal life. So she'd had a false start. Jeremy was ultimately a nice guy. He was handsome, sexy and kind. They'd had some rotten luck, but that happened every day. Isabel needed to get past the idea that her fresh start was ruined by one mishap.

She stepped to the sink, took a sip of water from the glass on the vanity and prepared herself to walk back out into the room. "Worse things have happened." When she opened the bathroom door, Jeremy was standing right outside, suit on but no tie. His briefcase was in his hand. For a moment, she wondered what he did for work. Probably a Wall Street guy. He seemed the type—cocky, good-looking, sure of himself. She wouldn't ask him now.

"Okay, then. You off?" she asked.

He nodded. "Yes. Thank you for tonight. It was really nice. I swear."

She had to laugh at what a sad and funny situation she'd gotten herself into. She stepped closer to him and stole one last kiss. "Jeremy. You were amazing. And I hope you have a lifetime of making money and finding fun wherever you go."

He smiled, but it wasn't a full-throttle grin, not the smile that had first sparked her curiosity or the chemistry between them. "I hope you find everything you're looking for, Isabel Blackwell."

With that, she opened the door and watched as he walked down the hall to the elevator. She hoped Jeremy was right. She didn't want to go too much longer waiting.

Three

Jeremy finally gave in at 4:37 a.m. His night's sleep was a lost cause. He climbed out from under his down comforter and sat on the edge of his bed, elbows on his knees, and ran a hand through his hair. A deep sigh escaped his lips, but he could have sworn he heard a word in it. A name. Isabel. *What the hell was that? What the hell happened?*

He'd never had a woman work her way into his psyche in such a short amount of time—mere hours. Sure, part of it was the fact that he was still stinging from the way he'd had to exit her room, and her life. When they'd been down at the bar flirting and she offered the invitation to come upstairs, his plan had been to leave her happy and exhausted, positively aglow from sex. Instead, he'd departed while she was bundled up in a sheet like a hastily wrapped gift, granting him a dispassionate kiss goodbye and leaving him with the crushing sense that they would always have unfinished business.

Another sigh came. He was going to have to stop letting this get to him.

With a long day of client meetings ahead, he decided to get in a workout. He sometimes managed to sneak away at lunch and go to the Sharp and Sharp gym, but that likely wouldn't happen today. He flipped on the light in his master bedroom, grabbed a pair of shorts, a T-shirt and running shoes, then made his way up one set of stairs to the fourth floor of this renovated brownstone. He had a small theater and gym up there, additions he made after his ex-wife moved out. Kelsey never saw the point in watching movies and didn't want the "smell" of a workout space. But now that he was all on his own, Jeremy could do as he liked.

It wasn't much of a consolation.

Forty-five minutes on the treadmill and a half hour of free weights was enough to work up a sufficient sweat and shake off some of the lingering thoughts of Isabel. He hustled down to the second floor and the gourmet kitchen, where he prepared entirely too many meals for one. Coffee was dripping into the carafe when he heard a familiar sound coming from the patio off the back of the house.

Meow.

It was December 9. It was entirely too cold for an animal to be outside. Jeremy padded over to the glass door, and as had happened many times before, a large orange tabby cat was winding his way back and forth in front of the window. The cat had been to the house many times, and Jeremy had even taken him in once before, over a year ago when it was unbearably hot. The cat's visit had lasted less than a day. He slipped out the front door when Jeremy came home from work that night. Jeremy wasn't a cat person at all—he didn't really see the point of a pet that didn't do anything other than lounge around all day. He'd called Animal Control to see if they could catch him, but they'd seemed unconcerned. He'd even had his assistant call the veterinarian in his neighborhood of Park Slope, but they couldn't do much until someone caught the cat and brought him in. Jeremy kept hoping someone else would take on the burden, but apparently not. At least not today.

Meow. The cat reared up on its hind legs and pressed a single paw to the glass, peering up at Jeremy with eyes that were entirely too plaintive.

Jeremy crouched down and looked into his little cat face. "Buddy. What are you doing out there? It's six in the morning and it's freezing."

Meow. The cat pawed at the glass.

Jeremy straightened. This was the last thing he had time for, but temperatures weren't expected to get above freezing today. He couldn't let the poor thing suffer. Resigned, he flipped the dead bolt, turned the knob and tugged on it. Bitter cold rushed in, but not as fast as the cat. Jeremy closed the door, realizing he now had a big task ahead of him—he had to feed the cat and figure out where to put him all day while he was at work.

He went to the pantry to look for a can of tuna, but that was a bust. Then he remembered that he had some lox in the refrigerator from the bagel shop down the street.

"I guess we're going to find out if you like smoked salmon." He placed a slice of the fish on a plate and broke it into smaller pieces with his fingers. Jeremy had a feeling this was going to be a big hit. The cat was now rubbing against his ankles.

Jeremy put the plate on the floor and the cat began to scarf down the food. Mission one, accomplished. He filled a cereal bowl with water for the cat, then went about making his own breakfast of eggs and a bagel. As he sat at the kitchen island, the cat wound its way around the legs of his barstool, purring loudly enough for Jeremy to hear. He had to get to the office, so he sent a text to his housekeeper, who would be arriving around eight. There's a cat in the house. Don't ask. Can you bring a litter box and show it to him?

Margaret replied quickly. You got a cat?

Jeremy laughed. Not on purpose.

After getting cleaned up and dressed, Jeremy left for the office, arriving promptly at seven thirty, just like every other day. Not only was the weather unbearably cold, it was gray and dreary, somewhat typical for early December, although Jeremy couldn't help but feel like it was somehow sunnier outside than it was inside the Sharp and Sharp offices.

The other partners typically arrived at eight, but Jeremy had learned long ago that his boss, who was also his dad, demanded that his own son deliver more than everyone else. Jeremy had worked twice as hard to make partner. He brought in nearly twice as much billing. He worked like a dog for two reasons. First, he hoped that he would eventually make his father happy enough to loosen his iron grip on the firm and afford Jeremy some autonomy. The second reason fed into the first. When Jeremy had been in the middle of his divorce, he bungled a big case. The Patterson case, a multimillion-dollar wrongful termination suit. It should have been a slam dunk and instead, Jeremy dropped the ball, mostly because his personal life was falling apart. His dad might never forgive him for that grave error, but Jeremy had to keep trying. He had to live the life of a workaholic for the foreseeable future.

In recent months, his father had been pressuring him to bring on a very specific sort of big-fish client, someone with a case that could attract media attention, even of the tabloid variety. In the internet age, one juicy headline brought a lot of free exposure. And although his dad was a traditional and upstanding guy, he loved the spotlight. He basked in it. He loved knowing the firm's coffers were piled to the ceiling with cash.

"Morning, son," his dad said, poking his head into Jeremy's office. He truly was the spitting image of Jeremy, only twenty-three years older. A bit more gray. A few more deep creases. The uncanny similarities in their appearance made the problems in their relationship that much more difficult—on the outside they were nearly identical. On the inside, they couldn't have been more different. "Are we a go with the Summers case?"

"We are. I'm just waiting for the signed agreement to come in this morning and then we'll be in contact with the legal department at Eden's."

His dad glanced at the chair opposite Jeremy's desk. "May I?"

"Of course." Jeremy took a deep breath and prepared himself for what might come—there was no telling with his dad. Some days, he was calm and reasonable. Other times, he hit the roof over the smallest detail. It had been like that since Jeremy was a kid, and he still wasn't used to it.

"What do you think is the real reason Mr. Summers fired Mulvaney and Moore?"

"Honestly? I met with Mr. Summers last night and he's a little off his rocker. He's dead set on getting revenge against the Eden family. This is about far more than money. I'm sure that scared off the senior partners at M and M. They're an incredibly conservative firm." Jeremy leaned back in his chair. "Why? Are you worried about it? There's still time to call it off if you want."

His dad shook his head, pulling at his chin with his fingers. "No. No. I think it's a good thing. Summers is desperate and he's willing to pay for it. I don't have a problem with getting our hands dirty. Your grandfather always avoided it."

Jeremy's grandfather had been the first Sharp in Sharp and Sharp. In fact, Jeremy's dad had declined to add an extra Sharp to the firm's name when Jeremy made partner. He'd simply waited for his own father to pass away. Jeremy missed his grandfather. He was the real reason he'd become an attorney, and things had been much different around the office when he was still alive. His grandfather had a love for the law and the myriad ways it could be interpreted. He loved the arguments and the strategy. His dad had a love of money and winning. He refused to lose, something that had been hammered into Jeremy's head countless times.

"I think it'll be just fine. I have it all under control." Jeremy knew nothing of the sort, but he had to lie. The truth was that the meeting with Benjamin Summers at the Bacharach had been chaotic. Thus the reason for the Manhattan. Thus the reason for perhaps not exercising the best judgment with Isabel.

"Don't let this one get away from you. If he's fired one firm, he'll fire another, and I don't think I need to tell you that it would be a real shame for our bottom line if we lost this billing. It'll be a scramble for you if you have to make up for it."

It was just like his dad to make not-so-thinly-veiled threats. "He's not going to fire us."

"At least you're only going up against the Eden's corporate lawyers. Those guys are so far out of their depth with a case like this. It should be a walk in the park if you do it right."

There went another insult wrapped up as praise. Jeremy wasn't about to point it out. It never did any good. "I'm not worried about it. I've got it all under control."

"Good." His dad rose from his seat and knocked his knuckle against Jeremy's desk, then made his departure. "Have a good day."

"You, too." Jeremy grumbled under his breath and got back to work, writing up the details for his assistant so she could set up the meeting with the Eden's legal team, which he hoped could happen tomorrow. It was the only thing he could do—try to move ahead. Try to make Dad happy. And after that, he'd need to dig into the mountain of work on his desk. Anything to take his mind off Isabel Blackwell and their amazing night that went horribly wrong.

Isabel arrived at Eden's Department Store shortly before 10:00 a.m. the morning after her rendezvous with Jeremy. Her lawyerly instincts normally had her keyed up and wide-awake before a client meeting, but she was so tired she could hardly drag herself out of the taxi.

She hadn't managed more than a few minutes of sleep. After his departure, Jeremy's warm smell lingered on the sheets, meaning the memory of his touch followed her with every toss and turn. If the condom hadn't broken, their night might have gone on to be nothing less than perfect. He might have asked to see her again, an invitation she would have eagerly accepted. She might have started her new life in New

York on a positive note. But the moment they had their mishap and Isabel witnessed firsthand how anxious he was to get out of her room and away from her, she knew he wasn't the right guy. It didn't matter that he was charming, sexy and one of the most handsome men she'd ever had the good fortune to meet. She needed more. She needed a man who would stick around, not run for the exits the instant things got serious.

Per her brother Sam's directions, Isabel took the elevator up to the top floor where the Eden's executive offices were. Sam was sitting in reception when she got there.

"Hey, handsome," she said as Sam got up out of his seat.

He was dressed in all black—suit, shirt and tie, just as most days. He placed a kiss on her forehead. "I'm so glad you're here."

Isabel wasn't quite so happy about it, but she was hopelessly devoted to her brother and that meant she was going to take one last dubious legal assignment before turning her sights to less messy work. "I'm still not sure I'm the right person for this job."

"Are you kidding me? You're the exact right person for this job. You're an expert at making problems like this go away."

The subtext of Sam's words made Isabel's stomach sour. This wasn't the sort of case that got wrapped up by legal wrangling and negotiation. Whenever you had very wealthy, powerful people fighting over something valuable, it inevitably turned into a race to the bottom. Who could dig up the most dirt? Who could make the other side cry for mercy first? "Sam, you know I don't want to tackle this like a fix. I just don't want to work like that anymore."

Sam put his arm around Isabel and snugged her close. "You worry too much. It's just a wealthy guy trying to get his hands on the store. You can handle this in your sleep."

First, I'd have to get some sleep. "But your girlfriend's family legacy is on the line. We can't afford to be cavalier about it."

"You mean fiancée." Mindy Eden appeared on the far side of the reception area and approached them, a big smile on her face.

Isabel knew full well that Sam and Mindy had gotten engaged. She'd merely slipped. Perhaps it was her subconscious reminding her how bothered she was that her younger brother had found the sort of happiness she desperately wanted for herself. "I'm sorry. Fiancée."

Mindy gave Isabel a hug, then wagged her fingers, showing off the square-cut diamond-and-platinum engagement ring Sam had given her. The thing was so big it looked like Mindy was walking around with an ice cube on her hand. "I honestly never thought this would happen."

Isabel didn't believe that for a minute. Mindy was lovely, but she seemed like the sort of woman who was accustomed to nothing less than getting exactly what she wanted out of life. "Why's that? You had to know my brother was over the moon for you."

Mindy elbowed Sam in the ribs. "I was oblivious to that for a while. I spent so much time focused on my career that I forgot to open my eyes."

Isabel took a shred of comfort in that. She and Mindy might have butted heads when they first met, but that was only because of Isabel's protectiveness of Sam. Mindy had hurt him and Isabel wasn't going to be the one to forgive her for it. Now that Sam and Mindy had reconciled, and the two women had gotten to know each other a little better, Isabel knew that she and Mindy had some things in common. They were both driven, determined and not willing to take crap from anyone. "I'll try to remember that when I jump back into the dating pool."

"Any prospects?" Mindy asked.

"I'm out of here if you're going to talk about guys," Sam said, turning away. "I don't do well with this subject when it comes to my sister."

Isabel grabbed his arm. "Oh, stop. We're not going to talk about that because there's nothing to say. I need to get an apartment. There are a million other things for me to accomplish before I can seriously think about dating. I have to find an office and get my new practice up and running."

"Don't put it off too long," Mindy said. She then cast her sights at Sam. "Are there any cute, eligible guys working for you right now? Maybe you can set her up."

Sam shook his head. "Something tells me she doesn't want that."

In truth, Isabel might not mind it. If Sam picked out a man for her, she'd not only know that he had been fully vetted, she'd have the knowledge that Sam approved. That was no small matter. "We'll see how I do. For now, let's sit down and talk about the case." Isabel was resigned to moving forward with this, and the sooner she started, the sooner she'd be done. So she'd delay her fresh start a few weeks. It wasn't the end of the world.

"Come on," Mindy said. "We're going to meet in Emma's office. It's the biggest. It used to belong to my gram."

Gram, or Victoria Eden, was the founder of Eden's Department Store, which at its height had more than fifty stores worldwide. Unfortunately, the chain was now down to a single location, the original Manhattan store. Mrs. Eden had passed away unexpectedly a little more than a year ago, and left the business to Mindy, her sister, Sophie, and their half sister, Emma. It was a bit of a tawdry story—all three women had the same father, and their two mothers were also sisters. Victoria Eden had brought the affair to light via her will, where she told everyone of her son's dalliance in an attempt to give Emma some justice.

Inside the office, Emma and Sophie were waiting. Isabel had met them both at a fund-raiser a month and a half ago, which was also when Sam and Mindy had finally figured out that they were desperately in love. Mindy made reintroductions and they all sat in the seating area—Isabel and Sophie on the couch, Sam in one chair with Mindy perched on the arm, and Emma opposite them.

"I guess we need to walk you through as much of this as we know," Mindy said. "I wish we had more information, but until a few weeks ago, we had no idea who Benjamin Summers was."

"He claims that our grandmother had an affair with his father, which is utterly preposterous," Sophie said. "Gram was devoted to our grandfather for as long as he was alive."

"Please, Soph. Can you not do this right now? Let me finish," Mindy said, returning her sights to Isabel. "This would have been nearly forty years ago if it really happened. Early days for the store, but our grandmother was doing well and by all accounts, very eager to expand. That's when Mr. Summers, the father, comes into play. Supposedly he lent our grandmother a quarter of a million dollars so she could open additional locations."

"That was a lot of money at that time," Isabel said. "And this is a handwritten promissory note?"

"Yes," Mindy said. "We've been going back through the store's old financials and bank records, but we can't find any record of an influx of money. There are large chunks of cash flowing into the store at that time, but it could have just been sales. Unfortunately, the accounting from that time is nowhere near as exact as it is now. Most of it is on paper."

Isabel's gears were starting to turn. As much as she'd said she didn't want to do this sort of work anymore—untangling the pasts of wealthy people—she had to admit that she had a real knack for it, and that made her feel as though she was ready to tackle it. "The first thing we're going to need to do is get the promissory note authenticated. There's a good chance it's not real."

"Do you think it could be a fake?" Emma asked.

"You'd be surprised the lengths people will go to in order to cash in."

"But Mr. Summers is so wealthy," Mindy said. "Why would he do that?"

Isabel sat back and crossed her legs. "It might not be the cash. It might be the store he's after."

"No. We can't let that happen," Sophie blurted.

Isabel didn't want to be the bearer of bad tidings. Losing the store was a real possibility. For now, Isabel needed to get up to speed on the materials in the case and see where the Eden sisters stood. "Let's not get ahead of ourselves. Give me some time to look over everything. I have several different financial detectives I've worked with in the past. They're going to need access to your records to see if we can figure out if the money ever flowed into the store at all."

"How long is all of that going to take?" Mindy asked.

"A few days to a few weeks. It just depends."

Mindy cleared her throat and Isabel sensed something bad was about to come to light. "Yeah. About that. We don't have that kind of time. Mr. Summers's lawyer sent a letter to the Eden's in-house counsel today. He's threatening a lawsuit right away if we don't come to the negotiating table tomorrow."

Isabel blinked several times while trying to absorb what Mindy had just said. "Mr. Summers not only wants us to start negotiating tomorrow, his lawyer isn't even aware the store is employing outside counsel?"

"We thought a sneak attack was the best approach. They're expecting someone else. Not Isabel Blackwell, Washington, DC, fixer."

Isabel cringed at the words. She didn't want to be that person anymore.

Sam sat forward and placed his hand on his sister's knee. "I have to agree. The store is too important to the Eden family for us to be anything less than completely strategic about this. They'll prepare for a corporate negotiation, not having any idea who they're dealing with."

Isabel took a deep breath, trying to ignore the way her already soured stomach grew even more uneasy. "Can I see the letter they sent?"

"Yes. Of course." Mindy hopped up from her seat and grabbed a thin folder from Emma's desk, handing it to Isabel.

Inside was a single page—the letter inviting Eden's Department Store's legal representation to the negotiating table. All looked in order until Isabel saw the name on the signature line. Then the blood drained from her face.

Jeremy Sharp. Oh my God.

Her big meeting tomorrow with the lawyer representing the man who wanted to take down Eden's Department Store? It would be the second run-in with her one-night stand. And apparently, they were about to go from the bedroom to the war room.

Four

"I don't want you to worry," Jeremy said as he escorted Benjamin Summers into one of the meeting rooms at Sharp and Sharp. "We have everything well in hand."

Mr. Summers turned to Jeremy and narrowed his eyes until they were only small slits. "Why aren't we meeting in the main conference room? The one with the big windows. The one you can see from the waiting room."

Jeremy pulled back a chair and offered Mr. Summers a seat. "Because this is more discreet." In truth, Jeremy preferred it because it meant his father couldn't interfere unless he walked right in on them. Jeremy had been in many client meetings where his dad paced back and forth outside that main conference room. It was unnerving as hell.

Mr. Summers sat in a huff. Jeremy hadn't spent a lot of time with him, but he'd always been like this—gruff and impatient. "I'm not worried about discretion. If anything, I'd prefer not to have it. I'd like the whole world to know that I'm going after Eden's. Victoria Eden destroyed my parents' marriage and this is the only way I can seek retribution on behalf of my mother."

Jeremy poured Mr. Summers a glass of water, hoping that might help to cool his temper. "I don't think it's a great idea to bring that up in this meeting. I know it's difficult to curb your personal feelings about the matter, but we need to focus on the bottom line, which is a very large unpaid debt."

Mr. Summers cleared his throat and tapped his fingers on the table. "Fine. I'll take your advice."

"Thank you. I appreciate that."

"For now."

One of the admins in the office poked his head into the conference room. "Mr. Sharp, the Eden's representatives and legal team have arrived. Shall I show them in?"

Jeremy turned to Mr. Summers, hoping he could get him to remain calm and collected. "Are you ready, Mr. Summers?"

"More than I've ever been."

Jeremy stood and straightened his jacket, then made his way to the door. The in-house counsel for Eden's was a crew of white-haired older men, much like his dad and Mr. Summers. He knew he could handle this easily as long as everyone could set aside their egos. But when he glanced down the hall, a stunning vision came into view—a woman who was not easy to handle. *Isabel.*

What the hell? For an instant, Jeremy shrank back from the door, his mind whirring with thoughts, even when there was no time to think. Before he knew what was happening, Isabel, along with another woman and a very tall man, were being led into the room by Jeremy's admin. "Mr. Sharp, this is Mindy Eden, COO of Eden's Department Store."

Mindy, willowy and poised with flame-red hair, offered her hand. "Mr. Sharp."

"Special adviser to Eden's, Sam Blackwell," his admin continued.

Sam, towering and dressed in black, shook Jeremy's hand. "Hello."

"And lastly, Isabel Blackwell, special counsel for Eden's."

Isabel stepped forward, but her beguiling scent arrived a split second before her. It filled his nose, and that sent memories storming into his mind—their white-hot tryst in her hotel room was not anything he would forget anytime soon. Unfortunately, he couldn't afford to think about what her luscious naked body looked like under her trim gray suit. He was too busy trying to tamp down his inner confusion. Had she known who he was when she seduced him? Had she seen him in the bar with Mr. Summers a mere fifteen minutes before the fire alarm sounded?

"It's nice to meet you." Isabel offered her hand. He'd noticed that night that her skin was unusually warm, but right now he felt as though he'd been burned.

Jeremy cleared his throat. "Nice to meet *you*, as well." He gestured to the other side of the long mahogany table, more rattled than when he'd worked his very first case. He couldn't help but feel as though they were being ambushed. He'd been led to believe that Eden's in-house counsel would be handling this. Unless Isabel was a new addition to their team, she was a ringer. "Please have a seat."

Isabel sat directly opposite Jeremy. The look on her face was difficult to decipher, but he reminded himself that he hardly knew her. What were her motives? What sort of person was she? Most important, what was her endgame? For a man with countless trust issues when it came to women, this was not only bringing all that to the surface in an uncomfortable way, it felt as though Isabel had opened an entirely new area of mistrust to explore. He deeply disliked the revelation.

Jeremy drew in a calming breath. *Focus.* He looked Isabel square in the eye. She met his gaze with steely composure. On the surface, she was quite simply stunning. Easily the sexiest woman he'd ever met. But he sensed now that beneath that flawless exterior was a woman who was at the very least, trouble. He didn't want to regret the other night, but perhaps he should. Would he feel as though he was at less of a disadvantage right now if it hadn't happened? "Ms. Blackwell, your client's grandmother borrowed 250 million dollars from Mr. Summers's father in 1982. She offered the Manhattan location of Eden's Department Store, the building, inventory and the land it sits on as collateral. By our calculations, with standard interest adjusted for inflation and compounded monthly, that unpaid loan now sits at a balance of just over 842 million."

"You have got to be kidding," Mindy Eden scoffed. "Why not just round it up to an even billion?"

Isabel placed her hand on Mindy's forearm, then smiled at Jeremy, the picture of cool composure. "And what exactly would Mr. Summers like for us to do about that?"

Jeremy had no choice but to continue. "As it's been nearly forty years, Mr. Summers expects the loan to be repaid in cash within thirty days or we'll begin proceedings to claim the property."

Isabel nodded, then licked her lips, making Jeremy

clutch the arm of his chair. "Any talk of property sei-
zure is premature, Mr. Sharp. Frankly, my client had
never even heard of Mr. Summers prior to the letter your
team sent to the Eden's offices, so I don't know how the
Eden family should be expected to simply hand over
the keys to a multibillion-dollar business and property
without exploring this matter as thoroughly as possible."

Jeremy knew he should be feeling as though he'd
been put on notice, but he only felt incredibly turned
on. Blood was coursing through his body so fast it was
making his head swim. Oh, Isabel was good.

"My first priority is to determine the authenticity
of the promissory note," Isabel continued, her cheeks
flushed with brilliant pink. "We can't be expected to
proceed without an expert analysis of the document.
I'm not convinced it's authentic or that it has Victoria
Eden's true signature on it."

This was not good news. And yet Jeremy noticed a
significant tightening in his pants.

"Are you calling me a liar?" Mr. Summers bellowed.

Jeremy turned to his client. "Please, Ben," he muttered. "I've got this."

"It's a handwritten note, Mr. Summers." Isabel's
voice was direct and cutting, while her chest was heav-
ing in a way that brought back entirely too many memories of the night at the Bacharach—having Isabel at
his mercy, in her bed. "Anyone could have produced it.
You could have fabricated it last week for all we know."

"It's real. I have no reason to lie," Benjamin said.

Isabel's eyebrows shot up. "From where I'm sitting,
you have 842 million reasons to lie. Do you have financial problems I should know about, Mr. Summers?
Is that what I'm going to find when I start looking into
your businesses?"

"Ms. Blackwell," Jeremy said as a warning, stopping himself from uttering what he really wanted to say—*Ms. Blackwell, you and I need to hash this out on our own. Alone. On this conference table.* But he had to get his act together. "Ms. Blackwell, I'll thank you not to speak to my client directly, especially when you're accusing him of things that have no basis in fact. Mr. Summers is not on trial here."

"If he's going to get ugly about the matter in front of my client, I'm afraid I have no other choice. This is not as cut-and-dried as you're trying to paint it."

Jeremy sensed this meeting was starting to go off the rails and he had to get it back on track. More than anything, he really needed to ask Isabel a few questions that were not appropriate in front of their respective clients. "Ms. Blackwell, would you mind asking your clients to wait out in the lobby? I'll ask Mr. Summers to adjourn to my office so that you and I can discuss the terms of determining the authenticity of the note."

Isabel lifted her chin and narrowed her sights on Jeremy, seeming suspicious. "I'll give you five minutes."

I'd rather have ten. "Certainly."

Isabel turned to Mindy and Sam, and they conferred with heads bowed. Jeremy took his chance to chat with Mr. Summers.

"I don't like being taken out of the negotiations," Mr. Summers said in response.

"I assure you, this will be nothing more than boring legalese. Plus, it'll give me a chance to find out more of what exactly their strategy is. This isn't the usual Eden's team."

"It isn't? I expect my lawyer to know details like that."

Jeremy looked over at Isabel as she got up from the

table and made way for Mindy and Sam to leave the conference room. "In my experience, these things rarely go the way you think they will."

Isabel accompanied Sam and Mindy out to the luxe Sharp and Sharp lobby. With dark wood, soft light and tufted navy leather settees, it spoke of old money and an organization steeped in tradition. Isabel could only imagine how her life would have been different if she'd come to New York instead of Washington, DC, and gotten her start at a firm like this, where business was done aboveboard. Sure, Mr. Summers had made a spectacle in the meeting, but it was nothing more than a man, accustomed to getting everything he wanted, kicking up dust because she and the Eden family were not going to go down without a fight. It wasn't a real roll in the mud, one where people make threats to destroy other people's lives.

"Is this normal?" Sam whispered at Isabel. His body language suggested pure agitation. His back was stiff as a board. "For the other lawyer to kick everybody out of the room?"

Isabel surveyed the lobby, which was unoccupied except for the receptionist, who was on the phone. If they were going to discuss this, they needed privacy. She placed her hand on Sam's arm. She wasn't entirely sure what Jeremy's motives were, but she was curious. Their short string of quipping back and forth had really gotten her running hot. And damn, the man could rock a suit unlike any other. "I think he was trying to get his client to cool down. Which I think is for the best. Plus, I didn't want him saying anything disparaging in front of Mindy."

"Why?" Mindy asked. "You know I can take it."

Isabel laughed quietly. "I know you can. It's more that we need to walk a fine line between being tough and not escalating anything. Summers and Sharp are going to be all about taking things up a notch. It's my job to walk everything back."

"But you were the one who threatened to look into his business," Mindy said.

"I know. He still needs to know we're serious. And I had to let him know that I won't hestiate to call his bluff." What Isabel really meant to say was that old habits died hard.

Sam turned to Mindy. "I thought that was a brilliant move, personally. We need to fight fire with fire. We need to dig up dirt on this Summers guy and it's not a bad idea to go after his lawyer, too. I don't like that guy. He's smug and arrogant, the exact kind of guy I'd love to take down a notch."

Mindy looked at Sam like he had a screw loose. "Do you seriously not know who that guy is? Jeremy Sharp? Ex-husband of Kelsey Kline? The socialite?"

"Shh, you two," Isabel snapped, eying the receptionist, who thankfully hadn't seemed to overhear their conversation. Still, Isabel's mind was reeling. Jeremy had been married? And to a socialite? Both details came as a big surprise, but Isabel had fought her urge to look into his personal life when she learned that he was handling the case for Mr. Summers. Only the old Isabel did that. Now she might have no choice but to do at least a minimum of digging. Otherwise, she'd die of curiosity. She glanced at her brother. How could she tell Sam that the man he found so unlikable was someone she'd fallen into bed with? Sam would never judge her for it, but he would be disappointed, and as far as Isabel was concerned, that was worse.

"Sorry." Sam shoved his hands into his pockets. "I'm stressed. I hate that Mindy has to go through this."

"It's okay," Isabel offered, loving that her brother was so focused on Mindy's well-being. "Look, let's focus on the merits of the case. We need to get an expert to analyze the promissory note and make sure it's legitimate. I've already hired the financial forensic experts. They're going through the old Eden's books to see if there's any evidence the money flowed through the store." She turned to Mindy. "And I was thinking, if this relationship between Mr. Summers's dad and your grandmother was this significant, don't you think there'd likely be some evidence of it somewhere in her personal effects? Maybe old papers? Letters of some sort?"

"I got Gram's apartment after she passed away, but I never moved in. I had planned to, but it's only been a year and, well…" Mindy looked at Sam with utter adoration. "Your brother came along and everything changed."

"Our offer was accepted on the house out in New Jersey," Sam said to Isabel.

"It's way too much room for two people," Mindy added with a smile that said it didn't bother her at all.

Sam shrugged it off, but his grin was also a mile wide. "I want us to start having kids as soon as possible. I've put my life on hold for too long. And I've always wanted a family."

Isabel understood exactly what Sam was saying. She wanted those things for herself. In many ways, she felt like she and Sam would never truly heal from the trauma of losing their parents until they were each able to start a family.

"I'd still like to get married first," Mindy offered.

If these two were going to continue to ruminate about

their shared future, Isabel would never get any work done today. "Mindy, if you and I could get together and go through your grandmother's apartment, that would be great. In the meantime, I need to go back in there and hash things out with Mr. Sharp."

"Unless you need us, I think we'll take off and grab lunch," Sam said.

Isabel nodded. "Excellent idea."

Mindy hooked her arm in Sam's. "Thank you, Isabel, for having our backs. My sisters and I appreciate it more than you will ever know. Something about having a woman in charge makes us all breathe a little easier."

Sam's forehead crinkled in confusion. "I realize she's an amazing lawyer, but what does being a woman have to do with it?"

It was apparent Mindy was doing her best not to roll her eyes. "I like to be in control, and your sister and I are a lot alike. I know that she won't allow herself to fail. She'll keep at it until we win. She won't try to settle."

Winning was Isabel's preferred result, but this case wasn't going to be that simple. And her brief history with Jeremy would certainly complicate it. "There will have to be some negotiation, Mindy. That's just the way it works," Isabel said. She didn't make a habit of lowering her own bar, but if the note was determined to be authentic, Eden's was in a very difficult situation, one that Isabel would have to work miracles to get them out of.

"*If* the note is real," Mindy said. "I think there's a good chance that this is all a hoax."

Isabel could only hope for that right now. "I'd better get back in there and get it settled." She straightened her jacket and strode back down the hall. Wanting to appear confident and strong, she marched right into the room. And right into Jeremy. She reflexively braced herself, planting her hands on his chest. He gripped her elbows. She gazed up into his soft gray eyes. He intently peered down into hers. Her lips twitched with electricity, their connection fiercely uncomfortable to endure. Of course she'd fallen into bed with him that first night. Of course they'd given in to this. It would be impossible not to.

But now they were standing in a law office with a messy case to unravel. This was no time for rubbing up against Jeremy.

However badly she wanted to do exactly that.

She dropped her hands, and he dropped his, creating distance by stepping away. Isabel stared at the carpet, a perfectly ordinary office gray, as she struggled to regain her composure. She wasn't regretting the fact that they'd slept together. She found herself again regretting that she'd ever taken on this case.

"Sorry," Isabel said. "I guess I was in a hurry for us to get back to work."

Jeremy cleared his throat. "As am I. Lord only knows what Mr. Summers might do if left to his own devices in my office for too long." He flashed a quick smile at her. "Kidding, of course. He's fine in there." He strode to the door and closed it.

Isabel swallowed hard. Something about the sight of his hand against the ebony wood made her pulse skip a beat. She needed to get a grip. She was in the throes of battle with this man. Constantly reminding herself how sexy he was would only put her at a disadvantage. It didn't matter that he smelled good enough to eat. It didn't matter how unbelievable he looked in that suit.

"So," he started. "I take it this is why you didn't want to discuss your career the other night? Very clever of you."

"That wasn't the reason. I truly didn't want to talk about work. Is that so odd?"

"For someone who seems so eager to embrace her role as attorney, I find that a little peculiar."

"Eager? I'm just doing my job." She sat down and crossed her legs, hyperaware of the way her skirt hitched up an inch too far. She tugged at the hem as inconspicuously as possible. She needed to wrestle her side of their sexual tension into submission. It wasn't good for her or her client.

"Well, I have to admit that you're good at it. Very good." Jeremy sat down and drew a circle on the table with his index finger, making eye contact with her the whole time. Her mind zipped back to the memory of his hands on her naked skin—her breasts, her butt, her most delicate places—the parts that made her want him just as bad now as she had the other night. If only things hadn't ended so disastrously. "I got a little worked up there. You're definitely the most interesting person I've had the chance to spar with in recent history."

Isabel had always been drawn to that side of the law, where you make an argument, the other side responds with their own, and it then becomes a battle of wills, each party strengthening their stance until someone has no choice but to beg for mercy. Of course, it only felt good to come out on top. It felt horrible to lose. "Hopefully there won't have to be too much of that. I'd like to come to an agreement, starting with getting that note authenticated."

Just then the door flew open and a handsome, well-dressed older man stormed in. The resemblance to Jeremy was striking. It was like someone had hit the fast-forward button twenty years.

"Excuse me." The man barely glanced at Isabel. "Jeremy, can I speak with you?"

Jeremy impatiently rose from his seat, so fast that the chair rolled and hit the table with a thud. "We're in the middle of something. Can't this wait?"

"Why is Mr. Summers in your office?"

"He can't keep himself in line, that's why," Jeremy whispered, but it was loud enough for Isabel to hear every word.

The man unsubtly eyed Isabel, then returned his sights to Jeremy. "I'll go have a chat with him."

"Please don't."

Jeremy's voice was exceptionally firm, sending a thrill through Isabel, one she tried to ignore. She pulled out a legal pad and made a few scribbles to distract herself.

"All right then," the man said. "Check in with me when you're finished."

Jeremy said nothing in response as the man exited the room, but he had that stressed look on his face—the same one he'd had when he left Isabel's hotel room. "I'm sorry about that. My dad. He's supposed to be in partial retirement, but it only means that he has fewer clients but spends just as much time in the office."

"Leaving him too much time to interfere with what you're doing?" Isabel asked.

"Yes. Precisely."

Isabel didn't know much about Jeremy other than the revelation from Mindy that he'd been married, and apparently to a woman of some social stature, but she did feel bad that his own father was causing him distress. "No worries. Let's get back to the authentication. I've only been in New York a few weeks, so I don't have an expert on hand in the city. I know several in DC. I'm happy to bring one up."

"DC, huh? Big Washington lawyer?"

"Not exactly." Isabel pressed her lips together tightly.

"Something tells me you're underselling yourself." Jeremy's phone beeped with a text. "I'm so sorry, but I've been waiting for a message. Do you mind?"

"No. Of course not."

Jeremy pulled his phone from his pocket, seeming concerned. "Do you think we could discuss the authentication of the letter over dinner? I actually have to run home right now."

Run home during the day? Did Jeremy have a family? A girlfriend? He was becoming more of a puzzle by the moment. "I hope everything's okay."

He sighed heavily. "I think so. I ended up taking in a stray cat. It's a long story."

"Sounds like a lot."

"It's like everything in my life right now. Just one more thing on an endless list of obligations."

Isabel nodded, a bit chagrined that she'd been so right about Jeremy—he was not the guy who liked to be tied down. "Okay, then. You can tell me over dinner. Eight o'clock? The Monaco?"

Jeremy looked surprised. "It's impossible to get a reservation."

Isabel shrugged. "I know a guy."

"But you've only been in the city for a few weeks."

"Trust me. I got this."

Five

Dinner with Jeremy—hot and absurdly handsome Jeremy—was not the best plan. To some, it might seem like a particularly poor one. Did Isabel have a choice? Of course she did. She never liked to think that she didn't. But wrapping up this case on Mr. Summers's proposed timeline would take some artful work on Isabel's part if she was going to come out on top. For herself, her brother and his new family, she wanted nothing less than a win.

She did not want to be quibbling with this in January or having it drag out into February or March. She wanted this done so she could move on to the next phase of her career, adoption law. It would be a lot easier to get something out of Jeremy if the two of them had a good rapport, and well, the way things had played out at the Bacharach the night they met had not been a great start. She wanted to put that behind them, and in her experience, nothing cured a few bruised feelings faster than a glass of wine and some conversation over a delicious meal. Plus, the pasta carbonara at the Monaco was to die for.

First, she needed to get back to the Bacharach from the Sharp and Sharp offices. Wanting to clear her head, she opted to walk, even if she had to do it in heels. A crisp December wind whipped between the tall buildings of Midtown Manhattan, bringing Isabel the focus she craved. All around her, the city was abuzz with the holidays. She strode past storefronts with extravagant window displays, hosting scenes of Santa and snowy ski chalets, candy canes and snowflakes. Red-cheeked shoppers bustled along the sidewalk, loaded down with department store bags, including silver-and-white bags from Eden's, which was only seven or eight blocks away. Isabel hadn't celebrated Christmas in years. Well, not for real, with a tree and gifts and the Wham! song some people try to avoid hearing. She and Sam typically got together on Christmas Eve and spent a few quiet days together, cooking and talking, content with each other's company. It had been like that since their parents died, when Sam was in high school and Isabel in college. The holiday simply didn't have the same meaning without their entire family together. Losing both parents in a six-month period had left them no time to adjust. So she and Sam slipped into a new tradition, made up of celebrating the one thing they still had—each other.

Isabel wasn't sure what would happen this year. Sam had Mindy now. With that big lovely ring on her finger, they were buying their big house and talking about children. Of course, Isabel was over the moon about the whole thing. Yes, she'd been reluctant to accept Mindy after the heartbreak she'd caused Sam, but in the end, she'd been won over by Mindy's magnetic personality and determination. Plus, Isabel had to be nothing but in awe of her future sister-in-law. She'd accomplished the impossible, something no one else had managed in his thirty-six years on this planet—Mindy had found a way to make Sam happy.

Isabel arrived back at the Bacharach and dashed in through the revolving door, crossed the lobby and pressed the button for the elevator. She couldn't help but notice the woman in the fire department uniform speaking to the man she knew to be the hotel manager.

"The entire system?" the manager asked.

"I'm afraid so, sir. One minute it passes the test, the next minute it fails."

The elevator dinged and Isabel didn't hang around to hear more about the hotel's faulty alarm system. Hopefully it would get fixed soon.

Upstairs, she keyed into her room, unwound herself from her black wool coat, which she tossed onto the bed. She kicked off her pumps, sat at the desk and opened her laptop. She probably should have just given in to the urge to look into Jeremy yesterday, when she first learned that her one-night stand was opposing counsel. Less than a second after hitting the return button on *Jeremy Sharp*, a flurry of tabloid articles appeared. The first headline suggested exactly what Mindy had: Kelsey Kline Leaves Husband, Says Marriage "Loveless."

Isabel wasn't much for pulp or gossip, and she'd never even heard of Kelsey Kline before that morning, but the story was fascinating. The only daughter of a shipping magnate, heiress to a vast fortune, Ms. Kline was well-known in NYC as a party girl turned fashion blogger turned wedding planner. She was flat-out gorgeous, fit yet curvy, with high cheekbones, full lips and a stunning head of chocolate-brown hair. Isabel didn't know Jeremy particularly well, but Kelsey seemed like the kind of woman he might choose—fun and carefree.

As Isabel read on, the story turned dark and sad. Kelsey claimed that Jeremy was inattentive and unaffectionate, not the marrying type or a guy who was meant to settle down. She said point-blank that he broke her heart, getting married to him was a mistake, and she might never recover. There were even a few hints that he might have been unfaithful, although it was a subject carefully tiptoed around. No matter whether that was true or not, this was all another sign that Isabel might have dodged a bullet.

Kelsey filed for divorce less than three years after she and Jeremy had tied the knot in a lavish ceremony at a historic cathedral in the city. Other than being blamed for the end of the marriage, Jeremy was hardly mentioned in the article at all. It said that he had declined to comment, which Isabel took as confirmation that everything Kelsey had said was true, at least on some level. Otherwise, why not stick up for yourself?

Isabel took in a deep breath through her nose and closed her laptop, not wanting to read any more. She felt that familiar crawl over her skin after having peered into someone else's life. She realized there were plenty of people who lived for such salacious details, but Isabel had seen too much of the personal toll. At least she was now certain that she had made the right call when she'd let Jeremy off the hook after their first night together. She would have dinner with him tonight, get this case worked out and move on. That would be the end of her chapter with Mr. Sharp. And from the sound of that article, that was the best case scenario.

* * *

A few minutes before eight, Isabel climbed out of a town car in front of the Monaco. From the outside, the restaurant was a mystery—a dark wood facade with a large arched center door, the name in gold above. No random passersby would ever bother to step inside unprompted, out of either ignorance or perhaps fear of the unknown. But it was one of Isabel's favorite spots in Manhattan, owned by a former client who had top-tier restaurants all over the world—London, Madrid, Los Angeles, DC. Isabel's last assignment for the restaurateur had been to get his college-age daughter out of jail when she was arrested in Belize on spring break. It had been Isabel's job to not only deal with the legal side of getting her out and back into the US, but to keep the story out of the papers and away from her university. Thus had been her life of a lawyer turned fixer.

Isabel ducked through the door and into a dimly lit vestibule with an ornate tile floor, coat check and host stand. The sounds of the restaurant, a steady hum of conversation and clinking glass, filtered into the small space, even through the heavy emerald-green velvet drape that obscured the entrance into the dining room. Isabel gave her name to the hostess just as a rush of cold came in behind her. She turned and there was Jeremy. He was clearly flustered, his cheeks full of color as he pushed his hair back from his face. Isabel endeavored to ignore the way her pulse raced when she saw him. He turned his shoulders out of a charcoal-gray wool coat, dressed in black trousers and suit jacket, with a midnight-blue dress shirt that turned his gray eyes an even darker and more intense shade. Isabel had to hope that at some point the zap of attraction would subside.

Hopefully it wouldn't always feel like this to be around him, as if her body was on perpetual high alert.

"Everything okay?" she asked.

He smiled thinly. "Basically, yes. Just a crazy afternoon."

"Crazy good or crazy bad?"

He blew out a breath. "The stray cat I told you about? I thought it was a male, but it's a female. And she's pregnant."

Isabel pressed her lips together tightly to stifle a laugh. For the guy who seemed to be bothered by responsibility, this was pretty funny. "What are you going to do?"

"I'm going to buy you a drink as soon as we're seated for dinner. That's what."

Isabel signaled the hostess with a nod and they were led into the restaurant, just as beautiful as she'd remembered it, with its signature emerald-green circular booths for two, soft lighting and glamorous clientele. Jeremy waited for Isabel to sit before he slid into the other side of the booth. It was a sexy and intimate setting, perfect if there had been the possibility of any romance between them at all. But the article she'd read a few hours ago had put that idea to rest. Instead, she hoped to lean on the privacy of their table to start cutting their deal. They each ordered a drink from their server—a gin and tonic for Isabel and a Manhattan for Jeremy.

"I haven't been here in years," Jeremy said, flipping through the menu. Isabel already knew what she was going to order: her favorite pasta. "It's pretty much a date-night spot."

Isabel hadn't considered the possibility that Jeremy might have memories of this place with his ex-wife. Or other women. Her mind then made the next leap—did he think she was trying to make a romantic overture? She deeply hoped that was not the case. She didn't want to embarrass herself. "I love the food, though. It's exceptional."

"Indeed."

Their drinks were quickly delivered and they placed their dinner orders. "I suppose a toast is in order," Jeremy said once the server had left. "To making a deal."

Isabel was happy to hear that Jeremy didn't have romance on the brain. It might make it easier for her to set aside the thoughts that kept creeping into her consciousness—sharing a drink brought back too many memories of their blazing-hot first kiss. "Yes." She took a sip and placed her glass back on the table. "So, the authentication of the promissory note. Do you have an expert we can call on? I'd like to speak to them, of course, and have a detailed outline of their process, their experience in the field, and have them sign an agreement of impartiality."

"I have one person we work with, but I can assure you that they'll do a great job and they'll get it done quickly."

"We wouldn't want to mess with Mr. Summers and his thirty-day timeline."

"We're already nearly a week in. The clock started the day we sent the first letter. And you can't blame the guy. The loan is long overdue."

"And my clients had no idea the loan ever existed. You can't pay off what you don't know about."

"They don't seem eager to repay it now."

Isabel stirred her drink. "It's not a simple matter to pull that kind of cash together at one time. Especially not with so little time."

Jeremy shrugged it off. "I don't want to sound like a jerk, but it's not my problem."

Isabel did not like the way this was going. She saw too little room for negotiation. This case might be even tougher than she'd thought. "I would never say you sound like a jerk. But you do sound like the lawyer of a jerk."

Despite being referred to as the lawyer of a jerk, being out with Isabel was far more enjoyable than the many work-related obligations Jeremy endured on any given week. "If that's what I am, at least it pays the bills."

"Good to know you have your priorities," she said, then took a long sip of her drink.

Jeremy had to hide his amusement as the waiter delivered their meals. Isabel was a far cry from the usual blowhard attorney. He genuinely enjoyed her company. She was more than simply beautiful and smart. The world seemed different around her, the air charged with mystery and excitement. Jeremy had learned a lot about her after she'd left his office that afternoon. While working in Washington, DC, she'd gathered a passel of high-powered clients—senators, billionaires and cabinet officials. Not a single controversy or scandal seemed to stick to any of them, even when lawsuits were filed and whistles were blown. Accusations and rumors all vanished into thin air, and Jeremy was smart enough to know that didn't happen on its own. Did Isabel's beautiful exterior and graceful facade make it easier for her to sweep things under the rug or keep secrets? If so, it made her even more dangerous than he'd thought that morning. "So, I have to ask, why didn't you call me as soon as you realized that I was the opposing counsel? That part of this whole thing seems especially sneaky."

Isabel dabbed at the corners of her stunning mouth with a napkin. He had an improper desire to kiss her until her lipstick was gone. Despite being on opposite sides of the negotiating table, that sexual energy between them wasn't going anywhere. "Honestly?"

"Please. I don't do well with anything less." Jeremy found himself cutting his steak a little more aggressively than was warranted. Even the manipulation of words bothered him, which made being a lawyer difficult. So much of the job was about the careful parsing of language.

"It was my brother Sam's idea. He thought it would give us an advantage if you didn't know who exactly you would be facing. I apologize if you felt ambushed, but it was just a tactic."

That morning in his office had likely only been Jeremy's first taste of the sorts of things to which Isabel might resort. "It made me look like an ass in front of my client. I certainly don't appreciate that."

Isabel nodded. "Fair enough. I guess it wasn't the kindest thing to do. Sam is just very protective of his fiancée, Mindy, and the entire Eden family for that matter. And since it's just Sam and me in our family, I guess that I'm part of that scenario, too."

Jeremy understood family loyalty, but only to a point. If his grandfather were still alive, he'd still have undying devotion to the Sharp name. But his parents certainly didn't inspire that sort of allegiance. They'd treated him horribly in the aftermath of his divorce, more preoccupied by the public embarrassment than the fact that their son had experienced a great personal betrayal. "Do you actually like working for the Eden family?"

Isabel shot him a quizzical look. "That's a loaded question."

"Why?"

"The tone of your voice for starters. You sound as though the Eden family disgusts you."

Jeremy was letting his personal bias get in the way, but he couldn't help it. The Eden family and his ex's family seemed to be very much the same—wealthy beyond measure, treating the world as their personal playground. "It's just the entitlement. It drives me crazy. The Eden sisters have been handed a vast fortune and now they're quibbling over this debt. I assure you that Mr. Summers would not dredge up this matter if he didn't desperately want it resolved. It's a very personal thing for him. The affair between Victoria Eden and his father destroyed his family. I don't think we can discount the personal component of the case."

Isabel set her fork down on her plate. "And surely you know it takes two people to tango. Mr. Summers seems to want to assign all blame to Victoria Eden. He wants to paint her as a home-wrecker, when the reality is that his own father was complicit as well if the affair happened as he says it did. For all we know, his father could have instigated the whole thing."

Jeremy felt his pulse pick up. His heart hammered. He did love it when Isabel delivered a smart jab, even if he was on the receiving end of it.

"*If* the affair actually happened," she continued. "We don't know that for sure."

She bit down on her lip, her dark eyes scanning his face. Damn, her skin was beautiful in this soft light and all he could think was how badly he wanted to touch it. To touch her. Every inch. He wasn't the type of guy to rest too much of his self-worth on how things went in the bedroom, but he was certain that he had rocked Isabel's world during their one evening together, and it was still aggravating him that it had ended on such an inelegant note.

She shook her head and looked down at the table, her dark hair falling across her face. "I'm sorry. I just get worked up. I don't like seeing a woman shouldering the blame for this. Men and women are equal and should be treated as such, good or bad."

"Don't apologize for your anger. I'd much rather go up against someone with some passion behind what they do than deal with a robot."

Her eyebrows bounced and one corner of her mouth popped up into a smile. "I run way too hot to be a robot."

An abrupt tightening of the muscles in Jeremy's hips made him shift in his seat. Isabel was going to make him crazy by the time this case was wrapped up. For once, Jeremy was glad for Mr. Summers's ridiculous timeline. The sooner this case was done, the sooner he could decide if he wanted to pursue anything with her. It seemed like he had to at least try one more time, leave her with a smile on her face rather than having her push him out the door. "I know that. Firsthand."

"I hope that doesn't make you uncomfortable. You know. That we slept together. I'm trying to look at it as an odd coincidence."

"So you definitely weren't spying on me and Mr. Summers in the bar at the Bacharach?"

Isabel's eyes went wide. "Is that who your meeting was with that night?" She clamped her hand over her mouth, much like she had when he'd mentioned that his new roommate, the stray cat with no name, was going to have kittens.

"It is. Summers loves the bar there."

Isabel reached out and clasped Jeremy's forearm. "I swear I wasn't spying. I would never do that. I was legitimately up in my room trying to get some sleep when the silly alarm went off. It had been a hell of a day trying to find an apartment and look for a new office space. It's a lot to deal with at one time, especially when you're starting on a case that could easily end up being all-consuming."

Jeremy couldn't help but look at her hand on his arm, her slender fingers on the dark wool of his coat, and quietly wish he wasn't wearing a suit. "I had to ask." He cleared his throat, knowing he'd never truly believed that Isabel had been up to something nefarious that night, but it did make him wonder whether she was someone he could trust. "You know, I looked you up on the internet this afternoon. Judging by the work you were doing in DC, I'm up against quite a formidable foe."

"Please don't judge me by that. As far as I'm concerned, that was a lifetime ago. I'm actually getting ready to go into a whole new area of practice. Adoption law."

Now Jeremy was even more fascinated. This was a full one-eighty. "There's not exactly a lot of money in that, is there?"

Isabel shrugged. "There isn't. I'm not worried about that. I just want to have a body of work that I can be proud of."

"I take it that doesn't include the things you did in DC?"

She shook her head. "Definitely not. But I'm putting all of that behind me. For good."

So maybe he'd read Isabel all wrong. He could hardly

fault a person for wanting to do some good with her career. "Sounds like you've got it all figured out."

"And speaking of getting things figured out, let's say we get the note authenticated. At that point, we'll need to set up a time for in-depth negotiations to hammer out the details. But I don't have an office right now."

Jeremy sucked in a deep breath. He had serious concerns that as soon as the note was deemed authentic, Mr. Summers would further dig in his heels. But it was part of Jeremy's job to at least move forward in good faith. "It's not easy for me to get much done at the Sharp and Sharp office. Too many interruptions." He cleared his throat, racking his brain for an idea. "Is meeting at Eden's an option?"

"They don't have the room. I asked about a work space there, but the building is old and they're bulging at the seams." She placed her napkin across her plate and sat back.

"I have a full office big enough for two people at my place in Brooklyn. In fact, I probably have too much space. I have meetings there all the time when I need quiet, or when a client wants more discretion than they'll get walking into the front door of a law firm. Would you be comfortable with that idea?"

"Hmm…" She squinted at him. "I don't know. Is this some sort of come-on?"

Jeremy could feel the heat rising in his cheeks. "Most women aren't seduced by the idea of negotiations."

"Ah, but I'm not most women."

Jeremy swallowed hard, finding it difficult to get past the lump in his throat. "I noticed."

Isabel granted him a small smile. "Would that mean I'd get to meet your cat?"

"She's not my cat."

"She's come up in conversation an awful lot for a cat that isn't yours."

"I'm not a cat person at all. I just took pity on her because she was outside in the cold. Ironically, the only reason I hadn't let her in before was because she was so fat. Now I know why."

"What are you going to do about the kittens?"

Jeremy kneaded his forehead. His meeting with his neighborhood veterinarian was still fresh in his mind. "For now? I'm fostering her. We had such a late summer that I guess there's a big surplus of cats and the shelters are full. The vet said the kittens should be ready for adoption by Valentine's Day." Jeremy could hardly believe the words out of his own mouth. Like he needed another complication in his life.

"Well, I can't wait to meet her. I love cats. We always had them when I was a kid. My mom was obsessed with them."

"You haven't had one since?"

Isabel's face reflected something Jeremy hadn't seen before—sadness. "No. Not one of my own."

"Well, good. Maybe you're the answer to my prayers. I'm a bit out of my depth." He glanced over at her, wondering why he was allowing himself to get further entwined with Isabel. He knew he shouldn't be, especially not now. He should be creating distance. That was how you won. "With the cat. Not the case."

Six

Isabel arranged to meet Mindy at her grandmother's penthouse apartment on Central Park West on Sunday morning. It was only eleven days until Christmas and the clock was ticking on Mr. Summers's timeline. The results of the promissory note authentication were due back tomorrow. Then Isabel would have to get back into it with Jeremy. She wasn't quite sure what to make of the invitation to meet at his house, but she knew from experience that there was no substitute for sitting down at the negotiating table and hammering out details. So she would risk having to endure the temptation of Jeremy, being alone and sequestered with him, just so she could move forward with her life—finish up the Eden's case and start the new year with a whole new direction.

"Hey there." Mindy answered the door, dressed in the sort of outfit Isabel had never seen her wear—jeans and a sweater. No designer dress or sky-high heels. It was nice to see her dressed down and relaxed. "Come on in."

"Thanks." Isabel stepped into a bright and elegant foyer with white marble floors and a crystal-and-chrome fixture overhead. She took off her coat, glad she'd also gone for pants and a sweater. Even hot-running Isabel found it too cold outside for a dress.

"Thank you for suggesting we do this. It was a really good idea. Sophie is convinced that this whole Summers case is bogus. But I'm not so sure, especially after your forensic accountants found the money yesterday. And discovered that it went into my grandmother's personal account, not the business."

"It's starting to make sense now, isn't it? No wonder we couldn't find any evidence of it in the Eden's books. It never touched Eden's. Or at least not directly." Isabel was struggling just like Mindy, wondering how this all went together. "But we still don't know for certain that the money came from Summers and we also don't know where it eventually went."

"Only that it existed."

"Right."

Mindy waved Isabel across the foyer. "Come on. Let me show you the place."

They progressed down a skinny hallway and then the apartment opened up, with an entire wall of windows overlooking Central Park. The vista ahead was frosted with snow, a lovely match for the mostly white furnishings.

"My grandmother was all about punches of color." Mindy picked up a magenta throw pillow from one of several plush sofas. Behind it was a sunny yellow cashmere throw. The walls were dotted with an eclectic mix of art, wildly varied stylistically, from impressionist to modern, featuring nearly every shade of the rainbow. It all looked to be original. The space as a whole spoke of a very chic woman with impossibly expensive taste. Of course Victoria Eden had lived in such a grand and unbelievable space.

"I've seen that same thing at Eden's, especially in her old office."

Mindy nodded. "Emma's been afraid to change a thing. Too much tradition. The specter of my grandmother always looms large."

Tradition. Another reason Isabel could not let Eden's fall apart on her watch.

"I can't believe you never moved in here," Isabel said. "It's incredible. Completely gorgeous." She wandered over to a set of French doors that led out to a stone balcony, admiring the wintry scene. Mother Nature had already gone big this December.

"I knew that no matter what I did, Sophie would criticize my choices unless I left everything exactly as it was. And I do not want to live in a museum."

"That's not really fair to you, is it? So you just leave this sitting here because of your sister?"

Mindy shrugged. "I have no business complaining. Emma never knew our grandmother very well, so she enjoys coming up here and poking around, looking at old photos. Sophie likes it for the same reason, and I'd be lying if I said that I didn't enjoy it, too. It's comforting to be here. I can feel our grandmother's presence when I'm here and we all miss it. I can't fault anyone for wanting to put the world on pause."

Isabel nodded, appreciating the whole sad story. She knew very well what it was like to miss someone so desperately. She still felt that same way about her parents, especially her mom. "If only we could do that. It would be nice every now and then."

Mindy gathered her glorious red tresses in her hands and draped them over one shoulder. "It's only been a year since Gram died, and so much has happened. Just when we thought we were getting the store back on a more profitable path, this happens. I'm honestly wondering if we're not better off just selling, paying off Mr. Summers and moving on. I know Sophie and Emma want to keep Eden's alive at any cost, but sometimes, things just don't work out."

Isabel carefully considered Mindy's words. She loved that her future sister-in-law was both savvy and sweet. She could make shrewd business moves and still take everyone's feelings into account. "Have I told you how happy I am that my brother found a woman who is not only smart, but also incredibly thoughtful?"

Mindy smiled. "That's not what you thought of me the first time we met."

"I know. And I fully admit that you changed my mind."

Mindy reached out and rubbed Isabel's arm. "I'm excited to have you for a sister-in-law. Although, honestly, I have a feeling that I should probably just call you my sister. You and I are a lot more alike than Sophie or Emma and I."

Isabel felt like her heart was growing to twice its normal size. She and Sam were impossibly close, but that was such a small circle of family. Here was Mindy, forging a connection of her own with Isabel. She was so thankful for it. "That sounds amazing. I've always wanted a sister."

"Consider it done." Mindy grinned and placed her

arm around Isabel's shoulders, pulling her close. "Come on. Let's go dig through my grandmother's office."

The pair trekked through the living room to what appeared to be Victoria Eden's private quarters, with a large master bedroom, elegant bathroom with its own view of the park, dressing room and, finally, a generous home office. Like the rest of the house, a neutral backdrop of white and cream made room for the more over-the-top elements, like a crimson velvet club chair. Mindy stepped behind her grandmother's grand desk and opened the closet to reveal six large filing cabinets.

"I'm guessing we start here?" Mindy asked.

Isabel didn't have a better suggestion. "It's as good a place as any."

They quickly set up a system, methodically going through one drawer at a time, file folder after file folder, page after page of surprisingly meaningless paperwork. For a woman who had been considered a business tycoon, Victoria Eden had been keenly focused on the smallest of things.

Mindy shook her head and closed one folder. "She kept nearly thirty years of electric bills. Who does that?"

"Someone who's watching every penny? Maybe that's part of why she was so successful."

Mindy's shoulders dropped in exasperation. "I hope this doesn't end up being a big waste of time."

"I don't know. Compared to most things I do, this is pretty fun. Plus, we get to spend time together."

"There you go. Good job looking on the bright side. I need to do more of that."

"Actually, if anything, I'd take all of this mundane stuff as a good sign. Anyone who kept electric bills likely also kept far more important things."

"Even superpersonal things?"

Isabel closed up the folder she'd been sifting through and handed it over to Mindy. "Especially that."

After two more hours of pulling apart the contents of the filing cabinets, they were down to the last drawer. Mindy pulled the handle, but it only opened partway. "Can you help me with this?" she asked, peering down inside.

Isabel rushed over and knelt down next to Mindy. Sure enough, there was a large wood box, turned on its side, preventing the drawer from being opened the whole way. Mindy and Isabel quickly pulled out the hanging files in front of it. Mindy grabbed a letter opener from her grandmother's desk drawer and slipped it under the bottom of the box, twisting and pulling until the box popped free with a clatter of wood against metal.

Mindy closed the drawer and sat spread-eagled on the floor with the box between her knees. She flipped the small brass latch on the front. She looked up at Isabel, her eyes wide with astonishment. "It's a bunch of letters." She examined the first envelope. "The return address says Bradley Summers."

Goose bumps popped up on Isabel's arms. She sensed that another piece of the puzzle was about to fall into place. "Bingo."

Isabel and Mindy spent the next several hours devouring the correspondence sent by Bradley Summers to Victoria Eden, which seemed to begin in the spring of 1979, years before the loan would have been made. They arranged the letters in chronological order, which helped them sort out how the affair began: after Bradley and Victoria had a chance meeting at a cocktail party in the Hamptons. Bradley made mention that he was glad their spouses had not been on hand—Bradley's wife because she'd had one of her "many migraines" and Victoria's husband because he couldn't be bothered to stay away from the racetrack. It was an epic love story that sprouted up between two people thrown together by chance, who just happened to fulfill what the other was so desperately looking for. For the senior Mr. Summers, it seemed to be the undivided attention of a woman. *My sweet Victoria*, he wrote, *When we're together, I feel like I'm the only man in the world. Every moment with you is priceless, worth framing and hanging in a museum.*

"Wow. This is so romantic. They were head over heels for each other," Isabel said, handing over the letter she was holding to Mindy. She couldn't help but be astonished by what had been between these two people, sentiments that served as a very plain reminder that Isabel hadn't come close to finding that kind of passion or affection with a man. She hoped she wasn't running out of time.

When Mindy finished reading the final letter in the box, she looked over at Isabel with a tear in her eye. It was a bit incongruous with Mindy's normally tough exterior. "Their love affair was real." Mindy's shoulders dropped. "I don't know what to think about this. Or how I'm supposed to feel. I really loved my grandfather, but it's pretty well known in our family that he was not a great husband. This is at least confirmation that my grandmother stayed in a loveless marriage for her entire life."

"That part is incredibly sad." Isabel glanced down at the pile of letters. "It was also pretty clear that your grandfather had a serious gambling problem. Bradley mentions several times that he hated your grandmother living with the burden of his many debts. Do you think that's where the money could have gone?"

Mindy shrugged. "I have no idea. I mean, going to the racetrack with our grandfather is one of the only things I ever remember doing with him, but we were kids and it was nothing but fun. We'd drink soda and eat junk food and he'd let us pick our favorite horses so he could place bets. Sophie always picked names like Fancy Frolic, and I always picked ones like Emperor King. My grandfather used to tease me, saying that I needed to learn to like 'girl things.'" Mindy made air quotes. "As far as I was concerned, I liked what I liked. No big surprise, but he handed those same ideas down to our dad. Even so, those days at the track are some of my fondest memories of my grandfather. He at least wanted to spend time with us, which is more than I can say for my dad."

Isabel was struck by how even a family with great wealth and power could have such a bittersweet legacy. "If the money went to gambling debts, it might be harder to track down, especially depending on who he owed money to. And it still doesn't change the fact that it appears that the loan was real."

Mindy again looked down at the letters in her hand, but it was for several moments this time. She brushed her fingers across the envelope at the top of the pile. "This means that the store is really on the line, doesn't it? We aren't talking hypotheticals anymore. I mean, chances are that the promissory note is real, and we're going to have to find a way to pay off the debt."

"No matter what I'm able to negotiate, chances are that it'll still be a huge chunk of money, and from everything I've seen of Mr. Summers, he's serious about wanting it in one lump sum, right away. Early January, right after New Year's."

"It's just hard to come up with that kind of cash without a loan. And the most valuable thing we have to use as collateral is Eden's. It's all Sophie has, aside from her apartment and Eden House, our family's vacation home, which she would never let go of in a million years."

"What about selling this apartment?"

Mindy nodded, looking around the room. "Yeah. I could definitely do that, but we're talking maybe fifty million, and that's if we get top dollar from the right buyer, which could easily take a year to happen. It's a drop in the bucket compared to what we have to come up with."

"Can Sam help?"

"He's looking into selling some bigger properties, but like I said, that all takes time, and it all costs money, too. Real estate agents need to get paid. It sort of feels like we're throwing money into a big black hole." Surprisingly, a smile crossed Mindy's face.

"And you're happy about that?"

"No. No. I was just thinking about Sam and his reaction to this whole situation. He wants to fix everything. He gets so worked up about it, wanting to hold everything together. It's just so damn sweet. Every time he gets upset about it, I fall a little more in love with him."

Now Isabel was the one having to fight back tears. The struggles she and Sam had been through when they were young had been much harder on him, and Isabel still had a good deal of guilt over having been away at college when it happened. "You really love him, don't you?"

"It might sound corny, and I'm not a super sentimental person, but he is my soul mate. We work together in every way. I can't imagine my life without him." Mindy gathered the letters in her hands and squared the edges on the floor. "And I nearly lost him. I pushed him away so many times."

Isabel had never pushed anyone away, but she'd had many men shutter her out of their lives. It hurt an unimaginable amount, which was a big part of the reason Isabel had not initially liked Mindy. She hated the thought of her brother having his heart broken. "I feel like everything happens for a reason. Maybe you had to go through those early tests to know for sure that you're right for each other."

"That sounds a lot nicer than my version, which is basically just me being an idiot." Mindy shifted to her knees and got up from the floor. "So what do you think is going to happen with Eden's?"

"I think we're going to have to count on Mr. Summers's good graces and hope that they'll agree to a reduced settlement and a payment plan."

"Do you think these letters might help?" Mindy asked. "What if we showed them to him? Showed him how much his father really loved my grandmother? It might make him see that the loan really was made out of love. It's not our fault his parents couldn't make their marriage work."

Isabel shook her head. "No. Absolutely not. I think you should put those letters back where you found them, and for the time being, I wouldn't tell anyone about them other than Sam and your sisters."

"Okay, then. What's next?"

"I'm guessing that I'm going to get a phone call from Jeremy Sharp tomorrow morning saying that the note was authenticated. And that's when we start negotiating from a disadvantage."

"You don't think you're better than him?"

Now it was Isabel's turn to smile at an inopportune time. "It's not a matter of better. Jeremy is plenty skilled. He's a shrewd attorney."

Mindy narrowed her sights, and Isabel immediately worried that her future sister-in-law was onto something. "Is it just me or is he superhot, too? I mean, I know Sam thinks he's a weasel, but there's no accounting for his taste. Especially not when it comes to hotness."

Isabel's cheeks flushed with warmth. There had been many times at dinner the other night when she'd caught herself holding her breath in awe of Jeremy's appeal. "He's extremely handsome. There's no doubt about that."

"It was sexy the way you two were arguing at that first meeting. It felt like there were sparks flying. Or is that stupid of me to say?"

Isabel already felt bad about not coming clean about Jeremy with her own brother the day of that meeting. She wasn't sure she could keep it from Mindy, too, especially when they were becoming so close. "I have to tell you something. But you have to promise not to breathe a word of it to Sam. At least not until the case is settled." She bit down on her lip, waiting for Mindy's response, hoping like hell that she could truly be trusted.

"I don't like the idea of secrets. But I also don't like the idea of you feeling like you can't tell me anything. Because you can." Mindy nodded eagerly. "So, yes. My lips are zipped. I won't say a peep to Sam."

Isabel took in a deep breath for confidence. "I slept with Jeremy."

Mindy slugged her in the arm playfully. "Shut up. Are you serious?" Her eyes bugged out. "Wait. When?"

"It was actually a few days before the first meeting. I had no idea who he was, and he had no idea who I was. It was pure coincidence." Isabel went on to share the most general of details from their night together, sparing Mindy the part about Jeremy's quick departure.

"So, how was it?"

"It was fantastic, but it was a one-night thing. You don't have anything to worry about. There will be no conflict of interest there. Jeremy's all business and he's devoted to his client. That goes much further than you might imagine."

"I trust your judgment, Isabel. Completely. I know you're an amazing lawyer and I'm sure you won't have a problem keeping it all aboveboard. So, how do you like our odds of saving the store?"

Isabel didn't want to sugarcoat anything, but she didn't want to set her future sister-in-law up for disappointment, either. "The optimist in me is thinking fifty-fifty."

"Really?" Mindy asked. "That bad?"

Isabel reached out and caressed Mindy's arm, wanting to be at least a little reassuring. "I'm going to do everything I can to keep you from losing."

"Everything?" Mindy asked with two perfectly arched eyebrows.

Isabel was now second-guessing the decision to spill the beans about Jeremy. She really hoped she didn't end up regretting it. "Nearly everything."

Mindy and Isabel put away the letters, tidied up the office, and went their separate ways. It was a chilly day, but the sun had come out, so Isabel decided to walk back to the Bacharach. When she arrived, there was a sign on the door: *All guests: Please see the front desk for information regarding your stay. There will be no new check-ins until further notice.*

Isabel strode inside to investigate, but there was a sizable line of seemingly upset guests at the front desk. "What's going on?" she asked a woman who was waiting for the elevator.

"The fire department has ordered the hotel to replace the alarm system. They start the work on Friday. Everyone has to be out by then." The elevator dinged. "It doesn't affect me, so I'm not too worried about it."

Isabel decided she wasn't going to wait with the angry mob in the lobby and instead took the elevator up with the woman. "Did they happen to say if they're sending guests to another hotel?"

"It's Christmas in Manhattan. There are no other hotel rooms. That's why everyone is so mad."

Isabel wasn't sure how things could get much worse. She'd just have to move in with Sam and Mindy for a few days until she could find something more permanent. If nothing else, she needed to get back to looking for an apartment in earnest.

The woman got off on her floor and Isabel rode up another two to her own. She'd hardly keyed her way into her room when her phone rang. It was Jeremy.

"Hello?" she asked, plopping down on the bed.

"Did I catch you at a bad time?"

Isabel disliked the way her body reacted to his voice, like a puppy that's just been told it's time for a treat. "No. It's fine. What's up?"

"We got the authentication of the note. I just wanted to tell you as soon as I knew."

Isabel reclined back on the bed and stared up at the ceiling. This was not surprising news, but it was certainly not what they wanted. "Okay, then. I'll notify my client. And I guess we need to get together to hammer out these negotiations."

"Yeah. About that. I talked to Mr. Summers and in light of the authentication, he has changed his terms. He wants an even billion or the store. By January 1."

She shot straight up in bed, her heart hammering. She could hardly believe what he had just said. "It's Christmas. Is he really that cold and heartless? I'm sorry, but your client is behaving like Ebenezer Scrooge."

"From where I'm sitting, he has an ironclad case."

Isabel fought the grumble in her throat. She also tamped back her natural urge to launch into her side of the argument. There was no point in that right now. Isabel had seen the letters. She'd known that this was coming. Victoria Eden and Bradley Summers had absolutely had an affair. And by all accounts, it had been a doozy. Her heart sank at the thought of the call she had to make, to break this news to Mindy and Sam, then let them break it to Sophie and Emma. It would take the wind out of their sails, for sure, but Isabel would not let this be the end of the story. It would not be the final chapter of Eden's Department Store. Somehow, they would pull this off. She would. "I'll talk to my clients and see what we can do."

"You'll get back to me?"

"I don't see that I have a choice."

Seven

Since the moment the promissory note had been authenticated, Isabel had been doing nothing but playing cat and mouse with Jeremy. His client was refusing to budge. Mr. Summers wouldn't give an inch. Jeremy was holding fast. She knew from experience that she'd never be able to exercise any influence over him unless they could meet in person, but he was insisting on phone calls, much to her dismay. He was avoiding her, and it was starting to feel personal.

By Friday, things were becoming dire. Sam and Mindy had spent the entire week moving assets, trying to sell properties, but they were finding the task more difficult the closer they got to the holidays. It would be nearly impossible to liquidate anything between Christmas and New Year's. There were simply too many people who weren't working. With Christmas six days away, time was running out.

As if life couldn't possibly get more complicated,

Isabel had to vacate the Bacharach by noon that day. She'd originally planned to stay with Sam and Mindy, but they'd both been working so hard that they'd managed to come down with a dreadful cold. Isabel's back-up plan was to fly to DC and stay with a friend for the weekend. This close to Christmas, there wasn't a spare hotel room anywhere in the city.

Before she left for the airport, Isabel was set to meet with Sophie and Emma at Eden's and if all went okay, Sam or Mindy would call in. Isabel arrived at Eden's first thing that morning. Eight o'clock to be exact, right when the offices were first open. A burly but friendly security officer named Duane met her at one of the main entrances.

"Sophie and Emma are already here," he said, walking her through the cosmetics department and back to the executive elevators.

"Thank you. Have they been here long?"

"Most of the night."

Isabel had been afraid of that. Coming up with a cool billion to get Benjamin Summers to go away was no small job and they were all going to extraordinary measures to attempt the impossible.

The store was eerily quiet, with only a handful of lights on. It would open early at 9:00 a.m. for holiday shopping hours, but there was still a sense that she was taking part in a death march. Just like the entire Eden family, she desperately didn't want the store to slip into Mr. Summers's hands. There were no guarantees that he'd continue to run the store at all. Isabel could imagine him taking a wrecking ball to the whole thing out of spite. What would happen to the employees? Or the history contained in this beautiful old building? And what would happen to the Eden sisters if they lost their birthright, this very permanent fixture of this city, emblazoned with their name?

Duane pressed the elevator button for her. "Do you know your way upstairs? Lizzie, the receptionist, should be here soon, but not yet. She just texted me to say her train was delayed."

"Eden's really is like a family, isn't it?" Isabel asked. Where else did the receptionist check in with the security guard when she was running late?

"Yes, ma'am. Lizzie is like a little sister to me. She tells me everything." His eyebrows bounced and he smiled. "Even about her new beau."

"Ooh. Anyone I know?" Lizzie was a total sweetheart and Isabel had grown to adore her.

"I shouldn't say anything." Duane's face said that he was dying to tell someone.

Isabel reached out and touched his arm. "Look. I'm very good at keeping secrets. You can tell me. I won't say a peep."

"It's James, one of the salespeople in menswear," he blurted. "He's a Brit like Emma's husband, Daniel."

As if there hadn't been enough excitement about the Eden family, Emma and Daniel had decided to get married at city hall last week. With a baby on the way, Daniel was eager to start the process of becoming an American citizen, apparently much to his mother's disappointment.

"I'll have to find a reason to sneak down to menswear later and see if I can get an eyeful of James."

Duane laughed and the elevator dinged. "Have a good meeting."

"Thank you." A minute later, Isabel arrived on the executive floor.

Sophie was waiting right outside the elevator bank,

pacing. She lunged for Isabel the instant the door opened. "Thank God you're here. We have an emergency and it's bad."

Isabel could hardly keep up anymore. She'd dealt with plenty of panicked clients, but this was turning into an hourly thing with the Eden family. Fortunately, she had a great deal of experience in this arena. "Whatever it is, it's okay. Did something happen with one of the deals Sam and Mindy were working on? Or something you and your husband were setting up?"

Emma strode out of her office. Her baby bump was now visible. Small, but apparent. "I read the article, Sophie. I really don't think it's that bad. I mean, it's not great, but I've seen worse things."

Isabel was starting to put this all together. "Something in the tabloids, I take it?"

Sophie waved her ahead. "Come on. My office. I'll show you."

Isabel was starting to bristle at Sophie's cloak-and-dagger approach as she found herself marching with Sophie and Emma down the hall to Sophie's office. Inside, a stack of newspapers sat on her desk. Even upside down, Isabel saw the headline: Eden's Matriarch's Secret Affair Exposed. Of course, those words—*secret affair*—leaped off the page. Isabel wasn't much for prurient accounts, but anyone would have to be intrigued. "How did this happen?" Isabel took the liberty of taking a copy and began scanning the story.

"We have no idea. I guess the reporter called Mindy last night but she was so hopped up on cold medicine that she barely remembers the conversation."

Isabel had to hand it to Mindy. For someone on cold medicine, the quote she'd given the newspaper was remarkably smart and diplomatic. She'd said precisely what Isabel would have coached her to say. Mr. Summers, however, was a different case. Clearly Jeremy had *not* had a say in the formulation of his comment. No lawyer would have allowed their client to say such a thing.

"It's so horrible. The things he said about our grandmother." Sophie plopped down on the couch. "And right before Christmas, no less. I wouldn't be surprised if people start boycotting the store. We need to hire a PR person and start fighting this. We need to put our own version of this story out there. We can't let Gram's memory be tarnished like this."

Isabel very pointedly shook her head at Emma, who was the only one paying attention to her. Sophie was dead wrong. "Actually, ladies, this is amazing news. I believe we finally have a leg up in this negotiation."

Jeremy had reached a new low—he arrived at the office having had no more than ten minutes of sleep. Granted, it was Friday morning and it had been an incredibly long week, which usually left him stumbling into the weekend. With his grueling job, he already didn't sleep well. but that had gotten progressively worse since his night with Isabel. She was this beautiful dangling string in his life, unfinished business, both personally and professionally. Situations like that had always bothered him.

When Kelsey left him, it was yet another situation where he was left with far more questions than answers. She took off with no warning, leaving only a note that he'd made her deeply unhappy. He never had the chance to ask how or why—she went right to the press and smeared him, telling them their marriage was over. It wasn't until later that Jeremy learned she'd been unfaithful, but he couldn't prove it, and the court of public opinion was squarely against him. He'd been painted as heartless, and since it was clear to Jeremy that the situation would not get better if he spoke up, he put his head down and gave in to her demands. Just to get her out of his life. He simply hadn't had the fight.

If Jeremy had learned anything over the past five days, it was that the Eden family would go down swinging. Isabel had been incredible to work with, and they'd talked every day, but she was doing nothing but push, even from her disadvantaged position. He loved the fight in her. He loved it a little too much. Every conversation with her was a turn-on, precisely why he'd made excuses all week and kept their back-and-forth on the phone.

Of course, last night before he left the office, Isabel had called him on it. "I'm beginning to think you're avoiding me, Sharp." She referred to him by his last name when she really wanted to put on the pressure. It was playful and toying and sexy. On some level, she *had* to know what it was doing to him. "Why don't we meet for a drink? Or I'll come out to Brooklyn. I still haven't met your cat. Does she have a name yet?"

"I'm calling her Cat."

"You have got to be kidding me."

Jeremy had not appreciated the inference. "No. I am a kind soul who took in an animal. But she's not staying and I don't want to get attached. Hence, I put only enough time into giving her a name as absolutely necessary. Her next owner can give her a real name."

"Any sign of the kittens?"

"Soon, I guess."

"You guess?" Isabel then went on to read him a laundry list of the things he should be looking for in Cat's behavior. He had noticed nothing she mentioned.

Jeremy's only response had been to change the subject. "My client refuses to budge, so unless you have a check for me to collect, I guess I don't see the point in a face-to-face meeting."

"I think that what you're really saying is that it's harder to negotiate with me when you and I are in the same room."

She was *not* wrong. In fact, that had been his number one fear—Isabel would get him to do something he shouldn't if they had to meet in person. Sure, he *wanted* to see her. He'd be an idiot to not want that. But was it a good idea? No. "Goodbye, Ms. Blackwell. Have a good night."

Jeremy had called Mr. Summers immediately after, but got nowhere. "There is no wiggle room," Mr. Summers said. "From where I sit, we have them right where we want them. They will pay or they'll hand over the store. They're lying and stalling."

"Every day they continue to delay is another day you have to pay me. We could expedite the process and get it all wrapped up if you were willing to concede to a payment plan. You'll still get your money, just on a different timeline."

"No. Absolutely not. And please don't ask me again."

Jeremy had a duty to give Mr. Summers whatever he wanted, no matter how punitive he was being about the whole thing. "Very well then. Have a good night."

Now back at work, he couldn't get his head screwed on right. Maybe Isabel was right. Maybe they did need to meet. He couldn't concede with anything, but he could at least see her. Let her beat him up with her words. It would likely be the only fun to be had with this case.

"Knock, knock." Jeremy's father appeared at his office door. "Good morning."

Simply hearing his father's voice these days made him cringe, and this reaction was starting to get to him. He didn't enjoy having this negative relationship. In fact, he hated it. His only real hope was to keep plugging ahead so that he could convince his dad to retire or at least taper down to far fewer hours in the office. Once they could lessen the day-to-day professional grind that was ever-present between them, Jeremy hoped they could return to being what they should be—father and son. "Hey. Good morning."

His dad took a seat on the leather sofa just inside the door of Jeremy's office. "I need to steal you for a few minutes. I spoke with Benjamin Summers on my way in."

Jeremy didn't need to hear another word to know that this was likely bad. "Why did he call you? I always make myself available to him. Always."

"He didn't. I called him."

Jeremy instantly found his hands balling up into fists. His neck went tight. His jaw, too. "He's my client. Why would you do that?"

"I'm seeing no movement on this case, Jeremy. I had to know that he was happy."

"Then ask me directly. I would've gotten you up to speed without you making me look bad to a client." Jeremy leaned forward in his chair and planted his elbow on his desk, closing his eyes and attempting to knead away the tension in his forehead with his hand. But the more he thought about it, the angrier he became. Finally, he pushed back from his desk and stood, marching over to his dad with determination. He wanted him to know that this was serious. He would not let this stand. "In fact, I'd say that what you did was wholly unprofessional. You don't just make me look bad, you make the entire firm look bad. And there's absolutely no reason for it other than the fact that you don't trust me to do what I need to do."

"I trusted you with the Patterson case. We all know how that ended."

"I was in the middle of getting a divorce and my soon-to-be ex-wife, who I thought loved me, was dragging my name through the tabloids. If I wasn't on top of my game at the time, I think it's understandable."

"You can't allow your personal life to get in the way of your job."

"And I might have let that happen one time, but it's not the case right now. Summers isn't budging on anything, and Eden's simply doesn't have the capital to pay him off in a single lump-sum cash payment, as he's demanding."

"Sometimes, it's a lawyer's job to convince a client that it's in their best interest to move the goalposts."

"I understand that. And I have tried. It's only been a few weeks. The trouble is that what I really think he wants is revenge. And I don't think that's possible."

His dad drew a deep breath through his nose, looking right at Jeremy, although in many ways it felt as though he was looking through him. Jeremy never felt that his dad truly saw him. "I just want you to get this done. Get together with Ms. Blackwell and remind her in person that she has no choice but to acquiesce to Summers's demands. I'm not buying that they don't have the cash. The Edens' war chest has to run deep."

Jeremy nodded. "I'll get it done. But it's not because you decided to interfere. I have it under control. I wish you knew that."

His dad stood, which was a great relief to Jeremy. Hopefully this meant he was leaving. "I don't care what it takes. Lock yourselves up in a room until there's only one person left standing."

Jeremy fought back a grin, which at least helped the tightness in his neck go away. How he would love a negotiation with Isabel that involved them locked away. The tougher she proved herself to be, the more he wanted to show her that he could match her intensity. In every way. "I'll suggest it."

"And another thing, you need to be careful with this Blackwell woman. I looked into her history and she's worked with some very high-level but shady clients. There's no telling what she'll pull to make Summers go away. We should be ready to torpedo her in the press if necessary."

Jeremy took a step forward. "Dad. No." Even he was surprised at his protective response. He might not know Isabel very well, but he didn't want his dad to go after her. Not like that. As someone who'd been taken down by the tabloids, Jeremy knew firsthand exactly how brutal it was. He didn't want that for anyone. Jeremy wasn't going to fault Isabel for the things she'd had to do professionally. He knew very well how lawyers could get pushed into a corner by a client and have no real choice but to work their way out. It was how you got ahead. It was how you made a name for yourself. "We're not doing that. It's unseemly and unnecessary."

"You're too soft, Jeremy. Always have been. You let Kelsey walk all over you. You're letting Summers do it to you, too."

I loved Kelsey. And I'm trying to make my client happy. "I'll get it done without torpedoing anyone. I will get both sides to meet somewhere in the middle."

His dad pursed his lips, a sign that he remained un-convinced. "It'd better be a lot closer to what Summers wants than the middle."

"It will be."

His dad turned to leave. No handshake. No pat on the shoulder. Just one lawyer leaving another lawyer's office. But he stopped when he reached the doorway. "Have you and your mother talked about the tree-trim-ming party?"

Christmas. Jeremy was so knee-deep in this case, his mother was the only thing reminding him that the holiday was just around the corner. "We did. A few days ago. Although there's not much to talk about, is there? We've been doing this every year on December 23 for as long as I can remember."

"And it's my job as your father to make sure you're going to be there. You're the only child and your mom looks forward to that night all year long."

"I will not disappoint her."

Jeremy's dad had hardly been gone a minute before Jeremy's phone rang. His heart sped up when he saw the caller ID. It was Isabel. "Hey there. Calling to give me a hard time about the cat again?"

"Have you seen the papers?" Isabel's voice could sometimes be cutting, but her tone was particularly icy.

"I haven't. I never read them."

"I suggest you do it right now. You can look online. Do a search for Eden's Department Store. I'm sure it'll come right up."

Jeremy took a seat at his desk. "Can I call you back when I'm done?"

"I'd rather wait on the line and hear your reaction."

This couldn't be good. "Ten minutes. I'll call you back. I promise." He ended the call and did exactly what she suggested. When the headline popped up in the search results, Jeremy's stomach sank so low it felt like it was at his knees. The words "secret affair" jumped right out at him.

Jeremy only had time to scan the article. He wanted to call Mr. Summers before he spoke to Isabel and he knew she'd hold him to the promise of ten minutes. The story laid out the facts as the two parties generally understood them. The bad of it was that these details had now become public information. The worst of it was the comments from Mr. Summers as contrasted with those from Mindy Eden. Mindy's only comment was, "Mr. Summers has made a claim and we're doing everything we can to negotiate with him in good faith. My sisters and I loved our grandmother very much and want everyone to know that she was a generous and kind person with a big heart."

Mr. Summers's comment wasn't quite so delicate. "Victoria Eden barged into my parents' marriage and destroyed it. She was a vile money-hungry woman who handed her naive granddaughters a business wrongly built on my father's money. I will get restitution if it's the last thing I do."

Jeremy physically winced when he reread it. Then he picked up the phone and called his client. "Mr. Summers. I saw your quote in the newspaper today. You have painted us into a corner."

"That reporter misquoted me."

"You might have to prove that to me. Do you know who fed the story to the papers in the first place?"

"I don't."

Jeremy wasn't convinced, but he had no evidence that his client had started this. "Okay, then. I'm calling to let you know that the Eden's team has read the article and they are not happy about the things you said. They could easily countersue you for defamation of character."

"You can't defame the dead. I looked it up."

"Ah, but survivors can make a claim that the defamation of their dead relative reflects on their reputation. Knowing Ms. Blackwell's previous legal work, I have no doubt she will make exactly that argument." Jeremy took in a deep breath and kept going. "Also, the Eden sisters are immensely popular in the city of New York. They are in the tabloids all the time. People love them and their store. So if you think that you could somehow get somewhere by bad-mouthing them to the press, you were sorely mistaken. Public opinion is important, Ben. And you have officially hurt your own chances by trying to mess with the Eden heiresses."

Mr. Summers cleared his throat. "What do you suggest I do? Call the reporter?"

"What's done is done. Nobody reads retractions, anyway. I want you to give me permission to negotiate with Eden's. You're going to have to give a little."

A distinct grumble came from the other end of the line. "Promise me you'll give up as little as possible."

"I'll do my best." Jeremy said goodbye and hung up, wasting no time returning Isabel's call. "I'm sorry," he said when she answered. "I saw the article. He claims he was misquoted, but regardless, people are reading it and I'm sorry that it happened in the first place. We need to get this hashed out."

"I can't negotiate with you if you won't give in on anything, Sharp."

He caught himself smiling. How could she do that when he was as stressed as could be? "Will you please stop calling me that? You've seen me naked. Can we go with Jeremy?"

"Are we starting negotiations already? Because I think you know that you're now the one at a disadvantage. Which means that technically, I can probably call you whatever I want."

Jeremy sat back in his chair and glanced out the window. It was starting to snow. He was tired. He really just wanted to get home. "If you're going to call me something bad, I think you should say it to my face."

"Oh, so now you'll meet with me in person? Now that you're forced to do it? That doesn't say much about your good faith, Jeremy."

Good God, it made heat rush through him to hear her say his first name. Inviting her to his place was not a great idea. But he had to get this done, get his dad and Mr. Summers off his back, and well, there was the matter of Cat, too. Isabel seemed to know what she was talking about when it came to his feline houseguest. "I know. I know. You were right all along. I owed you this meeting days ago. You can come to Brooklyn and meet Cat and we'll get things worked out."

"Actually, I was about to get on a plane back to DC. I've been kicked out of my hotel for the weekend and there are no vacancies this close to Christmas. My brother and Mindy both have some dreadful cold, so I don't want to stay with them. I can't afford to get sick."

Jeremy's mind was racing. He had more than enough room for Isabel. But could he resist her for a night or two? "I could put you up. If it's just for the weekend. In your own room, of course."

"You have that kind of space at your place?"

Jeremy wanted to keep things simple. He wasn't about to explain to Isabel that he had a big empty house because he'd been stupid enough to hope that someday he and his wife would have children. "I do. Plenty of room."

"Okay, then. Text me the address and I'll be there a little after noon, suitcase in hand."

Eight

Isabel had no idea what to expect when she got out of the car in front of Jeremy's brownstone. Overhead, the early-afternoon sky had darkened with clouds and big, fat flakes were falling steadily. Ahead, an ornate wrought iron gate awaited, with a long flight of stairs up to a beautiful arched wood door. It was straight out of a movie, but Isabel couldn't help but notice that Jeremy's neighbors all had Christmas wreaths or holiday garland adorning their facade. Not Jeremy. Not the guy who couldn't be bothered to give a cat a proper name. Which was just fine with Isabel. It wasn't like she was doing much better with celebrating the holiday.

She rang the bell and waited for Jeremy to answer. When he unlatched the lock and opened the door, she was presented with an image she admired a little too much—Jeremy with his salt-and-pepper temples wearing a black sweater and dark jeans. "You weren't kidding about the suitcase." He gestured with a nod.

"I never joke about imposing on someone for a night or two. Are you sure this is okay? Are you sure you have enough room?"

Jeremy rolled his eyes and reached for her bag. "I wouldn't extend the invitation if I didn't have the space. I've put up plenty of clients at the house."

"But never opposing counsel, I'm guessing." Isabel followed him inside, where a square of beautifully restored ebony penny-tile floor marked the landing. From this first peek, his home was a showplace, every detail exceptional. Above, the ceiling soared with graceful moldings, lit up by vintage fixtures of seeded glass and rich bronze. To her left, a staircase with neat white treads and a scrolled black railing led to the floor above, then doubled back, climbing to yet another level. Ahead, a glossy dark wood floor stretched the full length of the house, past what appeared to be living room and kitchen, ending when it reached tall leaded windows through which she saw only snow-dusted trees. Taking this all in felt like more than a view of Jeremy's residence. It felt like a look into his soul. For the man who seemed to bristle at any personal burden, keeping this home had to be, on some level, a labor of love.

He closed the door behind her, set down her bag and came up beside her, giving her a whiff of his irresistible smell. It was like the finest bourbon, rich and warm without any trace of booziness. "Actually, you'd be wrong about that. I did a negotiation here when another lawyer had a long layover at JFK. His flight got canceled and he ended up spending the night."

Isabel felt a little better about the propriety of this

now. Although given her history with Jeremy, their situation wasn't *exactly* the same. "I see."

"No need to be jealous," Jeremy said. "He wasn't anywhere near as cute as you."

Isabel blushed and smiled, but then a spark in his eye caught her gaze and she was immobilized by the zap of electricity only Jeremy could deliver. Mere inches separated them, reminding her body of how blissful it was to be pressed against him, comb her fingers through his thick hair and kiss him. The fact that he was tossing around words like *cute* wasn't making him any easier to resist.

"I hate that it's this close to Christmas and we have to do this," he said, leaning against the stair railing.

"As far as I'm concerned, as long as the fire alarm doesn't go off, this is a vacation."

"Brooklyn *is* lovely this time of year." It was Jeremy's turn to smile, but that only made her want him more. She was going to have to learn to ignore the four or five hundred irresistible traits he seemed to have. Too bad she needed the negotiations ahead to go smoothly. A little jerkish behavior on his part might help stem her personal tide of desire.

Isabel laughed. "It's fine. I don't celebrate Christmas anyway."

"Jewish?"

She shook her head. "No. Just a habit I got into a long time ago."

He pressed his lips together and nodded. "Come on. I'll show you the place."

Jeremy provided a quick tour of the main floor—a comfortable living room with chocolate-brown leather furniture in front of a stately fireplace with a carved white stone surround that had to be an antique. The kitchen was a cook's delight with a generous center island topped with Carrara marble and custom cabinets of creamy gray. The sink overlooked a courtyard off the back of the house, with a patio shielded from the outside world by a row of snow-flocked Italian cypress trees, the kind you see growing alongside the roads of Tuscany.

Isabel went to the window to admire Jeremy's outdoor retreat, an uncommon luxury, even in Brooklyn. "It's so lovely out there. It must be amazing to sit out there in the spring or summer with a book."

Jeremy came right up behind her and Isabel stayed impossibly still, keenly aware of her breaths as they filled her lungs. This house was a magical place, an oasis of calm and beauty in the middle of a bustling metropolis, and its owner a little too enticing. "Actually, it's even better in the fall, when there's a nip of cold in the air. I get the firepit going and can sit outside for hours."

That sounded like sheer heaven to Isabel. "The house is beautiful. Truly stunning." She dared to turn around and face him. In the natural light coming from the window, he was somehow even more handsome. More kissable.

"Thank you. It was a big project. It did not look like this when we bought it."

We, meaning he and his wife. She really didn't want Jeremy to know that she'd gone digging into his private history, so she kept that detail to herself. "Oh?"

He stuffed his hands into his pockets and cast his sights down at the floor. "Yeah. I was married until a few years ago. She really wanted a fixer-upper. I wanted a lot of space, so this was the perfect choice."

Before Isabel had a chance to comment, in traipsed an adorable orange tabby, clearly taking her time with her sizable belly. "Oh my God. That must be Cat."

"Unless I somehow managed to get another one, yes."

Isabel rushed over to her, crouched down and offered her hand. Cat rubbed up against the kitchen island, then did the same to Isabel's fingers. She immediately began to purr, pacing back and forth and brushing Isabel's knees with her tail. "She's so sweet. And so friendly." Isabel went ahead and sat on the floor, Cat purring even more loudly now that Isabel was able to pet her with both hands.

"Yeah. She's been coming to my back door for a while now. I saw her the other morning and it was so cold out, I couldn't leave her out there. My housekeeper put up flyers in the neighborhood and the veterinarian said she isn't microchipped, so we don't know who she belongs to."

"Must just be a neighborhood cat. We had a few of those around when I was growing up. My mom was crazy about cats." Isabel looked up at Jeremy. "They all ended up living at our house in one form or another. Even the ones who were too skittish to come inside got taken to the vet and immunized and fixed. My mom bankrolled it all."

"Wow."

Isabel's heart felt heavy just thinking about her mom. In her mind, she could see her out on their back patio, dishing up wet food for any cat who cared to show up. She talked to them all, gave them all names. She was a woman who was so full of love that showering her kids and husband with it simply wasn't enough. It said a lot about her—Isabel and Sam had never gone a day without feeling truly loved by their mom. "I need to get a kitty when I find a place." She'd never taken the time to get one when she lived in DC, but now that she was shifting her life in a more meaningful direction, a cat or even a few were an obvious choice.

"I know where you can get a pretty cute orange one."

Isabel grinned and looked Cat in the face. "If I adopt you, you're getting a new and better name. No question about that."

"Go for it."

"Are you seriously not going to keep her?" Isabel asked, getting up from the floor. "She has such a wonderful personality and she seems to be comfortable here."

Cat meowed and rubbed up against Jeremy's leg.

"I'm just not a pet person. My life is so crazy with work, it's hard to imagine caring for another living thing."

Isabel nodded. She'd felt that way for a long time. Not anymore. "Right. Work. I guess you'd better show me to my room so we can get something accomplished today."

Having Isabel in his home—a woman he'd kissed, laughed with, made love to and even argued against—was leaving Jeremy off-balance. A different energy had tiptoed into his private world, and it was both confusing and exhilarating to experience. There was just enough inkling of his past to make him again question what in the world he was doing by allowing himself to be so drawn to her. He and Isabel might be opponents professionally, but there was no denying that they could effortlessly slip into comfortable conversation. They seemed to naturally fall in sync. There was a part of him, deep in his core, that craved that so badly he would do anything to have it. But a bigger part of him had hardened around his needs and desires. That shell was there to protect him, but it was exhausting to carry around all day. He could set it aside when he was at home, and with the snow coming down outside and the weekend stretched out before them, he was in no mood to put it back on again.

With her suitcase in tow, he led her upstairs to the guest room, carrying it inside and setting it down on a bench at the foot of the bed. "It's no Bacharach, but the mattress is incredibly comfortable."

"I'd say it's a big step up for me. I haven't heard a single fire alarm since I got here." Isabel took her handbag and laptop bag and placed them on the bed. She smoothed her hand over the butter-soft duvet. "Ooh. Nice."

Just like the night they met, Jeremy was having to remind himself to slow down. It would be way too easy to kiss her right now and show her exactly how nice that bedding was. "You have your own bath." He traipsed over to the door and flipped on the light for her. When he turned back, she was sitting on the edge of the bed, looking as perfect as he could imagine.

"Thank you. Seriously. This works out great for me, and not just because I needed a place to sleep. I'm eager to get this case squared away. It's of monumental importance."

"To the Eden family or to you?"

"Take your pick. Yes, it's a job, and I'm being paid well to do it, but over the course of the last few weeks, Mindy and her sisters have been amazing to me. They've even invited me to celebrate Christmas with them."

"I thought you didn't celebrate."

"I haven't made the effort, but that doesn't mean I won't take part. I love this time of year and I used to be the sort of person who lived for every minute of

Christmas. It's just been a while since I took much joy in it. Like a bad habit, which I suppose is possible for anyone to fall into. Something doesn't feel as good as it used to and so you turn your back on it."

That got the gears in his head going. It was an incredibly insightful thing to say. Jeremy didn't want to tread too heavily on Isabel's personal life, but he was curious. "Any particular reason it stopped feeling good? Work? Career?"

"Work definitely kept me away from it, but this started way before that. My mom. And my dad." She pulled in a breath through her nose, her shoulders rising up to her ears. "They both passed away the same year. It's just been Sam and me since then."

"Oh, wow. I'm so sorry. I didn't know."

She nodded and painted a smile on her face, like she felt a need to comfort him. "So that's why it's important to me to make the Eden sisters happy. You don't luck into a new family very often."

"That sounds nice. A tidy little package." Jeremy decided against giving in to his greatest inclination at the moment, which was to express the depths of his skepticism. In his experience, families like the Edens would turn their backs on you just as easily as they welcomed you in. "Your brother must be part of this for you, too."

"Absolutely. I love seeing him happy for once in his life, and he's so over the moon for Mindy. They are so in love, it's amazing. I doubt they'll ever get around to planning a real wedding. They just want to get the show on the road."

"I wish them the best of luck."

"Don't you mean happiness?"

"Personally? I think luck plays a much bigger role." Isabel reached out with her foot and knocked it against his calf. "Hey. That's not nice. They aren't even married yet and you're acting like they're getting ready for a divorce."

Funny, but he never fully appreciated just how pessimistic he'd become until someone took the time to pick apart his words. "You're right. You're absolutely right. Just because I got burned doesn't mean that some people don't have a happy ending."

Isabel reached into her purse and pulled out a lip balm, glossing it over her sumptuous lips. "Sorry. It's so dry out this time of year."

Jeremy cleared his throat, trying to keep from admiring her mouth.

"And it's okay that you're down on love," she continued. "I get it. I've been burned a few times, too."

"Oh yeah? Anybody I know?"

Isabel smirked. "Like I would actually tell you. And no, I'm guessing you don't know him. He was…" She pursed her lips and furrowed her brow. "Let's just say that he wasn't much for the idea of commitment."

He nodded, knowing all too well what it was like to be on the business end of someone who was willing to take promises and devotion and toss them in the trash. "That's a problem for a lot of guys." It didn't used to be an issue for Jeremy at all. He was once the guy who said "I love you" at the drop of a hat. He used to be the sort of man who made romantic gestures any day of the week, not just on Valentine's Day, Christmas and anniversaries. But when you're endlessly giving, and that generosity is labeled as "not enough," it's hard to see the point in making an effort. At his age, Jeremy wasn't convinced it would ever be worth it to try.

"I was probably asking too much of this guy. But it was just the situation we were in. I try not to harbor too many bad feelings about it. Holding on to that stuff will eat you alive."

"What was he like? The guy who couldn't commit?"

Surprise crossed Isabel's face. "Why do you want to know?"

Jeremy shrugged it off as trivial, but he was so interested in the answer he wasn't sure he could take it if she declined. Perhaps it was because he was still trying so damn hard to figure out what made her tick. "I don't know. Curious, I guess."

She got up from the bed, placed her hand on his shoulder and peered up into his eyes. "Don't worry. He wasn't nearly as cute as you."

Jeremy fought to hold back the full force of the smile that wanted to spread across his face. He loved their back-and-forth. He loved talking to her. For the first time in his entire career, he couldn't have been more excited about negotiations if he tried. "Honestly, I'm surprised you ever had a single man walk away from you. You seem like the type of woman who does the burning."

"I may run hot, but I know better than to set a good thing on fire."

Jeremy swallowed hard.

"And on that note," she said, pulling a legal pad out of her laptop bag, "I think we should get to work."

Nine

The snow kept falling, and Isabel and Jeremy kept working. In the moments when the negotiation grew particularly complicated or even contentious, both Isabel and Jeremy would stare out the window of his home office, watching the fat flakes drift to earth. They were hypnotic and calming, and they both seemed to need the escape, and what a perfect setting, tucked away in Jeremy's cozy office, the room lined with books and decorated with masculine furniture in dark wood and leather.

"It's really coming down out there." Jeremy tossed a pen onto the small conference table they were working at and leaned back in his office chair. He stretched his arms high over his head, causing the hem of his sweater to inch up, revealing a peek of his stomach.

Isabel was nothing if not incredibly distracted by this subtle reminder that her hands, and her mouth for that matter, had once been all over his incredible torso. "It is. The sky's getting dark, too."

Chair tilted back at an angle, Jeremy consulted his watch. "It's nearly five. Do you want to keep going? Or we could take a break."

Isabel flipped through her notes—they'd made so much progress on a compromise for the interest calculations on the loan repayment, along with a schedule for getting Mr. Summers his money. But there were other options she was hoping she'd convince Jeremy to run by his client. "Depends on how generous you're feeling about talking through the alternate forms of repayment I've proposed."

"We've been over this, Isabel. Do you really think that's a good idea? Give my client a chunk of Eden's in exchange for the loan? Right now, both parties despise each other."

"Ten percent is hardly a chunk. It's not like your client would have any control. Just enough to make him a tidy sum every year."

"I really don't see it. With the volatility in retail, I'd have a hard time advising him to take that."

"The store is doing great."

He was still sitting with his chair leaned all the way back, hands clasped and resting on top of his head. He raised both eyebrows and looked down his nose at her. It was inexplicably hot. "If it was truly doing great, you'd be able to fork over the money and we wouldn't be discussing this at all."

"What about a piece of the online business? Would you be happier with that?"

"I'd need to see the numbers."

"Okay, then. Let's get it done."

"Such a shark. Gotta keep swimming, huh?"

"We're so close to figuring this out."

An hour later, everything but the smallest of details had been ironed out. "Did we really just do that?" Jeremy asked, seeming incredulous.

"We did." Isabel surveyed the landscape of the meeting table, which was strewn with papers, files and notes. She couldn't help but feel at least a little jubilant, even though she knew from experience that things could fall apart any time. For now, she would be happy. She held up her hand and reached across the table. "High five?"

"Yes." Jeremy smiled and smacked his hand against hers. "Good job."

From the doorway, Cat meowed loudly, then padded her way to Jeremy. It was at least the fifth or sixth such interruption.

"She seems restless," Isabel said. "I wonder if it's close to kitten time. Has she nested anywhere in the house?"

Jeremy reached down to show Cat some affection. "I have no clue what you're talking about."

"Nesting. Finding herself a safe and cozy spot to have the kittens."

"The vet had me put a blanket in a cardboard box, but I can't get her to stay in it. She's been sleeping on the floor of my closet since she got here."

It was adorable how truly clueless Jeremy was about this. "My guess is she's planning on giving birth in there."

"Seriously?" His eyes went wide with horror. "In my closet?"

"Why don't you show me?"

"Yeah. Absolutely. No more reason to hang out in here today."

Jeremy got up from his chair and Isabel followed

him out of the room, down the hall to the last door on the left. Inside was a magnificent and sumptuous bedroom, tastefully decorated with a warm touch. The bed seemed to go on forever, with a charcoal-gray duvet and plump pillows. Overhead, a wrought iron chandelier gave the space a soft glow. The windows, overlooking the back patio, brought in the perfect amount of natural light.

"No wonder you've never needed a sleep mask. This room is so peaceful. I think I could sleep in here for days."

Jeremy smiled. "You don't need that thing at home, do you? I mean, if you aren't staying in a hotel?"

Isabel brushed her fingers on the silky soft bedding. "Depends on how worn out I am." She instantly regretted her choice of words, especially when Jeremy cocked an eyebrow.

Cat sauntered into the room and darted right into the closet.

"I'm telling you, you're about to have a bunch of kittens in with your designer suits and Italian leather shoes." Isabel nodded at the closet. "May I?"

"Please. Be my guest."

Isabel stepped inside and Jeremy was right behind her, flipping on the light. Either Jeremy was an incredibly smart man or his ex had been highly concerned with her appearance. His closet had the sort of lighting you find at a cosmetics counter, gentle enough to make anyone look amazing. Which of course meant that Jeremy appeared flawless, even with his stubble showing the effects of late day.

"She's been sleeping down here." Jeremy pulled back a row of dress shirts to reveal the back corner, where sure enough, Cat had made herself a bed. "Hey. Wait a minute. That's my favorite T-shirt." He crouched down. Isabel knelt next to him. "I wondered where that went. I took it off the other morning to take a shower after my workout and never saw it again."

Isabel was momentarily stuck on the mental image of Jeremy in the shower, with droplets of water on his chest. She'd never wanted so badly to have a bar of soap in her hands. "Did you think it just disappeared? She clearly stole it. Dragged it in here to make her bed."

He shook his head in disbelief. "I figured I must have tossed it in the hamper and didn't remember doing it. I have a lot on my mind these days."

She couldn't help but notice the weighty drag in his voice. Not putting much thought into it, she placed her hand on the center of his back to comfort him, but that caused him to look at her, his gray eyes showing mysterious flecks of blue in this light. If they were a window into his soul, she wished she could see some true happiness in there. She was desperate for a reason *not* to kiss him. Make him happy. She could do that, at least for a little while, with the snow falling heavily outside.

Jeremy cleared his throat and returned his sights to Cat's nest. "I can't believe she stole my stinky, sweaty T-shirt."

"It means she loves you. Pets love things that smell like their owners."

"I'm not her owner. This is temporary." He stood up and stepped away, as if that could somehow extricate him from the situation.

"Uh-huh. Tell that to Cat."

He turned back to her, kneading his forehead. "How do I get her to not have the kittens in here? Won't it make a big mess?"

"First off, you don't get her to do anything. If she's

happy and feels safe there, you should let her do her thing. You do not want to get into a battle of wills with a mama cat. Second, we can put down an old towel or two and you can toss them out once the kittens arrive."

"What about the T-shirt?"

She patted his shoulder in consolation. "I think that's pretty much a goner."

"I never should have let her in that morning."

"Oh, Jeremy, no. You had to do it. She could have died out there. Her and her kittens. You did the right thing."

He twisted his lips, which made her think he was considering the other side of the coin she'd just shown him. "You really are good at forming an argument."

She loved not only knowing that she could show him when he was wrong, but that he would actually listen. She found that a rare quality in a man, especially a lawyer. "Thanks. I appreciate that. Now what do I have to do to convince you to open a bottle of wine?"

"You don't. It's six on a Friday and there's cause for celebration. I can't believe it's taken us this long to get around to it."

"You're speaking my language. I'm just going to grab my purse from the guest room. I can't live this time of year without lip balm."

Down the hall they went, making a brief stop so Isabel could fetch her bag, then descending the stairs and back to the kitchen. Isabel perched on a barstool at the kitchen island and watched Jeremy go to work. "Red or white?" he asked.

She glanced out the patio windows. The snow was still pretty and fluffy, but the wind had started to whip. "Considering the weather? Definitely red."

"Perfect. I have a Spanish rioja that's absolutely delicious."

"Sounds amazing."

Jeremy opened a tall cabinet at the far end of the kitchen, which had a waist-high wine chiller below and diagonal bottle storage above, the entire setup going from floor to ceiling.

"It's like your own little cellar."

"There's a real cellar downstairs on the ground floor. I got really into wine about ten years ago. I was starting to wonder if I was going to be a bachelor forever, so I figured I might get a hobby." He brought the bottle to the island and expertly opened it, then pulled two glasses from an upper cabinet near the fridge.

"And then you met the woman you married and the bachelor was reformed?" Isabel was indeed curious about the notion of Jeremy seeing himself as never getting married, and that apparently changing at some point.

"It had nothing to do with being reformed. I was on board from the beginning."

"Head over heels?"

"I guess you could say that, but she also had a way of sweeping you up into her world. Or maybe sucking you into the eye of her personal hurricane is a more apt analogy."

"She sounds lovely."

Jeremy laughed. "It happened fast. That's all I can tell you. I think she liked the fact that I wasn't the typical Manhattan playboy. She'd dated a lot of guys like that." He filled their glasses and handed her one. "Cheers. To not talking about my ex-wife."

Isabel took a quick sip. "It's delicious. Thank you. But not so fast." She had questions. A lot of questions.

Things weren't entirely adding up. "Okay, confession time. I looked you up on the internet after the first meeting at your office."

"Of course you did."

"You did the same thing to me, did you not?"

He brought his glass around to the other side of the island, but didn't sit with her. "Come on. If we're going to talk about this, we're going in the living room. I'd rather be comfortable while discussing unpleasant subjects." He didn't wait for her reply, but instead wandered off.

Isabel followed in earnest, worried she'd hurt him. "I don't mean for it to be unpleasant. I'm just curious because what you're telling me isn't matching up with what I read."

He set his glass and the bottle on the coffee table and began building a fire in the fireplace, crumpling up newspaper, then stacking logs across it and striking a match. She stood and watched him work. "Isabel. As a former Washington, DC, lawyer with a bunch of very high-profile clients, I have to think that you would know better than anyone that what's in the paper isn't always the full story. A lot of it has to do with who gets there first."

"Well, sure. Things get twisted. But they don't usually take a one-eighty."

He stood and brushed his hands off on his pants, then pointed to the couch. "Please. Sit."

She felt like she was in trouble, and just like upstairs when he'd admonished her during negotiations, she found it incredibly sexy. "Yes, sir." She did as she was told, sinking down into the comfortable cushions. The fire began to crackle and blaze. Between the wine and Jeremy, she never wanted to leave the room.

"Actually, a one-eighty is the perfect way to spin something." He took a long draw of his wine and Isabel admired his profile in the golden glow of the fire. "It's a believable story since it's true, so you simply take whatever you're guilty of and accuse the other person of it."

"So if I'm a woman who wants out of my marriage, but I'm worried about how that will be perceived, I tell the press that my husband isn't the settling-down type, or that he isn't loving."

He turned to her, his eyes full of resignation. She'd seen this expression from him before, the look of someone who was hurt and sad, but who had learned to live with it. Isabel hated the idea that anyone would have to live that way, especially a man as extraordinary as Jeremy. "Precisely."

Isabel took another sip of her wine, her mind still churning. No wonder the things she'd read about Jeremy had seemed so off. "I almost hate to ask this…"

A corner of his mouth shot up in a wry smile. "You don't hate to ask anything."

She leaned forward and grasped his forearm. "No. I really don't want to upset you. Truly. I don't. You've been nothing but gracious in letting me stay here."

"Go for it. I have no secrets."

Isabel found herself hoping that was really true. Because every minute with Jeremy was starting to feel like the start of something.

I really don't want to upset you. Even though Isabel was capable of a good sneak attack, he was sure of what she was about to ask. He'd never spoken about it to anyone. His parents spent their time making themselves the victims by claiming their own embarrassment at the way their son had been dragged through the tabloids. His friends made themselves scarce after the divorce. Nobody wanted to go out to dinner with the guy who was getting snide comments from perfect strangers who'd sided with the socialite. So Jeremy kept it all bottled up inside, another attempt at holding on to his pride.

"I shouldn't ask," she said. "Let's talk about something else."

"No. Please. Just do it. Let's put the whole thing to rest. Honestly, it'll be a relief."

"Was it all a one-eighty? There was a suggestion that you'd been unfaithful." She held up a finger. "And before you answer, I want to make it clear that I will not judge you. Everyone has their reasons for doing things."

Jeremy had every reason in the world to keep a wall up with Isabel, both personal and professional. But the reality of their situation was that they were close to wrapping up negotiations. Their clients would come away happy. As for the personal side, she was so easy to talk to. It had been like that from the moment he'd met her. There was something almost therapeutic about baring his soul to her. "Everything she did to sabotage our marriage, or every unpleasant feeling she had, she put on me. The thing about not being made for commitment, the thing about not being the settling-down type. So yes, there was infidelity, and it was all hers."

"I'm so sorry. That's such a terrible betrayal."

She wasn't wrong. It had been. But now that it was years later and he couldn't imagine himself with Kelsey at all, the pain wasn't quite so persistent. "I didn't find out about the affair until after she left. I've somehow convinced myself that it wasn't that bad because I didn't know about it while it was going on. That might be some faulty logic at work."

"Those are the things we say when we're trying to protect ourselves. There's only so much hurt a person can endure."

"Is there really a maximum? Sometimes life keeps throwing stuff at you, whether you want it or not."

"I have to ask why you didn't stand up to her. You had no comment in the article I read. I have a hard time imagining you taking that lying down. A lawyer always fights back."

"But a lawyer also knows when to quit. Some battles just aren't worth it. Plus, who wants to get into a fight over love? In the newspapers? Either it's there between you or it isn't. You can't just pull it out of thin air. And it wasn't like I was going to convince her to come back."

He watched as she sank farther back against the cushions, wineglass in hand. What kind of pain had she endured? Was that why she sometimes seemed like such a mystery? "Now that I told you my sad story, I want to know if I can ask about the guy who burned you."

She looked down into the rioja in her glass, swirling it round and round. "Bad timing. It wasn't all his fault. It was an unfortunate situation."

"Those are an awful lot of vague details."

"Okay, then. Here are the specifics. I got pregnant and he panicked. He couldn't handle it. We'd only been going out about six months and it had been very casual." She breathed deeply and sighed. "So I did him a favor and I called if off. I already knew that I wanted to have a baby, so I decided I would just deal with it on my own, but then life decided to throw me the cruelest of curveballs when I lost the pregnancy." Her voice cracked when she uttered those last few words. The room fell impossibly quiet.

"I'm so sorry. That must have been awful."

"Nobody knows about it. I mean, he must have figured it out when I never had a baby, but it's not like he ever checked in on me or asked."

"You never told your brother what happened?"

A sad smile crossed her lips. "You know, I thought about it, but I don't think Sam would have dealt very well with it. I think it would have made him feel helpless, and I didn't see any good in that. So I dusted myself off and I went back to work and I tried to forget."

She was so tough. So resilient. No wonder she made such an excellent attorney. "Back to being a shark?"

"That's the last thing I am." Isabel waved it off.

"A beautiful shark, of course."

Her eyes flashed in the soft light from the fireplace. "Flattery will get you everywhere."

"I'm no dummy."

"And I'm serious when I say I'm not a shark. It's an act. Acting is how you win. You can't tell me you aren't the same way."

"I'm not acting right now."

Cocking her head to one side, a dark strand of her hair fell across her cheek. The way she narrowed her sights on him made him feel as vulnerable as he'd felt in a very long time. "I believe that. But when you're working, you have on your armor. You're ready for battle. And if I'm being completely honest, I think you were playing an act the night we met."

Jeremy reached for the wine bottle and poured more into her glass before topping off his own. "Isn't everyone on their best behavior when they first meet? Trying to impress the other person?"

"Yes, and that's why I didn't want to talk about work. I wanted us to just be a man and a woman having a conversation."

"And you think I was faking my way through it? I guarantee you, I didn't fake a damn thing up in your room. That was all legit."

Isabel grinned, her cheeks flushing pink. "I believe that. I do. It's the first part of the night when you were acting. Playing the part of the fun-loving guy."

"Hey. I love fun. I just don't have a lot of it."

"But you're not as cavalier as you try to make yourself seem. You act like nothing bothers you, but you aren't like that. You're thoughtful and serious." She took another sip of her wine, then scooted closer on the couch. "And now that you've told me the story about your marriage, I know why. You're trying to hide your pain from everyone."

Jeremy swallowed back the emotion of having her see right through him. "I just don't want to feel hurt anymore. That's all that is. So I pretend like it's not there and I figure it'll eventually go away."

Slowly and evenly, she nodded, gazing up at him with her sweet and tenderhearted eyes. He loved that she had so many sides, that she was a woman of many facets. She could be determined one minute and gentle the next. "I know. I just want you to know that you don't have to pretend with me." She ran her finger around the rim of her wineglass. "We're nearly off the clock."

"Just a man and a woman having a conversation."

"No hiding."

Two simple words from Isabel and a wave of heat rose in Jeremy, starting in his thighs and rolling upward, taking hold in his hips, stomach and chest. He fixed his gaze on her, on the rise and fall of her breaths, the flush in her cheeks, the brilliant flash of life in her eyes. Electricity was arcing between them. A current. A jolt. One minute they were talking work and life and pain and now…well, he would have had to be a complete idiot to not notice that this was all leading somewhere he hadn't quite planned on.

What was it about Isabel that didn't merely tug at his heartstrings, but unraveled them? It was more than attraction, although that was its own powerful force. There was a connection between them, one that went beyond working together.

"I was hiding from you this week." The words rolled out of his mouth as if he'd planned to say them all along, which he hadn't at all, but it still felt good to own up to it. So good that he wanted to keep going. "That night at dinner, all I wanted to do was kiss you. But the pressure is on with this case and I worried I would end up sabotaging myself if I spent any time with you."

"So you invited me here because you didn't have a choice."

He shook his head. "No. I invited you because I had a reason. I finally had a legitimate reason to do what I'd wanted to do all along."

"I have an admission of my own." She sat forward, angling her body toward his.

Jeremy's pulse picked up, running along at a clip. "I'm listening."

"I thought about kissing you way before dinner. I thought about it that day in your office."

All he wanted was for her to bend at the waist and plant her soft lips on his. He wanted to feel her body pressed against his. He wanted to get lost in her and never be found. "And since then?"

"There's been a lot of inner conflict over it." She licked her lower lip and placed her wineglass on the coffee table, which felt like an ultimatum—kiss me, or don't.

Jeremy didn't want to leave any challenge from Isabel unaccepted.

Ten

Isabel was tired of waiting. She had to have Jeremy. The trouble was, the fragile parts of her ego really wanted him to make the first move. And he was being the perfect gentleman. Apparently setting aside her wineglass and biting down on her lower lip were not enough of an invitation.

She scooted closer to him on the couch, pulling her leg up all the way onto the cushion and facing him. Looking at him was both the easiest thing in the world and the most difficult—he was so handsome, it made the center of her chest burn. The fire popped and crackled, the heat warming one side of her face. He tossed back the last of his wine, as if needing liquid encouragement, and there was a very big part of her that wanted to just come out and say it—*I want you, Jeremy. Now.*

He finally placed his own glass on the table and turned to her, his eyes beautifully dark with desire. She'd wanted plenty of men in her lifetime, but none as bad as Jeremy. None so bad that it made it hard to breathe. Whether it was unfinished business or the notion of false starts, they both deserved this.

"I don't want you to feel as though I'm taking advantage," he said, reaching for her hand, caressing her fingers softly. "It's my house and you're vulnerable here."

Isabel's heart *and* body were aching for his touch. "I don't know that I've ever felt more comfortable. Anywhere." She inched herself closer until their knees were touching, then she took his other hand and raised it to her lips. Even that one touch of skin against skin left her nearly gasping for more. She had to be closer. She had to be next to him. And it had to happen now.

Isabel shifted up onto her knees and straddled Jeremy's lap. The pleased look on his face was her reward for bravery. She let her weight settle, pressing her hips into his, already the heat and need pooling between her legs. Her hands went to the hem of her sweater and she pulled it up over her head, her hair collapsing around her shoulders when she cast the garment aside. She loved falling under his appraisal, his dark eyes scanning her body. She didn't need him to tell her she was beautiful. She saw it all in his expression.

The first kiss was the softest, as if they were marking the moment. The beginning. His lips were just as firm and perfect as she remembered. Possibly more so. She set her elbows on his shoulders and dug her fingers into his thick hair, rocking her center against his. She could already feel how hard he was, even through the layers of denim between them. Their tongues wound together. He ran his across her lower lip. His warm hands roved the landscape of her back, then he finally had the good sense to remove her shirt and unhook her bra, pulling the straps forward to be rid of it. He took her breasts in his hands, cupping them completely and rolling her nipples between his fingers. Her skin gathered and grew hard beneath his touch, the perfect contrast to the softness of the kiss. But she wanted his lips and tongue everywhere, so she wrenched her mouth from his.

He took the invitation, licking and sucking one nipple, then the other, his hands squeezing her breasts firmly. Electricity zapped from her chest straight to her center, as if there were a line connecting the two. It felt so good that she wanted to close her eyes and simply languish in the sensation, but it was so hot to watch his face as he flicked his tongue against the tight buds of sensitive skin. Isabel curled her fingers into his shoulders, letting her nails dig into his skin. Jeremy's eyes popped open and he looked up at her, their gazes connecting before he took a gentle bite of her nipple. It was the perfect amount of pain, just enough to show how much he wanted her. It took every bit of pent-up desire inside her and ratcheted it up another notch.

Isabel reached down and lifted his sweater up over his head, spreading her hands across his glorious chest, firm and muscled with the perfect amount of hair. She kissed one sculpted shoulder, then across his clavicle, nestling her face in his neck, letting the stubble scratch at her nose and cheek while she inhaled his warm smell. Jeremy's hands were at both of her hips, squeezing hard and pulling her against him even more tightly. White-hot liquid heat pooled between her legs as she felt his erection against her center.

Both of his hands traveled north to the middle of her back and the next thing she knew, he had shifted her until she was lying back on the couch, the leather cool against her overheated skin. Jeremy stood and shucked his jeans and boxers, never taking his eyes off her. He was everything she wanted, long and lean and so primed for her that it was impossible to not feel lucky. She wedged her mind in the moment and focused on the physical, like the way her need picked up when she watched him take his steely length into his own hand and give it a few careful strokes. She loved seeing his own hand on his body, but it also made her desperate to touch him.

Isabel unbuttoned her jeans and lifted her hips off the couch, shimmying them and her panties down her legs. Jeremy helped her pull them from her ankles and then she was completely bare to him, ready and dying to have him inside her. "Come here," she said, her voice sounding a bit desperate.

"I want to see you touch yourself," he replied.

Isabel wasn't much of an exhibitionist, but Jeremy had her so turned on right now, she would have done anything he wanted. She dropped one foot to the floor and eased her knee up, spreading her legs. She brushed her fingertips against her chest, down along the flat plane of skin between her breasts. The anticipation on Jeremy's face was priceless. He watched her, both enthralled and speechless, standing next to her and stroking his erection. She studied what he liked, even as she relished her own touch as her fingers rode down her belly and finally between her legs.

A gasp left her lips when she touched her apex, the skin warm and slick with desire. She began to move her fingers in delicate circles, feeling as though she could rocket into space in no time at all if she wasn't careful. Jeremy lowered himself to a kneeling position before her, kissing the knee of the leg that was still up on the couch. Isabel didn't stop with the ministrations, even when it was pushing her even closer to her peak. She wanted to see what he would do next. She was desperate for it.

He kissed his way along her inner thigh and she moved her hands out of the way to comb his thick hair as he moved lower. His mouth found her center and he used his fingers to gently spread her folds and give himself better access. As hot as it was, Isabel's eyes clamped shut as he drove her to her peak with his tongue, which traveled in circles hard against her. She did her best to hold off on the pressure, but it eventually became too much, and she felt the dam break, the way her body gave in to him completely. She knocked her head back and called out as she rode out wave after wave of warmth and pleasure. On the other side of the room, the fire continued to roar, but Isabel knew that the heat coming from it was only a fraction of what Jeremy was about to give to her.

Jeremy took one more taste of Isabel, wanting to be immersed in the sensory delights of her unbelievably gorgeous body. Everything about her was soft and sweet, yet hot and carnal. If things between them never went any further than tonight, at least he'd always have the mental image of her touching herself, of her fingers rolling over her most delicate places, while the heat of the room flushed her skin with a breathtaking shade of pink.

But right now, he had more pressing needs. He had to be inside her. Isabel pulled her legs back, then knelt down next to him on the floor and pushed the coffee table a good foot or so away from them. Jeremy stretched out on the plush area rug as Isabel positioned herself between his knees, taking his throbbing erection into her hands and stroking delicately. Everything in his body went tight—his abs, his hips and thighs. She took her time and he loved watching as her slender fingers rode his length, up and down. As good as it felt, he wanted more of her, and as if she knew what he was thinking, she lowered her head and took him between her plump lips.

Her tongue was hot and wet on his skin, which was already straining from the tension. He couldn't think of another time he'd been so hard or wanted a woman so badly. He gently rolled his fingers through her silky hair as she swirled her tongue and made it nearly impossible to think about anything other than pleasure and warmth. Just when he was starting to feel as though he couldn't take much more of the pressure, Isabel released him from her mouth, kissing his lower belly.

"Don't move. I'm going to get a condom from my purse." She flitted off to the kitchen and was back in seconds, tearing open the packet and kneeling next to him. She then climbed on top of him, taking his length in her hand and guiding him inside.

As she sank down on top of him, he marveled at how well they fit together, how this was even better than that first night together, when logic said that it could never be better because the excitement of everything new tends to eclipse the familiar. They moved together, perfectly in sync, and Isabel lowered her head to kiss him. Their tongues wound together as his fingers roamed down her back to the velvety skin of her bottom, his hands encouraging her to raise her hips as far as she could, only because it felt so damn good to have her ride his entire length.

The pressure was building in his hips, and everything was pulling tight again. Isabel's breaths were ragged, but he wanted her closer before he came, so he slipped one of his hands between their bodies and found her center with his thumb. She countered with pressure of her own, pressing her pelvis into his harder and harder, grinding her body in a circle with every pass.

Isabel rounded her back, using her hips to force him closer to his peak. He clamped his eyes shut and his body gave way, pleasure pulsing and slamming into him. Isabel followed mere seconds later, burying her face in his neck and rotating her hips, making the final waves longer and even more pleasurable. She collapsed on top of him, warm and a bit sweaty, resting her head against his chest. He wrapped his arms around her tightly and kissed the top of her head over and over again. There were no words between them and Jeremy felt that was only fitting. They had exchanged plenty of them in the few short weeks they'd known each other. It was nice to get back to a place where they could let actions speak louder than words.

She rolled to his side and curled into him. He wrapped his arm around her waist and for a moment, they both got lost in the warm flicker of the fire. This was not how he'd imagined tonight going, but if he was being honest, it was everything he ever could have hoped for.

Eleven

Jeremy woke with a feeling he hadn't had in a long time—hope. He was also drunk on infatuation. Isabel was simply amazing, and last night had been unbelievable. Everything he'd thought about their sexual chemistry had been on the money. He hadn't made it up.

"Good morning, beautiful," he said, kissing her bare shoulder.

She smiled, eyes still closed, lying on her stomach. The early light of day filtered in through the windows, bathing her in a bright and beautiful glow. "Good morning."

He cozied up next to her, their naked bodies pressed together. It was so good to not wake up alone. "What do you want to do today?"

In response, Isabel's stomach rumbled loudly. "Food might be a good idea."

"We never ate last night, did we?"

She opened an eye and popped up onto her elbow.

"We did not. I feel like I should file a complaint, except you're still way ahead of the Bacharach. Not a single siren went off in the middle of the night."

"We never would've met if it weren't for that silly alarm."

She rolled to her back and clutched the covers to her chest. "We still would have met. It just would've been under far different circumstances."

Their first rendezvous had set the stage for last night, so he was immensely thankful that things had played out the way they had. "I'm glad the first time we encountered each other wasn't at the negotiating table."

"Me, too." She leaned forward and kissed him. "Now let's get some food. I'm starving."

Downstairs in the kitchen, Jeremy put some bacon in a skillet and began cracking eggs for breakfast. Cat had come downstairs for her own morning meal, which Isabel dished up for her before taking a seat at the center island. "I like watching a man cook."

"Lots of years as a bachelor," he said. "And my ex didn't cook anyway, so it was all up to me." Looking back, he should have known it was never going to last. Kelsey spent too little time in this house. She was always out, desperate for her next adventure. It had taken a long time for him to figure out that her absence wasn't about him. It was about the bottomless hole in her psyche that would always need filling.

"What did you and your wife plan to do with all of this space anyway?"

Jeremy dished up the bacon and eggs and grabbed slices of buttered toast, then ferried the plates to the island. "Madam, your breakfast is served."

Her entire face lit up when she smiled. "Thank you, sir."

He took the seat next to her. "I assumed we would have kids, and if we were going to create our dream house, it only seemed logical to me that we would have space for a growing family. That never happened, obviously. I wanted kids and she did not."

Isabel sipped her coffee, hands wrapped around the mug. "Did you guys not talk about it ahead of time? That's a pretty important topic before marriage."

"We did discuss it. I told her that I wanted a family and she said she did, too. But when it came time to try to get pregnant, she kept secretly taking her birth control pills. I guess she just never had the guts to tell me she'd changed her mind. Or she'd been lying to me all along." He was proud of himself for saying all of that without losing his cool. Something about Isabel made it so easy to confide in her. "Maybe I'm not cut out for parenthood, anyway. My own parents did not embrace their role."

"I wouldn't call your dad warm and fuzzy. At least what I saw of him."

Jeremy had to laugh, even if it was a sound born of sadness. "He's not. Neither is my mom, unfortunately. Although she has a softer edge to her. I'll give her that much. They've both always been more interested in what a person accomplishes than what kind of person they are."

"That's terrible."

"They've always been like that and I fed into it. I learned from an early age that if I did exactly what they wanted, and especially if I excelled at it, I was showered with praise. That was as close as they came to expressing affection."

"Is that why you became a lawyer?"

"Actually, it isn't. My dad wanted me to follow in

his footsteps, but it was my grandfather who inspired me to do it. He was all about the subtleties of the law and he loved the interpretation of it. He loved forming an argument." Jeremy turned to Isabel. "Very much like you, actually."

"He sounds like an awesome guy."

"He was. Those are all his law books in my office upstairs."

"So that's why you like to work here. Stay away from your dad and be surrounded by reminders of the real reason you got into this crazy business in the first place."

"Absolutely." Jeremy nodded, perhaps a little too eagerly. Isabel was an angel who'd dropped out of the sky. She understood him so naturally. "So, I was thinking, since it's Saturday and there are only a few days until Christmas, maybe we could do something holiday-related today."

"What did you have in mind? I hope not caroling. I'm a terrible singer."

"You and me both." He took another bite of his toast. "Shopping? I've already done mine. I get the same thing for my parents every year." A year's supply of monogrammed golf balls for his dad, who not only hit the links regularly, he was apt to lose them in the water hazards. For his mom, Jeremy went to Tiffany & Co. and bought the most recent offerings of earrings or a bracelet.

"I'm done, too. I got everything at Eden's. It was the first time in years that I've done that." She slid him a glance. "What about decorating? A Christmas tree?"

"I don't have an artificial one. There's a tree lot about seven or eight blocks away. Even with the snow, it's probably open. We could drag it back?"

Isabel turned and looked out the patio doors. "We don't need to buy one. You already have plenty."

"Out there?" This option had never occurred to him. Not once.

"Do you have any lights? Ornaments?"

"Well, yeah. I haven't used them since my divorce, but they're definitely still there."

"Let's decorate one of the trees out on your patio. It'll be so pretty at night. Plus you won't have to worry about Cat climbing it or messing around with it."

"You want to go out there in the cold? And decorate one of the cypress trees?"

"It's not snowing anymore. The sun is shining. It'll be nice. Plus, it'll be good to get some fresh air."

This was about the craziest idea Jeremy had ever heard. And he loved it. "We'll go hunting for everything in the attic in a little bit."

"We have all day, don't we?"

After breakfast was done and the kitchen cleaned, they trekked upstairs to the top floor of the house, where the attic was. It wasn't difficult to find the boxes of Christmas decor. They were some of the only things up there—thus was the life of the single guy with too much space. Jeremy certainly hesitated before he opened the first box. He and Kelsey had bought these decorations together, back when he believed they were building a life and would use them for years to come. Back when he'd thought that they might have kids and those children would eventually hang these ornaments on the tree. He didn't want to think about it too much as a reflection of the life he no longer had. Here with Isabel, his heart was nothing but light. If she'd never come along, these Christmas baubles might have spent many more years tucked away in an attic, collecting dust and going unused and unappreciated. It wasn't difficult to see the parallel between the boxes of ornaments and his own existence.

"I think four strands of lights will be enough. And I think these red and silver ball ornaments will stand up to the elements." Isabel tapped a fingernail against the shiny orbs. "They don't seem particularly breakable."

"Perfect."

They carried the boxes down a floor, then each went and changed into more suitable clothes for outdoors—jeans and sweaters. Back downstairs, they bundled up in boots, coats and gloves. "Do you have an extra hat I can wear?" she asked. "I don't have one with me and it looks really cold out there."

"I'm sure I have something."

Jeremy rummaged through his front coat closet, where he pulled out a red hat he'd had for years. "I haven't worn this one since college." He tugged it on her head, which pulled much of her hair over her face. With his fingers, he gently brushed it aside, tucking it neatly under the cap. She looked up at him while he did it, eyes big and bright, leaving him with only one logical thing to say. "You're so beautiful, Isabel. Truly." He was so deep in her orbit right now, it would be difficult to ever pull himself out. He wasn't sure he'd ever want to.

"You aren't half bad yourself, you know." Leaning into him, she slowly rose up onto her tiptoes and placed a soft kiss on his lips.

All he wanted to do was melt into her. Stay like this forever. *You're perfect. You're the best thing that's happened to me in recent history.* The words were right there, zipping around in his head, desperately wanting to be set free. But Jeremy knew his worst tendencies, the way he wanted to jump many steps ahead and profess his affection. It didn't matter how amazing she was. It was too soon. "Ready for our Christmas tree adventure?"

"I was born ready."

Isabel was beginning to think she'd gravely misjudged Jeremy that first night they met. Normally, she was an exceptional judge of character from the get-go. She was good at picking up on signals—the little things people do that tell you what drives them or makes them tick. The talent was part and parcel of being a lawyer and it'd been honed over the years. If anything, she should be getting better at it, not worse.

So where did she go wrong with Jeremy? Or was it simply that he was putting on an act, the one that kept him from sharing his pain with the rest of the world? She couldn't decide which it was, but also decided that it didn't truly matter. For the first time in years, she was actually enjoying herself. And she wasn't about to let her overthinking ways come between herself and a good time.

Trudging out onto the snow-covered patio with Jeremy, Isabel realized this suggestion of hers had been a bit unorthodox. "Thanks for indulging my peculiar idea."

"Are you kidding?" Jeremy asked, swiping snow from a patio table to give them a spot to put the boxes. "This is far less work than dragging a Christmas tree seven or eight blocks."

"It's more eco-friendly if you think about it, too. This tree's already here."

Jeremy trekked over to the back door and plugged in an extension cord, then returned to Isabel so they could begin stringing the lights. They worked in tandem, with her uncoiling the strands around her arm and Jeremy climbing up on a patio chair to loop them around the tree. It was a bright and sunny day, the air perfectly crisp and cold. Despite the temperature, Jeremy had opted for no hat, which gave her the perfect view of his adorable forehead wrinkles as he concentrated so intently on the task before him.

"I know it's probably my job to tell you where you missed a spot, but you're doing an amazing job," she said. "Not surprising. You're pretty much perfect at everything you do."

Jeremy looked down at her so abruptly that his sunglasses slid to the end of his nose. "You have got to be kidding."

"Um. No. I'm not."

Shaking his head in disbelief, he placed the remainder of the final strand of lights. "We'll have to wait until it's dark to see how it turned out." He then climbed down from the chair and opened one of the ornament boxes.

"I was serious about what I said. You're an amazing lawyer. Negotiating with you was one of the highlights of my entire career."

That stopped him dead in his tracks. "You're the one who's amazing." He swiped off his sunglasses and before Isabel really knew what was happening, he had his arms around her. His mouth was on hers, passionate and giving. It sent ripples of excitement through her entire body. She couldn't wait to go back inside with him.

"Wow," she muttered, sounding and feeling drunk.

"You make me want to do things like that, Isabel. You make me feel good. In every way imaginable."

Funny how making someone else happy could be such a lift to your own spirits. Not that Isabel needed a lift—she was already floating on air. "You make me feel good, too."

They finished the tree and headed back inside, stomping the snow from their boots and peeling off the winter layers. The moment clothes of any sort started to come off, it all had to go. Jeremy approached Isabel like a man on the hunt, lifting her sweater up over her head, peeling her bra strap from her shoulder and kissing her bare skin.

She shuddered, in part from his touch and in part from the ambient temperature in the room. "There's too much cold air from outside down here. Let's go upstairs to your bedroom."

He took her hand and led her through the house, zeroing in on his bed, sitting on the edge of the mattress and encouraging her to stand between his knees. He kissed her stomach, kneaded her breasts, and then pulled her down on top of him. She felt like a goddess, so admired and adored. That alone was nearly enough to send her into oblivion. The rest of their clothes were gone in a flash and they became a frantic tangle of limbs, mouths roaming and craving caresses. Isabel gasped when Jeremy drove inside her, relishing every delicious inch of him. He took deep strokes and kissed her neck, scratching at her tender skin with the stubble on his face. She wrapped her legs around his waist and used her feet to hold him tighter. It didn't take long until he left her unraveling, calling his name and breathless.

Jeremy climbed out of bed and pulled back the covers, Isabel quickly ducking under them to get warm. With the postorgasmic glow taking over, and after their eventful morning, she craved sleep. Her eyelids were heavy, her mind fuzzy. "You wore me out, Sharp. I guess all of that fresh air and sex did me in."

"Take a nap. You work like crazy and this weekend should be for relaxing. Plus, I remember that you told me the night we met that it's one of your favorite things."

Isabel grinned at the memory of them sharing their three universal truths that night. "It's the truth. I absolutely love it."

Jeremy reached over onto his nightstand for a book. "Perfect. You nap. I'll read."

When Isabel woke, she was nothing if not disoriented. Jeremy was gone, the room dark. She squinted at his clock: 5:12 p.m. She'd taken a three-hour nap, so much longer than she would normally sleep during the day. As she slowly woke, delicious smells filtered to her nose—garlic, herbs and possibly wine. Jeremy must have started dinner.

She padded down the hall to the guest room to grab a cardigan, popping into her bathroom to freshen her makeup while she was at it. Still not quite awake, she knocked one of her toiletry bags from the counter, sending the contents flying. She crouched down to pick up the mess, but her hand froze on a small box of tampons. For a moment, she stared at the blue-and-yellow swirl pattern on the package. It was as if she was standing on the edge of a realization, and reality was about to push her over the edge. *I'm late.*

Frantically, she fished her phone out of her pocket and pulled up the app she used to track her cycle. She was remarkably calm despite what the notification on her screen was telling her—she was six days late. Maybe this was the upside of having been a high-powered attorney for so long. Most panic-laden situations did not make Isabel freak out. Even when she could potentially have a very big reason for going into a tizzy.

Could she have gotten pregnant the night of the broken condom? It was the only possible explanation. Jeremy was the only man she'd been with in the last year. And if that was the case, what was she supposed to do about it? What would it mean? They were getting along amazingly and had an unbelievable chemistry, but this was going to throw everything on a fast track that Jeremy couldn't possibly be prepared for. If he'd gone into a panic over the broken condom, she couldn't imagine him reacting well to news of an actual baby.

She sucked in a deep breath. She had to get her act together. Phone still in hand, she flicked over to a different app and placed an order from the chain drugstore nearby. They could deliver her a pregnancy test tomorrow, along with a few other things to help hide the contents of the order, and she could take it Monday morning if she hadn't started her period by then. It was the responsible thing to do, most likely completely unnecessary. She typed in Jeremy's address, clicked Place Order and shoved her phone back into her pocket. It was probably nothing. Just her cycle being wonky.

When she reached the main floor and rounded the staircase to walk to the back of the house, she saw the tree lit up out on the patio. She ambled along the main corridor, her pulse thumping in her chest, while the aromas from the kitchen enticed her to move a little more quickly. She *was* hungry. And she'd been incredibly tired.

"Hey there, sleepyhead," Jeremy said, turning away from the stove.

Isabel's heart did a full cartwheel at the sight of him. "Are you making me dinner?"

"I'm making up for last night and the noticeable lack

of food." He wrapped his arm around her shoulders and gave her a soft kiss.

"It smells amazing. Although I hope that doesn't mean we don't get to revisit the events of last night. Or this morning. Or this afternoon."

Jeremy slipped his hand under her jaw and brought her lips to his. The kiss was enough to make her lose all sense of time and place, which was perfect. She couldn't stack another worry inside her head. "I can't wait to do everything we did last night."

"Neither can I." Goose bumps raced over the surface of her skin and she focused on the thrill of being with him.

"Did you see the tree?" He took her hand and led her to the patio doors. "It's so beautiful. You're a genius. I'm going to do this every year from now on."

"How wonderful. A new tradition." Isabel leaned into him and put her arm around his waist. The lights twinkled in the inky darkness outside and the wind blew enough to send snow from the tree boughs in puffs of white.

Jeremy wrapped his arm around Isabel. "Can I tell you a secret?"

Truly, the question could have easily been her own. "You can tell me anything."

"I'm so happy right now."

A heavy sigh left her lips, equal parts contentment and worry. "Me, too," she replied, hoping against hope that this happiness would last.

Twelve

Isabel's worries about being pregnant had manifested themselves in some very specific dreams. The truly odd part was that they were still lingering, at least in her head. Half-awake with her eyes still shut, she heard tiny cries—baby wails so peculiar they didn't sound human.

"The kittens." She bolted upright, blinking in the early light of Jeremy's bedroom. She reached over and shook his arm. "Jeremy. I think Cat had her babies."

"What?" He managed to make disorientation adorable, lifting his head off the pillow, then plopping it back down. "We don't have to do anything, right? You told me she can take care of them on her own."

Typical guy. "We don't have to do anything, but don't you want to make sure she's okay? That the babies are okay?" She tore back the comforter and tiptoed over to the closet door, turning on the light. She wasn't too worried about scaring Cat or the babies—it was plenty dark in their little corner. "Don't you want to see how many there are? Or what they look like?"

"Oh. Uh. Sure." He sat up in bed and flipped on the light on his bedside table, pushing his sexy bedhead hair off his face. "I'm coming."

Isabel tiptoed into the closet and pulled back Jeremy's shirts, peeking down into the box. Suckling Cat's belly were two tiny kittens; both appeared to be orange, although their fur was still matted. A third, with orange, gray and white patches, was blindly wandering around the box, crawling on its belly and mewing. Cat looked completely spent, asleep on her side.

"I thought they would be cuter," Jeremy said, peering over Isabel's shoulder. "Kittens are supposed to be cute."

Isabel shook her head and looked back at him. "Not at first. Not really. They'll be plenty cute in a few days."

"I'll have to trust you on that one."

He consulted his Apple watch. "It's nearly seven thirty, which seems way too early a time to be up on a Sunday morning, but I guess we're up, huh? Should I go make coffee?"

"That would be great. Bring me a cup?" She made herself at home on the floor, right next to the box.

"Are we spending our whole day in the closet?"

"I just want to sit here a little while. Make sure they're doing okay before we leave Cat to it."

He leaned down and pecked the top of her head. "I will not begrudge you your kitten time."

Isabel turned her attention to the box, watching as the stray kitten finally found her way to Cat's belly. It had been a long time since she'd been around this scene. She'd been a teenager the last time their family had newborn kittens in the house. Even all these years later, witnessing this made her feel connected to her mom. She pressed her hand to her lower belly, wondering what her body would ultimately tell her. She'd have been lying if she said she didn't desperately want a baby and to become a mom. But she wanted it all—true love and a partner. She would do this on her own, but it wasn't what her heart desired.

Jeremy returned and handed her a cup of coffee. "Good?" he asked, distracted by his iPad.

"Yes. Perfect." It was prepared exactly the way she liked it, with a splash of cream and one sugar.

"Good. Because here's where I have to ruin your day. There's a story in the paper this morning. Apparently somebody found love letters written to Victoria Eden by Mr. Summers's father. And the papers decided to publish them."

Isabel felt all of the blood drain from her face. *No no no.* She scrambled to standing and took the tablet from Jeremy when he offered it to her. There in black and white were the letters she and Mindy had discovered that afternoon in her grandmother's apartment. They had agreed to hide them away. They had agreed that no good came of anyone seeing them.

"How did you find out about this?" She felt her entire body go tight, fearing the answer.

"Summers, of course. Nothing gets past that guy. He texted me a link and asked me to call him, but I wanted to talk to you first. What the hell, Isabel? I thought we had a deal. I thought we were putting this whole thing to rest."

"We *do* have a deal." She hated seeing the expression on his face—the sheer disappointment was excruciating. Meanwhile, her mind was racing, wondering how this could have possibly happened. "Why are you looking at me like that? I didn't do this."

"Your clients must have done it. There's no other explanation." He took the tablet from her hand and stalked out of the closet.

She followed him back into his room. "But that doesn't make any sense. Why would they do this? Especially when I specifically asked Mindy not to?"

The look on Jeremy's face when he turned around told her what a grave error she'd made. She'd grown so comfortable with him that she'd let down her guard. He didn't know about the letters. She'd never said a peep about them, not even after he'd called to let her know that the promissory note had been authenticated. "Please tell me you didn't plan this. Please tell me this isn't a trademark Isabel Blackwell move."

That stung like no other thing he could have said. "Jeremy, no. I didn't plan this. I don't know what to tell you, but I didn't have anything to do with this story."

"Did you know about the letters?"

A sigh left her lips involuntarily and he stormed out of the room. "Jeremy, wait!" She ran out into the hall after him, grabbing his arm just as he reached the top of the landing. "Please let me explain. Yes, I knew about the letters. Mindy and I found them right before the promissory note was authenticated."

"But you still waited for me to call you and tell you about the authentication. Even when you knew at that point that it was all real? The affair between Mr. Summers's father and Victoria Eden was real?"

"Of course I waited. You would have done the same thing in my situation."

He closed his eyes and pinched the bridge of his nose, not saying a thing.

"You would have. You know it."

"Of course I would have, Isabel. My first duty is to my client. Which only illustrates how far you and I have crossed the line together. And now I have feelings for you and what in the hell am I supposed to do about that?"

She sharply sucked in a breath. "Feelings?" She had feelings for him, too, but she didn't have the nerve to express them now. The thought of sitting down and examining them, or daring to put a label on them, was too terrifying an idea. Meanwhile, there was no sign of her period and the drugstore was scheduled to deliver a pregnancy test at any time.

"Please don't throw my word back at me like I've said something horrible. We've had a great weekend together and now we're right back where we started except that it's quite possibly worse. I don't see any way that Summers is going to agree to a single term you and I so carefully worked out. The entire deal is off as far as I'm concerned."

Isabel's stomach sank. She'd not only disappointed Jeremy, she was about to crush the entire Eden family and her brother, for that matter. Best-case scenario, Eden's would end up embroiled in a legal battle for months, one that would cost them untold sums of money. Mr. Summers had been headed for the warpath from the very beginning and it was only understandable that this story in the papers would convince him it was the only course. Mindy and Isabel had found the letters extremely romantic when they read them, but there was no doubt that they were the flowery ramblings of a man smitten with a woman who was not his wife. They were a chronicle of lust, passion, obsession and ultimately, infidelity. They told the story of two people casting aside the sanctity of marriage.

"Please. Let me talk to Mindy and Sophie. Let me get to the bottom of this."

"I don't see what good it's going to do, but I'm not going to prevent you from doing whatever you need to do to take care of your client."

"Gee, thanks. That's so generous of you." Isabel retreated to the guest room, fuming and upset and uncharacteristically on the brink of tears. Normally when things went wrong with a case, she immediately went on the offensive. Right now, she wanted to crumple into a ball and hide. She got out her phone and called her brother.

"Hey. What's up?" he asked, sounding as though he was still recovering from his cold.

"Have you seen the papers?"

"No. Why?"

Isabel gave Sam a quick recap. "So I need to know if Mindy fed this story to the newspapers."

"I don't see how she possibly could have. At least not in the last few days. She's been completely out of it on cold medicine. The only person she's talked to has been Sophie."

Isabel felt like a light bulb had been flicked on above her head. Sophie was the most likely person to do something like this. When Isabel had tried to calm her down the other morning, she was all ready to hire a PR person and take Mr. Summers down. "Okay. Thanks. I need to call her and talk to her."

"Are we in hot water because of this?" Sam asked.

Isabel wasn't about to couch it. "I'd say we're about to boil."

Unfortunately, when Isabel called Sophie's cell, all

she got was voice mail. She left a message, asking—no, begging—for Sophie to call her back. Then she flopped back on the bed and stared up at the ceiling, wondering how she was possibly ever going to get herself out of this.

Jeremy had sought the solitude of his office, closing the door behind him. He wasn't interested in Isabel's excuses or reasoning. All he could think about were the things he'd learned about her the first time he'd looked into her career trajectory and discovered what she'd done in Washington, DC. This was straight out of the Isabel Blackwell playbook—when one party can destroy you, you destroy them first. Although he didn't want to make this situation about him, this was far too much like the things Kelsey had done to him. His heart legitimately went out to Mr. Summers. Who wants to read a newspaper article where their father, in his own words, professes his love for someone who isn't his wife?

He couldn't believe he'd fallen back into bed with Isabel. He couldn't believe he'd let himself get so carried away again. Even five minutes ago out in the hall with her—why had he uttered that word? *Feelings?* For someone who was supposed to be exceptionally good with words, he'd sure chosen a terrible one. Right now, he had a few too many feelings coursing through his system, anger being pretty high on the list. Everyone was pissing him off—the Eden sisters, the situation and honestly, even Isabel.

Jeremy's phone, which was facedown on his desk, beeped with a text. Then another. He flipped over the device and scanned the screen.

The first message was from his father. Summers case

is no longer under your control. We need to take down Blackwell.

The second was from a reporter, and just because today seemed to be hell-bent on destroying him, it was the same one who'd sought Jeremy's comment after Kelsey ran her smear piece. Can we talk re: the Benjamin Summers lawsuit?

Before he spoke to either of those people, he needed to call Ben. He didn't want to risk him talking to his father first. "Ben. Good morning. I got your text," Jeremy said, wanting to be as upbeat and diplomatic as possible, even though it felt like the world was crumbling around him.

"It appears that the shoe is on the other foot, doesn't it? I'm embarrassed beyond words at the atrocity in the papers this morning, but I suppose I should be thankful that the Eden's team has finally shown their true colors."

"I don't know about that. We're still trying to get to the bottom of exactly what happened." Why was it his inclination to try to walk any of this back? Logic said that he should be going for the jugular right now, but the truth was that he just wanted this done. He couldn't spend more time with Isabel. She'd shown that she was just as capable of inflicting damage as any woman he'd ever allowed himself to get close to. He needed this case to be over. "I have to tell you that Ms. Blackwell and I worked out some extremely favorable terms for you on Friday. It's an attractive offer, and yes, today might give us additional leverage for perhaps a few more concessions, but I don't think we should throw the whole thing out the window because of one story in a tabloid."

"And I'd think you would be happy about this. Don't lawyers love leverage?"

"Not when it means that we needlessly drag something out for longer than it needs to go." He could see this going on for months and months, during which he would have to battle Isabel. He didn't want that. Frankly, he wanted this whole thing to go away so he could decide for himself, without any outside intrusion, whether he could trust her. Whether they could be something.

"Do you have these supposed favorable terms for me to look at?" Mr. Summers asked.

"I'm in the process of drawing them up. We can meet tomorrow morning if that works for you."

"Fine. Nine o'clock. My office."

"Absolutely. I will be there."

"And if I'm not happy, I'm prepared to drop the gloves and go to war." The line went dead before Jeremy had a chance to respond. Not that he had anything to say. He'd wait until tomorrow to do battle with Mr. Summers.

Of course, now he had no choice but to call his dad and explain what was going on. As the phone rang, dread began to build in his system, and all Jeremy could think was that this entire situation was wrong, starting with the fact that he couldn't stand to speak to a man he should have been able to trust and confide in—his own father.

"I just got off the phone with Mr. Summers," Jeremy started. "We're meeting tomorrow morning. I'm presenting the terms of the negotiation to him. I'm hoping he can put aside what happened in the papers today and agree to everything. He'll get his money. He'll get that and more."

"That's not even my worry anymore, Jeremy. My concern is that you have caused irreparable damage to our firm's reputation. You're making us look like a bunch of hacks."

"Dad. I'm not a public relations guy. I have no control over what runs in the newspaper."

"But if you had put this case to bed at that first meeting, if you had the nerve to be ruthless with Ms. Blackwell, we wouldn't be having this discussion."

"It wouldn't have changed the tabloid story. That still could have run."

"And Summers would have had his settlement by then. At that point, Sharp and Sharp would only be bandied about as the firm who had come out on top. Instead, we're flopping around like a fish out of water." His father cleared his throat. "I think I need to level the playing field."

"By doing what exactly?"

"We need to get rid of Ms. Blackwell. Get Eden's to fire her."

"They won't fire her. Her brother is engaged to Mindy Eden. He's a special adviser to the store." Jeremy couldn't explain further, about how Isabel felt like she was part of the Eden family and how it all meant a great deal to her. He couldn't divulge his personal involvement with her. It would infuriate his father to no end, and Jeremy had to admit, he would be justified in being angry.

"Trust me, they'll get rid of her when she's a liability, and I know exactly how to make that happen. Then they'll hand it over to their in-house counsel. You can steamroller those guys in your sleep."

"Dad. Please don't do anything reckless. Just let me meet with Summers tomorrow morning and see where we get. Just give me this one last chance."

Thirteen

Monday morning had arrived, which meant it was do-or-die time. Jeremy would be leaving the house in a half hour to meet with Mr. Summers. He hoped that Ben had taken some time to cool off. He hoped that he could see that there was no point in letting pride get in the way. It was time for an agreement. An armistice. That was the best-case scenario for Jeremy and he wanted it so badly he could taste it.

Sunday had been horrible—Jeremy stewing in his office and Isabel in the guest room, tucked away. Their only real interaction came when she got a delivery and he brought it to her room.

"This came from the drugstore." He handed her the paper shopping bag, hating that he felt as though he had to stay out of a room in his own house.

"Thank you," she said, clutching it to her chest. "I got a call from the Bacharach and I can move back in on Tuesday morning. If you want, I can see if Mindy and

Sam can take me in. Or maybe I could stay in Mindy's grandmother's old apartment."

"Don't do that. Just stay. It's fine." He desperately wanted that to be true. It was killing him to not be where they'd been mere hours before that, enjoying each other's company, touching each other, kissing.

"I know this story just made everything worse. And I'm really sorry for that. I still don't know what happened, but I will get to the bottom of it. I wish I had something you could tell Mr. Summers, but I don't."

"Okay. I still plan to meet with him tomorrow morning. No telling what he's going to say, but I will present our agreement to him if you still want me to."

Isabel had picked at her fingernail, seeming to want any reason to not look at him. "I'll do the same and I guess we'll just see where we end up?"

He nodded in agreement. "Do you want something to eat?"

She shook her head. "Not right now. Maybe later. I'm tired and I have work to do."

"Okay then. Let me know if you need anything." He'd been about to walk away when she said one more thing.

"I checked on the kittens while you were in your office. I made sure Cat got some food and water. They seem like they're doing well."

"Good. Thank you."

"Of course."

With that, she'd shut the door, and Jeremy was left much like he'd been before Isabel had arrived on his doorstep—alone. It stayed like that for the rest of the day. And the night. And for all of that morning.

In his closet, he was choosing a suit to wear for his meeting with Mr. Summers when he heard one of the kittens mewing. In all of the commotion of yesterday, he'd frankly forgotten that they were there. The two orange kittens were nursing, but the other one was wandering around the box, bumping into the sides. Cat would nudge at her with her nose occasionally, but the kitten, quite frankly, seemed lost. Jeremy was unsure of what to do, but something told him he had to help the poor thing, so he reached in, picked it up and placed her next to her siblings, mouth near Cat's belly. He watched as she rooted around and latched on to nurse. There was some consolation in that one silly achievement—today wouldn't have to be a total loss.

After dressing, he went into his office to gather his things. That was when Isabel appeared at his door. She was just as beautiful as always, but he could tell that there was something on her mind. She wasn't her normal lively self, and the dread that prompted in him made him sick to his stomach.

"Do you have a minute?" she asked. "I have two things I need to talk to you about."

"Sure. I have to leave soon, but I'll always make time for you."

"First off, you should know that your dad tried to get one of the tabloids to run a smear piece on me. The reporter called me late last night for comment and after I spoke to the editor, they agreed not to run it."

Jeremy looked up at the ceiling, furious with his father for attempting to sabotage her while also relieved that he hadn't been successful. "I'm so sorry. I don't know what to say."

She waved it off. "Don't worry. I've had worse things happen to me. And I'm sure that whatever they wanted to print would probably be true. I've represented some people who aren't great. But I've always acted in accordance with the law. I don't have anything I'm ashamed of."

"Well, good. I'm glad."

"I simply don't want to be a part of any of this anymore. I can't deal with the mudslinging and the backstabbing and everyone trying so hard to disparage each other. I'm hoping we can wrap up the case, but if we can't, I think I will likely step away from it. I've had my fill of it. I love the Eden sisters and care about them deeply, but I also need my sanity."

"I can't say that I blame you. If my dad wasn't in the middle of it, I might be tempted to bail on Summers. None of this has been very fun, has it?"

She shrugged and a slight smile crossed her lips. It was like stepping into the sunlight for the first time—that small glimmer of happiness from her made everything better. "I don't know about that. I had fun with you. I had more than fun."

A grin that he was sure was quite goofy broke out on his face. "Me, too. I don't regret that part."

"Me, either. Which brings me to the other thing I have to tell you. There's no easy way to say this, so I'm just going to come out with it. I'm pregnant and you're the father."

Of the many things Jeremy had thought Isabel might tell him, that one piece of information had never occurred to him. Not even for a second. "The night we met?"

"Yes."

"But you…"

"I know. I thought there was no chance. I was wrong."

"I, uh… I don't even know what to say."

"I know. It's okay. You don't need to say anything.

This is all very sudden and it's a lot to deal with, especially given everything else that's going on." Now that she was talking, she was picking up speed, as if she had a long list of things she'd been dying to say. "I realize that the timing couldn't possibly be any worse. And we don't really know each other that well, so I understand that you would be wanting to distance yourself from me, and I can appreciate why. It's okay. I will be completely fine on my own. I don't want you to worry."

He got up from his desk and went to her, taking her hands. "Hey. Hey. Slow down a minute. Take a breath."

She dropped her head for a moment and when she looked up at him, there were tears rolling down her cheeks. "I've wanted a baby for so long, Jeremy. I've always wanted to be a mom. But this isn't the way I wanted it to happen. And I hate putting you on the spot. You're a good man. I know that. You're sweet and generous and you don't deserve to be in this situation."

Jeremy wasn't sure what to think about any of this. He'd wanted a family for a long time. He'd wanted a woman like Isabel for a long time. But this was traveling on a preposterous timeline. He wanted to put the entire world on pause, if only for a day so he could have time and space to think. A baby? With Isabel? How would this work? Would it be yet another negotiation? That was the last thing he wanted. And what if things didn't work out? He didn't want to be an absentee father, around every other weekend and select holidays. That wasn't what he wanted for himself at all. It wasn't what he wanted for Isabel, either.

His phone beeped—the reminder that he had to leave for his meeting. "Shoot. I'm going to be late to meet with Summers. He's such a stickler for punctuality. I can't afford to make him angry."

"I understand. It's okay. Just forget what I said. We can talk about it after everything with the case is over."

Jeremy grabbed his briefcase from his desk, then returned to her. "Hey. Will you stop trying to let me off the hook? I'm not like that guy who burned you. I don't turn my back on people who need me, okay? So just give me a chance to meet with Summers, and talk to my dad, and, and…" He looked at her, certain he couldn't possibly be in a bigger state of disbelief. "Then we'll talk about the baby."

That fresh start Isabel had wanted so badly? It felt like she was watching it crumble to dust in her hands. How could she possibly save Eden's now? How could Jeremy salvage this situation for Mr. Summers? Even more important, how could the two of them reach an understanding about impending parenthood? They'd hardly had enough time to fall in love.

The scene in the guest bath at Jeremy's house was still rolling around in her mind. She'd paced back and forth across the white marble floor, arms wrapped around her middle like she was giving herself a hug. She'd been unable to escape how lonely it felt to be doing that on her own, for the second time. It had played out like that when she found out she was pregnant with Garrett's baby all those years ago—Isabel enduring the painfully slow ticks of the clock while she waited for news that could change her whole life.

The timer on Isabel's phone had gone off, echoing in the bathroom. She'd closed her eyes for a moment to steel herself for the news, unable to decide what result she hoped for, although she'd known that there was no reason to reach a solid conclusion. Her heart would tell her with its own reaction.

She'd opened her eyes and grabbed the test from the counter. *Two blue lines. Positive.* She'd stumbled back into the bathroom wall, steadying herself with her hand. *Positive. A baby.* Her heart did the inexplicable, even when her stomach wobbled—it began to flutter in her chest. However imperfect her situation, a baby was something she wanted more than anything. She'd been waiting years for another chance.

She had to admit to herself that Jeremy had handled the news far better than expected. She'd been prepared for the absolute worst, and he'd kept everything on an even keel. He'd been a rock. She hoped and prayed that this wasn't another of his acting jobs. She didn't think she could take it if he wasn't at least going to play some role in this baby's life. She couldn't handle it if he was going to turn his back on her as Garrett had done.

In the car on the way to Eden's to meet with Sam, Mindy, Sophie and Emma, her heart was heavy. Perhaps her first mistake had been taking this job—she'd only agreed out of loyalty to Sam. But now she was so much closer to Mindy, Sophie and Emma than she'd ever imagined she could be, and it was all on her that they could lose the store. Isabel the fixer had not only failed to fix anything, she'd allowed it to get worse. She should have had the sense to take the letters into her possession that day at Victoria Eden's apartment. She never should have trusted her clients to keep them out of public view.

Arriving at Eden's, she waved to Duane the security guard and marched right back to the elevator, prepared to unleash a few unpleasant things on the Eden sisters if necessary. If they'd gotten themselves into this mess, she wasn't sure she could get them out. She strode into the lobby feeling determined, but the instant she saw

Sam, she burst into tears. He rushed over to her and gathered her up in his arms.

"What's wrong?" he asked. "Are you that upset about the case?"

She sank against his chest, unable to speak. As much as Eden's had weighed on her as recently as a few minutes ago, that was definitely not what was on her mind.

Mindy appeared in the reception area. "Is everything okay?" She stepped closer, but kept her distance. "Sorry. I'd hug you, but I'm still getting over this cold."

"Is Summers going to go after the store?" Sam asked.

"I still haven't talked to Sophie, but it has to be her," Mindy said. "I don't completely remember our conversation over the weekend, but I'm pretty sure I told her about the letters. Leave it to her to go to our grandmother's apartment, find them and leak them to the press."

Mindy's explanation was of little consolation. Isabel still felt as though she had let down her new friends. She'd let down their entire family. She'd let down Sam's wife-to-be. She'd failed in every way imaginable, at least when it came to her legal responsibilities. "I'm so sorry. I really wish I had better news. Summers is just out for revenge. I'm not sure we ever had a chance."

Sam placed his hands on Isabel's shoulders. "I know you did your best. Some of this has to be his lawyer. I didn't like Sharp from the very first meeting. He seems like a real weasel."

Isabel froze, looking up into her brother's eyes. Sam's opinion mattered. It mattered a lot. And she couldn't allow him to think of Jeremy that way. She also couldn't keep him in the dark any longer about the full scope of her relationship with him, especially now that it had become infinitely more complicated. "Jeremy's a good man. He's caught in an impossible situation. Summers is unreasonable."

"You have Stockholm syndrome. You were stuck negotiating with that guy. You've convinced yourself he's not that bad."

"I don't know about that," Mindy said.

Sam turned to her. "Don't you agree?" he asked.

"For Isabel's sake, I can't. If she says he's a good guy, I believe her."

"Why? This guy is about to destroy your entire family."

"He's not going to destroy our family. He might end up being part and parcel of ending our business, but it's not the same."

"Wait a minute. Why do I have the feeling you two have talked about him before?" Sam asked. "Am I missing something?"

"We did talk about him. The day we rummaged around in Gram's apartment."

Isabel had fond memories of that day, despite the things they'd discovered. She felt closer to Mindy afterward. She felt as though she was becoming part of the Eden family. "We talked about a lot that day." Isabel loved her brother deeply, and it was time to tell him and Mindy everything. "I need to tell you both something. There's more going on than just the negotiations breaking down. Jeremy and I are involved," Isabel whispered.

It wasn't easy to take Sam by surprise, but he noticeably reared back his head. "Are you serious? Why would you do that? That's so unprofessional."

Mindy grabbed both of their arms. "You two. In my office. We can't have this conversation out here."

As soon as they were behind a closed door, Isabel confronted Sam. "You're going to lecture me about professionalism? Seriously? I didn't even want this job to begin with."

"Wait. You didn't?" Mindy asked, incredulous. "I thought you did. Sam, you told me she wanted to help us."

"She took the job. That was all you needed to know."

Mindy let out a frustrated grumble. "You can't keep things like this from me. Isabel is going to be my sister-in-law. We've been getting along great and now I find out that the foundation of that is all a lie."

Isabel reached for Mindy's arm. "It's not a lie. As soon as we spent that afternoon together, I knew I was doing the right thing. I wanted to help you and your sisters. I wanted us to be close. That's why I told you about my thing with Jer..." Isabel stopped herself, but it was too late.

"Whoa. Hold on a minute. You were involved with Jeremy before? I'm so confused. And Min, you knew about this?"

Isabel couldn't allow Mindy to take heat for this, so she explained that she and Jeremy had a one-night stand before they were involved in the case. Then she told him about the broken condom.

Sam shook his head, holding up both hands. "Enough. I don't need to hear about that." He closed his eyes and pinched the bridge of his nose. "So when we met him in his office that day, you guys had already slept together? And you didn't say a thing to any of us."

"What was I supposed to do? He had his client and I had mine and none of that was going to change the fact that there was this case standing between us."

"And now what? Where do you two stand?" Sam asked.

Isabel knew she had to come clean. About everything. "I got pregnant that first night. With Jeremy's baby. I found out this morning."

Sam walked over and sat on the couch, but Mindy went straight to Isabel.

"Oh my God. Are you okay?" she asked.

Isabel had to take a moment to reflect. Was she okay? "I am. I mean, I've wanted to have a baby for a long time now. Ever since…" There were far too many details of her life she had kept from Sam. Perhaps it had been Isabel's way of protecting him. With both of their parents gone and Isabel being two years older, she certainly felt responsible for him.

"Ever since what?" Sam asked, seeming desperate. "Just tell me what's going on, Isabel. I feel like I am completely in the dark, which is not a good feeling when it comes to my own sister."

Apparently that day was for nothing but revelations and admissions. So she finally told Sam about the heartache of losing her first pregnancy, and how she so desperately wanted this child.

"What are you going to do?" he asked when she'd told him everything.

"Right now, all I can do is my best for me and the baby. I have absolutely no idea what's going to happen with any of it. The deal or Jeremy."

Fourteen

Jeremy left his meeting with Mr. Summers feeling as though he'd been hit by a truck. The man's ability to hold on to a grudge and to allow every perceived slight to fester…well, it was unparalleled.

Nothing had been resolved, but Mr. Summers promised him a phone call in an hour with an answer. Either he would accept the terms from the Eden's team or it would be all-out war. Which left Jeremy with one more thing to deal with—his dad. No matter what happened with the case, he was done.

He headed straight to the office and didn't even stop to drop off his things. "I need to speak to my father," he said to his dad's admin, striding right past her desk and opening the door. "I heard that your plan to smear Ms. Blackwell didn't work. I guess I should be thankful you failed."

Jeremy's dad was on a call. "I'm gong to have to call

you back," he said into the receiver before hanging up. "I can still make it happen. I just need to dig up more dirt on her."

"Just don't. Just stop all of this. You're as bad as Mr. Summers. There is no winning when you play the game like this. It's just a race to the bottom and I'm tired of it."

"You're complaining about your boss and your biggest client. Apparently you don't know who signs your paychecks."

"Don't posture with me, Dad. You know that the other lawyers and I are the ones who keep the lights on. You're just the head of the dragon, spitting fire and still trying to prove yourself because you know that no matter how hard you try, you will never be as good as your own dad."

"That's not true. The success of this firm begins and ends with me. It's my legacy."

That word didn't sit right with Jeremy. "I'm your son. Am I not your real legacy? The firm could go under tomorrow and I would still be here, trying to find a way to make you happy. Trying to find a way to get through to you."

Just then, the door to his father's office opened and in walked the last person he expected to see—his mother. "Jeremy. I thought it was strange that you weren't at your desk."

"Mom. What are you doing here?"

"Trying to get your father to go Christmas shopping with me."

"I'm in the middle of something," his dad said. "I can't drop everything and go shopping."

"Why not?" Jeremy asked. "Everything is under control here. The other lawyers and I have everything in hand."

"The Summers case isn't resolved."

"No, it isn't. But it will be. And I'll see it through."

"Then what?" his dad asked. "You'll get another client I have to bother you about?"

"You never had to bother me about this one. If you trusted me to do my job, it would get done. Grandpa trusted you. I don't know why you can't place that same faith in me." Jeremy stuffed his hands into his pants pockets, frustrated.

His mother turned to him. "Your grandfather never trusted him. Your dad was proving himself until the day his father died. He never had a chance to win his confidence."

Jeremy was frozen for a moment, letting that bit of information tumble around in his head. "What? Seriously?"

His dad drew in a deep breath, staring off into space as if he couldn't possibly handle the admission. "He never made things easy on me. That's for sure."

Jeremy's mom stepped closer to him. "As the person who had to listen to your father complain every night when he came home from work, I can tell you that it was far worse than that."

"Dad? Why didn't you ever tell me this? And why are you doing the same thing to me?"

"Because it made me stronger to be tested like that," his dad snapped. "It made me a better lawyer."

Jeremy wanted to laugh, but this was all striking him as incredibly sad. If only they'd had this conversation ten or fifteen years ago. He might be in a very different place. "You don't have to be miserable to be strong. That all comes from within as far as I'm concerned."

"It's the only way I know, Jeremy. I don't know what you want me to tell you."

Jeremy approached his dad's desk. "Dad. I love you. I hope you know that. I love you even though you make it very difficult some days. But I can't work with you anymore. Either you step aside or I do. I'll leave it up to you."

His mom came up behind him. "Son. Do you really want to do that? Close this door on your career?"

He turned to her and placed his hand on her arm. He really did love her. "My career isn't going anywhere. But at the rate we're going, the three of us aren't going to be much of a family. The situation at work has been bad enough, but we need to talk about how things went south after Kelsey left me. I didn't feel supported. And I never took the time to think about how unhappy it made me until I talked to a friend about it." Isabel had shown him so much in such a short amount of time. How had she done that?

"You never told us you felt that way. I thought we were supportive."

"I should have said something. I know that now. I shouldn't have kept it bottled in. But you were not supportive. You were embarrassed."

"Embarrassed for you. The things Kelsey said about you were horrible. No mother wants her son to go through that. To experience that kind of betrayal."

"But you never really said those things to me. All I heard were the things your friends were telling you."

Jeremy's mom frowned and her eyes grew misty. "I didn't?"

He shook his head. "You didn't."

She wrapped her arms around him. "I'm so sorry. I never, ever wanted to hurt you. You and your father are the most important things to me in the entire world. I love you. I love you both."

Jeremy returned his mom's hug. "I love you guys, too. Hopefully that can save us." As soon as the words left his lips, he realized that they weren't really his. They were Isabel's. From the night they met. *I believe that love is the only thing that saves anyone.*

The thought of Isabel sent goose bumps racing over the surface of his skin and that was when he realized it—he loved her. As improbable as it was, he'd fallen in love with her. Could love save him? Was it as simple as that? Was it meant for him? He'd spent the last few years so unhappy, convinced that his empty existence was something he must learn to accept. A fact of life. But did it really have to be that way? He wanted to believe that it didn't.

"Are we going to see you for the tree-trimming party?" his mom asked. "I look forward to it all year."

Jeremy was determined to keep building bridges, not tearing them down. He wanted to be the sort of man who made connections, not destroyed them. "My only problem is that I'd like to bring a date. Isabel Blackwell."

His dad's eyes became as large as dinner plates. "Excuse me?"

Jeremy wasn't about to go into a long, drawn-out explanation. He wasn't even certain Isabel would accept the invitation. "Yes, Dad. We actually had a brief romantic relationship before the case started. I never said anything because I thought it wouldn't be a problem. And honestly, it wasn't, until you decided to try to drag her through the mud today."

Jeremy's mother's face was full of horror. "Oh. Well, that's awkward, isn't it?"

Honestly, it couldn't be any more uncomfortable for

Jeremy than anything else he'd endured with his parents. "It doesn't have to be if Dad apologizes."

"You have to apologize," his mother blurted. "Otherwise, it'll ruin Christmas."

"You can't ruin Christmas, Dad."

Full of resignation, his father nodded. "I will apologize. First thing."

Jeremy could be content with that. "Then I will do my best to convince her to come."

Jeremy said his goodbyes to his parents, then marched down the hall, feeling as though a weight had been lifted. He'd finally said his piece with his family and the world hadn't ended. In fact, it had gone quite well.

Just then, his phone rang. He plucked it from his pocket and answered, striding down the hall.

"Yes?"

"Jeremy. It's Ben."

At this point, Jeremy was prepared for anything. "Do you have news for me?"

"I do."

"Am I going to be happy about it?"

"Depends on what you were hoping for."

Was Jeremy ready for the answer? He had to be. Because the truth was that he wanted to put this whole thing to bed and turn his attention to Isabel and the baby.

Isabel arrived back at Jeremy's place, and of course, it just *had* to be snowing. Again. As if the sight of his beautiful brownstone, with the grand steps and stunning front door, didn't hold enough vibrant reminders of what had happened between them. They'd not only fallen into bed, she'd fallen into the Christmas spirit for the first time in years.

Funnily enough, the most pressing thing she could think of as she looked at the facade of Jeremy's house was that it needed a wreath with a big fat red bow. She needed to rein herself in. There was no telling what that afternoon might hold. Jeremy was having a showdown with his father and Mr. Summers. There were too many things that could go wrong.

As she climbed out of the car and zipped up her coat, she had to admit to herself that despite her predicament, she wasn't feeling truly pessimistic right now. She accepted the reality of her situation. Jeremy had never asked for this—an undeniable tie to her, forever. And that was fine. She was strong and independent. She could care for a child on her own. And she'd wanted this more than anything for so long. Nothing was going to keep her from building her own little family. Life was once again proving to be quite unlike what she had hoped for, but she wouldn't put herself or her future on hold. She'd done that after Garrett left, and the pain of losing her first pregnancy had made her tread water for years.

But as she ascended his front steps, she was overcome with another wave of melancholy. She and Jeremy could be good together if they had a chance. They could be great. She cared for him deeply, and was holding on to feelings that sure felt an awful lot like love. Such was the case with bad timing. Only some things in life lined up perfectly. Not everything. At least not for Isabel.

She unlocked the door with the key Jeremy had given her and flipped on the light in the foyer. After taking off her coat, she made her way upstairs to check on Cat and the kittens.

"Hey there, Mama," she said when she carefully pulled back Jeremy's dress shirts to reveal the cardboard box. Cat was half-asleep with her eyes part open, the kittens nursing and kneading at her belly. Cat looked up at Isabel and blinked—such a simple thing, and yet Isabel was so taken by the beauty of the moment. There was this sweet and beautiful creature caring for her babies, at utter peace with the world. Isabel hoped that her future could be like that.

She hoped more than was probably reasonable.

"Hello? Isabel?" Jeremy's voice came from downstairs. "Are you home?"

Home. She was home. She wanted to believe she was. "I'm up here. With the cats."

She heard his steady footfalls on the stairs and moments later, he appeared at the closet doorway. "Of course you're up here."

"I had to get my kitten time."

"I'm wondering if I can steal a minute with you. Or maybe more." From behind his back, he produced a huge bouquet of red roses. "I'm hoping these will convince you."

Isabel popped up from the floor, planted her face in the flowers and drew in the heavenly smell. "I don't need convincing to talk to you. Although I appreciate the effort. They're beautiful." She then worried there might be a specific reason for the kind gesture. "Mr. Summers. Did you talk to him? Is he throwing down the gauntlet?"

"I did talk to him. For quite a while, actually. Turns out that when he got so mad about the story yesterday, he hadn't actually read the letters. After I talked to him this morning, he finally did."

"And that made things better or worse?"

"Better. Much better. He called and told me that he realized just how much his father loved Victoria Eden. Truly loved her. I guess that in the end, he stopped seeing it as this salacious affair and more as a love story between two people who met at the wrong time."

Isabel blinked several times, struggling to catch up. "So what does that mean?"

"He's agreed to the terms. A lump sum of the original loan amount by January 1 and 10 percent of the Eden's online business in perpetuity." Jeremy shrugged his way out of his suit jacket and hung it on a hanger. "So I guess what I need to know from you is whether the Eden family is definitely on board."

"They are. I heard from Mindy on my way back here and it was Sophie who leaked the letters to the press. I told her that they had to agree to the terms if we had any chance of wrapping this up."

"See? What a shark you are."

"I'm not. I'm just like you, Jeremy. I wanted this to be over so we could deal with the real-life stuff that's sitting in front of us. I know that I unloaded a lot on you today, and I'm not trying to let you off the hook, but I do want you to know that there is no pressure from me. You can take all the time you want to think about this and decide what you want."

"I already know what I want."

Isabel was surprised by his quick response. She only hoped that he wasn't going to say that he'd decided he didn't want her. "You do?"

"Yes. And it all came to me when I had it out with my dad this morning." He reached for Isabel's hand. "Come on. Let's go sit on the bed so I can tell you the whole story."

They traced into the bedroom and sat on the edge of

the mattress. He held her hand the whole time he was recounting what had happened with his parents and how relieved he was to finally clear the air.

"I'm so glad it all worked out. But I'm still not sure how that helped you figure out what you want."

"I ended up telling my mom something you said the night we met."

Isabel narrowed her eyes in confusion. "Good Lord, Jeremy. What in the heck were you talking to your mom about?"

He laughed so hard that she could see his body relax. "Love. We were talking about love."

"I don't remember us discussing that. At all."

"When you were telling me your universal truths. You said that you believe that love is the only thing that ever saves anyone. And as soon as the words came out of my mouth, I realized that you saved me. You brought me back to life."

He reached out and smoothed her hair back and she peered up into his eyes, which were full of tenderness and love, the things she most craved. "If I did that, Jeremy, it was only because you make it easy. You're so pure of heart. It's impossible to not get caught up in that. To admire it."

"If that's the case, it's because I'm better when I'm with you. That's all there is to it. And I don't want to walk away from what's already between us."

Isabel's mind raced. She felt the same way. Exactly. And it was only leaving her with one conclusion.

He sucked in a deep breath and blew it out. "It might sound crazy…"

Oh my God.

"I know we've only known each other for a little while…" he continued.

"But I love you." They both said it. At the exact same time.

For a moment, they sat there, staring at each other in disbelief. Then the laughter came and an embrace and finally a kiss that made every bad thing that had ever happened fade into nothingness. Isabel had waited her whole life for this moment, and she knew Jeremy had, too.

"The baby," she said. "I know it's a lot."

"Of course it's a lot. But I'm forty years old. I don't want to let life pass me by. I don't want to let you or this moment pass me by. We have to take everything life has given us here, Isabel."

"We have to take each other."

"Yes. Absolutely."

"And never let go."

Epilogue

"Do you think it's cheesy to get married on Valentine's Day?" Mindy posed the question to Isabel as they stood in the grand master bedroom of Sam and Mindy's splendid new home.

Isabel shook her head, helping her future sister-in-law adjust the bustle of her wedding gown. It was a jaw-dropping bias-cut silk charmeuse that hugged every curve. Isabel was guessing Sam might pass out the minute he saw her. "No. I think it's sweet."

"It was Sam's idea, you know. Who knew he could be such a sap?"

"I knew. I knew it all along." Isabel already found herself blinking away tears. It would be a miracle if she could get through the ceremony without sobbing. Pregnancy hormones were definitely getting the best of her, but she relished every frantic and slightly chaotic moment of it. She'd be twelve weeks along in six days, then she and Jeremy would finally tell his parents. It'd been a bit of a rocky road to start with them, but they were making strides, especially since Jeremy's dad had apologized for trying to drag Isabel through the mud.

"How are we doing in here?" Sophie ducked into the room with Emma at her side.

Emma, who was showing all five months of her pregnancy, clasped her hand over her mouth when she saw Mindy. "You look so gorgeous. Sam is going to freak."

"You do look amazing. But I figured you already knew that," Sophie said, wandering farther into the room.

Mindy shot her a look. "A bride still wants to hear it, you know."

Sophie sat on the edge of the bed, watching Mindy adjust her hair. "I'm still surprised you didn't opt for a big wedding, but I suppose you've always been a bit contrary."

"After Emma and Daniel got married at city hall, I started to see the wisdom of it," Mindy said. "Having something low-key means way less drama. Plus, Sam didn't want to wait any longer, and honestly, I didn't want to, either."

The question of not waiting for life to start was certainly on Isabel's mind. She and Jeremy hadn't discussed marriage aside from agreeing it was best for the baby if it happened eventually. It wasn't that she was expecting a grand proclamation of love, more that she just wanted that certainty in her life. If he didn't pop the question soon, she planned to do it herself.

Of course, Jeremy had a lot on his plate now that he'd convinced his father to retire and step aside. There were lots of changes afoot at Sharp and Sharp as a result, including Jeremy bringing Isabel on board to start a new family law division. It was not only a good move forward for the firm, it was a way to save on office space, and they agreed that it would make things much easier when the baby arrived. They would likely get a nanny, but they also wanted to be as hands-on as possible.

A knock came at the bedroom door. Reginald, Eden's creative director and by all accounts, the sisters' de facto uncle, poked his head inside. "Everybody decent?" He didn't wait for a response, waltzing into the room in a pink suit and black bowtie festooned with pink hearts.

"Reginald, Gram would have loved that outfit," Sophie said.

He took it for a spin. "You think?"

"Definitely."

Mindy glanced at the clock on the bedside table. "You guys should head out there and get your seats."

Sophie, Emma and Isabel descended on Mindy, giving hugs and the gentlest of kisses on the cheek so as not to mess up her makeup. Sophie in particular was getting extremely choked up by the moment. "I love you all so much. Emma, you're the light and joy of this family. You make everything better. Mindy, you're the one who manages to keep us all moving forward." She then turned to Isabel. "And Isabel, at this point, you're pretty much our sister. We love you, too, and not just for saving Eden's. You helped us preserve our grandmother's legacy."

Isabel was so overwhelmed with emotion as the four of them joined in a group hug. "This means a lot to me. I've always wanted sisters."

Reginald cleared his throat loudly. "What about the stand-in for the father of the bride?"

"Get over here." Mindy waved him into the fray, but he only stayed for a beat or two before getting them all on schedule.

"Ladies, I need you to clear out. I have a bride to escort to the altar."

Isabel, Sophie and Emma hurried down the hall and descended the grand staircase into the foyer where the chairs were assembled. It was a small gathering—a few people from Eden's, like Lizzie and her new boyfriend, and Duane, the security guard. There were some people from Sam's office and Mindy's company, as well.

Isabel ducked into the seat next to Jeremy. "Hi," she whispered, pecking him on the cheek.

He took her hand and smiled, but otherwise kept quiet. Honestly, he'd been a little on edge all day, but she tried not to read anything into it. They were happy together, but he was under a lot of pressure to keep Sharp and Sharp firing on all cylinders.

Soft music began to play and everyone's attention was drawn to the top of the staircase, where Mindy stood with Reginald. As they began to descend, step by step, Isabel couldn't help but turn to a different sight, that of her brother waiting for his bride. She and Sam had been through so much together, and it felt like both a miracle and a blessing that they'd each found love, that they'd both found professional fulfillment and that they were now living in the same city. Her heart swelled at the thought of him having the happiness he so richly deserved.

The ceremony was short and sweet, officiated by one of Sam's friends from college, who'd recently moved to New York from Boston to work with him. He'd been ordained online for exactly this occasion. As her brother took Mindy into his arms, she couldn't have kept the tears at bay if she'd wanted to. It was too beautiful a moment to believe. Jeremy held her hand tightly, not letting go, and she hoped that it meant that no matter life's ups and downs, he would stay by her side.

As soon as Mindy and Sam walked down the very short aisle, the music got louder and decidedly more up-beat. "Now we get to have a party," Mindy announced, grabbing a glass of champagne from a waiter who had appeared from the kitchen. "Let's get these chairs out of here for dancing."

Sam pulled Isabel aside and gave her a warm hug. "It means the world to me that you could be here for this."

"Are you kidding? I wouldn't miss it for the world."

He looked down at the platinum band now circling the ring finger on his left hand. "Did you ever think I'd get married? Be honest."

"I always knew it would happen. It just took finding the right woman."

He pulled her into another bear hug. "So, at some point, Mindy and I want to talk to you about a legal matter."

Isabel reared back her head. "Not something to do with Eden's again. I barely survived the last one."

"Not that. The store is just fine. It's the question of children. Mindy and I were talking and we're considering adoption."

This surprised Isabel. "Is something wrong?"

"No. We haven't even started trying yet. I just…" He looked around the room at this massive home he and Mindy now owned. "There's a lot of room here and there are a lot of children in the world who need a good home. I think we'd like to do both. Have our own kids and adopt."

"Yes. Of course, yes. I would love to help."

"So you'll take our case?"

"Don't be silly. Just try to keep me away."

Jeremy came up by her side and shook Sam's hand. "Congratulations. It's a big day."

"The best big day ever." Sam unleashed a toothy grin, then winked at Jeremy, which Isabel found odd but decided it was because he was goofy with love. "Now if you'll excuse me, I need to hunt down the bride."

Isabel and Jeremy held hands as they watched him disappear into the other room. "How long do you want to stay?" Jeremy asked.

"I guess I feel like we should stay for the whole thing. Is everything okay? You seem preoccupied." She didn't want to let paranoia get the best of her, but she couldn't escape the feeling that something was wrong.

"Everything is absolutely perfect. You know me. I always want to get you home."

Isabel fought a smile. "Well, if that's what you're getting after, I'm thinking we stay an hour, tops."

They ended up staying fifty minutes. Isabel was tired and they had quite a ride back to Brooklyn. Jeremy was quiet as they sat in the back seat of the town car.

"You sure everything's okay?" she asked for what felt like the one hundredth time.

"Yeah. I spoke to my dad today. You know how that goes. It's getting better, but I still feel like I'm feeling my way around in the dark."

"Talk about work stuff?"

He nodded. "And just trying to get to a point where I have a better relationship with him. I went ahead and asked them about dinner next week. So we can tell them about the baby."

"And?"

He smiled. "Obviously I didn't tell them that part. But yes, they said that they would love to have dinner. My mom really adores you. She says you're good for me."

Isabel squeezed his hand tight. "Somebody needs to tell her that you're good for me."

They arrived back at Jeremy's and performed their new coming-home ritual, which was checking on the kittens. Jeremy, never the big cat fan, conceded that he had "warmed" to them. Of course, Isabel was over the moon for them, and the thought of them being adopted out soon weighed heavy on her heart. They wouldn't have this fun to look forward to much longer.

Isabel sat on the floor of the guest room and played with the three kittens, who still didn't have names. For now, they were Things 1, 2 and 3—the orange male, the orange female and the calico respectively. Jeremy, however, excused himself and said he needed to get something. That only left Isabel to worry about what his dad had said and how that played into the future of their relationship.

"What do you think, Thing 1?" Isabel scooped up the kitten and kissed him on the nose. The cat squirmed to get down and frolic with his littermates. In the corner, Cat was watching over everything. "Is Jeremy acting strangely?" Isabel asked Cat.

"I don't know. Am I?" Behind her, Jeremy had walked into the room.

Isabel turned quickly. "Whoa. You are stealthy. I didn't even hear you open the door."

"I think that's only because you're so wrapped up in the kittens."

She returned her attention to them as they wrestled on the carpet. "I do adore them. I love them."

Just then Jeremy knelt down next to her. "Do you know who I adore and love?"

She eyed him with great suspicion. "Okay, now you are definitely acting weird."

"You, Isabel. I love and adore you." He reached into the pocket of his pants and pulled out a small velvet bag. "And the reason I've been quiet all night is because I have a big question on my mind."

Isabel sat perfectly still, her heart beating unevenly in her chest. She didn't want to miss a moment or a single word of what she hoped was about to happen.

He reached for her hand and held on to it tightly. His gaze met hers, and she saw exactly how sincere he was. The hurt that she'd once seen in his eyes was gone. And now, she saw hope. "I love you, Isabel Blackwell, and it's not just because you're brilliant or beautiful. And it's not merely because you're having my baby, although that's part of it. I love you because you make my whole life better. I want you to be my wife." With that, he let go of her hand and opened the velvet bag, presenting a beautiful gold-and-diamond solitaire. "This is why I talked to my dad. It's the ring my grandfather gave to my grandmother. He gave it to my dad, but my dad gave a different ring to my mom. He always felt bad about it, and I can't help but feel like this is all coming full circle now. As long as you'll say yes."

She had to laugh, at least a little bit, even as the tears streamed down her cheeks. "Of course the answer is yes. I love you, Jeremy. I love you for being strong and sensitive. I love you for not giving up on people. I love you for the way you make me feel like I'm the most important woman in the entire world."

"You *are* the most important woman in the world. No doubt about that." He leaned forward and kissed her, softly and sweetly, with just enough of that sexy Jeremy edge. She combed her fingers into his hair, wanting more.

Unfortunately, the kittens had different plans, tumbling around on the floor between them. In the excitement, Jeremy had dropped the velvet bag on the floor and they were fighting over it. "Bunch of hooligans," Isabel muttered, taking the pouch and pretending to scold them. "I can just see one of you choking on the string."

Jeremy laughed. "Can I make another crazy suggestion?"

"On top of marriage?"

"Yes. Let's keep the kittens. And Cat. Let's not give them up for adoption."

Isabel could hardly believe the words that had just come from Jeremy's mouth, which was saying a lot given that he'd just proposed. "But you don't really like cats."

"Like a lot of things, you managed to show me what I was missing out on."

"It'll be a ton of work. Four cats running around here."

Jeremy shrugged and pulled her closer. "So? I have spent years walking around this big house, hardly using it or enjoying it for that matter. And then I met you and the whole place sprang back to life. I don't want to hold back on that. So we have four cats and a baby. Bring it on."

Isabel smiled harder than she'd ever smiled, even more than she had while watching her brother say "I do" mere hours ago. "Oh, you know what I just realized? If I change my name to Isabel Blackwell-Sharp after we get married, you can still keep the firm's name as Sharp and Sharp."

"First off, I'm not doing the same thing to you that

my dad did to me. We will change the firm's name to whatever you want it to be. To whatever you want your last name to be."

She then realized what a pushover she was being. "You've got me into way too much of a charitable mood, Sharp. I should be negotiating with you, not offering concessions from the word go."

"I don't want to talk work, Isabel." He threaded his fingers through her hair, then rubbed his thumb along her lower lip. "I don't want to talk about who we know or what we do."

Isabel smiled at the echo of the magical night they'd met, when she'd dared to take a chance on Jeremy. How lucky was she that he ended up being the one? "Yeah? Then what do you want to talk about?"

"How do you feel about good views? Because there's a spectacular one in our bedroom."

* * * * *

COMING SOON!

We really hope you enjoyed reading this book. If you're looking for more romance, be sure to head to the shops when new books are available on

Thursday 14th November

To see which titles are coming soon, please visit

millsandboon.co.uk/nextmonth

MILLS & BOON

HEROES

At Your Service

Experience all the excitement of a gripping thriller, with an intense romance at its heart. Resourceful, true-to-life women and strong, fearless men face danger and desire - a killer combination!

LET'S TALK
Romance

For exclusive extracts, competitions
and special offers, find us online:

- facebook.com/millsandboon
- @MillsandBoon
- @MillsandBoonUK

Get in touch on 01413 063232

For all the latest titles coming soon, visit
millsandboon.co.uk/nextmonth

MILLS & BOON

THE HEART OF ROMANCE

A ROMANCE FOR EVERY KIND OF READER

MODERN

Prepare to be swept off your feet by sophisticated, sexy and seductive heroes, in some of the world's most glamourous and romantic locations, where power and passion collide.
8 stories per month.

HISTORICAL

Escape with historical heroes from time gone by. Whether your passion is for wicked Regency Rakes, muscled Vikings or rugged Highlanders, awaken the romance of the past.
6 stories per month.

MEDICAL

Set your pulse racing with dedicated, delectable doctors in the high-pressure world of medicine, where emotions run high and passion, comfort and love are the best medicine.
6 stories per month.

True Love

Celebrate true love with tender stories of heartfelt romance, from the rush of falling in love to the joy a new baby can bring, and a focus on the emotional heart of a relationship.
8 stories per month.

Desire

Indulge in secrets and scandal, intense drama and plenty of sizzling hot action with powerful and passionate heroes who have it all: wealth, status, good looks...everything but the right woman.
6 stories per month.

HEROES

Experience all the excitement of a gripping thriller, with an intense romance at its heart. Resourceful, true-to-life women and strong, fearless men face danger and desire - a killer combination!
8 stories per month.

DARE

Sensual love stories featuring smart, sassy heroines you'd want as a best friend, and compelling intense heroes who are worthy of them.
4 stories per month.

To see which titles are coming soon, please visit

millsandboon.co.uk/nextmonth

MILLS & BOON

MODERN

Power and Passion

Prepare to be swept off your feet by sophisticated, sexy and seductive heroes, in some of the world's most glamourous and romantic locations, where power and passion collide.